THE
13TH
TRIBE

ROBERT LIPARULO

THE 13TH TRIBE

THOMAS NELSON
Since 1798

NASHVILLE   DALLAS   MEXICO CITY   RIO DE JANEIRO

Published in Nashville, Tennessee, by Thomas Nelson. Thomas Nelson is a registered trademark of Thomas Nelson, Inc.

Thomas Nelson, Inc., books may be purchased in bulk for educational, business, fund-raising, or sales promotional use. For information, please e-mail SpecialMarkets@ ThomasNelson.com.

Scripture quotations are taken from the HOLY BIBLE: NEW INTERNATIONAL VERSION®. © 1973, 1978, 1984 by International Bible Society. Used by permission of Zondervan Publishing House. All rights reserved.

THE NEW KING JAMES VERSION. © 1982 by Thomas Nelson, Inc. Used by permission. All rights reserved.

Publisher's Note: This novel is a work of fiction. Names, characters, places, and incidents are either products of the author's imagination or used fictitiously.

Library of Congress Cataloging-in-Publication Data

Liparulo, Robert.
   The 13th tribe / Robert Liparulo.
      p. cm. — (An Immortal Files novel ; 1)
   ISBN 978-1-59554-169-7 (trade paper)
   I. Title.
   PS3612.I63A614 2012
   813'.6—dc23   2011051154

Printed in the United States of America

12 13 14 15 16 17 QG 6 5 4 3 2 1

For Don Liparulo
My big brother, my true friend

"For it is by grace you have been saved, through faith—and this is not from yourselves, it is the gift of God—not by works, so that no one can boast."

—Ephesians 2:8-9

"A preacher must be both soldier and shepherd. He must nourish, defend, and teach; he must have teeth in his mouth, and be able to bite and fight."

—Martin Luther

"Is it so dreadful a thing then to die?"

—Publius Vergilius Maro, *Aeneid*

[1]

Eddie Rollins didn't believe in ghosts or phantoms or the boogeyman, but at that moment he felt a chill run down his spine like a drop of cold water. Gun in hand, he inched through the darkness between two bulbs mounted above doors on the backside of MicroTech's large, squat building. Thirty yards ahead, a keypad beside one of the metal-skinned doors had just beeped and lit up. Seeing no one standing before it, despite the brilliance of the halogen lamp directly overhead, he'd drawn his weapon.

Unusual things made him nervous: eight years on the force had taught him that shifting shadows in a dark alley or unlocked doors that should be locked meant trouble. He believed it was this suspicious nature that had kept him alive and earned him the security position at MicroTech when he went out looking for a job to supplement the pittance Baltimore paid its finest. In all the times he'd made this late-night circuit around the building's perimeter, none of the keypads had ever beeped or lit up of its own accord. Then there were the noises: a faint whispering that could have been the wind, but his instincts told him wasn't.

He considered radioing for backup or at least asking Larry, who sat in front of a bank of monitors, to put down his ever-present magazine and tell him if the cameras were picking up something Eddie's eyes weren't. But until he knew more he didn't want to risk looking foolish or, worse, giving away his presence if someone *was* back here and hadn't already seen him.

He swept his gaze across the large parking lot, half full with only the night shift's cars. The few lights scattered around on high poles were dim and useless. Still, he thought he might spot something interesting—a dome light, a commercial vehicle—but nothing jumped out at him.

He smiled a little: *nothing jumped out at him*—not the best choice of words in this situation.

At the far back of the parking lot and circling around the sides of the building, a grassy berm rose to a tall chain-link fence topped with loops of concertina wire. Years ago, in an attempt to keep the employees from feeling like prison workers, the company had planted a row of trees midway up the berm. Pretty, but stupid from a security standpoint.

He scanned the trees, mostly defoliated this time of year. Something glinted in one of them, and he squinted at it. He could make out the fence through the branches and was thinking that's what had caught his eye when the keypad beeped again. Six beeps, actually, and the door's bolts disengaged with a metallic *thunk*. As the door swung open, Eddie crouched and hurried toward it, watching the lighted area draw closer over the sights of his revolver.

The light shimmered, a rippling current of air like heat waves coming off hot asphalt, then it was gone. The door was swinging closed now, and Eddie bolted for it.

"Freeze!"

It slammed shut.

He was almost to the door, recalling the code that would open it, shifting his gun into his left hand, when he tripped over something and crashed onto the concrete pad at the threshold. He rolled to see what he'd stumbled over and almost screamed—would have screamed, had his lungs not frozen solid.

A pair of eyes stared down at him. Just eyes, shaped by unseen lids, floating in the glow of the light. Where a head and body should have been . . . nothing. Beyond the eyes he could see the building's white-painted bricks, a crack running up from the foundation. The eyes blinked and moved toward him.

The same fear that had paralyzed him a moment before now spurred him to action. He scrambled backward, pushing himself away from the approaching eyes. He leaned on one elbow, swung his gun up and fired, instinctively aiming eighteen inches below the eyes, a center-mass shot—if whatever this thing was had mass.

The eyes sailed back and disappeared. A gout of blood appeared in the air and gushed down and around the point of impact in a thin sheet, coating a chest and stomach Eddie could not see. He gazed in awe as the eyes reappeared, this time as narrow crescents. They—and the growing sheet of blood—descended slowly, as though the invisible being was sliding down the brick wall.

The door burst open, fluorescent light from an empty hallway exploding over him. But the hallway *wasn't* empty: more eyes rushed out of it, bobbing up and down, coming toward him. And another object, floating, circling, as though dancing on the waves of light—a long blade: a knife or sword. It glimmered and sparked as it came at him. In the speed of it all, everything slowed down in the way wheels spin so fast they appear not to be moving at all. He swung the gun toward the eyes, the blade, and felt something strike his hand hard. He fired into the night sky.

A pair of eyes, angry slits with dark irises, stopped over him, and he felt a blow against his chin, knocking his head back. He felt the back of his skull collide against the pavement and an explosion of pain, making his vision go white. Then he felt no more.

[2]

Nevaeh knelt and grabbed the security guard's hair, yanking his head sideways as she brought her dagger to his neck. A firm hand gripped her shoulder and pulled her back.

"Nevaeh," Ben said behind her. "He's an innocent."

The blade shook under the strain of her anger. "He got in our way," she said, her gaze focusing on the man's carotid artery, pulsing just below the skin. "He shot Elias."

"NEV-ee-ah." Enunciating it with that deep orator's voice of his, like a father warning a child.

She sighed heavily and jerked her shoulder out of his clasp. She plucked the gun from the man's limp hand and cracked it across his temple to make sure he stayed down, then tossed it away. Her eyes met Ben's. "Happy?" she said.

From behind Ben, Phin's voice came at her: "Come on, come on." His eyes bounced in the doorway, and she knew his invisible body was bouncing, his arms jittering in front of him the way they did when he was excited or agitated, which pretty much defined his constant state of mind.

She glanced at the camera above and to the left of the door. It was slowly panning away from them, toward the darkness. It had captured the fallen man, but clearly no one had noticed; anyone who had would have overridden its automatic movement and held the focus on them. MicroTech made products that required both sterility and security, meaning lots of hermetically sealed barriers and doors, even in the corridors. She doubted the sound of the gunshots had reached anyone's ears.

She rose, brushed past Ben, and crouched where blood appeared

4

to float a foot away from the wall. She touched it and moved her fingers over Elias's body and down his arm. She slid a switch sewn into a tight cuff around his wrist, turning off the power to his suit, and he suddenly popped into existence, clad in a jumpsuit that appeared to be made out of sharkskin, scaly and gray. Something like a mouthless ski mask made of the same material covered his face and head, hands and feet. Constructed of negative index metamaterial, the suit effectively bent light around the wearer's body, rendering him—or her—invisible. The technology had something to do with each tiny scale transferring light to the adjacent scale, but Nevaeh didn't care how it worked, as long as it did. Ben had the brain for such things; she was much more interested in using it to rid the world of people who'd abused the life they'd been given by harming others. The mission at hand would go a long way toward that goal, and she didn't need Phin telling her to hurry.

But this was Elias—

He'd been shot in the chest. She pulled off a glove, careful not to detach the cord that kept it invisible. She probed the wound, and her finger slipped in. Something pulsed weakly against the tip, and she thought it was his heart.

"Nevaeh," Phin said, his voice squeaky.

"All right, all right." She brushed her fingers over Elias's facemask, leaving a streak of blood, and stood, slipping her hand back into the glove. She looked across the parking lot toward the trees, depressed a button in her own mask by her earlobe, and said, "Jordan."

The boy's voice came through an earbud. "What happened? Is that Elias—?"

"He got shot. I need you to hide him and the guard. Hurry."

"Both? I can't—"

"Wait." She leaned over and turned Elias's suit on again. He vanished. No way a camera would pick up the hovering bloodstain. "Okay," she said. "Just the guard. Drag him out between the cars, and don't let the camera catch you. Move it."

She watched the tree across the lot until she saw the silhouette of Jordan's eleven-year-old body descend from a branch and drop. Speaking to Ben's eyes, she said, "Let's go," then stepped toward the doorway. Phin turned away, taking his bouncing peepers with him. Nevaeh and Ben entered the hallway and shut the door behind them.

[3]

With the smell of Elias's blood still in her nostrils and her heart racing from the excitement of taking down the guard, Nevaeh hoped for more action—someone spotting their eyes or a security code that had changed since Ben's informant had given it to him—anything that would force them to take a prisoner and get the intel they needed through good old-fashioned violence.

And she meant *good*, as in God. After all, everything they did was for him. To get his attention, to please him. Anyone who had a hard time reconciling their methods with God's Word hadn't read the Old Testament. He ordered violence against his enemies, and all they were doing was carrying out those orders. Someone had to do it, and more people should; if they did, maybe the Tribe wouldn't be so necessary and God would call them home. Finally.

So bring it on, she thought. *His furious wrath moves our muscles and cuts with our swords.*

But there would be no cutting tonight. After the incident with the guard outside, everything else flowed without a hitch, and she supposed that was for the best. Ben had outlined a contingency plan to cover the break-in, but the farther into the building they could be traced, the more likely their true agenda would be discovered. And that would blow their grand plans to make a statement against evil that the world wouldn't soon forget.

Ben had memorized the layout, and every door opened at his digital command. They coasted past glass-walled rooms inside which workers in hazmat suits layered electronic circuitry into silicon wafers, tested them on monstrous computers, and etched or silkscreened model and lot numbers on their surfaces. The three intruders lowered their heads to keep cameras from catching their eyes and turned their faces away from assembly personnel and guards even as they breezed past them, close enough to smell their perfume, aftershave, and sweat.

Within minutes they'd found the company's most secure storage room and the vault inside. Ben punched in a code, passed an infrared security chip over a reader, and pressed a fingerprint on a square of transparent film against a biometric scanner. The vault door opened, revealing shelves of aluminum Halliburton cases, labeled with numbers. With his back to Nevaeh he was completely invisible, so when he pulled a case off its shelf, it appeared to spring up and dance in the air on its own. An identical case materialized, drawn from a metamaterial pack on Ben's back. It floated onto the shelf, and the original vanished into the pack.

The case contained twenty microchips that would give them access to sophisticated military weapons, enough to level a city. These chips were backups of ones already in the Pentagon's hands. Chances were they would be inventoried but never used, and the dummy duplicates Ben had left in their stead meant their theft would go unnoticed—at least until it was too late. Their tech wizard, Sebastian, had created them from specs provided by their informant, a man privy to top secret government contracts and who sympathized with their cause.

The vault door closed, and Nevaeh and Phin followed Ben back to their point of entrance. Before exiting, Phin produced a can of spray paint and graffitied the hallway wall: STOP HELPING BUTCHERS! And on the opposite wall: THIS TIME, THIS FAR. NEXT TIME, ALL THE WAY.

MicroTech had been the target of protests over their Pentagon contracts. The idea was to pin the attack on the break-in on radical peaceniks, content—this time—to demonstrate their ability to breach the company's security. The guard's claims of invisible beings would be chalked up to his head trauma, and the cameras would show that no one had penetrated any deeper than this hallway.

Ben punched in a code, and they stepped into the night.

[4]

Back on his perch in the tree, Jordan watched through binoculars as the rear door opened and closed. A few moments later Elias appeared, slouched against the brick wall beside the door; someone had turned off his suit, probably to check on his condition.

Lord, make him all right, he prayed. Elias was a bit scruffy, and sometimes his penchant for one-word answers came across as grouchy, but like Jordan he was partial to Western movies and comic books—Wolverine and G.I. Joe were their favorites. And over the years, Jordan had learned about God more from Elias than from any of the others, even Ben with his books and scrolls and big brain. Creed—who had remained home with Hannah, Toby, and Sebastian—once said that Elias's instruction was like God's "still small voice" coming to Elijah on the mountain, and Ben's was God's voice "like the roar of rushing waters and a loud peal of thunder" that the apostle John had heard in his dream.

Through the binocs he saw Elias rise, and Jordan's heart thumped with joy. Then he realized two of the others had lifted him, carrying him between them with Elias's arms draped over their invisible shoulders. He appeared to be skimming over the pavement, his toes dragging behind, arms outstretched and head drooped like a crucified zombie. And that was just creepy.

Jordan spoke into his mic, "Could you guys turn off your ghost suits now? You're freaking me out."

Nevaeh popped into view on Elias's left side, then Ben on his right. As they started up the berm, Jordan dropped down and looked around. "Where's Phin?" Then he jumped and yipped in surprise.

Phin's suit beeped and he appeared behind Jordan, his gloved hand on his shoulder.

Jordan swatted at it and stepped away. "Don't do that!"

Phin just laughed.

Jerk.

X I I I

Nevaeh wanted only to get back to their rented van, then to their private jet and out of this city. Elias's weight wasn't a bother—she'd lugged much heavier things—but that guard would be waking soon. Everything had gone too smoothly to get caught now.

She and Ben carried Elias past Jordan and Phin and pushed through the hole in the chain link they had let Jordan cut, which he had thought was "totally sick": after spraying it with liquid nitrogen, the metal had broken under his fingers like ice. They traversed a park on the other side and piled into the van, laying Elias on the floor in the back. Ben and Jordan crouched next to him, Ben peeling the mask off Elias's gray-bearded face.

Nevaeh got into the passenger seat and yanked off her mask, releasing long black hair that flowed over her shoulders. She shook it out of her face and looked at Phin behind the wheel. He'd already removed his mask and was rubbing at the metamaterial paint with which they'd coated their eyelids.

"This stuff is terrible," he said. "Every time I blink, I have to force my eyes open again."

"But you're so pretty," she said. "You'd have made a beautiful glam-rocker."

He scowled at her, and she could see the crazy in his eyes. She tried to remember if Phin had always been a bit bats. No, just hyper. The loony part had crept in slowly—like what, over a couple centuries? Seemed like it.

"So," she said, "what are you waiting for? Let's go."

He started the van, but before he could put it into gear, Ben stopped him. "A second, please." In the glow of the dome light he nodded at the others, bowed his head, and they began to pray. Correction: the three conscious males prayed; Nevaeh couldn't get into it, not this time. Ben intoned the same request for God to accept their work she had heard how many times? She'd lost count long ago. His voice was deep and measured, every word perfectly formed.

". . . guide our labor, for we are your obedient children . . ."

Oh please, she thought, then squeezed her eyes shut. *I mean, please . . . do guide us back into your arms at long last. At long, long last.* After so many years, it was hard to maintain confidence in their missions. But if she stopped believing, their torment would never end, and just the thought of that sent spiders skittering through her stomach. She felt as though she'd been hanging from a ledge by her fingers forever. The abyss of nothingness below her kept her fighting for leverage, spurring her to struggle and strain. But how long before her muscles simply could not take anymore?

Every mission, every killing was her cry for help, for *forgiveness*— so many cries that her soul was bleeding and raw. Still, every cry had apparently fallen on deaf ears.

She realized Ben had stopped talking, and opened her eyes. He was staring at her, his intense gaze piercing holes into her. Phin and Jordan were watching as well.

"Amen," she said.

Elias pulled in a loud, sharp breath and sat straight up. He pushed himself back to rest against the van's rear doors, reached into a pocket, and pulled out a hand-rolled cigarette and lighter. A shaking hand put the cigarette to his lips, and he lit up. He closed his eyes, leaned his head back, and blew out a stream of smoke. He shook his head, then rubbed his chest, finally ripping the suit open from neck to navel. Blood caked his chest hair into red paisleys. Over his heart, a dime-sized dimple showed mostly scar tissue. At its center was a pinprick hole from which a thin rivulet of blood snaked down his chest.

Nevaeh remembered the hole that been there thirty minutes before, large enough to stick her finger in and touch his heart. Couldn't do that now, and by morning it would look like nothing more than a vaccination scar.

Elias looked at each of his compatriots in turn, took a deep drag on his cigarette, and said, "Wow. *That* was a trip."

[5]

The blazing Egyptian sun baked Jagger Baird's face, and he tipped his head to let the brim of his boonie hat shade his eyes: his sunglasses were about as effective as tissue in a rainstorm. A gust of wind tossed sand at him, and he turned his back until it passed.

Standing outside the southeast wall of St. Catherine's monastery, he surveyed the tight valley stretching out before him. The hard ground dipped and rose, formed grooves and cracks, ravines and sharp ledges, as though it had been hacked into existence. Sand and loose rock had come down off the mountains and settled into a tiger-stripe pattern of treacherous terrain on top of bedrock—all of it sun-bleached to the color of old bones. The term that came to mind was *godforsaken*, which flew in the face of everything the area stood for. The mountain looming to his right, behind the monastery, was Jabel Musa—Moses's Mountain. Most of the world believed it to be the biblical Mt. Sinai, where God spoke to Moses through a burning bush and gave him the Ten Commandments.

On a pilgrimage here in the fourth century, Helena, mother of Constantine, claimed she had found the actual burning bush and built a small church around it. Two hundred years later, in 527, Emperor Justinian I ordered the construction of a protective wall around the church. The result became the monastery, no larger than a city block— with walls sixty feet high and nine feet thick. For 1500 years, the walls and monks inside had weathered crusaders and invaders, political and religious turbulence, famine and fires.

The latest onslaught was tourists, flocking to touch the bush, marvel at the monastery's ancient structures, and climb the mountain to the spot where Moses received the Decalogue. Probably why the mountains as they rose gradually took on a reddish hue, Jagger

13

thought: they were irritated by the bumbling trespassers, the way too much alcohol inflames a drunkard's nose.

His gaze moved from the mountain to the cloudless sky—denim blue at the northern horizon, brightening to brushed aluminum over-head—then down to the archaeological excavation that had brought him here as head of security. It consisted primarily of two Olympic-pool-sized rectangles, each stepping down to a depth of about twenty feet. They were positioned perpendicular to the slope rising from the valley floor to the base of Mt. Sinai. The hole—or *unit*—closest to the mountain was higher up the slope and had been dubbed Annabelle. The lower hole was Bertha. Ollie—Dr. Oliver Hoffmann, the lead archaeologist—had explained that their official designations were 55E60 and 48E122, respectively. These names indicated their positions in relation to a site datum, a point from which all dig activity was measured. On site, the lead arc was expected to christen them with easier monikers.

"So I did," he'd said with a grin badly in need of dental assistance.

"Meaning A and B?" Jagger had asked.

"Meaning two lovely ladies of my youth who left holes in my heart. Now I dig holes in their honor."

They'd been at a tavern in the nearby town of St. Catherine's, and Ollie had raised his glass to take a swig. The beer was Stella, an Egyptian concoction that many connoisseurs considered the best in the world. Judging by Ollie's consumption of it, he didn't disagree.

Downhill from the holes was a line of five beige tents, their aprons now fluttering in the breeze. Ollie used one as an office; the others provided storage space and shelter from the sun, a place to rest.

Ten yards below the tents, past a split-rail fence, ran the trail that led from the monastery to the two routes up Mt. Sinai—Siket El Basha, a gradually ascending, winding path; and Siket Sayidna Musa, a much steeper ascent of 3,800 steps chiseled into the mountain's granite by monks.

Jagger couldn't imagine the dedication required to accomplish that, kneeling on the harsh slope, pounding on hard stone in sweltering heat day after day for decades. But then, any faith that inspired such dedication was beyond him. He was fully aware of his sour disposition, and the reason for it: since a particular night fourteen months ago, his life had mirrored a *Reader's Digest* survival story gone wrong. His wife, Beth, had written a few of them; he knew the drill: an average person is thrust into the eye of a hurricane named Disaster and somehow finds the strength to overcome, even triumph. Take out *overcome* and *triumph*, and you got Jagger's story. He was still looking for his happy ending.

If Beth were plotting a piece on him, it'd look something like this: *Ivy Leaguer meets girl of his dreams. Whirlwind courtship. Wedding bells. Baby! Sheepskin. Commissioned as 2Lt, U.S. Army . . . Rangers . . . CID. Starts personal protection company with college/army BFF. Family/ career bliss. Car crash . . . other driver drunk! BFF + BFF's family dies. Arm amputated. Prosthesis. Depression. Survivor's guilt. Furious at God.*

Jagger crouched and picked up a stone. His boots had burnished a stable flat spot on the rocky slope. It was his favorite observation point, from which he could see the entire excavation with the monastery's wall protecting his back. Rolling the stone in his palm, he watched two university students carry buckets of dirt out of Bertha. They dumped them into a screen-bottomed box on wooden legs, then began shaking the box to sift for treasures. As fascinating as he considered the idea of finding traces of long-lost people, he had quickly realized it was grueling and boring work, something he could never do. He'd take a gun over a trowel any day.

Security-and-protection: *that* interested him, and through stints as an Army Ranger, a military investigator, and then a personal protection specialist—aka an executive bodyguard—he'd discovered a knack for it. Whether protecting a dignitary or an archaeological dig, he took his responsibilities seriously. More seriously, it seemed, than most archaeologists were accustomed to. When he'd arrived, the four guards already on site might have been recruited from a Cairo shopping mall. They'd worn no uniforms, except for what Jagger thought of as high school grunge, and, incredibly, spent most of their time playing cards on the other side of the monastery, where the gardens provided a measure of shade but no way to do their jobs.

It bugged him that here in Egypt the word *gun* was merely a metaphor for his profession. Firearms were stringently regulated, and Ollie had told him to anticipate at least a year for the government to approve his application, if it was approved at all. Used to be, Jagger wouldn't go a week without firing a weapon on a range. Now it'd been four months since he'd last felt the weight of a gun in his hand or smelled the clean fragrance of gun oil. He felt naked without firepower. He touched the hilt of a collapsible baton in a quick-release holster hanging at his hip where a pistol should have been. For crying out loud.

He tossed the stone, watched it clatter over larger rocks and settle among a thousand like it, and he changed his mind: this inhospitable land wasn't godforsaken; it was God-*embraced*, the perfect representation of the God he knew, a God more inclined toward punishment than compassion. Emotion stirred in his chest: not anger this time, but a grief at having lost something he'd once cherished.

Before he worked it into a melancholy that would carry him through the rest of his shift, he was yanked out of himself by a woman's screams.

[6]

She screamed again, and Jagger ripped off his glasses, scanning for the source. Workers were turning toward the tents, and he saw a canvas wall bulge out, then flutter back. He leaped forward, scrambling deftly over the treacherous surface—unlike his first few weeks here, when he'd spent most of the time twisting his ankles and landing on his butt.

No more screams, but the tent was shaking as though caught in a wind much stronger than the breeze coming through the valley. Jagger hit the strip of earth that had been cleared and leveled for the tents and picked up speed. Skidding to a stop, he whipped back the tent's entry flap.

A man was holding a woman facedown against the tent's plastic groundsheet, pulling an arm behind her back, pushing her face into the floor. Jagger recognized her kinky red hair: Addison Brooke, a doctoral student from Cambridge, here to work as Oliver's assistant.

Jagger grabbed the back of the man's collar and hoisted him off her. The man turned, swinging a fist at Jagger, who parried it with his prosthetic left arm. The man's face twisted in pain at the blow to his wrist. Jagger, still with a fistful of collar, got hold of the man's waistband. He spun, ready to hurl the guy into a shelving unit.

"No!" Addison yelled. "Not the shelves!"

At that moment Jagger didn't give a lick for the artifacts on them . . . but everyone else did, so he continued to whip his hostage around in a circle. He stuck out a leg, tripping the man. He put his muscles into making sure the guy hit the ground hard, then dropped his knee onto the man's spine. He rose enough to roll his adversary over, then pinned his knee into the attacker's sternum. Still the man struggled, ramming a fist into Jagger's thigh.

Jagger clamped the hooks that had replaced his left hand over the man's neck, an act that effectively hit the off switch on the guy's movements. Jagger glanced up at Addison, sitting near the front corner of the roomlike tent. "You okay?"

She brushed hair away from moist eyes and nodded.

"You know him?" he asked.

She said, "M-muscle." It was what the arcs called a local hired to move dirt and do grunt work.

The tent flap pulled away and Hanif, one of the site's guards, rushed in. Ollie followed and knelt beside Addison. "What happened?"

"He . . . he . . . ." She closed her eyes, covered her mouth with a shaking hand, and pulled in a deep breath. "I caught him stealing artifacts." Her voice was thin and tiny, like a little girl's.

The workman rattled out something in Egyptian. The words were raspy, squeezed through a windpipe pinched under Jagger's grasp. Jagger eased up on the pressure . . . a little.

"He says it's not true," Hanif translated, his own speech heavily accented. "He was simply putting away some new finds."

Addison shook her head. "Look in his satchel."

Jagger rose up off the man. He yanked him to his feet, but didn't release him.

Ollie grabbed the canvas bag hanging from the man's shoulder and pulled out what looked to Jagger like a broken ashtray. He shook it in front of Mumé's face. "A potsherd. We uncovered it this morning."

Hanif reached behind him and produced a set of handcuffs—a piece of equipment Jagger had insisted his guards carry, along with walkie-talkies, canteens, and batons. He'd also instituted uniforms—Desert Storm–style fatigues—and weekly training sessions. Hanif stepped behind the workman and forced his hands around.

When Jagger heard the ratcheting of the cuffs he let go, leaving a red mark on either side of the man's neck. He went to Addison and held his hand out to her. She grabbed it and smiled up at him. Bloody teeth caused his heart to skip. Her bottom lip had split open. Blood oozed out, and it was smeared across her chin. He turned and swung his fist into the culprit's face. The man flew back, out of Hanif's grip, and crashed into a makeshift table. He broke through cheap plywood, sending tools, papers, and unidentifiable debris flipping into the air. By the time they rained down, he had hit the floor and slid halfway through the bottom of the tent wall.

Hanif grabbed his feet and tugged him back in. The workman was shaking his head in agony, splattering blood from a shattered nose and wailing out a string of sharp words Jagger didn't understand.

Rubbing his knuckles on his hip, Jagger took in Ollie's stunned look and said, "Sorry."

Ollie grinned. "Only thing to be sorry about is beating me to it." He patted Jagger on the shoulder and turned to Addison. "Come on, I'm taking you to the clinic."

"Nonsense," she said. "Go back to Annabelle. Just let me clean up a bit."

Ollie squeezed her arm, then slipped out. His voice returned, "Okay, everyone, back to work! Nothing to see here."

Hanif got the workman to his feet. Snot and blood covered the guy's lower face like a veil. "I'll bring him in," Hanif said.

"Don't bother," Jagger said. The village's tiny police force didn't give a squat what happened at the dig and would let the guy go as soon as Hanif was out of sight. "Send him on his way and tell him if I see his face again, it won't be just a busted nose."

Hanif gripped his prisoner's waistband and tugged him out of the tent.

Addison touched Jagger's hand. "Thank you."

"You sure about the clinic?" It was in the village a mile from the monastery.

She made a face. "I've fended off boyfriends rougher than him."

Jagger didn't believe it—she was way too smart to get entangled with people like that. But he understood.

"You didn't have to punch him, you know."

"Yeah, I did." What he shouldn't have done was grip the guy's neck with his hooks. That could have gone terribly wrong. "Is the artifact he tried to steal worth much?"

"Probably not," she said. "We won't know until we date it."

Jagger nodded. He'd spent two years as a special agent for the army's Criminal Investigation Division. The more he learned about archaeology, the more amazed he was by how similar the two disciplines were. The best investigators never made assumptions, always pursued the smallest detail, and found connections that baffled others but in reality were based on a knowledge of human behavior—descriptors that equally applied to successful archaeologists.

Addison touched her lip, winced, then stared at the blood on her finger. She sniffed back a sob.

He suspected it wasn't pain that had her on the brink of tears: it was the feeling of helplessness, of being overpowered. Being at the mercy of another person, someone malicious, was staggeringly frightening. Jagger was muscular, agile, and trained to fight, all of which put him at the top of the food chain. But he had learned the hard way that there was always someone bigger and tougher. He picked up a roll of paper towels, unrolled two clean squares, and pulled them off. He poured water from his canteen onto them and handed the wad to her.

She dabbed at her lip and wiped her chin.

"Why don't you go see Beth?" he suggested. His wife and Addison had hit it off right away, and Jagger was grateful that Beth had a friend in this lonely place. He knew she would provide the balm Addison needed: a sympathetic heart and comforting words.

"I will," Addison said, "later. Really, I'm fine." She tossed the bloody wad into the rubble of the table and its contents. She started out of the tent, then stopped. "For a moment I thought you were going to kill him."

Jagger tried to smile but ended up frowning. "Me too." And what frightened him most was the realization that he wouldn't have felt much if he had.

[7]

Nevaeh strolled through a dark corridor, lighted only by a few candles set in small recesses carved close to the ceiling. This section of the tunnels had been wired with electricity, but she liked it this way better: she'd spent more time on earth without electricity than with it, and natural light calmed her like a warm bath.

As she walked, she raked the nails of her left hand along a wall of jawless skulls. They screeched over a fleshless forehead, then slid off to click against the temple of the next skull. *Screeeeech-click*, over and over again, like a vinyl record skipping back over two seconds of static. Her fingernail found a gaping crack, and she wondered if it had been inflicted postmortem or if it evinced the event that had separated body from soul.

Lucky you, she thought.

Her S.W.A.T.-style boots padded softly against the limestone floor. She imagined watching herself at that moment in a movie: her dark clothes and hair drifting silently in the shadows, only her face and hands standing out, as if disembodied, perhaps a spirit looking for her bones among the thousands around her. In this long-forgotten place, she could forever pace the length of the corridor, slowly wearing grooves into the skulls, and no one would notice.

On her right, the wall was made of stone blocks. Arched doors, spaced every thirty feet or so, marked the many rooms that lined the long corridor. In addition to the location's seclusion and secrecy, these rooms were one of the reasons the Tribe had chosen to call this place home for the past decade. Each of the nine remaining members had his or her own room, except the smaller children, Jordan and Hannah, who shared one. That left rooms for a kitchen and dining room, bathroom, storage area, an armory, and a cell for the rare "visitor." Most of the bedrooms doubled as something else: Ben's was also the Tribe's library and chapel; Sebastian's was used for planning and for their computer needs; Toby's was an entertainment center, with televisions and game consoles.

Nevaeh veered across the corridor to listen at Toby's door. Voices came through: Toby, Phin, and Sebastian were playing on the Xbox. She supposed *playing* wasn't quite right. They were using a flight simulator to train for their upcoming mission, the one that had taken a huge leap from dream to reality now that they had the chips from MicroTech in hand.

Good. Success of the Amalek Project, as Ben had dubbed it, depended on their ability to control the weapons.

She scanned the tunnel and didn't see light seeping under any doors. Though it was late morning, they had returned from Baltimore only hours before, and most of them had headed straight to bed. They could sleep on the jet, but it was never restful.

Nevaeh suspected Creed was in his room brooding. He opposed Amalek and was becoming more vocal about it as the date approached. Tough. It would happen with or without him, and the fact that everything was coming together was proof God approved.

But she didn't like dissent among the Tribe, and just thinking of Creed stirred the beginnings of a headache. As usual, it wouldn't be severe nor last long, but it intensified her exhaustion, and she considered heading for her own bed. No, as keyed up as she was about a lot of things—the events in Baltimore, Amalek, needing to kill something the way Elias needed his cigarettes—she'd only toss and turn.

Instead she returned to the wall of skulls and skimmed her nails over them as she walked by door after door. She passed the last one, then the last candle, into the stygian darkness at the end of the corridor. Here, another tunnel crossed, forming a T-intersection. Nevaeh sat on the cool floor, her back against the wall, looking down the entire length of the corridor. The candles flickered against the ceiling, their patches of light growing smaller as they receded toward the opposite end.

She heard a door click open but saw no new light until a flame kicked up and glowed on Elias's face. Smoke turned the flame into a hazy ball of light, then it went out, leaving only a floating red cherry. The lighter flashed again, this time low, at his side, and went out. He continued flicking it as he meandered down the tunnel toward the bathroom. He let out a loud sigh and groaned.

She knew how he felt. Their healing—which Ben said stemmed from the same biochemical change that prevented them from aging—was fast, but it wasn't painless. For a few days after the physical signs of an injury had faded, they felt queasy and weak, as though a bit of their life force had seeped out. More likely, it had gone into the affected areas, leaving the rest of their bodies less than whole.

The flicking lighter disappeared into the bathroom and the door clicked closed.

Nevaeh wondered if it was indeed the aftermath of his healing that had Elias groaning . . . or simply the burden of living so long, the weight of a sin for which they were still awaiting forgiveness. She'd thought about it a million times. Actually, 1,274,000 times, last she'd calculated: every single night for 3500 years. In a Dantesque twist on justice, her dreams were less about sorting through psychological baggage and more about the torture of reliving their transgression over and over and over.

The candles flickered, and her eyelids grew heavy.

"Arella!" someone called, using her birth name.

She snapped her head up and realized she had fallen asleep. The dream had been waiting for her, as it always was. She watched the candles dim as her lids drooped, and she lowered her head and stepped into the dream.

[8]

Arella gazed up at the mountain. Moses had been gone too long, almost forty days. Surely he was dead, slaughtered by his god for some transgression—leading all the people here without a plan, touching the wrong stone: his god was demanding and unforgiving. Or perhaps he'd left, gone to claim the Promised Land for himself. Day and night, the sky above the mountain was orange and red, flickering, waving. Not a good sign.

And what were they waiting for? What god required so long to do anything?

Moses's god. Was he also *her* god, *their* god? Was he the One and Only God, as Moses had said? If so, why would Moses instruct them not to worship *other* gods? Was the God of Moses the same as the God of Abraham? What about El and the Ba'als—Asherah, Melqart, and Hadad? Her people had bowed to *them*, hadn't they? And a good number had taken to including the gods of their Egyptian captors—Osiris and Thoth—in their worship. She was so confused.

She looked around. So many people, scared, angry, impatient, crowding up to the foot of the mountain, as though that would bring Moses back faster. Some were even on the rocks, the mountain itself, though Moses had instructed them not to touch it. And what was that, anyway—"Do not touch the mountain"? Forcing his authority with petty restrictions. He was old and clambering for power over others as he lost the power over his own body.

Who needed him?

Arella knew her body was young and strong, attractive to men. She'd seen their looks. Her dress of brown linen, falling to midcalf, fringes down to her ankles—it clung to her body like skin, and she made sure the colorful shawl spilled down her sides, like drapes open to what she had to offer. So many men, muscular from years of building Pharaoh's monuments. One would be hers before they left that desolate place. At least one.

Abdeel rushed to her, grabbed her arms. Thinking he was after her jewelry, she tugged away. He grabbed her again and said, "Arella! There's talk. Moses's god is dead, or never was. Our true gods are angry with us! Remphan wants worship for bringing us out of Pharaoh's clutches. Apis, Khnum, Sin—they demand our allegiance, our love! Come! Come!"

Naram-Sin, yes! This was, after all, his place: Sinai—the Wilderness of Sin.

Abdeel pulled her through the crowd. A group was gathering around Hur, whom Moses had left in charge, along with his brother, Aaron. Angry voices demanded that he craft an Apis bull for them to worship. Hur shook his head furiously and refused, spitting at their feet, saying he was disgusted by their impatience and ingratitude to the One True God, who had crushed Pharaoh's army for them, fed them, freed them.

Arella spotted something—a shadow gliding over the rocks, formed by nothing she could see—and her mouth opened in shock as she traced its movements. Human-shaped, but not human: its head bore spear-like spikes, and the angles of its shoulders, elbows, hips were too sharp. It skimmed past the crowd, sweeping sand and pebbles away as no mere shadow could. It stopped at the feet of a man Arella recognized: Gehazi, from the tribe of Asher. He was watching the rest of the crowd, wide-eyed at the rising tension around him, oblivious to the thing at his feet. The shadow swirled around his ankles, then rose, engulfing him in a whirlwind of smoke. In a blink it vanished—seemingly *into* him, as though through his pores.

She glanced around, but no one else seemed to have noticed; it had all happened too fast, and their attention was elsewhere.

Gehazi spasmed and fell to the ground. He writhed in the dirt, choking. As afraid as she was, Arella could not watch without trying to help. She pushed between two people to reach him, but before she could, he flipped onto his stomach and lifted onto his hands and knees, head hanging as if he were an old mule. After a few seconds he rose like a victorious warrior, spine straight, shoulders like planks, chin raised.

His face swiveled toward her, his gleaming eyes taking her in, caressing her like hands. He smiled, and she felt light-headed. He was the most handsome man she'd ever seen. How had she not noticed before?

She blushed and turned away. When she looked back, he was pushing his way to the front of the crowd. He stooped out of sight, stood again, and hurled a stone. Arella's eyes followed it to Hur's head.

Hur staggered back, grabbing at a bloody wound. Before he could gain his balance another stone struck, then another and another. All around Arella, men, women, and even children were picking up stones.

Yes! Because they would obey the gods, not old men.

She found a rock and hefted it. It felt good, doing something besides waiting. Her stone hit Hur's shoulder, and she quickly looked for another. Under a rainfall of rocks, he tumbled, and still the stones pummeled him. Finally the people backed away, and Arella witnessed the broken, bloody mess.

Gehazi moved in with a few other men and lifted Hur. The rabble flowed like the sea to Aaron, at whose feet they tossed Hur's corpse. Aaron covered his mouth, leaving his eyes to show the horror he felt. He raised his arms and begged for patience, for everyone to remember God's kindness to them.

"What kindness?" a man beside him yelled, and Arella realized it was Gehazi. "Confusion in the desert? Left with no leader, no home, and no way to make one? Their god has done nothing for us. He led us away from Remphan, Sin, Apis, and now we have no gods!"

The crowd screamed their displeasure. Arella forced her way to the front, wanting only to be closer to Gehazi, to be noticed by him and participate in his rebellion. But it was Aaron who caught her attention, the fear on his face, the shame. For a moment doubt seized her: what were they doing?

Then Gehazi picked up a stone and held it high, encouraging the crowd to do the same. And Arella felt the doubt shatter; she found a rock and shook it at the old man on a ledge of stone in front of her.

Aaron patted the air for calm. He lowered his head, and when it came up again, she saw resolve on his face. He gestured toward Hur's body and said, "Your sin is great"—blaspheming Naram-Sin's name by using it to mean a transgression against *his* "One True God," just the way Moses was wont to do.

The crowd screamed, calling for Aaron's stoning.

He said, "God will never forgive you, but let me take your transgression upon myself, that you may live. Give me your jewelry, all the gold on yourselves, your wives, and your children. I will give you the idol you deserve."

Disagreement rippled through the crowd. Their jewelry? Their gold? It was all they possessed of value. But then some started saying, "Give the gold, our gods will reward us tenfold." The women took off their bracelets and rings and earrings, stripped them from the ears of their children; the men too, and Arella followed, tugging each piece off like bits of her flesh.

A pile as high as Aaron rose before him, and the men went off to build a fire, a kiln. Aaron worked that whole day and night, and when Arella woke, she found that he had fashioned Apis, a god himself and servant to the greater god Naram-Sin. The calf had upturned horns, forming a crescent moon—the symbol of Naram-Sin.

People began to bow and sing before the golden god, but Aaron stopped them, saying he had to build an altar on which the godly calf would rest; anything less would be irreverent. The entire time he stacked the stones and shaped them, she saw him looking up at the mountain and sensed that he hoped Moses would return before he finished.

Another night passed, and in the morning the altar was complete with the Apis bull perched on it, awaiting worship. Gehazi stood in front of it and yelled to the crowd that the god demanded sacrifice, and Arella watched men slaughter cows at the base of the altar. Then around her a whispering started, and like the breeze that precedes a gale, it grew into shouting: Naram-Sin wanted human blood. Her skin chilled and her stomach and heart tightened like fists, but everyone around her was so sure: it had to be.

Somewhere a baby cried, a mother screamed, and men raised their voices. They'd found a child and wrenched it from its mother's arms, passing it from man to man until it reached the altar. Other men pushed through the crowd to stop what was happening, and Arella gasped when they too fell by the blade.

The deed was done, and she wanted to run, to fall on her knees before the mountain and cry out for repentance. Then the people started singing and dancing, kissing each other . . . and more. Someone grabbed one of her hands and someone else the other, and they danced, skipping in great spiraling circles around the golden god. A group of musicians picked up their instruments and played loud and fast, pounding drums, blowing horns.

People broke away to touch their fingers to the blood, then to their lips, and finally to the hooves of the calf. Arella found herself in front of the slaughter. A man beside her tasted the blood, touched the calf. A woman on the other side did the same, then a child . . . everyone. The throng shoved her and she fell, her palm landing in gore. Then she touched her bloody hand to her lips and reached high to caress the hoof.

God help me, she thought. *Gods help me—what am I doing?*

She saw Gehazi leaning against the altar. He smiled at her and nodded his approval. She spun off, thinking only of honoring her god, this god before her, who had brought joy back into the camp. She sang and danced and saw what the others were doing, the men and women. She found a man and joined them.

The clouds above swirled darkly, filling the valley with shadows. A voice rumbled like thunder over the masses of people playing and dancing. Silence came over them, a sudden calm that after so much merriment was as disturbing as the chaos. Heads turned toward the mountain, and there in the foothills on an outcropping was Moses. His beard and garments fluttered in a breeze, and his face was as dark as the storm clouds overhead. He raised two stone tablets, big slabs that appeared too heavy for the old man—any man—to lift. From them glowed a radiance that grew so bright it blotted out the hands holding them . . . the arms . . . the man himself. It was as though the sun had come down to expose what they had done. Arella shielded her eyes, but the light shone right through them, piercing her head.

The sun hung there on the mountain, then it flew toward them, brighter, hotter . . .

She woke up sprawled over the legs of a child. A woman in turn was draped over Arella's hips. This woman woke as well, then the boy. All of them waking at once, groaning, cupping their heads. Everything was blurry, but Arella could make out the people around her, stirring, rising. Some rubbed their eyes, and she realized they too were not seeing clearly. But other than their waking moans, no one spoke. They were ashamed, and whatever happened to them next, they would take their punishment in silence. Arella realized the calf and altar were gone.

She rolled off the boy and stood. Her clothes were ripped and half gone. She was filthy from hair to heels, mud and sweat and blood covering her. Her body reflected her soul, and she sensed that neither would ever be clean again. The boy, as dirty as she, flashed scared eyes all around, and then they settled on her. He started to cry, a quiet sobbing too mournful for a child so young. She helped him to his feet, and he clung to her. There were other children—all ages, in fact: boys and girls, women and men, dark-skinned and light, as though chosen as representatives of the whole encampment, the twelve tribes.

Taking the boy with her, Arella stumbled away, joining others who were trying to put distance between themselves and the site of their horrific deeds. The boy looked, but could not find his father.

A commotion drew their attention. A man was screaming, the worst obscenities, threats against everyone. Arella realized it was Gehazi, his handsome features twisted by hate. Soldiers held his arms and legs as he thrashed and shook his head back and forth. He paused a mere heartbeat of stillness, and he was gazing at her, the briefest smile bending his lips. His head snapped away, and his limbs tugged violently against his human restraints. He flailed and bucked as the men carried him into a crowd that closed after them, leaving only his screams as evidence of his insanity.

Arella and the boy continued until they came to a tight, undulating mass of people. They were being blocked from leaving the area. Whispers reached her: while they'd slept, Moses had called for repentance. Those who failed to bow had been put to death, 3000 of them. The people parted, and she saw it: bodies piled high, more being dragged toward the mound from all directions.

She took the boy away from the sight, from the nauseating stench of the blood, and they huddled beside a boulder. Before long, Moses came and walked among them. Levite priests accompanied him, whispering and wailing prayers, their arms raised and their faces turned toward the sky. Moses passed around a chalice, which he continually dipped into a vat carried behind him. She and the boy drank, too shamed to protest, too glad to be alive. Flecks of gold swirled in the water, pieces of the ground-up calf. The jewelry they had worn outside their bodies was now in them, the cow they had worshipped consumed.

The boy tugged on Arella's arm and whispered, "Are we to die too?" And she wondered if the drink was a prelude to death. She didn't care; it was what she deserved, what they all deserved.

After they all drank, the wall of guards dissolved, and they were free to return to their tribes. No one spoke of the calf or their transgressions, though Moses said that they would never see the Promised Land. God had instructed him to make them wander in the desert for forty years, until most of those who had been led out of Pharaoh's rule had died. Only their children would receive God's blessing of a land they could call home.

X I I I

In her dream Nevaeh wept, and could not stop weeping.

She woke with a start and stared down the long, dark corridor in front of her, its far end completely lost in the shadows. She wiped a tear off her cheek and thought about how the tunnel resembled her life: seemingly endless, only a few bright spots to mark the times she'd found something close to contentment, filled with the bones and ghosts of people who had, for a brief time, shared it with her and then died.

So much darkness.

It stood in utter contrast to the last time she'd seen God, that sun-bright radiance flying at her from the tablets. It had knocked her out and changed her—changed all of them, those who would eventually become the Tribe. They had stopped aging, stopped dying . . . destined to forever walk the earth without ever being with him in heaven.

[9]

Jagger had watched Addison hike to the upper hole and descend into it. He thought of the Greek myths in which a hero traveled into Hades to rescue a maiden or recover a stolen treasure. That was Ollie and Addison: descending into a pit, hoping to return with an armful of loot, maybe even a maiden, or at least the bones of one.

He stood outside the tent for a while, taking in the workers, scanning the ragged outcroppings on the mountain rising beyond the dig. Gradually his heartbeat slowed to normal, and he frowned at the thought that such a minor altercation had got him so worked up. If he stayed at the monastery for much longer he'd have to find a hobby that fed his need for adventure. Rock climbing, maybe. Or camel racing. The world here turned a little too slowly for his taste.

He looked down at the contraption that had taken the place of his left hand. He thought of it as RoboHand, but his son, Tyler, had described it perfectly: "Terminator G.I. Joe hand." Two metal hooks— one acting as fingers, the other a thumb—formed a circle similar to the action figure's hands, preshaped to hold weapons. The tips flared into a T, providing more gripping surface. Jagger flexed his arm, forcing the hooks apart, then relaxed, closing them again. He was getting adept at manipulating the device—called a *prehensor*—but mishaps still happened more often than he liked: clamping a plastic bottle tight enough to make the soda geyser out, bruising Tyler's head going for a clumsy embrace. Not that long ago he'd brushed away a fly and given himself a bloody nose. Twenty-nine years of flesh, one year of metal: it was a wonder he hadn't put an eye out.

Or crushed the thief's throat beyond repair. The prehensor had the strength to do it; only Jagger's conscious restraint kept the grip from its full potential. And in situations like the one with Addison's assailant—in fighting mode with high emotions—he trusted neither his mental capacity for restraint nor his skills at manipulating the hooks with precision.

But it wasn't that he was a physical man with a physically demanding job, suddenly disabled, that drove the despair Jagger had felt after the accident, not really. That was just a kick in the face when he was down. The real wound was everything else that had been lost in the crash: the Bransfords, four people he had loved as deeply as he did his own wife and child. Four powerhouses of compassion and potential, snuffed out like paper matches.

Move on, he'd told himself. *Don't dwell on it. Not now.*

He was getting better at tempering the perfect storm of self-pity, grief, and anger that swirled inside him . . . but as with RoboHand, mishaps still happened.

He remained self-conscious enough about his missing limb to wear his sleeves long, hiding the artificial forearm that slipped over a stub just below his elbow. Cables allowed his biceps, back, and chest muscles to open and close the hooks.

"Jag!" someone called. "Jagger!"

He looked between the tents and saw Hanif at the corner of the monastery walls. Jagger waved.

"Closing time!" Hanif yelled and tapped his wrist. As if on cue, a group of tourists appeared, streaming past him.

Jagger raised his thumb.

The monastery closed at noon, releasing scores of visitors to flow not to the parking lot but past the excavation on their way up Mt. Sinai to see the peak. The best time for the trek was at night, when the temperature was less oppressive and the reward was watching the sunrise on the God-trodden Mountain, as the locals called Sinai. The midday sojourners, however, hadn't heard that sightseeing tip, or had arrived too late to heed it.

Jagger headed for his closing-time position at the end of the split-rail fence, where his presence would discourage lookie-loos from lookie-looing too close to the excavation or becoming more than lookie-loos. It was at times like this—babysitting fat tourists like a museum guard—that he most missed being an Army Ranger or a bodyguard for foreign dignitaries and celebrities. At least then there'd been *some* action, even if only a false bomb threat or an overzealous autograph hound.

He gazed at the two big excavation trenches. Maybe digging around in a dirt hole ten hours a day wouldn't be so bad after all.

[10]

With posters of the latest muscles-and-mayhem movies and sexy women leaning on sexier cars, a lead guitar propped against an amp by an unmade bed, and dirty clothes scattered everywhere, Toby's room looked like a typical teenage boy's—except for the 9mm handgun on the nightstand, the bare bulbs under wire cages tacked to a stone ceiling, and the twin sixty-inch plasma TVs mounted to one wall.

The plasmas were displaying different images of the same video game: views of a city from what could have been birds swooping between buildings, diving to take in streets packed with cars or sailing up over rooftops. Could have been birds, but weren't. With a flick of Toby's finger on a control pad, a missile shot out as if from the bottom of the screen, sailed through the bubbling tip of a fountain of water spraying up from a pond, and streaked under a crowded portico right into a hotel lobby. An explosion sent glass and bricks, cars and people flying away on currents of fire and smoke.

"Yeah!" Toby said from a black leather chair.

"Pull up," Sebastian said, standing behind Toby with his hands on the back of the chair. "Pull up!"

Toby did, and the screen showed the hotel façade drawing closer, sweeping down as the camera angled up. Sky came into view, but the camera zoomed toward windows on the top floor.

"Pull up!"

"I am!"

The camera crashed through windows, and the monitor went black.

"I told you," Sebastian said, giving the back of the chair a fierce shake.

"I did pull up!" The boy twisted around to glare at Sebastian.

"You waited too long. You wanted to see the missile hit. You can't do that. I told you, release the missile and get away. Shoot and scoot."

"Like this," Phin said from a matching chair beside Toby's. On the plasma in front of him, a missile shot out from the bottom of the screen, heading for a building with a big sign mounted above the doors: POLICE. The camera banked away, climbing. He laughed, a pronounced *Ha-ha-ha!* The camera continued to turn and climb, and a building slid onto the screen from the right, panning across it like a swipe-away transition between movie scenes. It filled the screen, and Phin's monitor went black.

"Ha!" Toby said.

"Wait a minute," Phin said. "That building's in the wrong place!"

"It is not," said Sebastian. "You were supposed to study the maps."

"I did! It wasn't on my radar!"

"It was, I saw it."

"So did I," Toby said. "I was wondering what you were doing."

"You weren't looking at it," Sebastian told Phin.

"It's too small . . . down there in the bottom corner. How am I—?"

"You want it in the center of the screen?" Sebastian said. "Then how you gonna see where you're going, what you're shooting at?"

Phin tossed the control on the floor. "This is stupid." He stood and headed for the door.

Sebastian grabbed his arm. "If you can't even play the game—"

Phin pulled his arm away. "Don't worry about it. I'll beat that thing by tomorrow. Stop coaching."

They stared at each other for a few moments. Phin rolled his head, audibly popping out the stiffness, and said, "All right, one more go, then I'm done." He picked up his controller and dropped into the chair.

"Watch the radar this time," Toby said.

Phin glared at him. "When we're doing this for real, we'll see who gets the most kills."

"You're on," Toby said and pushed the button to restart the simulator.

[11]

Jagger had just swung his leg over the fence's top rail when he heard the distant voice of his son.

"Dad!"

He looked toward the monastery, over the heads of the streaming tourists. His vision landed not on his boy but on his wife. There was something about watching her unaware—ages ago, across a lecture hall as she bit her lip in concentration and furiously took notes; plucking a flower from their garden back in Virginia, smiling at its fragrance—that seemed not *better* than mutual attention but *special*, like sharing a secret.

The sight of her pushed aside the blackness in his heart, leaving a less volatile but more aching emotion: guilt. After the crash he had allowed depression to get the better of him. His feelings had grown numb to her charms . . . to everything. He'd been bitter and hurtful to the people he loved the most—knowing it and hating it even as he did it. He'd felt like a junkie constantly scraping for a fix, but instead of heroin he craved misery in himself and everyone around him.

Then Oliver had called, on the recommendation of a former client. It was an offer he hadn't taken seriously at first. Not only would he be leaping back into security work, but he'd have to transplant his family from comfort and familiarity to isolation and an environment completely alien to them—the last thing any of them needed.

But Beth had a different take on it: she saw the change as a fresh start, away from reminders, and he started thinking that the job could be a form of detox from his depression. And it was working: since moving to the Sinai, the close quarters, the challenge of living in a foreign country under isolated conditions, and his own renewed sense of purpose had energized them, individually and as a family.

Now he wanted time to stop so he could simply watch her—like that moment when falling asleep feels so good, you want to stay like that all night. She pushed her hair off her face and smiled at someone. Her eyes sparkled like sapphires held up to the sun.

He caught two more sparks of that light, as though refracted from her, and saw Tyler running ahead. His son was weaving through tourists on the path, his arms and legs pumping furiously. He wore a miniature version of a guard's uniform: desert camo shirt, matching shorts, boots, and canvas belt. The boy had begged to have Jagger's old utility case, a canvas-covered aluminum box the size of a fanny pack, originally designed to carry night vision goggles on a belt. The goggles were gone and so were the canvas covering and felt liner, leaving Tyler's stash of hard candy, coins, and rocks to clang around with impunity. With every step, the kid rattled like maracas.

Jagger climbed off the fence and opened his arms to receive the bundle of pure energy that was his boy. Tyler leaped and nearly knocked him off his feet.

Jagger *oofed*. "You're getting too big for that." He hoped Tyler hadn't caught his quick frown. After the crash—losing his best friend and watching his father suffer—Tyler had started acting younger than his years. He'd convinced Beth to bring his old raggedy "blankie" out of retirement, along with a handful of favorite toys from his younger days. For a while he'd called them Mommy and Daddy, and had even wet his bed a few times. His behavior was all the more jarring because he hadn't abandoned the introspective, logical thinking that Jagger had thought was advanced for a nine-year-old.

A child psychologist they'd consulted said such selective regression was common among children whose immediate family had experienced trauma: it was a defense mechanism, a mental retreat to more stable, comforting times. She'd assured them it was temporary. Tyler was slowly catching up with his age, but Jagger still found himself babying his son—a behavior he suspected had more to do with his own guilt than with Tyler's childish quirks.

"Mom made sahlab," Tyler said, his whole face smiling. "Are you thirsty?"

"Does a camel poop in the desert?"

Tyler laughed and squirmed his way higher in Jagger's embrace until his head was above his father's. He scanned the excavation. "Where's Ollie? We got some for him too."

"Dr. Hoffmann's working, Ty. Maybe now's not the best time." Tyler seemed to have made a hobby out of bombarding the archaeologist with questions and appeals for stories of previous digs.

"He said I can come see him anytime I want. He likes talking about archaeology." He leaned back in Jagger's arms to give him a serious look. "You know I'm gonna be an archaeologist."

"And what excuse do you use when you bother the monks?"

"*Bother?*" He punched Jagger's shoulder. "They like talking about what they do too. Mom says everyone does. That's why it's so easy to interview people for her articles."

Jagger scowled a little. The last thing *he* would want to do was talk about himself or his work.

Tyler said, "Did you know young monks are called brothers and old ones are fathers? Except when they talk to each other, then they always say brother."

"Even when they're fathers?"

Tyler nodded, eyes wide, like it was the craziest thing. "Anyway, I never told them I wanted to be a monk."

Jagger shook him up and down, making his treasures rattle. "How about a candy?" he said.

Tyler expertly opened the utility case without looking and produced a gumball. He popped it into Jagger's mouth. "Can I go see Ollie?" the boy asked.

Jagger relented. "I'll walk you over."

Beth reached them and held up a battered lunchbox emblazoned with *Clone Wars* stormtroopers. "Guess what I brought you?"

Jagger shifted Tyler into his left arm. For all of the trauma that limb had suffered, his biceps were as powerful as ever. In fact, given the metal prehensor, carbon fiber socket, and nylon harness that crossed his back and anchored around his other arm, the "disabled" arm was stronger than his real one.

He reached out, bypassed the lunchbox, and slipped his fingers around Beth's wrist. He pulled her close, said, "This?" and kissed her.

She smiled up at him. "Actually, I brought two." Her lips found his again.

Tyler made kissing noises.

Jagger dropped Tyler onto his feet, and the boy started for the excavation. Jagger snagged the back of his collar with his hook.

"Just to the fence, Dad. Promise."

Jagger released him, and Tyler climbed onto the fence's top rail to sit and watch the workers milling around the dig.

[12]

Jagger turned back to Beth. "School out already?"

She homeschooled Tyler in their tiny apartment in the monastery's visitors quarters. After learning that Jagger had brought his family, Gheronda, the monastery's abbot, had graciously offered it. Only Oliver had secured another room in the monastery. Everyone else hiked to the village's one hotel.

"We're meeting Gheronda in the library later," Beth said. "He's going to show us some illustrated manuscripts and explain how he classifies and catalogs them."

"Ah, the old AMREMM supplement to the Anglo-American Cataloging Rules," Jagger said with an air of professorial authority. He smiled at Beth's surprise. "Father Gheronda cornered me on my rounds and gave me an earful. You'd think he built the library himself."

The monastery boasted an impressive collection of early codices and manuscripts, second only to the Vatican in quantity and importance.

Beth laughed. "You know it's just 'Gheronda'?"

"I'm not going to call a guy I barely know by just his last name. He's been nice to us. I'll call him President Gheronda, if he wants."

"Gheronda means *elder*. The monks bestowed it on him out of respect, to honor him."

Jagger turned away, then looked at her out of the corner of his eye. "Yeah, I knew that."

She slapped his shoulder, and they watched Tyler assume a wobbling standing position on the top rail. "This is a great experience for him." She pushed herself into Jagger's side and put an arm around him. "For me too. I'm glad we came."

Jagger nodded.

41

"Dad," Tyler said. "Which hole is Ollie in?"

"Annabelle. Addison's with him."

The boy jumped down, grinning. "Let's go!"

Beth whispered, "He likes her British accent."

"He likes everything about her," Jagger said. He almost added, *But not as much as I like everything about you*—and it was true—but that he didn't have to say it was one of the things he loved about her. Beth was more comfortable in her own skin than anyone he'd ever met. It wasn't that she thought she had it all together; she was simply okay with *not* being all together.

She opened the lunchbox, handed him a paper cup, and uncapped a thermos. She poured out a white liquid, thick as motor oil. Made from spices and salep flour—ground orchid tubers—sahlab was a favorite Egyptian drink. The locals, however, served it hot. Beth's brilliance was in icing it.

"So," she said, "did you have a crush on someone when you were his age?"

"Of course. My fourth-grade teacher, Ms. Duncan." He blinked, furled his brow in thought. "I think."

Since the crash he'd suffered from long-term memory fragmentation—not amnesia, but a sort of fracturing of memories, so they were often recalled with no context: swimming in a lake as a boy with no memory of getting there or with whom or the events surrounding the swim; driving a car for the first time, but not knowing the make or model or where he'd been. He remembered his parents had died in a plane crash, but couldn't conjure being told of their deaths. And the faces of the foster families who'd taken him in, but not how many there were or the age he was with each one. Sometimes two unrelated pieces of memory would butt up against each other, making him believe—at least until he did the math—that they were part of the same event. He distinctly recalled coming home from delivering newspapers on a cold, wintry day to find his mom making him a grilled cheese sandwich and tomato soup. But by the time he'd acquired his first paper route, his parents had been dead for years.

Worst, his memories would sometimes pull images from things he'd never done—swashbuckling on a pirate ship, hugging a rifle in a foxhole—only seen in movies or heard from someone else; yet they were as vivid and real to him as watching Beth walk up the aisle toward him in her white gown or holding his newborn son. *Confabulation*, the doctors had called it.

It all had something to do with damage to his *parahippocampal gyrus*, where the brain stored its photo albums and home movies. But CAT scans had revealed no trauma there, so the doctors scratched their heads and wondered if his problem was psychological.

Just another jab from the Man Upstairs, he thought. *In case losing my arm, my best friend, and my best friend's family didn't knock me down enough notches.*

"Or maybe she was the one I didn't like," he said. "But that alien that abducted me when I was ten sure was cute."

Beth didn't laugh, just smiled sympathetically and rubbed his shoulder.

They watched Tyler climb over the fence and pick something up out of the dirt, brushing at it and blowing away the dust.

"I wish we'd met as little kids," she said. "Wouldn't that be wonderful, to have known your soul mate for your entire life?"

"You wouldn't have liked me."

She slapped his arm. "Don't say that. How could I not?"

"I'd have pulled your hair and called you names."

She made a smug face. "That'd just mean you liked me."

Jagger nodded and tugged her closer. "You're really glad we came?"

"We needed this."

"What about your writing? Do you miss it?"

"I'm writing," she said. "Just not articles. I'm making notes for my book."

"This would be a good setting for a murder mystery."

"It's nonfiction. Stories of the people who've come here throughout history."

"I know. Will we have our own chapter?"

"Nah, too boring."

"Dad!" Tyler called. He had edged halfway to the line of tents. "Come on!"

"When do you need him back?" Jagger asked her.

"Gheronda's expecting us at two."

He raised his arm to look at his watch, then realized he'd raised the wrong one. He closed his eyes and sighed. He didn't know which was worse, that after more than a year he still hadn't mastered the change in his body or that he'd suffered the involuntary change in the first place.

Beth squeezed his shoulder. He forced a smile and checked the time. "By two," he said. "No problem."

She returned the thermos to the lunchbox and handed it to him. "There are some extra cups in there for Ollie and Addison. And a sandwich for you."

He took it, kissed her again, and watched her walk toward the monastery until she turned to smile back at him and wave. Then he watched a little longer.

Tyler had returned and now tugged at his hook. "Come on, come on, come on."

Jagger scooped him up and deposited him on the other side of the fence. "Last one there does the dishes tonight."

As the boy bounded away, Jagger turned to look back toward the monastery, but Beth had disappeared in the crowd.

[13]

From her position in the center of the dark intersection at the end of the tunnel, Nevaeh watched Phin storm out of Toby's room. He turned back and said, "There's something wrong with the controls. I should have cleared the building that time!"

Sebastian stepped into the corridor and put his hand on Phin's shoulder. "Don't worry about it. Get some rest and we'll try again later."

Phin jerked himself free. "Fix the controls and we will." He stormed away and entered his bedroom, slamming the door behind him.

Sebastian shook his head, walked to his room, and disappeared into it. Light splashed into the corridor. Nevaeh waited for him to shut the door, but he didn't.

A minute later Toby came out of his room, strolled to the kids' room, and opened the door. The light clicked on, illuminating the skulls opposite the door. "Come on, guys," Toby said. "Let's do something."

Nevaeh could hear Jordan's groggy voice, but not his words. She guessed they weren't very pleasant.

She rose and walked through the first flickering sphere of candlelight. The kitchen door was open, and a light over the stove showed an empty room. She continued past Ben's door and stopped at her own. Three doors away, Jordan bolted out of his and Hannah's bedroom. He grabbed two skulls to keep from crashing into the wall, then looked back into the room as Hannah pattered out, giggling. Jordan's hair stood up on one side, and he wore pajamas covered with cartoon skateboarders; Hannah had on a pink nightgown and slippers like pink clouds. It didn't matter that Toby had just rousted them, nor that it was just after noon: in this windowless dungeon, night reigned around the clock, and the kids had taken to never wearing street clothes unless they were heading out.

Jordan looked in Nevaeh's direction, stiffened, and squinted into the darkness.

She stepped into the light of a candle so he could see her. He smiled and pressed a finger to his lips. He grabbed Hannah's hand, and they ran the other direction.

Toby's voice came out of the bedroom: ". . . six . . . seven . . . eight . . ."

The children flashed through three pools of light, then disappeared into the black throat of the corridor.

A few seconds later Toby stepped into view. The teenager had on his typical uniform of layered shirts and fashionable jeans: heaven forbid he should ever be caught in pj's. He looked both directions and addressed Nevaeh in a loud whisper: "Where'd they go?"

She shrugged, and Toby took off. Nevaeh knew he'd never find them: ever exploring, Jordan had found a place where the skulls had crumbled, revealing another room beyond. And she was sure that was only one of many hiding places the boy had discovered.

She thanked God for Jordan. He had been like a son to her since she'd woken up with her legs draped over him on that awful day so long ago. She was thankful, too, that the children's personalities and mental states had remained childlike. Ben had a biological explanation for that too, but she knew it was God. Without their constant youthful energy, quick laughter, and optimistic outlook, she would have gone crazy a long time ago. Maybe Phin should spend more time with them.

She walked the corridor to Sebastian's room and looked in. He was sitting at a table against the far wall, his back to her. Three laptop computers crowded in front of him, like children listening to a story. Another device, which resembled a black soda can capped by a glass dome, sat off to one side. Wires ran from it and disappeared behind the computers.

She walked silently toward him, past a big workbench on which he'd arranged his shark fishing gear: rod, reel, fighting harness, sonar. Stacked in a basket on the desk were hand-annotated underwater topographic maps from places like Vigo Port, Spain; Terceira, Azores; and Osa Peninsula, Costa Rica. The chair in front of the workbench was the floor-mounted fighting chair from which he'd caught a record-setting marlin—1,362 pounds and 15 feet long. Displayed on the wall was a selection of old whaling harpoons: two-flue and one-flue, toggling, and a bomb lance. They had nothing to do with shark fishing, but Sebastian was nostalgic about them, having used them on a Dutch whaling expedition in 1880. When Nevaeh protested his hobby—reminding him that even Peter Benchley had become a shark conservationist—he'd said the only reason she didn't shark fish herself stemmed from a general distaste for cannibalism.

Sebastian's fingers clicked over the center keyboard. He paused to watch numbers and graphs construct themselves on the monitor. Before they stopped moving, his hands flashed over the keys again, restarting the process.

She stopped behind him and watched him work. She considered grabbing hold of his close-cropped Afro, then thought her nails on the back of his neck would give him a better scare. She raised her hand.

"What do you want, Nevaeh?" he said, clicking away.

She slapped the back of his head. "You're no fun."

"I'm busy. Go away."

She turned and rested her backside against the edge of the desk. "Have you cracked the code on the microchips yet?"

"You just got back with them."

"And we should be heading for the zone of operations by now, but we can't move until you have the chips ready for the control panels."

"Can't stand still, can you? I had a dog like that once." He glanced at her. "Had to put him down, made me too nervous."

She picked up the soda can thing, drawing its wires tight against her side as she examined it. Under the glass dome rested an octagonal computer chip about the diameter and thickness of a dime. At each of its corners, a thin gold peg disappeared into a hole in the top of the can. It looked to Nevaeh like a spider caught in a trap.

"Hey, hey," Sebastian said, standing and taking the can from her. He replaced it on the desk. "Do you want me to decode this thing or not? Get out of here, Nev. I mean it."

She crossed her arms. "Give me an ETA."

He sighed and dropped back into the chair. He waved a hand at the monitors, as though tossing sand at them. "These chips are designed *not* to be decoded. Each UAV requires two chips onboard and two matching chips at the control console. All four have to communicate with each other as well as the rest of the fleet for the drone to work. Thanks to your success at MicroTech, we now have duplicates of the control console chips. But they're encoded and unusable until unlocked by the commanding officer—or me. Trouble is, each one has its own AES-256 encryption block." He smiled at the confusion on her face. "That's the most secure encryption in the world—NSA standard."

"Can't you just give me an ETA?"

"How long until the field test?" he said. It was their one window of opportunity, the only time the particular combat drones they planned on hijacking would be fully armed outside a theater of combat. The U.S. military had ordered beefed-up versions of their premier hunter-killer drones, each with enough firepower to bring down a skyscraper. They also wanted *fleets* of these flying killing machines to work in unison, with the ultimate goal of creating the most powerful conventional warfare unit of destruction ever. The field test was slated to be a demonstration of an operational ten-unit fleet. It was the Tribe's intention to make it a demonstration of much more.

"Two weeks."

Sebastian made a dismissive sound with his mouth.

"But Ben's inside man says they always change the date for security purposes. Could be anytime."

Ben—forever cultivating connections within multiple countries' seats of power—had been particularly secretive about this one. The source must have had umbra-level clearance: he'd told Ben about the drones' field test, the microchips that controlled them, and how to get the manufacturer's secret spare set.

"I'll have them cracked by tomorrow, okay?"

"I knew we could count on you. How're Toby and Phin coming along? I heard them practicing their piloting skills on the Xbox."

"They need a couple more days."

She shook her head. "The field command center has been set up for *weeks*. All we need to do is plug in the manpower and the chips. You got the chips, and they're still not ready?"

"It's not as easy as it looks, Nev," Sebastian said. "Lot of things to learn, and it has to be second nature to them, no time to think once they're moving. They've been practicing all day. They need a break."

"We should go as soon as you've cracked the chips. Let's at least get on-site."

"Talk to Ben."

"I don't *need* to talk to Ben."

Sebastian shrugged. "Whatever."

They stared at each other for a few beats. They both understood the balance of power. Ben was calculating and meticulous; Nevaeh swift and impetuous. Every mission required a mix of both personalities. How much of one or the other depended on a number of factors, such as the levels of risk, covertness, and political sensitivity. Either Ben or Nevaeh would take charge once they'd determined the mix. The Baltimore trip exemplified the concept. Ben had acquired the intel and planned the theft. Once there, however, Nevaeh had pushed them into action and taken care of the guard. Ben was the Tribe's head; she was its muscle.

No one doubted that this new project's size and importance—its potential impact—pushed it firmly into Ben's purview.

She nodded and strode toward the door. "We'd better not miss it," she said. She turned left into the corridor and stuck her head into the next room. Phin was sitting on his bed, balancing a bottle of whiskey on his knee and moving his head to music she couldn't hear. When he saw her and plucked out an earbud, she said, "Want to kill someone?"

"Who do you have in mind?"

She pulled a sheet of paper from her back pocket and held it up. "A bad guy, who else?"

[14]

By the time Jagger had reached the first pit, Tyler was running around the next, uppermost dig to reach its shallow end. The boy hopped in and disappeared. Jagger waved to the dozen workers in the first hole. Several nodded in return, their hands occupied by a shovel and a trowel, a wood-framed screen and a camera. He passed Bertha, crossed the ground between the holes, and stopped at the edge of Annabelle's deep end. Twenty feet below, Oliver, Addison, and Tyler crouched around a small lump protruding from the floor. Oliver brushed at the object while Addison made notes on a clipboard. Tyler was leaning close, as though inspecting a new kind of insect.

"Playing in the dirt again?" Jagger said.

Oliver cranked his neck to look at him and laughed. "In grad school I had a T-shirt with those very words. How're things, Jag?"

"All quiet on the Middle Eastern front."

Oliver flashed a big smile. "For now," he said. He turned back to his brushing.

"Expecting trouble?" Jagger said.

"I hope so," Oliver said without looking. "When we find what we're looking for, the looters will descend like vultures. And the anarchists. Then you'll really earn your keep." He glanced up. "Not that you don't now."

"Something like this?" Tyler said, leaning closer to the protruding clump. "Is it special?"

"Probably not," Oliver said. "Just a piece of pottery. Not even from the right era."

"Then why are you being so careful?"

Oliver leaned back onto his heels and sighed. "Because you never know."

Addison nudged Tyler with her elbow. "Some villagers in Jordan once found what they thought was a headstone," she said. "They broke it up to sell pieces to tourists. Turns out it was an ancient memorial celebrating a Moabite ruler's victories over Omri, king of Israel."

"The stone mentions the House of David and Yahweh, the Jewish name for God," Oliver added. "It pretty much shut up some groups who said there never was a King David."

"People said that?" Tyler said.

"Anything to disprove the Bible."

"But why?"

Addison shrugged. "They think religion is stupid, I guess. They want to live by their own rules, not God's."

Jagger squatted at the edge of the hole and set down the lunchbox. "We talked about that, Tyler," he said. "That's why Dr. Hoffmann's digging here."

Tyler chimed in. "'Cause some people say there was no Moses, right, Ollie?"

"They specifically deny the Exodus, that Moses led the Israelites out of Egypt."

"Even that the Red Sea parted?" Tyler said.

"Especially the miracles," Oliver agreed. "Just too crazy for them."

Tyler looked out of the hole at the mountain rising above them. "Or the Ten Commandments?"

"They don't believe any of it," Oliver said. He stood and brushed dust off his khaki trousers. "Thing is, no one has found any proof that the Israelites were ever here, which is sort of amazing, considering how many of them there were."

"Like . . . how many?"

"Oh, about two and a half million," Addison said.

"Or twenty thousand," Oliver said, "depending on whom you listen to. Either way, it was a lot of people. They should have left some evidence that they were here."

Tyler stared at the find Oliver had brushed. "Like what?"

"Bones, a gravesite. When Moses came down from the peak with the first tablets God had given him and found the people worshipping a golden calf, he had the Levites kill three thousand people. The bodies have to be somewhere."

Tyler made a face. "They just killed them?"

"For disobeying God. The rest of them had to wander in the desert—*this* desert—for forty years, until most of them died off. God wanted their children to inherit the Promised Land, not them."

"Wow." Tyler turned a horrified expression toward his father.

Jagger said, "And you think a spanking is bad."

Oliver continued: "Normally, archaeologists would look some distance away from encampments or settlements for gravesites. But scholars believe Moses would have had the slain buried right here at the base of the mountain, to warn the others of what happens when they sin against God. Plus, here's where we have the best chance of finding other evidence . . . like jewelry, lots of it. Moses said they didn't deserve to be decorated with ornaments, so the Israelites stripped off all their jewelry before leaving this place."

Tyler started to say something, but Oliver held up his hand to stop him. "Oh, and what if, just what if, we found"—he raised his hands and gaped theatrically at Tyler—"the holy grail of the Old Testament?"

"*What?*" Tyler exclaimed. "The real holy grail, like in that old Indiana Jones movie?"

Oliver laughed. "No, no. *My* holy grail, the greatest discovery I can imagine."

Tyler just stared.

"A piece of the original tablets," Oliver said. "A shard of the tablets that Moses broke when he saw the Israelites worshipping the idol. Written in stone by the finger of God himself."

"Really?" Tyler said. He looked at the walls of the dig. "Here?"

"If anywhere," Oliver said. "Can you imagine?"

He looked up, and Jagger could see on Oliver's face the wonderment that children display so easily and adults rarely rediscover. He realized it was what kept the man digging in the dirt, and he hoped it was never lost under too many potsherds and bottle caps.

"How would you know?" Jagger said. "If you found it . . . how would you know it's really from the tablets?"

"I think," Oliver said, furrowing his brow. "I think we'd just *know*. I mean, they couldn't be just *rock*, could they?"

Jagger smiled. "You don't sound much like a scientist."

"I'm a Christian first, Jagger," Oliver said. "I believe in miracles." He shook his head vigorously, as if shaking his dream out of his mind. "Besides, I'll settle for any evidence: a trinket . . . the gold dust Moses made them drink after grinding up the calf . . . coprolite."

"Copro-what?" Tyler said.

Addison grinned. "Poop."

"Huh?"

"Human waste," Oliver said. "There were a lot of people; they had to go to the bathroom somewhere."

Tyler stood quickly and studied the ground where he'd been kneeling. "What's it look like?"

"Like lava rock," Addison said. "It's rare, though. It usually dissolves into the ground. Sometimes you get lucky."

"Lucky?" Tyler said. "To find poop?"

"Proof," Oliver corrected.

"Still want to be an archaeologist?" Jagger said.

Tyler looked at Addison, who nodded. "Sure," he said. "Yeah."

Oliver slapped the boy's back. "You want to help unearth the potsherd?" He handed him a tool.

Tyler examined it. "This looks like a chopstick."

"It is," Oliver said. "I'll show you how to use it."

Tyler smiled up at his father. Jagger checked his watch. He said, "Go for it. I'll make my rounds and swing back in a little while."

He stood and ran his fingers around the inside of his waistband to tighten his shirt. The stream of tourists had vanished from the front of the excavation site. He turned to see the last of them struggling up the mountain. The peak was out of sight, beyond the first towering slabs of rock.

At the place where Moses had encountered God now stood a tiny chapel. The monks had told Jagger that under the chapel's floor, in the surface of the stone mountain, were the perfect imprints of two knees, left there by Moses as he knelt before God.

In the pit, Oliver was gently scraping the potsherd with the chopstick as Tyler watched, waiting for his turn.

"And, Ty?" Jagger said. "If it's poop, don't bring it home."

[15]

Sunlight reflected off the rippling water and played against the room's arched ceiling like electrical currents. Reclining in a poolside lounge chair, Philippe Gerard blew smoke into the air, adding to the illusion that he was in a dream, just floating in clouds and waiting to wake up. If only . . .

He had never thought his carefully constructed scheme to get rich would fall apart as suddenly as it had done. But like a house of cards, once the first fell, the rest followed.

Above him, the imitation lightning storm dissipated. He reached down to a box of tennis balls and tossed one into the pool, restarting the sun's reflected dance.

While it had lasted, his empire building had worked like the hand of God, relentless and unseen but for the things it left in its wake. It had built the lavish mansion around him; given him friends who controlled countries and starred in blockbuster movies; funded vacation homes, cars, global travel—everything he'd ever dreamed of owning and doing. But now that everyone knew the money had flowed out of retirement accounts and trust funds, diminishing them to near nothing, not only were the friends gone and the bank accounts frozen, but Philippe was days away from being sentenced to decades in prison.

He flipped the cigarette into the pool. He would miss this place, its opulence and proximity to the opera houses and nightclubs. The sunlight danced on the ceiling, calming him. At least that, the sunlight, he would not miss, because he was taking it with him. Different walls, different water, but equally beautiful, equally tranquil. He had no intention of ever seeing the gray drabness of a prison cell. Years ago he had purchased a villa in the resort town of Yalikavak, on Turkey's Bodrum Peninsula. Panoramic views of the Aegean Sea, a private beach, rooms with glass walls that levered up to let in the warm sea breezes.

His mother had been Turkish and had always insisted that he maintain citizenship in her native country. Now her conceit seemed providential. With Turkey's notoriously rigid extradition laws, he was a short car ride and private flight away from leaving his troubles behind.

Jacquelyn and the kids were already in Yalikavak, preparing for his arrival. He'd finished tying up loose ends with just enough time for one last meditation by the pool before the car came to whisk him away. He picked up the pack and tapped out another cigarette.

A loud rapping on glass made his fingers fumble, and the smoke fell to the tiled floor. He jerked his head around to see a figure at one of the French doors. At that angle, the pane's many bevels prevented a clear view. Only a journalist would be so bold as to broach the walls and gates around his property and make his way around back after receiving no answer at the front door.

"Go away!" he yelled.

More rapping, loud and sustained.

He sighed and rose out of the lounge chair. He pulled his robe closed and tied the belt, then picked up the revolver that had been under his leg. Holding it behind him, he approached the doors. A beautiful woman smiled at him from the other side. Long black hair, finely chiseled cheekbones and nose, exotic dark eyes—pretty enough to be the on-camera talent for any number of news agencies. But she was less modestly dressed than the ones who'd been shoving microphones in his face recently: tight black slacks, what appeared to be a matching bodice that accentuated her hourglass figure. A long black trench coat, open in front, fell below her knees. He glanced past her, saw no one else, no cameramen or sound guys lurking behind a topiary.

Hope goosed his heart. A fan, maybe? A going-away gift from one of his attorneys? He stopped in front of the door, only thin panes of glass between him and what he now realized was one of the most beautiful women he had ever seen. Perhaps thirty-five, she was one of those rare wonders whose appearance had obviously refined with age.

He shook his head. "No interviews," he said.

She pouted and said, "Do I look like I'm here to interview you?"

Behind his back, his finger slid over the trigger. His other hand unbolted the door, and he pulled it open. A breeze pushed her scent to him, overpowering the pool house's chlorine and tobacco. It confused his imagination—not altogether unpleasant, but dusty and old, with a touch of sweetness, an orchid ground into dirt. "What do you want?" he said. "This is private—"

Her hand came out of the trench coat pocket, holding a piece of paper, which she unfolded with the same hand. He saw a printout of a newspaper article, his face prominently displayed. She looked at it, then at him. "You're more handsome in person," she said.

He fought a smile. "What is this? Who are you?"

Her features hardened, as if solidifying into a statue—just as beautiful, but unattainable now, someone else's vision of beauty cast forever in stone. "Justice," she said.

"What?" He began to pull the gun around. Someone slapped it out of his hand. He spun. A man glared at him with wild eyes, a big crazy grin. Twin white wires snaked from a bulge in his shirt pocket to his ears. Midtwenties, short-cropped hair, patchy facial fur: Philippe immediately pegged him as a punk and realized the situation had exploded into something horrible. The young man lifted a flat blade, replacing half his face with the reflected image of Philippe's stunned expression. Squiggles of blood cracked the image like veins through marble.

Philippe looked down at his gun on the floor and saw his hand still clutching it. Blood pumped out of the stump of his wrist. For the briefest moment, all he could think about was how sharp the knife must be to slice through flesh and bone so easily. He reeled back and felt a sharp pain in his lower back and the solid form of the woman pushing against him.

The punk's blade flashed toward him.

X I I I

When it was over, Nevaeh gazed down at the bloody corpse.

Phin bobbed up and down on the balls of his feet, absently shaking blood off his blade. He tugged out his earbuds and let them dangle over his shoulder. "Like a cold glass of water in a desert," he said. He bent, dipped two fingers into a pool of blood, and held them under his nose. He stopped fidgeting long enough to cast a puzzled expression at her. "What's wrong?"

Staring at the body, she said, "I just keep thinking, *This is it. This is the one.*" She looked into Phin's eyes. "But it never is."

"Someday," he said, his head nodding like a bobblehead. "He can't ignore us forever."

"Can't he?"

With that she spun around, sending her hair sailing behind her like a cape, and strode through the backyard toward the gate.

[16]

"You see on this page," Gheronda said with more excitement than should be legal in a man his age, "the artist put a representation of each of the four evangelists in the corners." Under his cotton-gloved finger was a colorful and intricate illustration of an angel. "This one is Matthew." He pointed to a lion: "Mark." An ox: "Luke. And the eagle is John."

Tyler stood beside him, in front of the table on which the thirteenth-century book lay. He held his hands up like a surgeon stepping into an operating theater and continuously flapped them, making his oversized gloves wobble like ghosts.

Beth stood on the other side of Tyler, rubbing his back. She could tell Gheronda was losing her son's interest under a barrage of technical terms. Tyler had temporarily perked up when Gheronda described the process of making vellum from animal skins, but then it was back to *rubrics* and *drolleries* and *insular majuscules*, which elicited from Tyler yawns, roving eyes, and fidgetiness. It hadn't helped his enthusiasm when Gheronda asked him, despite the gloves, not to touch the delicate manuscripts. *Don't touch* was as grating to a nine-year-old as the word *bedtime*.

Trying to help, she said, "The illustrations are so *detailed*. It's incredible."

"Yes, yes," Gheronda said. "The transcribers fancied themselves artists—and certainly they were—but many of them abbreviated words to accommodate more illustrations, making translating the text a chore, to say the least. Look here . . ." He began methodically turning pages.

Tyler backed away, and when he was clear, turned to check out other parts of the library. He glanced back, seeking tacit approval, which Beth gave him through a smile. He stripped off his gloves and shoved them into his back pocket.

Beth scanned the long, two-story hall of the library—clean and white and modern looking, utterly at odds with the ancient dusty jumble of buildings beyond its doors. Nor did it resemble the Vatican's archival libraries she'd read about, with their hermetically sealed, temperature- and humidity-controlled rooms. Here invaluable books, manuscripts, paintings, and icons were stored on shelves and in cabinets and hung on walls. Apparently the dry desert air was the perfect preservative.

"Oh," Gheronda said, drawing her attention. "I believe we have a truant." He watched Tyler stroll past shelves of books to a window, onto which he pressed his palms and then his face. Instead of the admonition Beth expected, Gheronda laughed. "If I had his energy, I wouldn't spend an ounce of it on an old man's ramblings either."

She put her hand on his arm. "It's very interesting," she said. "Please go on."

The long hairs of his mustache and beard rustled into a grin, and they turned back to the book.

A few minutes later Tyler said, "Hey, what's this?" He was standing at the far end of the hall, where a door led to the icon archives. Beside the door was an antique sideboard, and on that stood a large painting with an arched top and heavy frame.

"Ah, that," Gheronda said, heading down the hall. "It's a diptych. Do you know what that is?"

"It looks like a dartboard," Tyler said.

As Beth approached, she saw what he meant. The painting was split down the middle: It had been painted on two panels that apparently opened to reveal something behind. That and the curved top resembled the dartboard cabinet they'd had in their den in Virginia—except instead of an old-fashioned Coca-Cola logo, this one displayed a baroque painting of what appeared at that distance to be an angel rising from a crypt. It was also at least three times larger.

Gheronda laughed. "Not a dartboard, no. A lot of polyptychs were created for the altars of—*Wait!*"

His bark made both Beth and Tyler jump. Tyler had been reaching to open the front panels. He froze with his hand hovering an inch from them. His saucer eyes stared back at them over his shoulder. His expression mirrored Beth's panic.

"Tyler, get away from that!" she said.

He snapped his hand away and jumped back.

Gheronda reached him and laid a gentle hand on the boy's shoulder. "I'm sorry I scared you. It's just that . . . well, a portion of the painting inside isn't suitable for all eyes."

"We can't see it?" Tyler said, disappointed.

"Not all of it," Gheronda said, reaching behind the sideboard. "Occasionally we host young people like yourself and others with sensitive spirits, so I made this." He withdrew a length of cardboard about four feet long by a foot tall. One of the long sides was irregularly shaped, reminding Beth of the surface of stormy seas. "Now, turn around, go on." He made a circle over Tyler's head with his finger.

Tyler made a face at his mother—*Oh brother!*—and reluctantly turned away.

Before Gheronda opened the panels, Beth realized that what she'd thought was an angel was a man, tearing himself out of a earthen grave as though from the flames of hell. Soil fell from his hair, cheeks, and open mouth. If Michelangelo had painted zombie scenes, they would look like this. No wonder it had intrigued Tyler.

The man split in two, and half of him swung toward her as Gheronda opened the panels. Her eyes landed on the lower half of the painting within, and shock unhinged her jaw. Animal parts lay at the base of a stone altar—heads, legs, cleaved bodies. Blood everywhere, and somehow she felt not all of it came from animals. People writhed in the gore, some on their knees, arms raised in worship, some fighting, others . . . She swallowed and tried to divert her eyes, but they would not obey. The others were naked, and not alone in their nakedness and debauchery. Then it was gone, covered by the cardboard.

Her mind could not process all that she had seen in that momentary glance, but her body was ahead of the game: nausea stirred her stomach, and she pressed a hand over it. As bad as the activities of the people were, their faces were worse. Fear, torment, delight—the artist had managed to capture them all on each face. The mixture produced expressions that were, if not demonic, then at minimum, evil. She felt light-headed and unsteady, and grabbed the corner of the sideboard, wondering how a painting could have hit her so hard. It was as though the very act of painting such vileness had imbued the artwork with a repulsion that assaulted viewers like a noxious gas.

She stepped to Tyler and took his hand. "Come on, we're going."

"But, Mom—!"

"Beth," Gheronda said, touching her arm. "It's worth seeing."

"I *saw.*"

"The *rest* of the piece. I promise there's nothing like the lower portion."

Tyler started to turn, and she grabbed the top of his head, holding it straight. Gheronda nodded encouragement and swiveled his eyes toward the diptych. She followed his gaze, ready to slam the shutters over her eyes at the first hint of depravity. The hint was there—in the faces, sly ecstasy—but they were only dancers, *clothed* dancers. It was a fascinating painting, and she understood why it held special meaning for Gheronda.

"What is it?" Tyler said.

She let go of his head and guided his shoulders around.

"Wow," he said.

[17]

The left panel showed Moses kneeling on a stone mountain, head bowed, hands clasped in front of him. A few twigs and leaves of a fiery bush encroached from one side, casting golden light on his face. Much as the bottom portion of the main painting had disgusted her, this one brought peace: humble man in communion with his loving Creator. In the right panel, Moses's demeanor had swung in the other direction. Face contorted in fury, he stood on a boulder, two stone tablets raised above his head. The same golden glow seen emanating from the bush radiated from the tablets. Instead of feeling his fury, Beth felt only sadness.

Both panels were masterfully crafted, but it was the center panel that commanded attention. It depicted the Israelites worshipping the golden calf. Men, women, and children danced around a large, gleaming-gold bull perched high on a chiseled stone pedestal. Several had joined hands, but most were engaged in their own private spinning and hopping, laughing and singing. Coming around the far side of the pedestal was a line of skipping musicians, playing their instruments with all the gusto and passion of a modern-day rock band. Behind them, the mountain—the one Beth marveled at every day—rose out of sight. Bodies packed the sides of the painting, giving the impression they went on forever, thousands, tens of thousands partying, reveling, worshipping the wrong god. Hair flew, clothing whipped around, a small child had tripped and was being dragged by an oblivious adult. Beth could almost hear the dissonance of music, singing, and shouting—blurring into a sustained, undulating scream. That she had to remind herself it was a painting and not a window onto a scene happening at the moment was a testament to the artist's talent.

"Who . . . ?" Beth said. She lost the thought among all the activity on the panel.

"No one knows," Gheronda said. "Experts have compared it to Rubens, and it's been dated to around his time, the early 1600s. Marvelous, isn't it?"

"That's not the word I would use," she said.

"Are they happy?" Tyler said. His eyes roamed over the painting as though following a particular string among a tangled mass.

"I think they're trying to be happy," Gheronda said. "In their hearts they know what they're doing is wrong, but they let their impatience and need to worship *something* get the better of them. That contradiction drove them a little crazy, I think."

"A little?" Beth said.

Tyler pointed at the cardboard covering the lower foot of the six-foot-tall painting. Its contours perfectly covered the most offensive images. "What's under that?" he said.

"You don't need to know," Beth said. "Just people doing bad things."

"I don't usually censor art," Gheronda said. "But in this case . . ."

"I'm a writer," Beth said. "I'm opposed to almost all censorship, except the kind each of us does in deciding what we will and won't let in. What you've done in covering up that part isn't censorship, it's decency." She shook her head. "Why would someone with the talent to paint like that, paint *that*?" She waved her hand at the covered portion, as though swishing it away.

A voice spoke behind them: "Because it's the truth."

The three of them spun toward it.

Father Leo was leaning against a pillar, arms crossed over his chest. Leo was the collection's curator. He had a scraggly beard clinging to his jawline, chin, and upper lip—considering his baby face, Beth suspected it was the best he could do to match the long, bushy beards the other monks sported.

He came off the pillar and stepped forward. "The artist did his homework." He mussed Tyler's hair. "Hey, Ty."

Tyler grinned.

"Think about it," Leo said, addressing Beth. "False gods corrupt the spirit. How can they *not*? They draw you away from the real God, from his love and protection and moral laws. Then we start looking for things to make us feel better, and we turn to"—he pointed at the lower portion of the painting—"that."

"That may be," Beth said. "But we don't need to *see* it."

Leo tilted his head, raised his eyebrows. "I disagree. Sin is a car wreck of the spirit. They show high school kids pictures of accidents, bodies and all. 'This is what happens when you drink and drive—or text and drive.' Why not show the result of sin: depravity, death."

"I believe focusing on positive rewards works better than negative reinforcement."

"We're wired to respond to both." He made a grab at Tyler's nose. "What works for your son?"

She gave him a lopsided smile and conceded, "Both. But I don't want to be *scared* into heaven."

Leo's smile grew wider. "When it comes to eternal salvation, don't you think the best strategy is whatever works?"

"Still, I don't need to see it or read it or watch it to know sin is bad for us."

"I think we all need reminders: Michelangelo's depiction of souls being dragged to hell on the ceiling of the Sistine Chapel; Hieronymus Bosch's paintings of demons eating sinners, skinning them alive. Scandalous during their times, but now most of us can appreciate that the artists weren't trying to titillate us, but tell us the truth about sin." He scratched at the sparse hair on his cheek. "Can you see yourself as one of the women in this painting?"

"No," Beth said definitively.

"Thank God for that," Leo said. "Thank him with all of your heart because you *know* how bad it can be—how bad *you* can be—without him."

"I don't—" Beth stopped herself. She was going to say she didn't have to hear the details of child abuse to understand how awful it is. But a thought occurred to her: Didn't she hate drunkenness and irresponsibility a thousand times more than she had before the accident that had taken Jagger's arm and the lives of an entire family? Hadn't she come to hate those things maybe as much as God did? Didn't it make sense that intimate exposure to sin and the grief it causes—even through art—would nudge her closer to the level of abhorrence for sin that God felt?

She nodded, giving Leo this debate.

"So can I see it?" Tyler said.

"No," she said. "Not yet." There was still such a thing as age appropriateness.

"Mom," Tyler whined.

"Tyler, I said—"

"I have to go to the bathroom. *Now.*"

Gheronda raised his hand to point out the restroom, but Beth said, "I'll take him back to the apartment. We've already kept you from your work too long."

"Thank you," Tyler said, rushing along their good-byes. He was squirming now.

"And you too, Father Leo," Beth said, "for the food for thought."

He bowed his head. "Bon appétit."

She took Tyler's hand and headed for the door at the other end of the hall. He broke away and ran, kicking up the treasures in his utility case: *kich-kich-kich-kich-kich* . . .

"Don't run!" she hoarse-whispered. She glanced back. The two men were appraising the diptych, as though they hadn't done so countless times. It didn't matter if she ever saw it again—she would never forget the depravity it depicted, the twisted delight of its faces, or the nausea it had stirred in her.

[18]

Nevaeh pushed her palm against her forehead, willing her headache to go away. "Creed, listen," she said, without looking at him, "it's never bothered you before."

"It does now."

The sadness she detected in his voice surprised her. Until moments ago, his words had been sharp with defiance and anger. She realized his face had softened; his eyes were pleading. She glanced at Ben, sitting behind his big desk, a book open in front of him. His finger was still pressed against a passage he had quoted a minute before. *And he went after the man of Israel into the chamber, and thrust both of them through, the man of Israel, and the woman through her belly. So the plague was stayed from the children of Israel.*

Creed hadn't wanted to hear it—or any argument against his opinion—and now Nevaeh didn't want to hear *him.*

He spoke anyway: "It's one thing to mete out justice to a criminal, but this . . . this *plan* . . . There will be too many innocents."

"'Now kill all the boys,'" Ben said, "'And kill every woman—'"

Creed slapped his hand on the desk. "Stop quoting Scripture to me," he said. "I know it as well as you do." He sighed and said quietly, "That was then . . . this is now."

Ben leaned back in his chair and rubbed his goatee. "What's changed?" he said. "Did God?"

"Yes!" Creed said and paused. "No."

Nevaeh said, "'All have sinned and fall short of the glory of God.'"

"That doesn't give you the right to kill them, not like this," Creed said. "Everyone deserves a chance."

Nevaeh tilted her head. "At what?"

"Salvation," Creed said. "Redemption."

"Do *we*?"

Creed blinked. "Yes."

"Then where is it?" Nevaeh snapped. "Where is it, Creed? How long do we have to wait?"

"That's another issue," Ben said. His deep voice and crisp diction imbued the words with authority. "Right now we're addressing Creed's concerns regarding our plan."

"We're not *addressing* anything," Nevaeh said, waving a dismissive hand at Creed. "It's like talking to a brick wall."

"Creed," Ben said patiently, "when God's people crossed the Jordan into Canaan, they cleansed the land of the pagans living there. Everyone: men, women, and children."

Nevaeh said, "They were directed by God to do so."

"Where's *our* directive?" Creed demanded. It'd been a point of contention among them for centuries: just how *did* God communicate with his children once burning bushes and pillars of fire fell out of vogue?

"It's come through prayers," Nevaeh said, "dreams."

"Inspired by you and your desires," Creed asked, "or his?"

"He paves our way," Nevaeh said. "We listen when he foils our efforts . . . and when he aids them."

"You can't say that because God allows it, he wants it."

Ben said, "Our actions have always been consistent with his revealed word."

"As you interpret it," Creed said. "The people of Canaan would have corrupted the Israelites, seduced God's people into worshipping false gods, acting like pagans."

Ben spread his hands. "And you're saying the ways of the modern world don't?"

"You can't rid the world of blasphemous influences," Creed said. "Trying to is just pointless . . . and cruel."

Ben tapped the Bible in front of him. "More than cleansing Canaan of bad influences, the destruction of those towns was *symbolic*, a sign for everyone who came after—everyone who reads the Bible now or who ever did—that God demands loyalty, and death will come to everyone who betrays his will."

"So you're planning the destruction of an entire city to prove a point? To try to teach religion to a world that won't listen?"

Ben sighed. He lowered his face into his hands. Finally he said, "Yes."

"That's just wrong," Creed said. "It turns us into the very criminals we've been trying to rid the world of."

"Round and round," Nevaeh said, heading for the door. "Chat about it all you want. We resolved this a long time ago." She strode into the dark corridor, feeling the eyeless sockets of the skulls watching her. "We have a precedent for this," she called back. "A *divine* precedent."

[19]

Nevaeh stormed past her own room and stopped before reaching the next one. The heavy wooden door was open, allowing light, music, and the children's voices to spill out. Their laughter and playful banter calmed her, reminded her not to take everything so seriously.

She took a deep breath, stepped into the entrance, and leaned against the doorframe. It was a big space, lighted by two bare bulbs whose wires had been tacked to the stone ceiling. Two beds—plump with blankets and pillows—and two dressers were situated on opposite ends. Heavy wooden chests of varying shapes and sizes ran the length of the back wall. Stuffed with toys, they nevertheless failed to hold the children's collection, which was piled against the chests and walls, scattered around the room: dolls and pull toys; board games and puzzles; containers of Play-Doh, Silly Putty, Legos, Erector Sets. It looked like a missile had struck a toy store.

The left side of the room was Jordan's, and its walls marked his territory as clearly as a dog claimed a backyard: a slingshot; BB, Airsoft, and paintball guns; an oak dartboard so pocked and pitted that it was concave, its markings long gone. Posters displaying hot-dogging skateboarders, exotic sports cars, sharks. If a glance didn't tell you the age and gender of the occupant, you didn't know eleven-year-old boys.

Conversely, the right side was all little girl: stuffed animals, princess gowns, children's purses and daypacks with monogrammed names. Small shelves held snow globes, frilly dressed dolls, and porcelain figurines. Posters depicted cartoon characters, Disney princesses, and teddy bears posed in a variety of human activities.

A large area rug—in a gender-neutral lemon—filled the center of the room.

Crouching atop a chest, Jordan was aligning an army of wooden Roman soldiers, each a foot tall, in bowling-pin formation. Toby sat against the wall by the entrance, tossing a beanbag in the air and catching it.

Nevaeh nudged him with her foot. "Why aren't you practicing?"

"Sebastian's goofing around with the simulator. Like this song?"

Nevaeh listened. It was a ballad, "Forever Young," the version by Meatloaf. "Funny," she said, without any humor.

Toby just grinned.

Jordan balanced the last soldier, then raised his arm. "Go!" he said. Toby chucked the beanbag, and half of the soldiers scattered across the floor.

"Five! Ha!" Jordan said. "That's . . ." He wiggled his fingers, calculating. "Thirty-two. If you don't get nine on the next throw, I win." He tossed the beanbag back to Toby and began resetting the centurions.

"I'll get in on this," Nevaeh said. "My *dao* says you don't get nine, Toby." He'd had his eye on the ancient Han-era sword for some time.

Toby squinted up at her. "Seriously? Against what?"

She smiled. "The obol."

He laid his palm over his thigh, where she knew he could feel the medallion in his pants pocket. "No way," he said.

She shrugged. "A punch, then."

"I'm not going to punch you, Nev."

"You won't have to." She could tell he didn't like her confidence in his failure.

"All right, then. Start thinking about which arm you want numb for a week." He hardened his jaw and eyed the targets, which Jordan was still arranging. Jordan's hand bumped one, causing three to tumble.

Lying facedown on the floor, her chin propped on a pillow, Hannah giggled. Her hands gripped the ever-present Rebekah, a threadbare doll with an olive wood face and stone eyes. She smiled up at Nevaeh and said, "Look at my feet." The little girl's legs bent up at the knees, and she crossed and uncrossed her ankles as fast as she could. "Is that funny?"

The things that entertain a six-year-old mind, Nevaeh thought. "Very funny," she said and sat on the rug beside her. She began rubbing Hannah's back. "Getting close to bedtime, Hannah, honey."

Hannah craned her head around to look at her. "I don't want to be Hannah anymore," she said.

"You don't? Who do you want to be?"

"Alexa."

"You were already Alexa," Toby said without looking away from the soldiers. "About a hundred years ago."

"I don't remember. I like it."

Nevaeh nodded. "Okay, then, Alexa it is."

"And I want dark hair." She flashed teeth as tiny as kernels of corn.

Nevaeh lifted a handful of the girl's locks and let it fall onto her back. "That'll be very pretty," she agreed.

Toby gave Nevaeh a double take and tapped his cheek. She rubbed her face, felt a crusty smudge, and scraped at it with a fingernail. Dried blood.

"Whose?" Toby said.

"Nobody you know."

"You went without me?" Sounding disappointed. "Does Ben know? Is that why you're fighting?"

"Not with Ben," she said. "Creed's the one being difficult."

Toby nodded. "For a long time. Just like Kayla and Saul and . . ."

"Shhh," she said. "Creed's not going anywhere."

Jordan got all the dolls aligned and stood on the toy box. "Go," he said.

Toby raised the beanbag and shook it, closing one eye.

"Hey, batter, batter," Jordan said.

"Quiet," Toby said. He hurled the beanbag, picking off a single soldier.

"Oh yeah!" Jordan said. "I've beat you like ten thousand times."

"Right," Toby said.

"*More* than ten thousand. I wrote it down."

"Show me, then, you little puke."

"*Tobias,*" Nevaeh said. "How old are you?"

"Fifteen." He grinned. "Give or take."

She shook her head. "Be nice."

"Tell that to them." He cocked his head toward the door. Ben's and Creed's voices had grown loud. The accusations and insults reverberated off the stones and bones and drifted into the bedroom.

She said, "Takes a lot to wear down Ben's patience, but I guess—"

Something crashed in the corridor, followed by a pained scream and angry yelling.

Nevaeh sprang for the door. Toby hopped up, and as she passed him, Nevaeh punched him hard in the chest, knocking him back against the wall and onto his butt. Rubbing his chest, he groaned and said, "How old are *you*?"

"You know I always collect," she said and winked. She went through the doorway. Framed by the light coming from Ben's room, the two men struggled in the corridor. Creed had Ben pushed back into the skull wall and was pounding at his head with a book. Ben had a handful of Creed's shirt, while the other hand pistoned into his ribs.

Hurrying toward them, Nevaeh considered letting them beat each other senseless. Creed deserved it, and heaven knew she'd wanted more than once to shove Ben's books down the old man's throat. But without really thinking about it, she ran up behind Creed and hooked her arms under his. She shot her foot out, striking Ben in the chest harder than she intended, and pulled Creed away. Before Ben could follow, Toby inserted himself between them and stiffened his arms.

"Now, boys," Nevaeh said. She glared at Ben over Creed's shoulder.

Sweat glimmered on Ben's bald dome. The book had opened a small cut at the corner of his eyebrow, and blood trickled over his cheek. He panted and stared Creed down. Then he knocked Toby's arms away, snatched the book out of Creed's hand, and brushed past them into his room.

Nevaeh shoved Creed down the hall. He stumbled and fell to the floor between Hannah—*Alexa*—and Jordan, who'd pushed themselves against opposite walls. He rolled over to scowl at Nevaeh.

She jabbed a finger at him, said, "We're a family, Creed. A tribe. Sometimes you have to just go along with what the rest of us do."

Creed ran the back of his hand over his lips, smearing blood. "Not this time," he said.

"It's happening," she said. "Live with it."

Jordan stepped forward and held a hand down to Creed. Nevaeh knew the boy wasn't used to strife among them. It wouldn't surprise her if he also gave Creed a hug and expected everything to be better. But when Creed was up, Jordan simply backed up to his spot against the wall.

Alexa sniffed and wiped away a tear. Creed ran a hand over her head and smiled softly at her. He frowned at Nevaeh, turned, and walked away.

X I I I

Ben dropped into the chair behind his desk. He pulled a handkerchief from a drawer and dabbed his forehead. He looked at the blood and shook his head. What had gotten into him? He was used to debating theology with the others. He should not have let Creed get to him.

But he knew what was bothering him. For some time, doubt had been seeping into his thoughts, trying to corrupt his convictions the way moisture rusts metal. Creed's words had rattled him; he'd felt them strike his heart—and had felt his heart repel them. It wasn't logic combating illogic. It was stone ignoring the stroke of a gloved hand. He was hard, yes; all the Tribe were, they had to be. What he felt now was something different. He didn't know what it was, but something wasn't quite right.

He lowered his head. *God, is that you? Are you talking to me through Creed? Soften my heart, Lord, make me hear . . .*

But before long, all he could think about were the plans they'd made to attack the city, about their massive strike against evil. He tightened his lips and nodded. It was the right thing to do. It had to be.

His fingers slid under the Bible on his desk and slammed it shut.

[20]

The knife slipped, pinging against Jagger's metal hook. He sat in a stout wooden chair on the third-floor walkway in front of their apartment, whittling on a thick branch he'd found in the monastery's gardens. The physical therapist in Virginia had suggested the craft as a way of becoming dexterous with RoboHand. At first he could barely hold a piece of wood, let alone clamp it tight enough to accommodate the knife's pressure. But now his biggest worry was leaving indentations in an area of wood he'd already sculpted. He'd even mastered using his non-hand to work the knife, which he did to initially shape the piece. Then he'd switch the knife into his real hand to whittle in delicate details.

He blew on the unfinished product and held it up into the glow of an amber porch light. Carved into the branch was the face of an old man—his scraggly beard flowed into the grains of bark; deep wrinkles etched his forehead, formed perfect crow's feet, and arched from his nostrils to the corners of his mouth. A bulbous nose perched over a grim mouth. Almond-shaped eyes awaited pupils.

"It's Gheronda!" Beth said, stepping onto the terrace from their apartment. "Shame on you." She held out a wine glass. When he set down the knife and took it, she filled it from a green bottle.

"A face like that," Jagger said. "How could I *not* carve it? I'm flattered you recognized him."

"Michelangelo has nothing on you," she said. She set the bottle on the wide, flat arm of the chair next to him and brushed wood shavings off the seat. "That boy needs to learn to clean up after himself."

"He was tired," Jagger said. "I told him I'd take care of the mess. He's getting pretty good too."

"He showed me. A man, I think."

"It's going to be a Union soldier. He wants to make a whole regiment. Confederates too. Is he asleep?"

"Soon as his head hit the pillow." She dropped into the chair with a long sigh. "This place is an endless playground for a little boy . . . and exhausting for his mother." She filled her glass and took a sip.

Together they scanned the monastery laid out before them, a box about the size of a football field. Moonlight cast a silvery radiance into the compound, which looked to Jagger like the Lego construction of an impatient six-year-old. None of the buildings was quite squared to the exterior walls; a few—such as the single biggest building, the basilica—canted diagonally away from the wall. Over a millennium and a half, structures had been built on top of others and squeezed into gaps. This left rooftops at varying heights, tunnel-like alleyways, and small irregularly shaped open areas. Many rooftops doubled as terraces and walkways, with stone flues popping up at odd locations like memorials to long-forgotten events.

Defying this mishmash was the newest of the structures. Built against the interior of the south wall—to Jagger's right—was the Southwest Range Building, which housed the library, icon gallery, a hospice, a chapel, and quarters for many of the monks. Its façade boasted a double series of arches, fanning out from a central monolithic tower with its own two-story arch and domed roof. Closest to Jabel Musa, the already-tall building was on high ground, giving Jagger the impression that it watched over the compound, a well-dressed parent calmly protecting its ragamuffin children.

"Beautiful, isn't it?" Beth said.

"The Southwest Range Building? Yeah." The lunar glow caught its edges, accentuating the arches and giving it the appearance of having been carved out of the mountain rising behind it, like the temples of Petra a 150 miles to the northeast.

The compound itself lay mostly in shadows. A small scattering of amber lights glowed slightly brighter than the moon, illuminating a terrace, a couple walkways, and the space between the basilica and mosque, which had been built in the tenth century to placate Egypt's Arab rulers.

"All of it." She crossed her wine glass in front of her, inviting his eyes to behold the ancient setting. "So much history. Centuries of worship. Just think of the love for God that went into the placement of every stone."

"Lot of sweat," Jagger said.

She smiled. "Listen."

He did, though he already knew what he would hear: nothing. It was one of the eeriest aspects of the Sinai. No muffled radios or televisions, no barking dogs, no far-off hum of traffic. Even the occasional breeze seemed to pass without stirring a leaf or finding a scrap of litter to push over the ground. At this time of evening—just past ten—the monks had all retired to their quarters, taking with them the noises of human life: footsteps, closing doors, the clearing of throats. During the day it seemed one monk or another was always scraping a straw broom over the silt that settled everywhere.

And with Tyler asleep—the only time he didn't rattle or stomp or make gun sounds with his mouth—Jagger and Beth had come to treasure this hour. The world had shut down, seemingly just for them.

Jagger felt pressure on his shin and leaned over to see a cat rubbing against him. He scratched its head, which it appreciated for about five seconds. Then it leaped away as if he'd pinched it. He slid back into the chair. The backsides of countless people who had sat there before him had polished the wood to a smooth gleam. The armrests were nicked and scarred by, as far as Jagger could tell, fingernails, knives, pens, and cigarettes. Even so, the chair felt like a throne to him, and he liked the idea of surveying a kingdom that wasn't his, next to a queen who was. He lifted his wine glass. "To you," he said, "for sticking with me."

She tapped her glass to his. "I never considered doing anything else."

"I know," he said. He sipped the scarlet Egyptian wine. It was a cabernet sauvignon from Chateau Des Reves, the best they could find, which wasn't saying much. When it came to wines, Egypt was no France. This blend, with grapes imported from Lebanon, exhibited the varietal characteristics of flowers and cherry cough syrup. "I just mean, you've put up with a lot, and we haven't really talked about it that much."

She touched his arm. "I figured we would when you were ready."

He smiled at her, then stared into the glass. "I just . . ."

"What?"

"I never would have guessed I'd crumble like I did."

"Your grief ran as deep as your love."

He squinted at her. "You loved them too."

"We all grieve differently. I threw myself into my work."

"I *couldn't* work," Jagger said, feeling that old smoky, choking sense of self-loathing rising up from his gut. He shook his head. "I don't know how you did it."

She squeezed his arm. "I laid a lot of pain at the foot of the cross. I just figured he could handle it better than I could."

"I *blamed* God," Jagger said. He pushed his lips tight. The anger was still there. "A *whole family*, Beth." As if she needed reminding. "Here one minute, gone the next. All because—" He turned away, didn't want her to see the fury on his face. It was something he was supposed to have left behind in the States. He gazed at the simple, thin cross rising from the basilica's peaked roof. "All because some idiot thought he could drive plastered out of his mind."

Beth half turned and tucked her legs beneath her on the chair. She leaned close to him, her fingers stroking his forehead and running back through his hair. "Shhh," she said into his ear. Her hand slid over the side of his head and stopped on his neck, holding him while she brushed her nose against his cheek. "Let it go," she whispered.

He turned toward her. Her eyes looked into his, calming, understanding, sharing his burden.

His lips paused before touching hers, and only their breath kissed. To them, it was more intimate than full contact. It had started with their first kiss. Unsure eighteen-year-olds, wanting it, but frightened of feelings they'd never before felt so strongly. Neither had moved to close the paper-thin gap between their lips. After what had seemed like an eternity of tasting each other's essence but nothing more, she had giggled. Spell broken, he went in, pressing his lips to hers. During their most tender moments, this was how they kissed. Now their lips touched, barely, and she parted from him, returning to her throne.

"I love you," she whispered.

"Right back in your face." Another youthful praxis they'd held on to. He scanned the grounds. "It scares me," he said, "how fast it comes rushing back. The anger, frustration . . ."

"You did the right thing," she said, "getting away, bringing us here."

"What else could I do? I fell apart." He offered her a thin smile. "I couldn't even *drive*, for crying out loud."

A hint of the concern that had defined her appearance in the bad old days touched her eyes. She parted her lips, then closed them. He knew she wanted to assure him that it wasn't his fault, that he'd crumbled for good reason. But she knew him better than that: Regardless of the circumstances, he took responsibility for his own behavior. He never blamed outside causes, because it wasn't what happened to you that made you the person you were, it was how you responded to those things.

But he *had* blamed outside causes—God, the world—and he hadn't handled himself very well.

"A lot of people would have just kept sliding away," Beth said. "You took steps to get better. That's who you are, Jag. You fall—sometimes hard—but you always get up."

"I wasn't sure I could this time. I'm still not sure."

"You're up," she said. "Maybe on wobbly legs, but you're up. Don't think you aren't."

"Like I said—" He raised his glass. "To you." He took a swig and stood up. He stumbled into the railing, and Beth reached for him.

"Jag?"

"It's these wobbly legs," he said, casting a sideways glance at her. He made his knees go out and in.

She smiled and stood, pressing her side to his and wrapping her arm around him.

"Don't worry," she said. "I got you."

[21]

Nevaeh was in her favorite time and place: almost midnight in the corridor of skulls. She loved the way it was now, lighted only by candles. She imagined this was the way it looked when the skulls were originally stacked, before someone had added the electric lights.

The candles were spaced twenty feet apart on the stone-wall side of the corridor. The limestone above each one bore the blackened smoke stains of thousands of previous flames. Their flickering made the skulls appear to move, as though they were snapping their attention back and forth, watching for visitors or chatting with one another.

She strolled past the closed doors. Ben's . . . her own . . . the kids' . . . heading toward the far end a hundred meters away. *Screeeeech-click*: feeling the texture of fleshless foreheads. She imagined the sights each set of now-gone eyes had witnessed, the torrent of memories each brain had stored and the emotions they sparked. A mother's kiss. A father's wink of approval. A spouse's embrace. Childbirth. Love. Loss. Grief. At the time important, monumental—now gone, smoothed into insignificance by death.

She stopped at a skull that appeared more agitated than the rest, jerking around in the light of a sputtering flame. She slipped her finger into the skull's eye socket and traced its rough edge.

"Who were you?" she whispered to it. "Did I know you? Did we laugh together? Fight?" She leaned over to glare into the sockets. "What sights do you see now? Angels and gold . . . demons and fire . . . eternal nothingness? Are you basking in heaven or burning in hell?" She hooked her finger around the ridge of bone between the sockets and pulled. It cracked. She withdrew her finger and pushed the bulging septum back into place. It gave off a chalky, dusty odor, like everything else down here, dust and earth.

A sound reached her—the scuff of a shoe on stone—and she spun toward it. The corridor appeared empty, then a shadow shifted in the gloom between the light of two candles. It was too far away for her to make out the shape, if indeed it was anything more than a trick of the flames. She reached behind her and touched the butt of the ever-present pistol nestled into her waistband at the small of her back. She stepped forward. The shadow moved, solidified into a human silhouette.

"Who—?" she said, then it moved away from her, into the radiance of a candle. "Creed?"

His eyes were wide, frightened.

"What are you doing?"

He ran, flashing through the cones of light toward the end of the corridor. A duffel bag bounced against his side.

Nevaeh bolted after him. "Creed! Stop!"

As she approached Sebastian's room, she saw a dim light glowing inside. She glanced in as she passed: a desk lamp was on, and Sebastian lay sprawled on the floor. Picking up speed, she pulled out the gun. She had no hope of killing Creed with it, but they'd learned a long time ago that they were indeed human: Their muscles tore, their blood flowed, their organs failed—for a while. And they could hurt. Over time, each of them had felt more physical pain from lacerations, gunshots, and broken bones than entire armies combined. But only by severing the head from the body could they end their immortality; God had at least spared the world the horror of animated headless bodies and bodiless heads. Sometimes Nevaeh found that infinitely comical, at other times eternally sad.

But shooting Creed would stop him long enough to deal with him—either locking him up until he came to his senses or eliminating him altogether. That was something they'd have to vote on as a tribe.

She fired, intentionally wide—a warning shot. A skull shattered behind Creed. Bits of it pinged off the opposite wall. Other skulls tumbled to the floor.

Creed zagged left, then right, continuing toward the dark end, almost there.

Nevaeh stopped and braced herself, steadying the gun in two hands. Creed darted through the last of the light, and she fired twice. He sailed into the shadows, throwing back a guttural scream. She heard him tumble. She shot into the darkness, low, where she thought he'd fallen. The bullets sparked on the stone floor.

Staying close to the wall, she walked quickly, ready to shoot again. She imagined him lying there, bleeding, but capable of lifting his own firearm, waiting for the chance to put a couple slugs into her.

Doors crashed opened behind her.

"What is it?" Ben yelled.

"Shots," Phin said.

Other voices joined in—Elias's, the children's.

"Stay back!" Nevaeh yelled. She stopped in the semi-gloom between two candles and squatted, squinting toward the blackness, expecting starbursts from Creed's weapon. She yelled, "It's Creed! He's running . . . did something to Sebastian."

Footsteps pounded behind her. Without looking, she knew it was Elias and Phin; neither knew the meaning of caution.

She fired at nothing she could see, hoping to hit Creed again or at least draw his fire, giving her a target. Elias and Phin tromped to a stop beside her. They raised handguns and began blasting away at the darkness. The noise was deafening, a long series of explosions like grenades igniting each other. Shell casings tinked over the floor, ejected from Phin's semiauto. Nevaeh held her pistol, ready to shoot at Creed's return fire, but it never came.

The gunshots echoed against the stone after the men had exhausted their ammo. Through billows of swirling, eye-stinging smoke she saw them lower their arms. Elias eyed her and said, "What'd he do?"

Nevaeh stood and gazed back toward the rooms. Ben was just entering Sebastian's room. She said, "I don't know."

Elias nodded and moved forward. Nevaeh grabbed his arm and stepped in front of him. She inched ahead, gun raised. When they reached the last of the light, where she'd pegged Creed, she broke a candle from its wax moorings. It pushed the darkness away, revealing blood glistening on the floor. A wide smear ended in a single handprint. A few feet farther, a thick ribbon of it snaked away. They reached the end of the corridor, where it joined another passage, running left and right. The blood continued down the left passage, as she knew it would: it led to the nearest exit. She held the candle to the wall. Creed had left a bloody handprint.

"Where'd you get him?" Phin said.

Nevaeh shook her head. She squatted again and held out the candle. The blood trailed into the darkness, drizzled near the right-hand wall, as though Creed needed its support. She thought of the many hunting expeditions she'd been on, how animals rarely fell where they'd been shot. More often, they ran—sometimes for miles—until finally succumbing to the blood loss.

A flashlight beamed past her, illuminating the passage's limestone walls far past the candle's reach: more blood, but no Creed. Jordan stepped beside her with the light. He also held a revolver, big in his small hand.

Five shots, she thought. *I fired five times.* Her small Beretta held nine, leaving enough to bring him down—if she caught up with him. She took the .357 from Jordan and handed it to Elias. Then she grabbed the flashlight and pushed Jordan back. "Go back to your room," she said. Then the three adults went after Creed.

[22]

Nevaeh, Elias, and Phin returned fifteen minutes later. They found the others in Sebastian's room. Jordan and Alexa sat on the cot, with Sebastian lying between them. A wet cloth was draped over his forehead.

Alexa spotted them first and said, "He won't wake up."

"Creed conked him good," Toby said, pushing off the wall. "Did you get him?"

Nevaeh shook her head, and Phin said, "He couldn't have gotten far."

"Far enough," Nevaeh said. They had followed Creed's blood trail until it tapered to nothing. Either he'd found something to staunch it, or the wound wasn't as bad as Nevaeh had thought and it had stopped bleeding on its own.

"What I want to know," came Ben's voice, "is why you shot at him."

For a moment Nevaeh thought he'd slipped into an invisibility suit, but then the fighting chair rotated and there he sat, glaring at her.

"None of us is a prisoner. We are all free to come and go. That's the way it's always been."

"Not when he's talking about stopping us," Nevaeh said. "Not when he knows our plans. Anyway, I didn't shoot until I saw Sebastian on the floor. Stop grilling me." She glanced around at the Tribe—the *eight* of them remaining, she thought achingly. Their faces reflected both sadness and anger—at Creed, not her, she hoped.

Ben stood and leaned against the edge of the shark-fishing workbench, turning a reel in his hand, pretending to examine it. He said, "It would be nice to know that you aren't going to shoot *me* someday when I step out for air."

"Don't knock anybody out on your way, and I won't."

Ben headed toward the cot, passing Sebastian's computer-laden workbench. Nevaeh's heart skipped a beat at what she saw there. She strode to the bench and picked up the black soda can with the glass dome. The dome was shattered, and the chip it had displayed was gone. She waved it at Ben, scattering bits of glass across the floor. "Creed took the chip."

Ben instantly looked sick, which told her more than words could.

She said, "He can convince authorities of our intentions with it, can't he?" She went to Sebastian and leaned over him. "Sebastian!" She slapped him.

Jordan grabbed her arm, and Alexa said, "Don't! He's hurt!"

Nevaeh shook her arm free and slapped him again. Sebastian moaned. His eyelids rose a bit.

"Sebastian!" She held the top of the can toward him. "Creed took the chip!"

His lids fluttered and stayed open. He put his hand to his forehead and pulled off the cloth. "What happened?"

"Creed clobbered you," she said. "He took the chip and left. How bad is it?"

He moaned again. "I woke up, and he was at the workbench. I said something and he rushed me. That's all I remember. Headache, but I'm okay."

"Not you," Nevaeh said. "How bad is his taking the chip? What does it mean to us?" She snapped her head around to address Ben. "Even if he doesn't use it to alert the authorities, we're down one drone. Sebastian's simulation says we need them all."

"No," Sebastian said, his voice barely audible. "Without even a single chip, we're dead in the water. They talk to each other, like a net over the entire fleet. It's a safeguard to prevent hijacking one. Nobody has the resources to grab the whole lot . . . that's the thinking, anyway."

"So it's either all or none?" Ben said.

Sebastian nodded.

Nevaeh leaned a knee against the edge of the cot and hung her head. "Does Creed know that?" she said.

"He was in here yesterday, asking about how it all works."

"And you told him?"

He stared at her as though a third eye had just appeared in her forehead. He said, "We're . . . *family.*"

She straightened and turned to Ben. "I'm not letting go," she said. "It's our only chance to do this. We were *made* to do this. What if this is it? Our ticket home? We have to go after him." She looked at the others.

Phin and Toby nodded. Elias was Elias: leaning back against a wall, one leg cocked up and his foot on the wall. He was rolling a cigarette, licking the paper and pushing it down. He stuck it in his mouth and lit it, then squinted at her through a cloud of smoke and nodded. All eyes turned to Ben.

Ben looked at each of them in turn, then at the floor for a long time. Finally he nodded. "Creed wants to stop us. Not once, but forever. It's not just this project . . ."

"Not—" Nevaeh started, intending to reiterate the importance of this one strike and how long they'd been planning.

But Ben held up a hand to stop her. "With that chip, he can raise an army—quite literally, an army—to stop us, to find us. It'll be the end, and not the way we had hoped." He turned away and seemed to speak to himself. "Hoped . . . for so long, so long."

"Okay, then," Nevaeh said. "Where's he heading? How do we find him?"

Ben paced back past the workbench, running his hand over its surface. "He'll seek help," he said. "Sean, maybe."

At the name, Nevaeh's stomach cramped. She'd spent years forgetting him, and now she wanted to deny Ben's logic. But she couldn't; he was right.

"Sean?" Phin said. "Why?"

"They're allies now," Nevaeh said. "On the same side. Sean will know how to best use the chip and Creed's knowledge against us."

"But how can Creed reach him?" Toby said. "*We* don't know how."

"One of the Keepers," Ben said. "They'd know. Plus, they'd give him shelter."

"Yeah, yeah," Phin said, pointing at Ben. "A Haven."

Set up millennia ago, Havens were safe houses designed to give them shelter from anyone wishing them harm. *Anyone*, including their own kind. Originally, they were established as part of a truce between the Tribe and a group of former Tribe members—a group their leader, once called Gehazi but now known as Bale, half jokingly called the Clan. Bale disagreed with the Tribe's targeting of only "sinners," people who abused the privilege of life by hurting others; he was bent on causing destruction, of taking his pain and anguish out on *everyone*.

For hundreds of years, Bale had been content to let the Tribe go about its own business. Then, as some members of the Tribe began embracing the teachings of Christ, Bale's hatred for them grew. In the fourth century he declared an all-out war on them, leading to bloody attacks that caused more pain than death on both sides. Neither Tribe nor Clan had been able to pursue its own mission, outside of planning against and attacking one another, and recovering from their wounds to start it all over again. They'd finally called a truce. The Tribe kept clear of the Clan, but witnessed their existence in random murders, hospital fires, school shootings . . . Ben was convinced that Bale and his Clan were instrumental in sowing the seeds of malice and insanity in many mass murderers.

Keepers were mortals entrusted with their secret. Most were the monks and priests who maintained the Havens. Once the elders of their orders believed in the stability and faithfulness of younger acolytes, they'd pass the secret on to them . . . and so it went, in perpetuity. At any given time, a handful of other people around the world knew immortal beings walked the earth: some had been doctors who'd witnessed their miraculous healing, others had been spouses—the Immortals were not prohibited from marrying, but all of them had tried to abstain from falling in love; watching their loved ones age and die was simply too painful.

That Creed would head to a Haven was all but assured.

"But which one?" Phin said.

"Want to make a wager over it?" Nevaeh asked.

"I told you," Phin said, "I'm done betting with you." He rubbed his left pinky finger, which bent unnaturally at the first knuckle—the result of losing his last bet.

Ignoring their banter, Ben said, "We'll have to surveil all three."

"I'll take Trongsa," Nevaeh said. It was a town in the center of Bhutan. Getting there was time-consuming and treacherous, which made it perfect for Immortals who needed to lie low. A small Christian monastery had operated there, in the shadow of a monstrous Buddhist temple, for nearly a millennium. She headed for the door to get her ready-pack.

"No," Ben said. "I want you here. You need to be on the recovery team—you, me, and Phin."

She nodded. She and Phin were the most aggressive. They worked together well and got the job done. Elias was equally effective, but too laid back for a shock-and-awe raid on a monastery.

Ben continued. "Sebastian, you stay here and make the arrangements for the others. We'll need three charters. We'll keep our own jet here so the rest of us can go as soon as Creed surfaces."

"I can watch for him," Jordan said.

Ben appeared uncertain.

Nevaeh saw the hope on the boy's face. He was always looking for ways to help, to contribute to the Tribe. And over the years they'd found he made an ideal sentry, thanks to his "youth" and ability to watch without appearing to do so. She told Ben, "It *is* his job."

Ben thought about it, then said, "Okay, yes, that works. Jordan, you have London. But if Creed shows up, let us know and do nothing more."

Jordan was smiling proudly at Toby.

"Boy, you hear me?" Ben snapped.

"Yes, sir."

"And that goes for you two as well." He pointed at Toby and Elias.

"When we know where he is, we'll get there as quickly as possible. Elias, you take Trongsa."

Elias blew out more smoke and nodded.

"Have fun with that," Toby said and laughed. "That's a twelve-hour flight, dude. Then another ten on the ground."

Elias shrugged.

Toby raised his eyebrows. "Hey, does that mean—?"

Ben nodded. "You're going back to where it all began. Mt. Sinai."

[23]

Jagger was having the same dream he'd had at least once a week for over a year, and he knew it. But knowing he was dreaming did not reduce the sheer terror he felt, or allow him to change anything about it.

As if intentionally designed to compound the horror, the dream forced him to be in two places at once.

Jagger the Observer stood under a starry Virginian sky, feeling the icy breath of approaching winter on his cheeks and hands. He waited in the grassy median between the westbound and eastbound lanes of State Highway 287, watching for the familiar SUV.

Jagger the Participant rode in that SUV with the Bransfords. Beth had stayed home with Tyler, who'd been feverish and vomiting all day. She'd insisted that Jagger go to celebrate Cyndi Bransford's birthday. After all, saying the Bransfords were like family underrepresented their closeness. Mark had been Jagger's best friend all through college. They'd joined the army together, managed to transfer into intelligence at the same time, and jointly left military life for gigs in private security. Nothing weird about it: they thought alike, bounced ideas off each other, and what sounded good to one sounded good to the other.

So maybe it wasn't so strange that when Beth started dating Jagger, her BFF Cyndi fell for Mark. Though a year younger, the Bransfords' son, Robby, became Tyler's best friend, naturally. When the Bransfords welcomed baby Brianna three years ago, everyone wondered when the Bairds would hurry up and produce *her* best friend. If Frank Capra were still around, he would have bought the film rights.

Jagger and the Bransfords were heading home to Sunset Hills

from the birthday dinner in Sterling Park. They'd eaten at the family's favorite haunt, the creative—but uncreatively named—Dinner & a Show. The place was a converted theater in which the seats had been replaced by rows of tables, with chairs all facing a huge screen. Dinner was served to everyone at the same time, then the lights dimmed and a movie started—always an older film, available on DVD, but the novelty of the experience kept the restaurant packed. That evening's entertainment was *Return of the King*, the extended, four-hour version. Before the show, the waitstaff had delivered a birthday cake and flowers to Cyndi, and all the patrons had sung "Happy Birthday." Now it was late, they were almost home, and the Bransfords were happy and satisfied that they'd done Mom's birthday right.

Lights flashed over Jagger the Observer as cars passed, not as many as there would have been a few hours earlier, but in the end that didn't matter. Goose bumps rose on his arms, a condition that had nothing to do with the temperature. The headlights of Mark's Highlander had just come into view, less than two minutes from their Reston Parkway exit.

Jagger the Participant rode shotgun beside Mark, who always drove with his hands at ten and two and observed the speed limit with maddening regularity. Jagger twisted around to laugh at Robby in the back, sandwiched between Brianna in a booster seat and Cyndi. The movie had acted like a jolt of cinematic caffeine on the boy, and the entire drive home he'd recited scenes—verbatim, as far as Jagger could tell.

Jagger the Observer ran onto the highway, waving his arms.

Robby was retelling the scene in which Eowyn slays the Witchking.

You fool. No man can kill me.

I am no man!

Cyndi and Brianna dozed, their heads canting toward the windows, away from Robby, as though avoiding his wildly swinging arms.

Jagger the Observer spun, and his heart constricted. Coming the other direction, a van weaved between lanes. As he watched, it careened onto the right shoulder, skimmed a guardrail, and shot diagonally across the highway. It bounced into the median, churning up sod and dirt. Instead of stopping, it picked up speed and flew out of the median in a roar of revving engine, bottoming-out shocks, and protesting metal. Jagger signaled to the driver, as to a taxiing plane, to simply cross over these lanes as he had the others and sail into the field on the other side. But the van's tires screeched and smoked and jittered as the driver aligned it with the highway. It zoomed past Jagger, heading the wrong direction, and crashed head-on into the Highlander.

The sound pierced Jagger's head, but it wasn't crushing-tearing-colliding metal, shattering glass, or rupturing tires; it was screams, louder than physically possible, extending longer than the lives of the family producing them, melding with his own pointless *Nooooo!*

They were gone. All of them. Just like that.

Except for him. In the car, he was conscious. His left arm was smashed and pinned between the hard folds of the dashboard, which had accordioned as the front end crumpled into the passenger compartment. He was drenched in blood—not all of it, not even most of it, his own.

Jagger the Observer blinked tears out of his eyes and stared at the demolished Highlander. Smoke and steam—lighted by a single burning headlamp, angled upward—roiled over the demolished front end. Tiny squares of glass glinted like jewels on the blacktop. Blood leaked from the car onto the road, mixing with oil, gasoline, radiator fluid.

In reality, it had taken two hours and the Jaws of Life to extricate the van's driver from the wreckage, and almost as long to remove Jagger as he drifted in and out of consciousness. Each time he revived he heard screaming, and prayed it was coming from the Bransfords.

Scream, he thought. *Scream because you're alive.*

He'd learned later that the van's driver had made all the noise, in agony from a shattered femur and cracked sternum.

It didn't go down that way in Jagger's dream. In this realm the man pushed open his door and stepped out. He saw Jagger and smiled—the same smile he had tried to hide from the cameras as he left the courtroom three months after the crash, a free man. A nurse had botched the blood test, using an alcohol-based swab to clean his skin before inserting the syringe. State law required a nonalcohol-based swab, in the mistaken assumption that the wrong swab would produce inaccurate results. Despite having a blood-alcohol level of .17—more than twice the legal limit—the D.A. had no choice but to dismiss the charges.

"Do it," a gravelly voice said beside Jagger.

He turned to see Mark standing there. Half of his face was gone, and glass peppered the other side like freckles. Smoke coiled out of a hole in his skull. One shoulder drooped as though his arm started at the base of his neck. His chest was caved in, his shirt pushed in with it, clinging to broken ribs. The crater was the size and shape of a steering wheel. At the bottom, over his breastbone, blood seeped through the material. It formed the Toyota logo, then spread into an indistinguishable mass. He glared at Jagger, then rolled a lidless eye toward the drunk driver. "Do it," he repeated.

Jagger felt weight in his hands and realized he was holding an M240 belt-fed machine gun, the pride of the Rangers in Iraq. He looked up at the driver, who was facing him now, holding his palms up as if to say, *Whatcha gonna do?*

"Shoot him," Mark's corpse said. "For me, for Cyndi, for Robby, for Brianna." He nudged Jagger's shoulder with bloody fingers.

Jagger hefted the weapon and took aim.

"Come on, man, you know he deserves it," the corpse said and nudged him again and again, making it impossible for Jagger to lock onto the drunk. Over the gun's wavering sights the guy started laughing. Then he broke up and disappeared.

Jagger's eyes snapped open. A spear of light cut across the ceiling over his head. He groaned and squeezed his eyes tight. Always the same nightmare . . . leaving him grieved and angry and frustrated.

Mark's corpse nudged him again, and he jumped, rolling in bed to face the monster come to life.

Tyler was hunched beside the bed, shaking him. His lips formed the word *Dad?*

Jagger reached to his ear and pulled out a bullet-shaped wedge of foam. The loud clanging of a woden scmantron in the monastery's bell tower rushed in, waking him as surely as a splash of cold water. There was no need to look at the clock; the tolling sounded every morning at 4:15, calling the monks to matins, the first service of the day.

"Tyler," he said, "what is it?"

"The gonging woke me."

Jagger craned to see Beth. She shifted and murmured quietly, but remained asleep. He rolled back and put his hand on his son's shoulder. "Where are your earplugs?"

"I can't sleep with them. All I hear is my heartbeat, filling my head."

"Better than waking up this early."

Tyler frowned. The boy had something on his mind.

Jagger propped himself up on an elbow. "What are you thinking, son?"

[24]

Although it was the dominant building within the monastery walls, the Church of the Transfiguration was small by modern standards. Built between 542 and 551, it was designed as a place of worship for the monks, not the public. Within, its marble, gold, and rare art could buy Trump Tower with a few million to spare.

Jagger quietly pulled open one of the heavy cypress doors, which had hung at the basilica's entrance since it was new. He held it for Tyler, who stopped to gaze up at the inscription overhead. It was too dark to see the Greek words; still, Tyler recited from memory: "This is the gate to the Lord; the righteous shall enter into it." As rambunctious as he was, the boy accorded the monastery a deference Jagger found hard to muster. It may have come from talking to the monks, or from his mother's awe of the place's venerable traditions and sites, but Jagger didn't think so. He suspected it came from someplace more primal, someplace at the heart of Christ's admonition to "become like little children."

The righteous shall enter.

He almost said, *Maybe I should wait outside*, but he didn't think his son would appreciate the joke.

Tyler smiled at him and stepped inside. Jagger followed and eased the door closed. The service had started. Across the nave's floor of intricately patterned tiles, a monk stood at a lectern, chanting a prayer. The language was lost on Jagger—Byzantine Greek, he had learned—but its singsongy cadence and the reverence in which it was delivered instantly calmed the remnants of the nightmare's emotions.

Jagger followed Tyler into the dark nave. The only light came from a lantern above the praying monk. They found a wooden bench against a wall and sat. Slowly, monks in black robes lowered brass lamps suspended from the ceiling, lit them, and raised them again. The lamps turned and swung, filling the room with an undulating amber glow. The chains and chandeliers, granite columns, and ornately decorated walls seemed to pulse with life. Above the altar, mounted to a beam that spanned the room, hung a massive gold-painted crucifix—upon which Christ appeared to be gasping for breath. As the lamps settled, Christ's breathing slowed and stopped. Jagger felt, simultaneously, a shiver along his spine and a warmth filling his chest.

The monk at the lectern finished and backed away. Another monk stepped up and began chanting a passage from a leather-bound book the size of a gravestone. Moving as stealthily as shadows, monks roamed the church, stopping at icons to light candles and pray. A monk appeared from one of the nine tiny chapels that lined the sides and back of the church, waving a smoking lantern. The smell of lilacs and charred timber filled the room.

The fifteen-centuries-old structure . . . the religious relics from every century since . . . the strange combination of majestic splendor and subdued humility . . . the ancient words and bowed servants: at that moment, the church felt like a bit of heaven on earth, like one of the mansions Jesus promised to prepare for his saints. It wasn't hard to imagine God himself setting this place here, at the base of the mountain on which he spoke to Moses.

Jagger felt like a trespasser. It wasn't that he didn't believe in God; he had spent too many years studying the Word, praying with Beth, attending church to completely reject the idea of the Almighty. He just wasn't so sure he *liked* God, wasn't so sure God liked him . . . or any of his creations. Intellectually, he understood what C. S. Lewis called the "problem of pain" as it related to reconciling human suffering with a loving God. He grasped the concept of Isaiah 55:8: *For my thoughts are not your thoughts, neither are your ways my ways.* That is, humans don't establish the standards of what is right. And Jagger would have argued God's position—until it had leapt off the pages of theological and Christian-living books and gouged out his heart. He felt bloodied and beaten, left for dead in a ditch, the glassy eyes of the Bransfords glaring at him.

Still, Jagger hoped that it was *he* who had the problem, not God. If it were God's problem, all was lost; life was meaningless. But if he, Jagger, just wasn't getting it, then there was a chance of finding peace once more, of reclaiming the comfort he'd known back when he believed God was good and caring.

It was this hope, small as it was, that had driven him to take his present job. If he couldn't bring his spirit to God, he could at least put his body someplace where God's presence was everywhere: in the work being done, the conversations being shared, even the mountains being climbed.

Beth, smart gal that she was, had agreed. Last night he'd almost told her he was coming around. He was happier—with her, with Tyler, with life in general. God was more on his mind than he'd been in the States. How could he *not* be, here? But Jagger wasn't sure he felt any closer to him or that his attitude about the Big Man's disposition toward mankind had improved.

A monk floated past them, the hem of his robe whispering along the floor. Jagger leaned into Tyler's shoulder to tell him it was time to go. He glanced over to see the boy's head bowed, hands clasped in his lap. His son was praying. Jagger wondered what he was bringing before God. He thought he knew, and his heart ached. He wanted to give Tyler something—hope, maybe—so he mimicked his son's body language, interlacing his fingers and closing his eyes. He vowed to stay that way until he knew Tyler saw him, but then a strange thing happened. He forgot about Tyler and found himself tentatively, even reluctantly talking to his Creator.

[25]

Elias stared out of the charter jet's cabin window, absently rubbing through his shirt the nearly healed bullet wound over his heart. Only a few lights dotted the Hungarian terrain below Elias's jet, like a small handful of diamonds scattered over black velvet. Behind him, pinpricks of light illuminated the otherwise empty cabin, so his bearded reflection in the Plexiglas window appeared to be a ghost among the stars.

He turned back to the thick book on the table in front of him. It was a modern printing of the Septuagint Bible, in the original Greek. As much as he enjoyed talking comic books with Jordan, sports cars with Toby, and firearms with Phin, he loved dissecting theological issues with Ben. Usually he'd let Ben rant and expound ad infinitum, then he'd drop a bomb on the man's logic, correcting a misinterpreted Hebrew phrase or reminding him of a cultural context that flipped Ben's opinion on its head. And always he'd do so in fewer words than a Chinese fortune cookie: a word to the wise really was sufficient, and he had no patience for fools.

He cracked open the Bible. On every page lines glowed under yellow, orange, and green highlighting. The margins were packed with his scribbled notes. He'd taken to squeezing memos between the printed lines. The ink or pencil he'd used at the time and the handwriting itself helped him remember what he was thinking when he wrote it, even years later. It was one reason he ignored Ben's encouragement to switch to an e-book reader. Lugging the heavy book—or any of his other favorite reads—was a small sacrifice for the history of his thoughts.

He found himself reading the same passage a third time before realizing his mind wasn't in it tonight. He closed the book and leaned back into the seat. From his shirt pocket he pulled a thin box of rolling papers and a bag of tobacco. He rolled himself a cigarette and stuck it into the corner of his mouth. He found his Zippo and sat there flipping open the top, lighting the wick, and closing it again, over and over. He wondered if Creed would really go as far as the Trongsa Dzong. It was easier to climb Everest with a Sherpa on your back, or so it seemed to Elias: the twelve-hour flight to Paro, which hosted Bhutan's only airport, followed by a painfully slow drive on coiling roads to Trongsa. He doubted Creed would undertake the journey if he was seriously wounded. Then again, he'd want to get as far away as possible, and Trongsa was both distant and a Haven.

He shook his head at Creed's defection. The man had been with them so long. Why now? It was the Amalek Project that bugged him. But there'd been others in which Creed had participated. Okay, none so . . . ambitious. Still, to leave and sabotage the whole thing was beyond Elias's comprehension. Fool.

He eyed the duffel bag in the ridiculously luxurious chair across the aisle from his seat. Protruding from the duffel was the handle of a falcata, a brutally powerful sword. He hoped he wouldn't have to use it, but there it was, just in case.

X I I I

Jordan's chartered flight arrived at London Luton Airport's private jet terminal well before sunrise. After checking through customs and finding the chauffeured car Sebastian had arranged for him, he instructed the driver to take him to the corner of Fleet Street and Inner Temple Lane.

"Your dad told me," the driver said, adjusting the rearview mirror to make eye contact with Jordan in the backseat. "He a barrister, your dad? Or solicitor?" They were heading for the heart of London's judicial district.

"My dad? Yeah, something like that."

"What are you, eleven? Pretty young to be traveling alone."

Jordan unzipped the daypack he'd brought and pushed his hand past a change of clothes and a satellite phone to the wad of cash Ben had given him. He peeled off a ten-pound note and handed it over the seat to the driver.

"What's this for?" the driver said.

"Peace and quiet," Jordan said. He smiled at the mirror, which the driver then returned to its original position. Thirty minutes later Jordan gave the mute driver another ten pounds and climbed out. At that hour, the area was nearly deserted. Only a few cars cruised the street. Jordan wore khaki slacks and a green polo shirt, hoping anyone curious about him would mistake him for a student. It was a weak disguise he didn't want to test.

A block away, a dark figure jangled keys in front of a storefront. *Probably a restaurant or bakery*, Jordan thought. Gotta get ready for a rush of breakfast customers. He knew how the people would come, like a spring rain with a few drops leading to a light sprinkle, then an all-out downpour. He had to get into position before then. He moved south on Inner Temple and within a few steps saw the portico protecting the west door of Temple Church. Lamps mounted high on the surrounding buildings left few shadows to cover his approach. No one around as far as he could tell, but still he stayed close to the walls and kept his steps quiet.

The church's famous round structure came into view, and Jordan stopped. Looking past the rear of the church, he spotted one side of the Master of the Temple's big brick house. It was there that Creed would seek help. A wall and gate kept tourists from approaching.

Jordan adjusted the daypack's straps over his shoulders and passed the church's west door into the front court. It was a wide-open area whose only adornment was a statue of two Knights Templar riding a horse. He had brought his soccer ball, hoping to kick it around—maybe get a few local boys to help with the ruse—while watching for Creed. But he realized now that the Master's house was out of sight from the court. He crossed to the far side of the church, where another wall and gate stretched between the church and another building. Through the gate he could see the front of the house. Between him and the house lay a grassy lawn lined on both sides with bushes and trees.

"Okay, then," he said, slipping off his pack and tossing it over the brick wall. He followed and dropped onto the grass. He circled the house and didn't find any lighted windows. If Creed had beaten him here, injured or not, at least some lights would be burning. There was a rear door, but anyone heading for it would have to cross Jordan's sightline from where he planned on stationing himself in front. He returned to the grassy area and pushed himself behind a heavily foliated bush at the northeast corner of the church. He had a clear view of the house's front door, its west side, and the alleyway leading to it from the east.

He sat and pressed his back against the church, knees bent up. He pulled the pack into his lap and unzipped it. He made sure the satellite phone was set to vibrate and pushed it down the front of his shirt so he'd feel it against his chest if it rang. Then he withdrew a Carambar and slid the pack to the ground beside him. As he unwrapped the candy, he looked at each of the house's dark front windows. He wanted to be the one to spot Creed, but he felt guilty about it. Creed was old enough to be his father, but he'd always acted more like a big brother. He took the time to play with him, and he'd always been patient about explaining things when the others wouldn't. In the end, however, Jordan's loyalty was to the Tribe, and anyone who threatened it was the enemy. Besides, all they wanted was the chip. Creed would be okay, and maybe someday he'd come back.

He stuck the end of the candy in his mouth and flattened the wrapper against his thigh. He leaned sideways to put the backside of the wrapper in the glow of a lamp and read the riddle printed there in French:

> *The strongest chains will not bind it,*
> *Ditch and rampart will not slow it down.*
> *A thousand soldiers cannot beat it,*
> *It can knock down trees with a single push.*

He worked the caramel soft with his tongue and teeth as he thought about it. "Wind," he said, scrunching up the wrapper and shoving it into the pack. He wiggled his rump until the dirt yielded a more comfortable seat and squared his shoulders against the wall. Then he watched the sky lighten to day and waited for Creed.

[26]

Ollie had convinced Gheronda to let him use the apartment below Jagger's to catalog and store the site's discoveries. It was there Jagger was headed, with Addison and a hand-carted crate, when a noise stopped him. Faint, almost not a sound at all. If it weren't for its repetition—*tap-tap-tap*, like the bass beats of a distant lowrider—he never would have noticed. From his position in front of the outside wall of the monastery he could see out of the valley, past St. Catherine's Village to the Plain of el-Raha stretching to the horizon. A black dot in the sky grew larger as it approached: a helicopter. The sound of its blades chopping the air rushed ahead of it and bounced off the valley walls.

"Isn't this restricted air space?" Jagger said.

"This and almost every tourist site in Egypt," Addison said. "Before the ban the things swarmed like flies, ruining the experience for everybody else."

Jagger pulled a small notepad and pencil from his breast pocket and checked his watch: 10:07. He recorded this, then turned in a complete circle. Tourists in front of the monastery gate either watched the helicopter with mild interest or ignored it altogether. The excavation workers displayed slightly more intrigue, but nothing that signaled expectation, excitement, or nervousness.

The helicopter buzzed over the village a mile away. It resembled a black Plexiglas egg, what the military called Little Bird. Good for moving six people tops in and out of a hot zone fast.

"Any idea who it is?" he said.

"Rich tourists," Addison said. "Probably kept slapping down Egyptian pounds until the pilot couldn't say no."

The helicopter slowed, then hovered over the gardens on the

outside of the monastery's east wall. It rotated to give the passenger a better view. Hard to tell at that distance, but Jagger thought the passenger was either a woman or teen. The person scoped the area with binoculars. Jagger reached behind him to a pouch hanging off his belt and pulled out his own binocs. As he raised them, the helicopter straightened and flew closer, putting the big outer wall between them. Its steady thumping told him it was hovering over the compound.

He ran toward the entrance gate, first dodging tourists, then pushing through them. He stumbled into the monastery's courtyard. The helicopter floated above the center of the compound, slowly rotating. When it faced the Southwest Range Building, it paused. Gheronda faced it from the third-floor walkway, his long gray beard fluttering in the machine's downdraft. The old man and the helicopter passenger seemed to be simply staring at each other. Jagger ran toward the proctor, cutting between the apartment complex and archive building. When he reached the courtyard of St. Stephen's Well, the helicopter swooped over him and disappeared.

X I I I

Toby was almost certain he'd beaten Creed to the monastery, if indeed this was his destination. Just before Toby had landed in Sharm el-Sheikh, Sebastian had called the helicopter charter companies and learned that no one had yet hired them for a trip to St. Cath's. Just to make sure, Toby had instructed the pilot to give him a close look around. Nothing appeared suspicious: no furtive monks playing sentinel, no ambulances, no disruption of the tourists. Plus, the old monk had expressed surprise and anger at his presence. If Creed had arrived first, the monks would have expected someone to show up looking for him. They might have tried to shoo him off, but most likely they'd have avoided him.

Banking away from the monk, Toby had caught sight of a man running through the compound. It had not been Creed. The patch on his sleeve and his utility belt made Toby believe it was a guard; of course he would come running.

Toby pointed to an outcropping on the mountain above the

monastery. "I want to end up there," he told the pilot. "How close can you get me without anyone at the monastery seeing us?"

The pilot made a hand motion like a jumping dolphin, then gave Toby a thumbs-up.

Toby's stomach dropped into his knees as the helicopter shot up toward the peaks.

[27]

Jagger considered it his job to worry about unusual events like the appearance of the helicopter. Obsession came with the territory, and it irked him that Gheronda had shrugged it off. "Tourists," he'd said.

But Jagger suspected something else: What tourist would hover right down between the monastery walls? And the person inside had binoculars, not a camera.

Jagger spent an hour on Ollie's satellite phone trying to track down the tail number—SY-RSN—but between language and bureaucratic barriers, he'd learned only that it was registered to a private company based in Sharm el-Sheik, the resort town 140 miles south of St. Catherine's. His suspicions grew stronger when he discovered no such company listed with any of the directory services.

Now it was just past noon—closing time—and all he could do was take his station at the far end of the split-rail fence and look politely intimidating. He'd told Hanif to be particularly watchful for suspicious behavior. With any luck, it would be the last he saw of the black helicopter and its mysterious passenger.

The stream of tourists heading up the mountain tapered off, and Jagger began walking toward the monastery. This was his routine, checking out the tourists still milling about out front and climbing up the foothills of the mountain on the opposite side of the valley from Mt. Sinai. He remembered being surprised upon their arrival to see how narrow the valley was. The opposite mountain started almost where Mt. Sinai ended. It was generous to say the valley had any kind of "floor" at all, which made the monastery's presence there all the more amazing.

Hanif walked toward him, starting an inspection that would take him completely around both the excavation site and the monastery. The man turned his head right to take in the dig, glancing up at the mountain as he did. His attention came back to Jagger, then snapped back to the mountain. He stopped, and Jagger followed his gaze.

The mountain rose in jagged clusters. High on one of these spinal outcroppings, a figure stood motionless. He was far off the path that led to the peak, in a place where he could observe the entire excavation and monastery. Occasionally a tourist would ignore the signs to stay on the path and appear as an insect scurrying around the dangerous precipices. Bedouins too sometimes popped up in unusual places, but these desert dwellers would rather sell trinkets, camel rides, and guide services than explore their own backyard by themselves.

Jagger reached behind him for his binoculars. As he thumbed off the lens caps, Hanif jogged up to him.

"The helicopter and now this," Hanif said, panting. "You think coincidence?"

"No," Jagger said and glassed the figure. The 150x zoom put him twenty feet in front of the man. No, not man . . . "It's a boy," he said. "A teenager, fifteen or sixteen. I think the one from the copter."

The boy's hair whipped around his face. It was cut stylishly short around the ears, longer on top. He wore safari clothes: khaki pants and shirt, both sporting more pockets than anyone would ever use. He glared down, seeming to stare directly at Jagger. The boy lifted a pair of binocs to his eyes, and the sun flashed off the lenses. He lowered them, scowling, then dropped out of Jagger's view. Jagger gazed over the top of his binocs. The boy was gone.

"I'm going up there," he said.

"But a boy," Hanif said. "Just a boy."

"There's been a rash of violence against archaeological digs lately. Tanis got hit last month. A couple weeks before that, it was Qift." He scoped the outcropping again, saw no one. He panned over the rocky contours. "I saw this in Afghanistan," he said, without lowering the binocs. "Al-Qaeda used woman and children as lookouts and spies, eyes and ears. Less suspicious, and it freed the men to plan, train, recruit, raid." He looked at Hanif. "Plus they're expendable."

"That was Afghanistan," Hanif said. "This isn't Cairo, no war here. Tanis, Qift—that was locals angry they didn't get jobs at the dig or crazies who don't want any digging in Egypt. The most they have are those—" He waggled his hands, grasping for the word. "Those . . . petrol bottles."

"Molotov cocktails," Jagger said. He raised his eyebrows. "You want to get hit by one?"

"I just mean . . . I mean . . ."

Jagger clasped the binoculars with RoboHand and used the other to pat Hanif on the back. "I know," he said, smiling. "Don't worry, I'm not seeing terrorists under every rock. I just believe in erring on the side of caution. If you think every kitten might be a tiger, you won't get eaten."

"You won't have any pets either. It is no way to live."

"Just gotta learn to turn it off." He started toward a hut on the other side of the footpath up the mountain. He had contracted with the Bedouin who manned it to provide camels for his guards. A month ago they had begun a weekly inspection circuit that took them farther out from the excavation and monastery than they could perform on foot. He looked at his watch. "If I'm not back by—"

That sound again: *thump-thump-thump-thump* . . .

When he looked over the Plain of el-Raha, the helicopter was already closer than the earlier one had been when he'd first spotted it. But this one was harder to see; it was white. "Different copter," he said. He turned toward the mountain and saw that the boy had returned. He scoped him. The teen was leaning forward and using his own binocs to follow the new helicopter's approach. He took a step, lost his balance, steadied himself—all without moving the binocs away from his eyes. If Jagger knew anything about body language, the kid was excited to see the newcomer.

Jagger shoved his binoculars into Hanif's chest. "Keep your eye on the boy," he said and ran toward the monastery. The copter came in fast, then stopped over the gardens on the far side and descended out of sight.

At least it's landing outside *the monastery*, Jagger thought. He knew right where it would come down. Unlike the raw terrain on the monastery's east side, where Ollie dug for artifacts, the west side had been built up, improved. It consisted of three tiers of flat ground, most of it paved with stone. The lowest level was at the front, where it was even with the ground. Ten yards in from the front wall, it stepped up eight feet to the next level, and again at the rear of the monastery. On the middle level, a wide court separated two parts of the gardens. That was the only place a helicopter could land.

Traversing the length of the front wall, Jagger weaved through tourists. He rounded the corner to the garden side and saw the copter on the next level up, where he had expected it would be. He jumped against the wall between the tiers and hooked his arms over it. By the time he pulled himself up, the copter was lifting off again. Jagger rushed toward it, waving his arms. The pilot made no indication he saw him. Its downdraft whipped the branches of the trees, blowing leaves off them and pelting Jagger with sand and debris.

Jagger spotted a man climbing to the third level, which was also the roof of a building the monks used to store garden tools and supplies. The guy rolled onto it and lay there a moment. He got to his feet and staggered. He didn't look well: the giveaway, besides his wobbly gait, was white gauze wrapped around the crown of his head. He moved toward the rear of the monastery, and Jagger took after him. "Hey!" Jagger yelled. "Stop!"

The man glanced back and redoubled his efforts to reach the back wall. Then he made a mistake: he stopped at a three-foot-square iron door, fuzzy brown with rust, set into the wall. He dropped to his knees and began pounding on it. During Jagger's initial risk-assessment tour of the monastery, Gheronda had told him that the old door once acted as an emergency exit in case of fire or siege. It had never been used, and decades earlier had been welded shut on the outside and bricked up on the inside.

Pound away, Jagger thought as he lifted himself onto the top level. He wondered how close he'd get before the man gave up on the door and resumed running. When he was twenty feet away—sure now that he could overtake the guy if he ran—Jagger stopped to catch his breath. He stooped to put hand and hook on his knees and chugged in air like a locomotive. The man kept pounding, and Jagger noticed that blood had soaked through the bandages, drying into a brownish-maroon patch the shape of Texas. He shook his head and said, "Don't bother, buddy. Look, man, I only want to ask you—"

The door opened, screeching like a tortured spirit. It swung inward, and the man collapsed onto his hands to crawl in. He threw a frightened gaze back at Jagger and disappeared.

Jagger sprinted to reach the door before it closed. "Wait!" he said. He dived for the door, reaching . . . The spirit screamed again as the door swung shut. At the last second, Jagger jammed his hook between the jamb and the door. The metal clanged into it, opened a few inches, slammed again.

"Wait," he repeated. "It's me, Jagger. I just have a few questions." He got his knees under him and positioned himself to shoulder his way in. Something struck his hook—a metal bat or pipe. The hook twisted and flattened against the floor. Shock waves blasted up his arm, from stump to shoulder, and he instinctively pulled what he still thought of as his hand away from the source of pain. The door slammed and rattled as bolts and locks engaged on the other side.

[28]

Jagger held RoboHand against his chest, hoping the electric-shock feeling in his elbow, biceps, and shoulder would fade quickly. He beat against the door with his fist. "Open up!"

Yeah, that would happen after they hit him with a bat to get the thing closed. *Oh, I'm sorry, sir, didn't see you there.*

He ran to the edge of the tier and dropped down, crossed the court, and swung himself down to the lowest level. Tourists crowded at the corner. They gawked, pointed, snapped pictures. He pushed through them, heading for the main entrance, mentally working through the logistics of where he needed to go. The small door was near the monastery's back wall. It would have to lead into the Southwest Range Building, on the side that housed the monks' quarters.

Inside, he passed in front of the basilica on his way to the stairs near his apartment, which would take him to the Southwest Range Building second floor and main entrance. He turned right around the mosque and spotted Father Leo heading for him. The monk's worried expression quickly turned charming.

"What just happened?" Jagger said, closing the ground between them. "Who was that? Why was I told that door had been bricked up?"

When he angled himself to walk by without stopping, Leo side-stepped to block him. Jagger pulled up inches from him, encroaching on what the average person considered his personal space. He'd found the tactic rattled people, just enough to give him a slight advantage in a verbal confrontation. Leo didn't seem to notice. Close to the same age, the two men couldn't have been more different. Where Jagger's inner being was a raging river, Leo gave the impression that his was a peaceful lake. It was a quality Jagger admired and hoped to attain someday. He just wasn't sure it was a disposition that could survive outside a monastery.

"What's going on?" Jagger said.

"Monastery business." Leo's irises flicked back and forth, searching Jagger's eyes for . . . what? His temperament? Signs of his intentions?

"I'm head of security and—"

"Of the excavation," Leo clarified.

"When Gheronda allowed my family to stay here, it was my understanding that he would appreciate my assistance in monastery security as well."

"You're here at Gheronda's pleasure," Leo said, maintaining that infuriating little smile of his, "and right now his pleasure is to keep monastery business private. I'm afraid this is a need-to-know matter, and you don't need to know."

"Look, within three hours, two helicopters violated restrictions governing their use around St. Catherine's, and some guy is up on that mountain keeping an eye on this place with binoculars. I think—"

"What guy?" Leo blinked several times, the only indication that something had disturbed the surface of his lake.

"A teenager, the same one who buzzed the compound this morning. He seemed particularly interested in that last copter."

"Where was he, exactly?"

Jagger took a step back. Maybe he was getting somewhere. "Where he could scope out the excavation and the monastery. He was watching . . . all of it, as far as I could tell."

"You didn't see anyone else?"

"Not with the boy. You know him?"

"I didn't see him." His gaze drifted away. Then it returned, and he put his hand on Jagger's shoulder to guide him back toward the gate.

Jagger didn't resist. He didn't like it, but Leo was right: he was out of his jurisdiction. If push came to shove, the monastery could shove him and the entire archeological team out of the valley, probably out of the country.

Leo said, "We appreciate your concern, Jagger, we really do. But

I can assure you, this has nothing to do with the excavation, and we have everything within these walls under control. Please trust me about this."

"Just tell me who he is, the man who entered through the small door."

Leo shook his head. "I can't. I'm sorry."

"Is he all right?" Jagger said, fishing now. Often, a little information led to more. "He was injured."

"He'll be fine."

Jagger stopped. "How can you know that? As soon as the guy got in, you must have run to cut me off."

"He made it this far."

"From where? Why here?"

The monk's face was inscrutable.

Jagger nodded. "I can find my own way out." He smiled. "I've been thrown out of nicer places than *this*."

Leo's smile grew into a grin. He nodded, then turned and walked away.

On his way to the gate, Jagger considered the conversation and came to a conclusion about it: whether by Leo's charisma or his steely resolve, Jagger was pretty sure he'd just been played.

[29]

With Creed's arms draped over their shoulders, two monks half carried, half dragged him down a dark corridor. Gheronda followed, praying loudly. They approached another monk, who ushered them into a small room: water-stained plaster walls, the smell of candle wax, spartan in every way. They lowered him onto a bed—no more than a raised board covered with blankets—and immediately forced his head around so they could inspect the bloody bandages.

"I'm all right," he said, weakly pushing at them.

Brother Ramón tugged the bandage up and off, taking with it a profusion of hair.

"Ahhh!" Creed complained, grabbing the back of his head and glaring at the monk.

Brother Ramón unclipped the strap from the duffel bag and pulled at it.

Creed yanked it back. "This stays with me!"

Ramón leaned in, grabbed Creed's chin, and turned his head.

Creed said, "All right, all right," and shifted to face the wall. Ramón pushed away clumps of bloody hair.

Leaning around Ramón, Gheronda saw the wound, and it wasn't what he'd expected. It was several inches long, as though the bullet had struck at an angle, gouging up the flesh. Scar tissue appeared to be already forming along the edges, making it look like a mouth with leprous lips. Ramón touched the hair just below it; blood welled up and spilled out. Ramón snatched his finger away and looked back at Gheronda.

Gheronda smiled. "I'm sure he'll be just fine."

"I told you," Creed said, turning to face his audience. He rubbed the back of his head, examined his bloody palm, and returned it to the wound. "Fierce headache, though."

Gheronda pulled the monks away. He said, "Let's give the man some room. Brother Ramón, I'll leave it to you to keep the bandages fresh."

Ramón nodded and walked to a writing desk, where he began rummaging through a satchel.

As if remembering an urgent task, Creek yanked the duffel up to his chest and unzipped it. He pulled out a mobile phone, ran his thumb across the screen, and squinted at it. "Oh, come on," he said. He shook it, held it up high, then tossed it into the corner of the room, where bits of it shattered off.

"Shhh," Gheronda said soothingly. "There's time for everything you need to do." He tugged a blanket up from the bottom of the bed, covering Creed, and gently pushed on his chest. "Lean back. What you need now is rest."

Creed grabbed a handful of the monk's cloak and pulled him close. He gazed into Gheronda's eyes with a mixture of insistence and pleading. "What I need now, *right now*, is a phone."

[30]

Owen Letois rushed along the dirt road, a teenaged girl draped over his arms. Her blood soaked his shirt, splattered his bearded face. He passed rickety houses pieced together with discarded scraps of wood and sheet metal, and huts of timber and straw—most of them long abandoned.

Gunfire behind him made him look. The heart of the village was beyond a rise in the road, out of sight. He saw no fighters, only a few civilians fleeing in his direction, ducking with each burst of gunfire. Dongo was barely a pinprick on Central Africa's Oubangui River, but it was the current flashpoint in the hostilities between the Enyele and Munzaya tribes over farming and fishing rights. The clash had been going on for years, and Owen suspected none of the militiamen understood or cared about the reason they fought; they were in it to avenge old grudges and recent atrocities, and because man's darkest demons were opportunistic creatures.

The girl groaned, and Owen tried to ease the jostling she received in his arms. The blade had gone deep, cutting through the muscles of her shoulder and upper chest; it had probably broken her clavicle. He angled off the road and started up a grassy slope, aiming for the cinderblock clinic of Médecins Sans Frontières—Doctors Without Borders.

Roos Mertens came out of the building and ran toward him. She was the only nurse who'd remained when MSF had evacuated the other physicians and staff. Owen was glad someone had stayed, and especially that she had; she was competent, compassionate, and professional.

"Prep a table," Owen called out in Flemish, the colloquial Dutch of Roos's Belgian hometown. "Fentanyl, Hespan, a subcutaneous suture kit . . ."

Roos held something up, and Owen recognized his private satellite phone. "It kept ringing," she said. "I found it in your backpack. I'm sorry."

He shook his head: he wasn't worried about her invasion of his privacy or the call or anything but getting the girl stabilized.

"A man on the line," Roos continued. "He says he must speak to you, an emergency."

"*This* is an emergency," Owen said, irritation making his words harsher than he had intended. He gave her a weak smile to convey this, but fully intended to trudge right past her if she insisted on not helping. His left foot squished against a blood-soaked sock, and he realized that his entire left side, from where the girl's shoulder bumped against his chest on down, was drenched as well. He quickened his gait and began a mental checklist of the equipment, instruments, and supplies he'd need for her surgery, pausing on each item to curse its disrepair or shortage or absence. The escalating violence that had driven out MSF, along with its flow of supplies, also increased the need for both.

As he approached, Roos waved the phone. "Doctor, he was very insistent. He said to tell you . . ." She hesitated, looked puzzled.

Owen barreled on.

"*Agag?*" she said.

He stopped. "What?"

"Agag. I don't know if that's his name or—"

"Give me the phone. Put it here." He shrugged a shoulder, then pinched the phone between it and his cheek. Still talking to her, he said, "Get the QuikClot out of my belt pack, see what you can do." In the field, there was nothing better than QuikClot for stopping blood flow. The gauze was impregnated with kaolin, which absorbed blood and accelerated the coagulation cascade. "Got a packet of gloves in there too."

Switching to English, he said into the phone, "Who is this?"

"Creed . . . You haven't forgotten, have you?"

"How could I ever forget? Is it true—the Agag?"

"Do you think I'd say it if it weren't?"

Even through the bad connection, Owen detected exhaustion, defeat, and fear. He glanced at Roos, packing the gauze into the girl's wound. He dipped his arms, giving her better access, then he closed his eyes. "The Agag" meant a specific catastrophe that would make the horrors in the Democratic Republic of the Congo look like a Disney cartoon.

The man on the other end of the line said, "You told me you'd help. You said anytime. Are you still willing?"

"That depends," Owen said. "You've . . . reconsidered?" He knew what the man was: just a man, cursed to be one forever. Several times Owen had tried to convince him to use his extraordinary lifespan and the wealth and knowledge that accompanied it for good instead of for the atrocities he'd been committing. He'd told him that when he changed his mind, Owen would help—whatever that entailed.

Creed explained his situation and why he needed Owen's help.

"Are you all right?" Owen said.

"I took morphine for the pain. Knocked me out flat on the plane. Used to be like popping a couple aspirins, you know? I must be getting old." He laughed, but it was cold and hard, like ice cubes dropped in an empty glass.

"Where are you now?"

"Sinai . . . St. Catherine's monestary."

Owen wasn't surprised. He'd been tracking the Tribe for years, trying to convince all of them, not just Creed, to amend their ways. The Tribe maintained relationships with people, organizations, places around the globe, and Owen had gone to all of them—the ones he knew about—to appeal for their help in stopping the Tribe's activities. None of them—including the old man at St. Cath's—wanted anything to do with him. Apparently they felt it was a sacred calling to protect the Tribe any way they could; what the immortals did was between them and God.

Creed continued: "Owen, either they'll get me and the microchip or find a way to replace it—only Ben knows if that's possible. I need you *now*. Promise me you'll come now."

"I'm on my way."

Roos stripped off the gloves and retrieved the phone.

"I have to go," he told her.

She looked stunned. "When?"

"Now, this second."

"But, Doctor . . ." She indicated the girl in his arms.

"I'm taking her. You too. I'll drop both of you off in Bétou." It was in neighboring Republic of Congo, where many refugees were now located. He started for the clinic. "We need to ABORh her."

The ABORh card, designed for battlefield use, would type her blood in two minutes.

"And take blood with us. Pack a bag for yourself and one with everything we'll need to stabilize her until we get to Bétou. We should be there in fifty minutes on the outside."

"Doctor, I really don't think—"

He stopped her with a look. "I don't have a choice, and I'm not leaving you here." As if to punctuate his point, a fresh burst of sustained gunfire rang out from the town. He looked back at a thick column of black smoke rising from the other side of the hill, then sidestepped through the open door of the clinic. He laid the girl down on a table and stepped back. The gauze was already soaked through, but the flow out of the wound had diminished substantially. When he pressed his fingers to her neck, he felt a pulse in her carotid artery. It was weak, but any measurable pulse meant a blood pressure of at least sixty; he suspected that most of her blood loss was exiting from the wound and not leaking into her body cavity, a good sign.

He sighed and pushed his fingers into the rat's nest that was his hair. Two days of walking through smoke, rolling in dirt, and being spattered by blood had taken their toll on his already shaggy and perpetually mussed hair. He took the phone from Roos and dropped it into a backpack, which he carried to the door.

"I'll be back in ten." He left and jogged around the building toward the jungle behind it. The stench of animal carcasses, fish entrails, and other refuse assailed him forty yards before he reached the offal-filled trench. The Dongo men he'd enlisted to help him keep visitors out of the forest had suggested it, and not a month had passed before it proved worthwhile: a group of soldiers from the Republic's army looking for God-knew-what had ventured that way, caught a whiff, and turned around.

Owen arced around it and entered the forest. He pushed through a fencelike line of foliage and into the shadow of a dilapidated barn. One side angled in, and the crumbling roof drooped toward the ground, a collapse waiting to happen. In truth, Owen had forced the look and stabilized both the wall and roof in that precarious-looking position.

The clearing in front was hemmed in by tall trees. At one of these trees, he used a pocket knife to saw through a thick rope, which sprang away, pulled by a falling tree. The dead sapele tree in turn yanked away a wide rectangle of chain-link fence that had been foliated with vines and branches. The new gap was directly in front of the barn doors and opened onto a grassy field.

Moving to the side of the barn, he located the end of a square wooden beam eight inches from the front wall. Gripping it, he hefted back and tugged it out slowly. When ten feet of beam jutted from the barn, he stopped. The huge front doors were now effectively unlocked. When he pulled them open, sunlight fell on a monstrous pile of dried straw, leaves, and tree limbs. He reached into this mess and pulled. A section of shrimp netting and all the agriculture glued to it flowed toward him and fell to the ground. He did this five more times and stepped back.

Resting in the center of the barn, gleaming despite the dirt and dust, the bits of straw and leaves clinging to it, was a sleek white Cessna 501 corporate jet.

[31]

Toby held the satellite phone to his face and waited for it to connect. He stood outside a shallow cave on a flat area of ground, which if it were not so far off the beaten path would make a perfect rest stop for trekkers on their way to the peak. Spires of stone rose all around, giving him the impression of standing at the bottom of an ice-cream cone. There were three gaps in the spires: one leading down the mountain, another up, and the third heading in a slightly upward but more lateral direction.

He stared straight up and hoped the oval of bleached sky was enough for the phone to find an up-linkable satellite. The Iridium service the Tribe subscribed to kept sixty-six satellites in low earth orbit, constantly zipping around 600 miles overhead—supposedly covering every inch of land.

Except here, he thought, listening to dead air. *Just my luck.*

He had just lowered the phone to looked at its screen when it beeped and displayed a single word: *Connected*. Ben's voice came through the small speaker.

"Toby, is that you?"

He raised the phone and said excitedly, "He's here. I just saw him."

"At the monastery?"

"Yeah. He's got bandages around his head. He must've got medical help before leaving, 'cause I got here a few hours before him."

"He only now arrived?" Nevaeh said, and Toby realized Ben had put him on speakerphone.

"A helicopter brought him about forty minutes ago. I watched for a while to make sure he was staying."

"Don't tip them off that you're there," Nevaeh said.

"Uh . . ." As soon as he said it, Toby knew he should have said *Sure* or *No problem*—anything but *Uh*.

"What?" Nevaeh said. "They saw you?"

"Like they wouldn't have guessed we'd be coming for him after they find out he stole our stuff."

"Great . . . ," Nevaeh said, and she and Ben began arguing about the consequences of losing the element of surprise. Toby crouched in front of the cave—more of a finger-poke, really, but large enough to keep his backpack and sleeping bag out of the weather and out of sight.

"It's a *Haven*, Nev," Ben said, as if explaining manners to a child. His voice, even over the satphone, was deep and soothing. "They'll expect us to respect that. If they anticipate we won't, they'll have no idea of our timing. That'll be our advantage."

Toby said, "I thought you liked challenges, Nevaeh?"

"Shut up, Toby. Okay, here's what we'll do—"

"Wait, wait," Toby interrupted. He listened, and the sound reached him again: rocks, tumbling down the mountain, scree sliding with them. "I gotta check on something."

"Toby . . . ," Ben started, but Toby set down the phone and didn't hear the rest. He stood and turned toward the closest opening in the ice-cream-cone cliffs, the one that led down the mountain. More tumbling rocks . . . and the crunching of footsteps. He edged up to the opening and peered around. A man was hiking up the gravelly slope. He was leaning forward and scanning the ground for decent footing, giving Toby a clear view of the top of his hat. Despite the angle, Toby could tell he was muscular and fit. No one he wanted to tangle with. The sun sparkled on something in the man's hand, then he realized it *was* the man's hand: a black hook poking out from a long shirtsleeve. He wondered what kind of damage it could do in a fight. It seemed like an unfair advantage. Behind the guy, where the mountain leveled off for a few feet, a camel was tethered to a rock. The hat tilted back, and as the man's face began to appear, Toby ducked behind the slab of rock.

He crept back to the satphone. "I have to go," he said quietly.

"What's happening?" Nevaeh said.

"A man's coming," he said. "He's wearing a security guard's uniform."

"Get out of there, son," Ben said. "Do not kill—"

"I have to!" A firm whisper. He could hear the man's heavy breathing now.

"No, Toby, listen—"

Toby disconnected.

X I I I

Jordan had been kicking the ball around the courtyard in front of Temple Church with three other boys, fresh out of school, when two bobbies shooed them away. It had taken him less than a minute to circle the buildings. When he returned, the cops were gone. So now he stood on the east end of the court, where he could see the front of the Master's house—only the front, but he'd decided that's where Creed would show up—and juggled the soccer ball with his knees. His stomach growled. He was out of candy and energy bars, and he wondered if it would be so terrible for him to slip away for twenty minutes to grab some food. Just the thought of a basket of fish and chips made his stomach noisy again.

No, no, I can't. The Tribe's depending on me.

Maybe he could pay a kid to get something for him, tell him his mum said he couldn't leave the courtyard. But no local lads were there now, just a few tourists and businesspeople hurrying past.

Okay, think of something else, take your mind off your stomach.

He started counting the number of times the ball shot up from his knee without going astray. But he'd practiced so long he could do it in his sleep. It was instinctive, thoughtless, no distraction at all.

He kicked the ball as high as the church's window tops, and a tingling shot up his spine. He froze, wondering what crazy thing his body was up to. Then he remembered that he'd taken the satellite phone out of his shirt and shoved it into his waistband at the small of his back so he could kick the ball around. It'd been there so long, he'd forgotten about its bulk and how it pulled his belt too tight in front. The ball hit the stone ground and bounced away as he struggled to get the phone out.

"Hello?"

"Creed's in Egypt," Ben said. "Toby spotted him."

"Awwww."

"He could have gone anywhere, Jordan. We needed the Temple covered. Good job."

It would have been a better job if *he'd* gotten Creed. "Okay."

"Sebastian's already booked your charter," Ben said. "A car will pick you up in fifteen minutes."

"Can I get some food?"

"Sure. We won't be here when you get home."

"I want to go with you." He almost whined it and mentally kicked himself for doing so.

"We can't wait for you."

"Can I go straight to Egypt? Hello?"

Ben had hung up.

X I I I

Elias rages through the streets, following the other men, all of them roaring. Their fury has less to do with their enemy's ageless enmity than with its being the only way they can get through what they have to do. Each of them is allowing the high emotion of war to swallow him, dulling all other feelings, severing all other thought. Countless men sweep over these perimeter dwellings like wildfire, spreading, growing, consuming. The soldier directly ahead swings toward a wooden door and, without pausing, kicks it open and rushes in.

In the street ahead of him, one of their own—Bale—grabs a woman by the throat and raises his blade. He turns a wicked grin toward Elias and laughs. He enjoys this, Elias thinks, his already sour stomach roiling with new distaste.

Elias runs past as screams rise up behind him. The next door is his. He arcs toward the center of the dirt street, then swoops into the door. His shoulder blasts it open, and he's in. A man bellows obscenities and charges him, swinging a blade. Elias raises his forearm, and the blade sparks against the metal strapped to it. He decapitates the man with a single swing of his sword. He spins toward the sound of crying. A family cowers in the corner—a woman, two children, eyes huge and streaming. He hikes his sword over his shoulder and rushes toward them. The children first, he thinks, end it for them. His sword slices through the air.

Elias startled awake so violently, his foot struck the table, sending the Bible and lighter into the airplane cabin's center aisle. A chirp sounded, but it hit his ears without sparking a thought. He hunched over and buried his face in his palms, pressing his fingers into his eyes. The chirp again, and this time he recognized it. He groaned and leaned across the aisle to grab his duffel bag. He shifted it to the table, pulled out the satellite phone, pushed a button. He took a deep breath before raising it to his ear.

Ben was already talking: "—my first call?"

"What?" Elias's voice was gravelly and slurred by the remnants of sleep. "Say that again."

"I asked why you didn't answer my first call."

"I was asleep." Sunlight filled the cabin, and he leaned his face toward the window, blinking against the brightness. Clouds stretched out below him like the snowy plains of Antarctica.

"Where are you?" Ben said.

"Hold on." Elias placed the phone on the table. A burled walnut ledge ran the length of each side wall of the cabin, into which the designers had crafted glass holders, ashtrays, and various controls. He poked a finger into one of the ashtrays, found two inches of a burnt cigarette, and put it into his mouth. He stood, then stooped to retrieve the Bible and lighter. Once he got the cig smoking, he sat again and examined a panel of buttons set into the ledge. He jabbed one, and a large plasma television at the front of the cabin came to life, showing a map and a little airplane icon. He grabbed the phone. "Almost there. We just passed New Delhi."

"Toby located Creed," Ben said.

"So, Horeb?"

"He's at the monastery. Nevaeh, Phin, and I are heading there now." In the background Elias heard Hannah or whatever she was calling herself these days. Ben said, "We're taking Alexa. Sebastian will keep making arrangements for us from here."

Jutting from the duffel, the handle of the falcata caught his eye. It was the same sword Elias had used in the dream. He turned his gaze to the dwindling cig, watched it burn for a moment. "I'll meet you in Egypt."

"No, we've got it covered."

"Ben . . ." Elias pinched the bridge of his nose. "What about the Haven? If Creed's holed up there—"

"We have to do this, Elias. We'll make amends later."

No, we won't, Elias thought. Once they breached the sanctity of a Haven, there was no going back. No place would ever offer any of them sanctuary again.

When he didn't say anything, Ben said, "Creed brought this on himself. This is the end for somebody, us or him."

Maybe it should be us this time, Elias thought. *Just let it happen.* But that went against everything they believed in. Go down fighting: it wasn't just machismo or stubbornness; it was a mandate that bore eternal consequences.

"You're the boss," he said. "Happy hunting." He disconnected and pushed another button on the console.

"Yes, sir?" the pilot said through a speaker over Elias's head.

"Turn this bird around. We're going home."

[32]

Jagger worked his tired legs, cursing the loose gravel under his feet. Away from the two paths that led from St. Catherine's to the peak, Mount Sinai's rocky, steep incline was grueling in the best of places. The gravel made it a Sisyphean challenge: every step forward resulted in a backward slide that reclaimed at least half his progress. He stopped and squinted up at the outcropping ahead of him, atop of which the teen had surveilled the excavation and St. Cath's. From the front there was no obvious way to reach the spot without climbing equipment. He assumed the backside offered easier access.

He started up again, heading for a fissure between the target outcropping and another to its left. When he reached it, he took a minute to catch his breath, then stepped through the fissure and onto a flat area. In special ops fashion, his mind instantly analyzed it: the ground here was hard, granite with a dusting of sand—not enough to capture footprints. It was protected partly by mountain cliffs and partly by the large, jutting outcroppings. These cliff walls were pocked and serrated, as though God had raked his fingers down them.

Even grassless, the area would have made a decent picnic area; at least he knew Beth would think so. He pictured Tyler falling off one of the rocks and not stopping until he tumbled into the excavation site 1,500 feet below, and decided he wouldn't tell her about it.

Back to operative mode. He stood in the clearing's seven o'clock position; at eleven o'clock another fissure or opening—apparently leading uphill, judging by the ground's steep incline there and the scree that spilled out into the clearing—and at two o'clock a third way out, leading to the right. At five o'clock, almost directly to his right, was the waist-high mouth of a cave. It couldn't have been deep, given that it penetrated the outcropping on which the teen had stood, which was no more than ten feet thick at its base.

Still, it was a hiding place, and a good one at that: shaded, out of the way, near the boy's stakeout location. Jagger pulled the baton from its scabbard and flicked his wrist to snap it into its full twenty-six inches. It was simply a precaution; he didn't expect any real danger. Jagger would be fierce and demanding and he'd let the intruder know he was serious about protecting the excavation and monastery. Maybe it would be enough to dissuade whatever plans the boy or his cohorts had in mind. In law enforcement and security, the appearance of readiness and efficiency was as important as *being* ready and efficient.

"Hello?" he called. "I just want to talk." He repeated the phrase in Arabic, which Hanif had told him. Jagger arced out into the clearing, eyeing the cave for a glimpse of a body part. When he was looking straight into it, he realized shadows cloaked its deepest reaches. He moved out of its line of sight—or, more accurately, a shooter's line of fire—and approached from the side. He pressed himself against the cliff beside the cave's mouth, took a deep breath, and moved fast: he spun into the cave, dropping onto his knees to accommodate its low ceiling, and scampered toward the rear with the baton thrust out like a lance. First the baton, then his arm disappeared into blackness. The tip of the baton struck the rear wall.

Nothing. No one.

He realized that the rock at his knees was in fact a rolled sleeping bag, and he caught the glint of two eyes in the darkness, their moisture reflecting the light behind Jagger.

"Hello?" he whispered.

He shifted to sit back on his heels. As he pulled back on the baton, something seized it. A hand, gripping the baton, slipped out of the shadow and into the light.

"I'm not here to hurt you," Jagger said. "I—"

He froze. The boy's face leaned into the light. He was a *young* teen. Fourteen? And he didn't appear frightened. A pistol came into view. Its large muzzle stared at him.

"Don't move," the teen said.

Jagger let go of the baton and rammed his forearm into the boy's wrist under the gun's grip. At the same time, RoboHand grabbed the barrel and twisted it up and around, counter to the direction Jagger was forcing the teen's wrist. It was a standard disarming technique, which— fortunately because of the confines of the cave—didn't require feet and body movement. He wrenched the gun out of the boy's hand. Jagger switched the pistol into his right hand and pointed it into the darkness.

Less than three seconds after first seeing the gun, Jagger possessed it. Under normal circumstances, in the open, Jagger would have quickly stepped back, out of the assailant's reach. It was a luxury he didn't have here, and the boy immediately took advantage of that.

The teen swung his forearm into Jagger's wrist, grabbed the barrel, and took the firearm back. It wasn't a matter of mimicking Jagger's tactic; the kid's movements were fast and sure. He had been taught and had practiced the maneuver.

Jagger acted before the teen could either fire, pull the gun away, or position himself more strategically. In a flash, he repeated the steps: slap and push the wrist . . . grab and twist the barrel. This time, when he had possession he swung his arm back and pitched the gun out of the cave, into the clearing. It had taken maybe eight seconds for them to exchange the weapon three times. He didn't want to make it four.

With his right arm crossing his chest and dropping away from the teen's wrist and RoboHand returning from its mission to rid the cave of the gun, Jagger was in no position to protect himself. So when the baton came off the ground and flashed toward his head, all he could do in that nanosecond of recognition was flinch. The hard molded-plastic grip struck his right temple, and he pitched left, slamming the other side of his head into the cave wall. He went down as the shadows engulfed him.

He was vaguely aware of the boy pummeling his body, kicking and punching it, but he couldn't keep an eyelid open, let alone fend off the attack. Light cut into the shadows in dancing, jittering flashes, and Jagger realized that the boy had scrambled over him. Jagger rolled to see him scurry from the cave on all fours.

"Wait," Jagger called, but the word came out on the weak breath of a whisper.

The boy grabbed the gun, and his black-khakied legs sprinted away.

[33]

Jagger remained in the cave until the exploding balls of green and purple light diminished from his vision. He rubbed his temple where the baton had made contact, feeling a big goose egg there. His brain pounded, and he laid his palm over his right eye, waiting for the drummer in his head to take a break. He found the baton, tossed it out of the cave, and backed out on all fours, dragging with him the sleeping bag and a backpack he'd found under it.

He wasn't worried about the intruder coming back to hurt him. If that were his intention, he would have shot Jagger from the safety of the clearing while Jagger was incapacitated in the cave. He suspected the boy might have used the gun when they were playing hot potato with it, but he'd been cornered; the kid merely wanted his freedom and nothing to do with Jagger. Fair enough.

But everything about this boy bothered him: his brash helicopter entrance, his gun, his knowledge of hand-to-hand combat, his surveiling St. Cath's at the precise moment the monks mysteriously took in a wounded stranger. It all pointed to trouble at the monastery, and there was nothing he could do but wait for it to play itself out and hope no one got hurt.

Crouching in front of the cave, he opened the backpack and rummaged through it. Clothes, energy bars, beef jerky, a small first-aid kit, a candle and lighter, a flashlight and spare batteries. He removed a tattered X-Men comic book and thumbed it open: *Dobbiamo ottenerli da qui prima che Logan trovi che fuori è ancora viva.* Looked Italian, but he wasn't sure. The boy had spoken English—only two words, but Jagger hadn't detected an accent.

He unrolled the sleeping bag and patted it down. If the boy had identification or a phone, it must be in those multipocketed pants. He pushed the unrolled bag and the backpack into the back of the cave—no sense denying the kid his food or a warm place to sleep. As he backed out, something in the sand glinted. He picked it up, exited the cave, and sat back on his heels to examine the object. It was a medallion or coin stamped with a human skull. Clutched between its teeth was a banner bearing an engraved word, almost worn away, nicked in spots. He thought the word could have been *Choroutte*. It appeared to be old, but what did Jagger know? Probably something an Egyptian fast-food chain handed out with its kid meals. He slipped it into his shirt pocket.

When he stood, the pounding in his head turned into something fast and loud: Deep Purple or Led Zeppelin or the Rolling Stones. He closed his eyes, and after a few deep breaths felt a little better. He retrieved the baton, collapsed it, and returned it to the scabbard. He walked a dozen yards along each of the other paths leading away from the clearing and didn't spot any sign of the boy, or anything else interesting. He returned to the camel—mostly sliding over the scree on his butt—and headed back to the monastery, all the way wondering if the boy was just a boy or an omen of more bad times ahead.

X I I I

Toby pulled the sleeping bag out of the cave and shook it, watching for anything that fell out of its folds. He got the backpack and dumped the contents on the clearing's stone ground. He brushed his fingers over the objects, spreading them out. He crawled into the cave and sifted through the sand. The obol was gone. He'd kept it in his pants pocket with the Glock. When he'd drawn the gun, it must have fallen out, and the security guard must have taken it.

Should have killed him, he thought, sitting in the cave, feeling as gloomy as his surroundings. He'd had the obol for years and really liked it; it was both a lucky charm and sentimental memento. Nevaeh had tried all sorts of ways to get it from him, to add to her collection of death memorabilia, but he'd always resisted her wagers and appealed to Ben when she tried to claim the obol as his punishment for some misdeed or another.

The satphone in his pocket vibrated. "Yeah?" he said into it.

"No trouble with the man?" It was Ben.

"No."

"He's alive?"

"You said not to kill him, didn't you?"

"Since when have you listened to me?"

"Since forever," Toby said. "When are you getting here?"

"We're en route. We'll meet you at Deir Rahab. You know it?"

"Yeah." Toby pulled a map and compass out of a pocket. Deir Rahab was an oasis—probably with a single farm—where the mountain met the plains about two miles north of his position.

"Sebastian's arranged for someone to drop off a Jeep and supplies," Ben said. "Can you be there by eight?"

"Tonight? I can crawl there by then."

"As long as you're there. We'll arrive an hour or two later."

After they disconnected, Toby wondered if Nev and Ben would let him participate in the night's activities, and if he'd have a chance to get the obol back. He didn't get a good look at the man who'd taken it—he was just a dark shape silhouetted by the light coming through the mouth of the cave—but how many security guards could St. Catherine's have?

Guess they'd find out soon enough.

[34]

Three iron-clad doors—layered against each other like sliced bread—blocked the monastery's main entrance. Inside the compound, Jagger pounded his fist on the one facing him. Solid as the stone walls around it. A single lamp bathed the courtyard in an amber glow. He turned in a circle, noting the few still-lighted windows scattered among the buildings. Most of the monastery's twenty monks had gone to bed, and tonight only five other people called the place home: Jagger, Beth, and Tyler; Ollie, whose habit was to read in bed until about ten; and the stranger.

The stranger.

Jagger shook his head and tried not to think of him.

He let his eyes rise above the Southwest Range Building's central dome to Mount Sinai, a looming presence, darker than the sky. Last night, sitting with Beth, it had been magical and holy; tonight it seemed like a dark being maliciously lording over a colony of caged insects.

He shifted his attention to the third floor of the guest quarters. A light burned in their apartment. He imagined Tyler asleep in his bedroom, Beth in the living room—which also served as dining room and kitchenette—studying C. S. Lewis or Thomas à Kempis with a Bible in her lap and a pen in her hand. The image made him want to get his rounds finished faster.

He turned and stepped into the deeper shadows near the mosque and switched on a flashlight. A white beam cut down an alley, exposing two startled cats. They darted away, and he followed slowly, swinging the beam between the walls.

After the teen had handed his butt to him on a platter, he'd cornered Gheronda and told him about it, gun and all. The old monk expressed concern, but in the end patted him on the shoulder and told him he was sure the boy and the arrival of the man were coincidental. He'd proven as closed-mouthed about the stranger as Leo. Jagger had then visited the little police station in St. Catherine's Village. Predictably, the two cops inside had nodded, mumbled assurances, and continued playing cards.

Jagger tried not to let his frustration turn to anger, tried to convince himself he was being as paranoid as everyone else apparently thought he was.

A noise startled him. He spun around in the ally, flashing the light back toward the main gate. No huge figure with twin machine guns. No monster loping toward him. Nothing at all.

"Hello?" His voice echoed and faded.

He willed his heart to calm down, but he couldn't quite release his grip on the baton, still resting in its quick-release scabbard. He continued down the alley, keeping the beam away from the windows.

The noise came rushing up behind him, reverberating off the walls. Loud, jangling, insistent. Jagger swung around, yanking out the baton, snapping it open. A wobbling light blinded him for a moment, until he ducked away. It was sailing down the alley at him. Then in the moment before his own flashlight beam landed on his attacker, he knew who it was.

Kich-kich-kich-kich-kich . . .

Tyler's grinning face glowed in the light, bouncing up and down as he ran—his hair bounding a second out of sync. "I scared you!" he said and laughed. He grabbed Jagger's waistband as he ran past, snapping to a stop like a dog reaching the end of a chain and nearly tugging Jagger off his feet. They spun toward each, and Tyler doubled over with laughter, his face turned up to show Jagger slits of eyes and a mouth stretched wide.

It took all of a quarter second of that face, that laughter to rid Jagger of worry and anger over the noise his son was making in this preeminently quiet place.

"You!" he said and threw a couple soft punches at his son's belly and chest.

Tyler slapped Jagger's fists away. "You . . . you . . . shoulda . . ." Tyler sucked in a deep breath. "Shoulda seen your face." He laughed harder.

"Okay, shhh." But Jagger himself had to laugh. He grabbed Tyler's shoulders and pulled him into a hug.

"I thought you didn't get scared," Tyler said.

"I never said that. A lot of things scare me."

"You never jump," Tyler said. "Not when I wake you up or jump out at you . . . not *normally*." He laughed again.

"I guess you caught me in a scareable mood." Jagger released him. "What are you doing up anyway?"

"Mom said I could come find you. She said you need help patrolling."

"She did?" He looked around. Amazingly, none of the windows facing the alley showed fresh lights. "Not a good time tonight, sport."

"Why? You hardly ever patrol the monastery . . . and never at *night*." He said it as though it was the coolest thing ever.

"There's a reason I'm on guard tonight," Jagger said.

"*Danger?*" Tyler's eyes flashed big.

"Maybe."

"Just for a little bit? Please?" He looked up the dark alley to where it ended in the jaundiced glow of another light. "Just to the burning bush?"

Jagger ran his fingers through Tyler's hair. "All right, but then I'll walk you home, and you go to bed."

"Deal." Tyler raised his hand and Jagger slapped it.

"And no more scaring me," Jagger said.

His son's grin stretched wide. He said, "I'll try to restrain myself."

"And can you not rattle? Didn't you see the sign that read 'Hush, monks asleep'?"

Tyler put his hand on the utility case. "It only rattles when I run."

"Don't run."

Tyler agreed, and the two of them continued on down the ally, flashlight beams bobbing and weaving. Tyler shifted around to Jagger's right side so they could hold hands.

After a few steps he said, "Dad?"

"Hmm?"

"What would you do if you found a bad guy?"

"I'd arrest him."

"What if he fought you?"

"I'd fight back, get him in handcuffs."

"What if he was tougher than you?"

Jagger looked at Tyler and smiled, then they did what they always did when Jagger's masculinity was questioned: they both laughed.

And Jagger tried to push aside the memory of the teenager whupping him in the cave.

[35]

The Jeep shook and rattled over what was suppose to be a dirt road, but Toby suspected the only thing that differentiated it from the desert was that the Jeep was rolling over it. Its wheels seemed to jump on their own into pits and rocks his night vision goggles had not revealed. They traveled without headlights, so only he could see the terrain, a luminous green wasteland rushing toward them. He wondered how well the roar of the engine and clattering of the suspension carried through the desert air. He strained his arm muscles to keep the vehicle from whipping side to side and rolling, and still the steering wheel pendulumed his hands back and forth as though he were helming a schooner on high seas.

A hand gripped his shoulder from behind. Ben said, "A little slower, please."

Toby said nothing and kept his foot on the gas. Nevaeh had appointed him driver, which meant he would stay outside the compound with the engine running while the others took care of business inside. He hadn't complained—it wouldn't have done any good, never did, and whining just made him sound like a kid—but he didn't have to like it.

In the passenger seat beside him, Nevaeh pulled metamaterial gloves over her hands. The neck hole of the scaly gray shirt was rolled down, exposing her throat. She reached into the footwell and came back with a gorget. The metal collar was about four inches wide with outwardly curved edges. It hinged in the middle, which lined up with the center of the throat and clamped in the back. Nevaeh slipped it on, groaning as she did.

"Are these absolutely necessary?" she said.

"This time especially," Ben said. "We fight a knowledgeable enemy."

Nevaeh rolled the shirt collar up over the gorget. She reached behind her and pulled the hood over her head and face. The suit's battery pack and computer resided in a paperback-book-sized box situated just below the shoulder blades, forcing her to sit forward in her seat. She twisted around.

"Ben," she said, "check me."

She switched on the suit, and when Toby glanced over she was gone, invisible even through the goggles. Only her eyes remained, hovering between him and the door pillar.

"You gotta do something about the eyes, Ben," Toby said. "That's really creepy."

"And a major glitch in the suit's effectiveness," said Phin from the seat behind her. He stretched his eyelids open with his fingers and glared at Ben.

Toby suspected Phin's bouncing was only partially the result of the jostling Jeep.

"So is your 'cologne,'" Nev said.

"It's psychological warfare," Phin said. "The odor of blood freaks people out. It makes them pause, gives me an advantage, if only for a second."

Toby caught Phin's eyes in the rearview mirror. "Well, it freaks *me* out that you wear it like perfume on missions."

"'Here's the smell of blood still,'" Phin quoted. "'All the perfumes of Arabia will not sweeten this little hand.'"

"Lady Macbeth was referring to her guilt over killing the king," Ben said matter-of-factly. He was fiddling with something on the cuff of his suit. "As far as the problem with making the eyes invisible, DARPA's working it. My associates there are still trying to develop a photocell that can bend light and remain transparent when viewed from behind. That's what we need, two-way metamaterial goggles. It'll take an amorphous silicon ferromagnetic thin film to achieve it, but the technology hasn't been invented yet. It's just a matter of time."

Toby rolled his eyes. Throwing big words at him was Ben's way of telling him to shut up. He said, "That's what I thought."

The Jeep hit a rut, tossing them into the air. Toby's thighs smacked the steering wheel; his head brushed the canvas canopy.

"Tobias," Ben said evenly, "five minutes sooner or later makes no difference. Our arriving in one piece does."

Nev's suit beeped again, and she reappeared. In the skintight suit she appeared more like a mannequin than a flesh-and-blood woman, but Toby had to admit she made a *fine* mannequin. She leaned into the footwell again. When she straightened, she set a pistol and machete-like sword on her lap. Toby's stomach rolled. That she'd brought the sword instead of her daggers reminded him of their reason for being here. Maybe his role as driver wasn't such a bad gig after all.

Nev slipped the gun into a pocket stitched into the invisibility suit under her left arm. Toby knew she'd wait to stow the sword. The pocket for it ran the length of her upper leg, from hip to knee. It was a pain to get it in and out while sitting.

Ben tapped Toby on the arm and pointed at the GPS unit suction-cupped to the windshield. "Main road in two minutes. We should hit it on the monastery side of the police checkpoint."

The Sinai was nasty with police and U.N. checkpoints, left over from the Israeli-Egyptian hostilities of the 1970s and more recent terrorist activities.

"Turn right and we'll be there. Bring us close, but not *too* close."

"Got it," Toby said. Whether or not he liked his role, the mission was on, and he didn't mess around when it came to missions. None of them did. In the rearview he saw Phin insert two earbuds and drop an MP3 player into a pocket. Phin pulled on his mask, and a few seconds later everything but his eyes evaporated.

Behind him, Ben yanked the slide back on a semiauto pistol and let it slam back into place, chambering a round.

"Ready, everyone?" he said. "Three minutes."

[36]

Jagger and Tyler had walked for five minutes and still hadn't reached the burning bush. Tyler had suggested they take the "scenic route," which was anything but. They traversed a tight tunnel between two buildings, with a ceiling created by structures built on top of them and spanning the narrow alley. Jagger knew of three such tunnels in the monastery, and he wasn't sure there weren't others. None was a straight shot from end to end; they all zigged one way, then zagged the other, making them eerily cavelike. The erratic placement and angles of the buildings, the dead ends, stairs, levels, and bridges from one rooftop to another all conspired to turn the complex into a labyrinth on par with the trickiest mouse maze. It was a nine-year-old boy's dream and a security specialist's nightmare.

They made loop-de-loops along the walls and ceiling with the flashlight beams till they emerged from the tunnel at the base of a narrow flight of stone stairs. Tyler started up, pulling Jagger with him. At the top they walked along a terrace to a rooftop, lighted by an amber bulb and sporting a single wooden chair. Jagger stopped in the light.

"Hold on," he said. "I have something for you." He dug into his breast pocket and pulled out the coin he'd found in the cave with the teen's belongings.

Tyler took it from him and held it up to the light, turning it to examine both sides. "Wow."

"I showed it to Dr. Hoffmann," Jagger said. "It's not Egyptian. He thought maybe a tourist dropped it, and it would be okay for us to keep it." He didn't mention the "tourist" it may have belonged to. "Ollie called it a 'Charon's obol.' People put it in the mouth of a loved one they were burying. That way the dead person would have money to pay the ferryman who brought souls across the river that separated the living from the dead."

"This was in some dead guy's mouth?" Tyler said. "*Cool.*" He stretched out the word, like a fascinated gasp. He looked at both sides again, then unsnapped the lid of his utility case and dropped it in. He smiled at Jagger. "Thanks."

Tyler gripped Jagger's hand again, and they started down a gradual slope of wide steps that arced around a curved wall. When they descended the last step, they were standing behind the basilica, where they'd attended services that morning and Jagger had prayed for the first time in sixteen months. Across the walkway, an eight-foot-tall round wall of rough stones and sloppy mortar protruded from another chapel and acted like a giant planter. Sprouting from the top was an enormous bush, billowing up six feet and cascading down like a fountain. It hung over the walkway, within touching distance of daytime tourists who'd stripped the leaves off the last foot of its stems. Its official name was *Rubus sanctus*—Holy Bramble. The monks believed this was the actual burning bush through which God had spoken to Moses, still alive and flourishing. Centuries past, a chapel had been built around it, but lack of sunlight had distressed the bush, so it was moved a dozen feet to its current location.

Jagger started toward it, but Tyler held him back.

"Wait," the boy said. He sat on the bottom step, put his flashlight into the utility case, and tugged off a sneaker. "It's holy ground. God told Moses to take off his sandals." He stripped away his sock and started on the other sneaker.

"We're not Mo—" Jagger began, then sighed and sat beside Tyler to unlace his boots. Before the first one was off, Tyler was barefoot and standing, scrunching his toes on the stone ground.

"Do you think God was really in that bush?" he said, eyeing the scraggly bramble.

"*In* the bush or *was* the bush, I don't know," Jagger said. "But yes, I believe the story."

"Why do so many people come here? You know, to see it and go up the mountain too?"

"Like you said, it's holy."

"When they see the mountain and the bush, they're so . . . so . . ."

"Amazed?"

"No . . . kind of like the way you look at Mom."

"In love?"

Tyler thought about it, nodding slowly, but not quite sure.

Jagger understood what Tyler was grasping for. Some visitors had the look of *This is it? That's all? I came all this way, spent all this money, hiked and sweated in the sun—for what, a bush, a mountain?* But Tyler was thinking of the others, the ones who seemed in awe of being here, so near the bush and mountain. They seemed at peace. They prayed. They had a glow about them, as people say of pregnant women. They didn't see a brambly shrub, a rock; they saw God.

He said, "I think it's a mixture of a lot of things: love, respect, awe, reverence . . ."

"Because God was here, because he touched it?"

"That's part of it," Jagger said, working on his second boot.

Tyler turned to face him. "But isn't God everywhere? Hasn't he touched everything? That's what you and Mom say."

Jagger squinted up at him. "That's true too."

Tyler thought a moment. "Then isn't everything holy?"

"In a way . . . I guess." He wasn't sure now was the time to launch into a theological discussion about original sin and free will.

Tyler made a firm face, coming to some conclusion.

"What?" Jagger said.

"If people love what's holy, and people are holy, then they should be nicer to each other."

Jagger's heart ached for Tyler's idealism: the beauty and simplicity of it. "I wish that was the way it worked, Ty."

"Well, I say there's something wrong when people treat a *bush* better than they treat each other."

Jagger stretched out to grab Tyler's hand. "And I say you're right. You're a smart kid, you know it?"

He *was* smart, but more important, he had a big heart for people. At his school in Virginia, he had stuck up for kids being bullied, but also had a way of sympathizing even with the bullies ("Maybe something's wrong at home") that Jagger himself had difficulty comprehending.

Jagger felt pride for his son well up in his chest. And he thought about how Tyler's praying that morning had led to his own prayer and to this conversation. He wondered if he'd find his way back into the fold of the faithful not through his physical presence in a holy place but through his family, the two people who'd stuck by him when even he couldn't stand himself.

[37]

Jagger stood, sweeping Tyler up with him. He carried his son to the bush and held him up so he could brush his fingers along the tips of the dangling stems. Then he set the boy down and playfully stepped on one of his bare feet with one of his own.

Tyler pulled his foot out and laid it on Jagger's. "Do you ever wish you'd lost a leg instead of an arm?"

"You know," Jagger said, "I do. I think it would be easier to adjust to."

"But then you couldn't run so good, and wouldn't it be hard walking around the dig and chasing bad guys?"

Jagger nodded. "I guess—"

An explosion boomed through the compound—a loud concussion, repeated in diminishing echoes as it bounced off the stone walls, followed by the sharp clatter of debris striking hard surfaces, raining down on roofs and walkways.

Tyler jumped, and Jagger instinctively wrapped himself over his son. Gripping Tyler's head with his arm, he looked around. The explosion had come from the other side of the monastery, near the front gate. The basilica blocked his view of the sky in that direction, but he imagined a cloud worthy of the sound: smoke and dust billowing up, drifting away. And then a light fog did reach him, coming from the alley between the basilica and the north wall. Smoky, with the bitter odor of burning plastic.

"Dad?"

"It's okay, Ty. Shhh."

Someone was coming for the stranger. He could be wrong, but he doubted it, and he didn't have time to consider any other possibilities.

He had assumed the man was holed up in the monks' quarters in the Southwest Range Building. If so, the attackers would cross through the entire complex, passing between Jagger and Tyler's position and their apartment; he couldn't send Tyler there. He glanced up at the top of the wall holding the burning bush. It was too high to push the boy up there.

"Come here," he said and led Tyler to the corner formed by the rounded wall and the chapel. "Sit." He eased him down, then went back to the overhanging bush. He pulled a folding knife from his pocket, opened it, and clapped RoboHand's hooks onto the handle.

The sound of running footsteps bounced off the walls. Lights came on in windows overhead. Deep in the compound, someone yelled in a foreign language.

Jagger jumped up, grabbed a handful of stems, and pulled them down. He reached high to get into the leafy branches and hacked them off the bush. He did it a second time and brought the cluster of foliage to Tyler. "Hold these in front of you," he whispered. "Don't let them shake. Stay here till I get back, you hear? Don't move."

"Dad, what's happening?" Tyler said in a small voice. "I'm scared."

"Everything's going to be fine. Just stay here and don't move."

Someone screamed, and Tyler gasped.

Jagger reached around and squeezed the boy's shoulder. "Shhh. Be brave, son." He moved to the stairs where they'd left their shoes and looked back. Tyler was in shadow, but the reflected glow of the bulb that illuminated the bush caught his trembling hands and the vibrating tips of the branches. Jagger would have broken the bulb, but it was twenty feet overhead. The best camouflage was anything that broke up the shape of a human body, and the branches at least did that.

He rushed up the stairs.

[38]

Be brave. Be brave. Be brave.

The words flashed in Tyler's head like a flickering neon sign. But the explosion had been so loud it had even scared his dad, he could tell. People were yelling. Footsteps grew louder, then faded away. It was like everyone was running around, all confused and scared and bumping into the things they were trying to get away from. He hadn't seen many monster movies, but he'd watched enough to know they were like this.

He squeezed his eyes shut and felt tears streak down his cheeks. He hadn't even known he was crying; he wasn't really, only frightened enough to make his eyes water. That's all.

The branches in front of him shook, and he snapped his eyes open, stopping a scream by cutting off his breath. He looked up, knowing some gruesome creature had found him. But there was nothing, only his shaking hands, and he stiffened his muscles to make them stop.

Be brave. Be brave. Be brave.

He remembered something his mother had read to him from a story about Joshua: *Be strong and courageous. Do not be afraid, because God is always with you.* Something like that.

"God, are you there?" he whispered. "Make me strong and courageous." He closed his eyes again, releasing another tear. "Make me be okay. Make Dad be okay. And Mom. And Gheronda and Father Leo and Father Jerome and . . ."

Footsteps were coming down the stairs. Tyler held his breath and stared out through the leaves. No one appeared, and the footsteps echoed away.

"Dad?" he said quietly, then louder: "Dad?"

He squeezed farther back into the corner and adjusted the branches in front of him. His stomach hurt, and his heart was pounding so hard he was sure it would burst out of his chest. He rested the branches against his legs and pressed his palm over his breastbone. *Pa-dump, pa-dump, pa-dump.*

All he wanted was to be back in the apartment with Mom and Dad, all of them cuddled up on the couch, reading something cool like *Diary of a Wimpy Kid* . . . actually, he'd settle for anything, even one of those boring books Mom liked.

God, please, I'll even do the dishes. Just get me out here. Make everything okay, make it—

He heard his name . . . thought he did. Had Mom just called him? His breathing was too loud in his ears. He forced his lungs to stop, and listened. Footsteps, all over the place, running, echoing. Then: "Tyler!" It *was* Mom! But not close by . . . he'd heard it many times before: she was calling from the walkway in front of their apartment.

Someone yelled back. Dad, had to be, but the voice was quieter and Tyler couldn't make out the words. Did he want him too?

He tossed the branches aside and sprang up. He took two running steps toward the stairs, kicking up the stuff in his utility case—loud as a siren—and stopped. *Stupid, stupid!* Last birthday, Grandma Marilyn and Grandpa Tony had bought him sneakers with lights in the soles that flashed when they hit the ground. He'd never worn them, because how could you sneak around in the dark with lights marking your every step? But he'd never considered how unsneaky his utility case was. Around the monastery—uncovering its secrets and spying on monks—he'd always *crept*. He'd never thought about *running* quietly.

He worked the belt buckle, but it was a "friction style," Dad called it, with a post that tightened the belt against the back of the buckle. He liked it because they'd found it in an army surplus store—a real army belt—but he could never get it undone. After a few seconds of frustrated tugging, Tyler decided walking quietly at least got him moving, and he padded up the steps, past the shoes and socks he and Dad had left behind.

[39]

Following their plan, Phin had scrambled through the smoldering hole where the monastery's gates stood thirty seconds before and hooked right into the compound. He'd seen Nevaeh's invisible body float through the plumes of dust and smoke, like a bubble in champagne, beelining into the heart of the monastery. Ben would be moving left, all three of them pushing back toward the rear of the mini-city in search of their prey.

Phin ran on light feet, his right hand at his hip, ready to whip his sword from the suit's thigh pocket. He felt for the MP3 player in his pocket and cranked up the volume. A symphony of percussion instruments—chief among them kettle drums and an insistent, rhythmic gong—slammed his eardrums at a rate of 200 beats per minute. His heart raced to catch up, feeling as though it possibly could. As often as he'd done this—hunted, killed—it never lost its high. The smell of blood helped. True, what he'd told the others, that its odor instilled fear and panic in those whose nostrils it reached, but more so it excited him as it did any wild beast: an olfactory cue to become stealthy, agile, ruthless.

He took a big whiff, disappointed that the mask caused his breath to dilute the fragrance, and sprinted past the Well of Moses toward the northwest wall. That would take him past the guest quarters, into a tunnel, and right to the big structure along the rear wall that the monks called the Southwest Range Building. Toby had reported that Creed had entered the structure through an emergency door, and it was there that he expected to find his prey. The building was large, with numerous rooms, and housed many of the monks, who were now in protection mode.

Phin had turned between the wall and the corner of a building when a light washed over him from behind. A monk wielding a heavy walking stick was standing in the doorway of a small homey structure. He pulled the door shut and rushed toward Phin, who had his sword half out before remembering that the monk could not see him. He released the blade and pushed back against the wall.

As the monk approached, Phin saw that the "walking stick" was in fact a shotgun. Of course they would be armed; protecting the likes of Creed was their sworn duty, and that aside, the brotherhood here hadn't survived sixteen centuries by merely throwing prayers at their attackers. Over the years, they'd been known to pour boiling oil over enemies at the gate, conduct sophisticated bow-and-arrow defenses, and even sneak outside to kidnap the kings of besieging armies. They adhered to a doctrine in which God expected ferocity of body as well as gentleness of spirit. The time for beating swords into ploughshares had not yet arrived; these monks—and Phin too—believed the era would be ushered in by the godly, and without the occasional use of the sword, the godly would be Abel to the rest of the world's Cain.

Bobbing up and down on the balls of his feet, he pushed a button through the suit, stopping the music, and prepared to spring. He'd shove the monk face-first into the wall and find out where they were keeping Creed. Didn't matter that the man would surely resist divulging the location; Phin knew techniques involving eye sockets, genitals, and the brittle joints of fingers that coud pry information from the tightest lips.

Someone yelled, snapping his attention away from the monk. A woman was standing on the third-floor terrace of the guest quarters, leaning over the railing.

Phin let the monk hurry past him.

"Tyler!" the woman yelled again. She was closer than Phin to the Southwest Range Building. If she came down to ground level, he'd have to pass her.

Someone responded in a loud whisper: "No . . . Beth, shhh!"

Phin followed the woman's gaze and saw a man on the roof of a building across from her. He was patting the air with one hand, signaling her to be quiet. Other voices sprang up around the compound, queries and commands, but they didn't seem to bother the guy. He said, "Tyler's safe. Don't call him. Go back inside until I come."

"But—" the woman started.

"Beth! Please!"

Listen to him, Beth, Phin thought. You *don't want to be out here.*

She looked around and slowly moved into the building behind her. The light from her room disappeared with the click of a door. The man waited a few seconds, then turned and vanished.

Phin ran to catch up to the monk.

[40]

Tyler paused on a landing halfway up to the rooftops. Continuing up would take him the way he and Dad had come, which meant passing the apartment and doubling back through the center of the compound. Instead, he took a different flight of steps down into an alley. It was dark, but he knew the route home: straight to the back corner of the compound, where the Southwest Range Building met the building that housed the guest quarters. Their apartment and the stairs leading to it were at the opposite end of this building. A tunnel ran its length; the left side was lined with the doors to the first-floor rooms. It opened up into a small courtyard, where he'd also find the stairs leading to their third-level apartment.

As he moved through the black alley, running his hand along one wall, he forced himself to think not of the sharp yells and pounding feet or the explosion and whatever had come into the monastery, but only of the way home: *Straight to the three-way intersection . . . turn right into the tunnel . . . courtyard . . . stairs . . . home . . . Mom.*

Directly ahead, the intersection glowed dimly. He pictured the source of the light: after about ten feet or so, the tunnel to the left ended in a door to a monk's cell. Beside the door was a narrow, curtained window—curtained, he knew, because he had tried to peer in many times. The light must be coming from the window.

Footsteps echoed out of the tunnel, growing louder. Tyler stopped and pushed himself against the wall. A figure flashed past, heading for the room. Bushy beard, wild hair, black habit—one of the monks. He continued forward and was about to call out when something stopped him: a flickering shadow that was not quite a shadow; it *sparkled*, just a few pinpricks of bright light, there and gone. He squinted but saw nothing other than the heavily mortared wall of the tunnel.

A rap sounded—a code upon the door: a single knock, three fast ones, two more.

Bolts rattled and the door creaked open, spilling bright light into the intersection. Still, no more shadows, no more sparkles. Then, as the closing door pinched off the light, something glistened. Tyler gasped as a sword appeared, growing long and floating in midair at the center of the intersection. Above it, two eyes were glaring at him, and he slapped both hands over his mouth just in time to catch his scream.

[41]

Phin stared at the kid, mostly obscured by shadow, but obviously terrified. He chuckled quietly, and the boy's eyes grew even larger. He waved his sword, shooing the kid away. The boy backed up, taking two steps before tripping and sitting down hard, causing something to rattle, as though his butt were made out of Legos.

Phin almost laughed again, but dancing shadows drew his attention to the window, where a face was pressed against the glass. Phin closed his eyes and slowly twisted the sword so its thin edge faced the viewer. When he looked again, only swaying curtains moved behind the window.

And the boy was still sitting in the alley. "Go away," Phin whispered. "The monsters are out tonight." The kid began pushing himself back, crabbing farther into darkness.

Phin turned toward the door. He had made a quick calculation that the odds favored finding Creed by following the monk instead of torturing him for information. The guy had a gun: where else would he be heading other than to the location of the man he was attempting to protect?

Phin walked to the window but couldn't see beyond the curtains. Faint shadows moved within. Monks' cells were tiny, barely enough room for a bed and small dresser. He guessed that if Creed was inside, there would be no more than two, three others.

It didn't concern him that no one stood guard outside; that would be like hanging out a neon *He's in here!* sign. If they were to keep an external watch, he suspected it would be from afar: the alley where the boy was or the tunnel entrances. But Phin was invisible and he'd been fast, faster than the monks would have been getting to their posts.

He stepped in front of the door and kicked it hard. It rattled against its bolts, but didn't open. He ducked away, crouching under the window. One of the monks inside opened fire: a blast blew a head-sized hole through the center of the door, spraying splinters into the tunnel. A second later the window blew out. Glass and bits of curtain sailed over Phin's head. The glass played a chaotic, chimelike rhythm against the tunnel's walls and stone floor.

Phin hopped up and kicked the door again. It crashed open, and he was in. Through a haze of smoke he quickly assessed the situation. The monk directly in front of him was busy breaking the shotgun open and fumbling to extract the spent shells. On his right, another monk was pressed into the corner, near the window. He was waving a revolver at the destroyed door like a frocked Harry Callahan, looking for something to shoot. His mouth was open and his eyelids beat like butterfly wings, probably stunned by his brother blasting out the window he was so near.

Creed sat on the bed, his back up against the wall, his own handgun leveled at the door.

Phin tossed his sword into the far corner beside the shotgun-toting monk and dropped to the floor. Dirty Harry fired two quick rounds at the sword, causing his brother to flinch away and lose a handful of shotgun shells. Creed did as Phin had expected: he began firing, panning the gun from one side of the room to the other, returning it to chest level after each recoil. He would know his attackers could be invisible.

Phin slammed his foot into Dirty Harry's knee, snapping it backward. As the man came down, Phin grabbed the gun, twisted it out of his hand, and cracked it hard into his temple. He rolled to the monk who was stooping to pick up shotgun shells and introduced the top of the guy's head to the butt of the handgun. He spun and hooked his arm over the bed, leveling the pistol at Creed's eye. But he had already heard the *click-click-click* of Creed's empty revolver.

Phin stood, plucking a gorget from Creed's lap. Apparently he'd been about to clamp it around his neck when the action started. Phin tossed it away and Creed slumped, his gun hand lowering to the covers, his shoulders drooping, his chest deflating. It made Phin think of a melting ice sculpture captured with time-lapsed photography.

"Who?" Creed said. "At least tell me that."

Phin found the switch in his cuff and turned off the suit. He peeled back his hood and facemask. He shuffled his feet in a kind of dance and threw open his arms: *ta-da!*

Creed nodded and glanced toward the door. "The others?"

"Nevaeh and Ben. They're either on their way or preventing monks from reaching us." He took in Creed's head bandages, his pallor, the posture of a defeated man. So unlike the Creed Phin knew. Where were his strength, his militaristic demeanor? Getting away had drained him, as years spent on the front lines of many wars hadn't done. "You look ready."

"Aren't you?"

Phin grinned, bobbing up and down, excited. He examined the handgun he'd taken from the monk, a Taurus Protector. "Nice gun," he said. "I expected something about a hundred years older." He slipped it into a pocket, then stepped over a monk to retrieve his sword. When he turned around, Creed was holding something up in his fingers, a small container with a hinged top, open now. Inside, Phin could see the microchip.

"This is what you came for," Creed said. "Take it and go."

Phin's head canted to one side, as if he were examining a curiosity. "You know I can't do that. Dude, you should have just skedaddled." He wiggled his fingers through the air, imitating a bird. "Others have." He nodded at the chip. "You betrayed us, man. We can't trust you." He stripped off one glove and reached out to take the chip in its container, but Creed closed his fist around it. He leaned forward.

"Listen," he said, pleading, shaking his fist, "this isn't the way. Not anymore. Times change."

Phin laughed. "You're not really trying to convince—"

In a flash, Creed's legs tucked under him and he propelled himself at Phin.

Phin jumped back, simultaneously raising the blade and swinging it at Creed, severing first his hand and then his head.

[42]

At the junction of the alley and the tunnel—where he had returned on hands and knees when the gunshots had made his curiosity stronger than his fear—Tyler dropped his face into his hands. He tried to scream, but all he could do was gasp for breath. His stomach retched, and he waited for the vomit to come. But like his scream, it stayed inside. He hitched in breath after breath. He blinked, blinked, opened his eyes, and saw the detailed texture of the stones through his fingers.

His heart clenched tighter. He had crept out from the alley—not realizing it at the time, but pulled by the fascination of an invisible being suddenly taking the form of a gray-scaled Shadow Man—and when the sword had . . . had . . . he had dropped his face right then and there. So here he was, exposed in the light of the open door.

He raised his head, turtle slow, sure he'd find Shadow Man standing over him, the sword poised high like a guillotine's blade. But Shadow Man was still in the room, his back to the door. He was working to get something into a backpack; while his shoulders see-sawed up and down, his hips swayed back and forth.

The man touched his ear the way Secret Service agents do in movies and said, "I got it . . . Yes, Ben, I *saw* it, all right?" He laughed. "Oh, and I guess they're having a two-for-one special today, because I got Creed too." Pause. "Right. Meet you there." He moved his finger from his ear, hefted the pack, and spoke again: "You're welcome, buddy."

The words confused Tyler, but then another assault on his mind pushed everything else away. The thing in the backpack was the shape of a bowling ball, and a dark stain was spreading over the bottom of the pack.

Tyler's vision focused for a brief moment on the headless body hanging off the edge of the bed, spilling blood into a pool on the floor. He dropped his gaze and saw the severed hand midway between the bed and the door. Its fingers were splayed open, as if it were waiting for someone to hold it.

And rolling toward Tyler like a marble on the flat stones of the walkway was the black thing the now-dead man had offered his killer. It stopped barely an arm's length away. Instinctively, Tyler reached out and snatched it up. It wasn't a marble or any type of ball: more like a partial roll of Life Savers. As he pulled back with his prize, Shadow Man's sharp voice stopped him.

"Hey!"

Tyler raised his head. Shadow Man was bouncing toward him, slinging the backpack over his shoulder, raising the sword.

"Drop it, kid! Now!"

Tyler scrambled to his feet and shot down the alley the way he had come. His reasoning for choosing that path instead of the tunnel home didn't catch up with him until a few seconds later: The tunnel didn't bend until it was close to the courtyard at the far end; if Shadow Man threw the sword or used the gun he'd taken, Tyler would have had no chance at all. He was fast on his feet, especially turning, zigzagging, and generally acting rabbit-ish. And he knew the monastery's crazy layout.

Yeah, good job, he told himself. *Keep thinking, don't be stupid.*

Stupid? Like what? Like taking that little black thing? The thing the murderer with the big sword wants?

Stupid, stupid, stupid. Drop it, just drop it.

But his hand wouldn't obey. His fingers tightened around it. Somebody killed for it. Somebody died for it. He didn't understand why that mattered, why that meant he shouldn't let it go, but that's the way he felt.

He and Dad used to watch a TV show, *What Would You Do?* or something like that. In one, a woman was hit by a car that just kept going. Some people on the show panicked and froze, others ran to see how the woman was. Dad had said, "Call 911, people! Get the license plate!"

Tyler had understood calling 911, but "Get the license plate"?

"Justice," Dad had said. "Make the person responsible pay for his actions." Dad was big on justice.

If you're not going to drop it, Tyler thought, *run faster!*

Nothing reached his ears but his own panting and the loud *kich-kich-kich* of the utility case. If he was going to lose the man chasing him, he had to get rid of the case. He tugged at the buckle, but it didn't budge. He glanced into blackness behind him and saw Shadow Man flash through a ray of light twenty feet back. Clenching the Life Savers thing in one hand, he used the other to reach into his pocket and fish out his knife, his whittling, prying-cool-things-out-of-the-dirt, fingernail-cleaning knife. His father had taught him how to open it with one hand, using his thumb to flip the blade out. Without slowing, he opened it and tried to slip it between his pants and belt so he could cut the belt's canvas. But he missed and jabbed his hip . . . twice.

A hand gripped his shoulder, squeezing, tugging him back.

Tyler yelled. *How'd he get so close?* Shadow Man's panting-grumbling was right there, right in his ear; his boots were loud on the stones.

Stupid! Pay attention!

He swung his arm above his head, crossed it over his face, and plunged the knife down into Shadow Man's wrist.

The man yelled, and his hand slipped away. A string of sharp words reached Tyler's ears, along with the unmistakable sounds of the man tumbling to the ground.

That's it! That's it! Yeah!

He turned to head up the stairs to the rooftops and looked back.

Shadow Man was already rising—gripping at the wall to help himself up. He roared, and Tyler heard all the rage he could not see on the man's shadow-hidden face. He burned up the steps, crossed a bridge, and started toward a waist-high wall that separated terraces.

He stopped. Behind him, Shadow Man raged on as he pounded up the stairs.

Tyler knew what he had to do. He took off in a different direction. He darted to a gap between two living quarters that had been built centuries apart. The alley—if you could call it that—was wedge-shaped, with the far end barely wide enough for him to squeeze through. A square of glass bricks set into the right-hand wall showed that a light had been left on inside the building and illuminated the far end, making it appear wider than he knew it was. *Perfect.*

He waited at the entrance until the man appeared on the bridge and spotted him. Then he shot into the gap.

[43]

When the shooting started, Jagger was on a rooftop terrace. He had pursued footsteps, but every time he thought he was right on top of whoever was making them, he'd found no one. Coming to believe the phantom sounds were tricks of the compound's jumbled buildings, he'd started back toward the front gate. He'd seen boot prints in the blast's sediment and had been following them when the footfalls led him a different direction.

The first gunshot—the deep boom of a shotgun—got him spinning and reaching for a firearm he didn't have. Another blast. He ran toward the sounds, the back corner of the compound. Then a barrage of small-arms fire. Two guns, at least. He pictured a monk facing off with a hit man, blasting away at each other. He wasn't sure what he could do without a firearm of his own, but he'd figure that out when he got there.

More than anything, Tyler dominated his thoughts. He remembered a gut-wrenching news clip of a schoolboy killed in the crossfire of rival gangs and pushed himself to move faster. He vaulted over a short wall and leaped from one roof to another. *Please, Tyler, be where I left you. Please—*

Hands shoved him off the roof. Turning as he fell, he saw that the walkway was vacant, no one there to push him off. But he'd felt the shove, two distinct points of impact, on his left bicep and left side. At the same time, a leg had swept his feet out from under him. He came down on his back, the wind burst from his lungs, his head cracked against the stone ground. As he heaved for air, shadows rushed over him from the alleys and eaves and corners. His vision went dark.

[44]

Tyler's head and rear end scraped the alley's side walls, then he popped out behind the buildings, where a ledge hung over another rooftop six feet below. He turned and slipped his lower half over the edge. Bracing his forearms on the ledge, he balanced over the drop-off and peered into the alley.

Shadow Man skidded to a stop at the other end. His sword was gone, and he was holding his wrist with bloody fingers. He glared at Tyler and started for him, becoming a silhouette, merging into the darkness. When he appeared in the light, he was turned sideways and already rubbing the walls. He shimmied closer. The guy was thin, but there was no way he'd make it through.

Relief made Tyler's gut feel better. The alternative route to the rooftop below Tyler's feet was long: across several other rooftop terraces, down a flight of stairs and up another—and that was if you knew the layout. He smiled, but lost it when Shadow Man smiled back. The man edged back a bit, jostled his arms around, then pointed the gun at Tyler.

Tyler dropped just as the gun fired. He hit the roof and fell onto his back. Sandy fragments of the ledge sprinkled down on him. He rose, rubbing his tailbone, and backed away, watching the edge in case the man found a way through or was waiting to catch a glimpse of Tyler through the crack.

A noise chilled him. He'd scampered over enough rooftops not meant to be scampered over to recognize it: the scraping of terra cotta tiles over one another. He heard grunting and knew for sure: the man was climbing *over* one of the small buildings. He'd be there in seconds.

Tyler darted to another ledge. Across a five-foot span was the wall of a building that rose way above his position. In the space between, a flight of stairs descended into darkness one way; in the other direction it rose and turned out of sight. He lay on the roof and pushed himself over the edge. His feet landed on different steps and he flipped backward, striking his head on the opposite building. The thing he'd taken fell from his hand. It rattled down the stairs, spilling out a tiny item as it did. He crawled to this new something and picked it up. It had little prongs that poked his finger. He dropped it into the utility case, then used both hands to sweep the steps below until he found the original item. It was a container with a hinged lid, which he closed.

He caught movement from the corner of his eye and turned to see Shadow Man hurl himself from the ledge. The man hit the wall, then crashed onto the stairs and began tumbling. The backpack's strap slipped from his shoulder to the crook of his elbow. The pack bumped down a step, seeming to pull Shadow Man down with it. The pack opened, and a human head rolled out. It picked up speed—hair flying like fire, eyelids open to white orbs, the mouth locked in a curled-lipped grimace—and bounced directly at Tyler.

Tyler screamed, a horrified, sustained release of all the screams he'd been denied: over the invisible man with floating eyes and magically appearing sword; the ear-splitting firefight; the *beheading*. He whirled away from the head, somersaulted down the steps, found his feet, and ran.

[45]

When the shadows retreated, giving Jagger a view of the stars and the buildings crowding around him, he was still trying to fill his burning lungs. He couldn't have been out long. He rubbed the back of his head, felt a bump, and rolled over to push himself up. While the lights were out, his heart had moved into his head. It pounded in there, making his eyeballs and forehead, jaw and ears as miserable as his heart apparently was about its new accommodations.

For a few moments he forgot what he'd been doing when he fell . . . was *pushed*. He'd been running . . . gunfire . . . Tyler!

Someone had been shooting at Tyler! No, that wasn't right. It came back to him the way reality did after a particularly nasty nightmare. The gunfire was unrelated to Tyler, except that he was outside somewhere, only possibly in the vicinity of it. Jagger had been hoping, praying Tyler was nowhere near it.

He took a step and stumbled, catching himself against a wall. He shook his head, aggravating his misplaced heart, making it pound harder. The gunfire had stopped. He had to find out what had happened, had to get to Tyler, get him home. He looked around and knew where he was, only a couple buildings from the back-corner shootout.

Okay, he thought, *move*.

He walked, breathed, felt the pounding subside a little. He picked up his pace, began considering what he might find: dead monks . . . dead bad guys . . . live monks and bad guys gearing up for another volley. In that instant he didn't care. His sole desire was to find his son. He couldn't help believing the monks had brought this on. Taking that man in, being so secretive about it, about a lot of things. So help him, if anything happened to Tyler or Beth, the people who'd blown through the front gate would be the least of Gheronda's problems.

A shot rang out, and he spun toward it: in the center of the compound, closer to the Burning Bush, closer to Tyler. He wanted to call out him, to let him know he was coming, to hear that he was all right, but if Tyler was safe somewhere, calling to him could draw him out into danger. He ran all out, forgetting about himself, about caution, about anything but getting to his boy.

Less than a minute later he arrived at the Burning Bush. Tyler was gone, the branches that had hidden him fanned out from the corner on the ground. Unthinkingly, disbelieving Tyler's absence, he lifted them, expecting . . . what? His son? A clue to his disappearance? Had he left on his own or had someone taken him? Was he home now, curled up on the couch with Beth . . . safe somewhere else . . . kidnapped . . . ?

Jagger's mind slammed the door on other possibilities. He turned in a circle, hoping first to see Tyler—coming to him, cowering in a different corner—then scanning for clues. His boots and Tyler's sneakers, their socks were on the steps where they'd left them.

Meaning to yell, it came out a whisper: "Tyler?" He raised his face to the sky, drew in a deep breath, but before he could send his son's name into the compound, Tyler screamed, a long, terrible, little-boy scream. It turned Jagger's heart to stone.

"Tyler!"

The scream had come from the compound's most jumbled, stacked section of buildings. Getting to the Burning Bush, Jagger had run through a tunnel under it. He bounded up the steps to the rooftops. "Tyler!" He crossed terraces, bridges, leaped over alleyways, looking, looking and calling. He traversed the roofs, descending a level, then re-ascending, heading toward their apartment. The Basilica's obsidian-like roof floated across a chasm to his right; the Southwest Range Building ran the length of the rear wall to his left. Beyond that, the black presence of God's Mountain watched.

He descended into a valley formed by two buildings rising on either side of a walkway, which was itself composed of the rooftops of buildings below it. At the end was an arch, beyond which was a wide terrace running perpendicular to the walkway.

Right or left? he thought as he hurried toward the T. *North or south?*

The maracas rattle of Tyler's utility case started as suddenly as a flipped switch. Close, but the walls around him tossed the sound around, and he couldn't be sure how close or even from which direction it came. He stopped, held his breath.

On the terrace, Tyler flashed past the arched opening.

"Tyler!" Jagger dashed to the terrace and swung right just as his son's bobbing head disappeared down the stairs at the terrace's north end. "Ty—"

Footsteps rushed toward him from behind. He spun to see a man dressed from toes to neck in a gray skintight suit. He had short-cropped hair, wild eyes, and the maniacal grin of a butcher who loved his job. Most disturbing was the handgun he clutched in a bloody, gloveless hand. He was pumping his arms in an all-out sprint.

All this Jagger registered in a glance. The guy was nearly on top of him. Jagger's sudden appearance had not given Tyler's pursuer time to slow; the man's eyes were just now growing wide in acknowledgment of his presence.

That this nightmare was chasing his son sent a flood of rage through Jagger's body. He stiffened his muscles and narrowed his focus on one thought: this guy was going down.

[46]

Faced with a charging madman, most people would freeze or jump out of the way. Jagger attacked. He took two quick steps toward the man, crouched, and threw his shoulder into the guy's midsection. He rose, flipping the attacker over his head, sending a backpack tumbling across the terrace. Before the body landed, Jagger had pulled his baton, snapped it into full extension, and swung it into the hand holding the gun.

The man howled, but kept his grip on the weapon. Jagger raised the baton, taking aim at the man's head, which lay between Jagger's feet where it had landed. In a move out of Cirque du Soleil, the attacker executed a backward flip, raising his legs over his head and planting a foot squarely into Jagger's crotch. Jagger dropped the baton and doubled over . . . then sprang forward, tackling the man as he tried to stand. There was no time for pain; two seconds of incapacitation meant death.

Jagger fell on top of him. He clambered up his back and pushed down on the man's head with his prosthetic forearm, grinding his face into the terrace. He gripped the gun hand, lifted it, slammed it down, over and over.

The man drove his head back into Jagger's chin. He slipped his body out from under Jagger's and began kneeing him in the hip. He twisted and shoved his foot into Jagger's ribs, thrusting Jagger off him. The man rose up on one elbow and crossed the gun under his body to fire it.

Jagger completed the roll he'd started when the man shoved him, winding up on his back. This put RoboHand inches from the gun. As the hammer fell, he flicked his hook, knocking the barrel away. The gun roared, and the bullet could have parted Jagger's hair, it came so close. He pushed RoboHand under the man's chest and clamped it over the hand and fingers that gripped the gun.

The man tried to jerk his hand away, but it might as well have been bolted to Jagger's hook. He tugged and tugged, casting a stunned expression at Jagger. Jagger flexed his biceps, deltoids, trapeziuses, and the rest of his upper-body muscles—all of them contributing to the power of his grip. In the second it took the man to draw breath, Jagger heard his fingers break—like eggshells and Fritos under a booted heel—then his scream obscured all other sounds.

Jagger released RoboHand's tension, slid the prehensor off the fingers, clamped the gun barrel, and pulled it away. He swung it around to his real hand, which found the trigger and grip wet and sticky with blood.

A locomotive drove into his cheekbone. As his head snapped back, he realized the man had elbowed him: a bony joint, powered by a muscular arm and backed by the weight of the man's upper body. Considering the excruciating pain his attacker must have been in, it was impossible for the man to have risen so quickly and launched such a precise counterstrike, but the exploding nerves in Jagger's face screamed otherwise. The man spasmed upward like a bucking bronc and came back down on him. His left knee pinned Jagger's gun arm; his right foot slammed down on the prosthetic.

Jagger rocked back and forth, twisted and pulled his arms. He kicked his legs up, but the man leaned forward, out of reach. His mangled hand was tucked to this chest, and he was grinning. He reached to his side and produced a sword. Its blade was about two and a half feet long, three inches wide, and marbled with blood.

Jagger squirmed, rocked, pulled, tugged, kicked.

"First you," the man said. His tongue slid over his lower lip. "Then the boy. What's his name?" He looked around and called, "Tyler! Tyler!"

"No!" Jagger said. He rocked left and twisted his fake arm. It popped free of the man's boot. He shot it up to the man's neck and squeezed. The hooks slid over a hard surface, ripping away the scaly material and exposing a metal collar.

"Pretty cool, huh?" the man said and laughed. He swung the

sword down at Jagger's face. Jagger caught it with RoboHand, kicking up sparks and stopping the blade six inches in front of his face.

Through gritted teeth Jagger said, "Not as cool as mine."

He twisted his arm and wrist, but with his back and other arm pinned, he couldn't generate enough strength to wrest away the blade. The best he could do was not let go, and he wasn't sure that was enough. The man was strong, and knew the kind of fighting moves that made him dangerous beyond his strength and weaponry. Jagger could think of a dozen ways the guy could push the sword into his face or weaken him enough to maneuver it free.

The man leaned over and rested his forehead on the back of the blade, which quivered under the pressure of converse forces.

"You know," the man said, "we were going to leave you alone. But you got in our way—you and the kid—and that gives us permission. Not just that, an *obligation*." He straightened, looked around again. "Tyyyyler! Here, boy!"

Under the man's knee, Jagger's right arm was out of action, but not his wrist. He tucked it in as far as it would bend, gave it every bit of concentration not already allocated to keeping the blade out of his flesh, and pulled the handgun's trigger.

A red blossom bloomed on the man's cheek, instantly followed by another, larger one on the other side, higher up. He spat blood. It ran over his lip and down his chin, along with a white chunk of tooth. He released his grip on the sword and toppled.

Jagger flicked the sword away and reached for the man's wrist, thinking he was going for the gun. RoboHand snagged his sleeve, ripping it along a seam. The man thudded down over Jagger's gun arm. The man's own arm extended overhead onto the terrace, as if reaching for something. The tear in the sleeve revealed a glittering gold tattoo on the inside of his forearm—a comet or fireball, as far as Jagger could tell.

He held the torn-off swath of scaly material over his face, watching it shake as his muscles tried to process the flood of adrenaline coursing through them. He closed his eyes.

The man remained conscious, but not fully there. He squirmed and gurgled out unintelligible words. With the man's chest over the gun, Jagger thought about how easy it would be to twist the weapon again and put another slug into him.

He heard footsteps and opened his eyes. Rising onto an elbow, he scanned the terrace. It was empty. The fight had taken him away from the arch, so he couldn't see the walkway on the other side of it.

"Tyler?"

He reached for his baton. It moved away from him, scraping on the stone tiles, then it lifted off the ground. His mouth dropped open as he watched it dance in midair. It rose high, and that's when he saw the eyes, only eyes. They blinked, and the baton sailed down at his head.

[47]

The blow didn't knock him out, but it might as well have. A spike of pain pierced his brain, kicking up incongruous thoughts like disturbed bats:

—*Tyler, get to bed*—

—*technically speaking, the brain itself does not possess the sensory nerve endings to feel pain*—

—*ha ha ha ha ha*—

—*I did not come to bring peace, but a sword*—

—*the children! not the children too*—

—*the monastery was founded by the Roman Empress Helena in 330 AD*—

—*you're here at the pleasure of Gheronda*—

—*and that gives us permission*—

—*you and the kid*—

—*you and the kid*—

Jagger groaned, touched the new wound, and pulled his fingers away to visually confirm the blood he felt. It took his eyes a few seconds to focus.

Fast breathing drew his attention toward the man lying on his arm. His back rose and fell far more slowly than the quick breaths Jagger heard. He noticed the eyes: they were hovering near the man's head, which teetered one way then the other unnaturally.

A woman's voice whispered, "Phin . . . Phin!"

The eyes moved higher and stared at him. White sclera formed twin almond shapes, irises that appeared black in the dim light. They shifted down, and the man's body began to roll over. Jagger tugged his arm out and pulled it close, tucking the handgun under his leg.

The eyes rose straight up and disappeared. Footsteps pattered around him. The backpack the man had dropped floated off the terrace, its strap forming a triangle above it. It swooped around, and the strap became an upside-down teardrop over what must have been someone's shoulder. He was looking at the part of the pack that ordinarily pressed against a wearer's back.

Jagger caught a glimpse of the eyes and said, "Who are you?"

The pack bounced in the air until it hovered over the man's feet. One of his legs rose, the pack rotated, and the man slid away, trailing a slick of blood over the terrace. His unelevated leg cantered out, bent at the knee. The man gurgled, shook his head, lifted it.

"Ev-ah," he said through blood and shattered teeth.

Jagger wondered if his tongue was intact.

He shook his head again and said, "No, no, wait"—or so Jagger interpreted from the "*oh, oh, aith*" the man gurgled out.

His leg came down. The pack moved around to his head and lowered, stopping a foot off the ground. His head rose—too steadily and too high to be his own doing. Jagger imagined the hand that must be holding it, the invisible woman crouching beside it. There was whispering, gurgling. The man's head turned, and he spat. More whispering. The head lowered and the pack rose. The eyes stared at Jagger.

"Where's the boy?" came the woman's voice.

Jagger felt ice crystals form in his blood. He regretted not finishing the job, not pulling the trigger one last time. He sat up, bending his legs to keep the gun hidden.

"He has something of ours," she said.

"Leave your address," Jagger said. "I'll mail it to you."

Silence. Then: "We'll find him."

Jagger closed his eyes, then slowly opened them. "Just . . . leave. Please."

"Not without what's ours." A beat. "Is he yours, the boy?"

"What does that matter?" Jagger said, but his words felt like denying Tyler. "Yes, he is."

"All we want is what we came for. If he . . ."

Jagger stopped hearing her words. Tyler had appeared behind her, rising up from the stairs. He smiled when he saw Jagger but recognized that something was wrong—not the least of which, Jagger thought, was the backpack floating between them. His boy froze, except for his lips, the corners of which drooped.

Go back, Ty, Jagger thought, hoping beyond hope that somehow, some way his son would hear him, would understand. *Back up, Tyler . . . go . . . away.*

Jagger forced his attention back to the floating eyes, but it was too late. She'd caught something in his expression or in the flick of his gaze. The eyes disappeared, and the backpack rotated around.

"Tyler, run!" Jagger yelled. "Go! Go now!"

The pack began bouncing in midair, heading toward his son.

Tyler spun and descended the steps.

Jagger lifted the revolver and pointed it at the backpack. "Stop!" he yelled, then added the word that had become, in the culture of cops-and-robbers entertainment, weighted with a specific consequence: "Freeze!"

The pack stopped and shifted sideways; it rotated back and continued toward the stairs. Jagger wondered if she had forgotten about the backpack, that it betrayed her location.

He nudged his aim a few inches to the right of the pack and fired.

When faced with something not only new but contrary to everything one has ever learned about the world, some humans are prone to suspect the supernatural or otherworldly—that hovering saucer must be from outer space because planes need wings and helicopters need rotors; those flickering lights, dropping temperatures, and self-opening cabinets are, of course, evidence of poltergeist activity. Upon first encountering the invisible being, Jagger's mind had flashed through the possibilities—*angel . . . demon . . . alien . . . ghost . . .* But then he'd seen human eyes and heard a human voice, and he'd put it together: ordinary bad guys with extraordinary technology. What happened when his bullet struck the invisible thing sent his mind spinning back into the Twilight Zone.

A small explosion sprayed fire and smoke from the point of impact, as though the weapon had been loaded with exploding ammo, followed by an eruption of sparks—not the empty Bic lighter sparks the blade had kicked up when it struck RoboHand, but big, Fourth-of-July sparks. A body appeared, sleek and charcoal-colored, with blue electrical currents flashing lightning-like around every contour, every limb.

At that moment it seemed to Jagger more of a probability than a possibility that the thing was some sort of space-aged robot, a real-life Terminator who'd come from the future not for John Connor but for Tyler Baird.

The creature—definitely female, or at least constructed to resemble one—reached back with both arms to claw at the sparking point of impact. She spun around like a dog chasing its tail, like a man on fire. She pulled off the backpack and slung it aside. She slapped at her arms, stomach, head, trying, it seemed, to catch the quick squiggles of electricity coursing over her. But her hands always landed after the current had passed. In desperation, she gripped the scaly flesh of her shoulder and tore at it, spinning away from him as she did.

After ten or fifteen seconds, the sparks sputtered and stopped. The blue streaks of current diminished to a few random bursts, except in one area: they congregated around her neck, concentrating into a pulsating color of bright blue threads that flew like shooting stars over her shoulders, up around her head.

The figure turned back toward him. Both hands grabbed her neck, and in a quick upward motion she peeled off her face, revealing—Jagger realized with some relief—her true identity: very human and very beautiful, an observation coming more from the part of Jagger's mind that told him marauding psychopaths who attacked monasteries and kids should *not* look like this than from the part that appreciated pretty things.

She had already torn away the material over her shoulder, arm, and chest, revealing a black athletic halter top. At first he thought her bare skin was dappled with shadows, but they were too crisp and formed images: thorny vines, a grinning skull, crosses in a variety of styles. Black, gray, blue tattoos. Among them one stood out: on her forearm, the same gold fireball he'd seen on the man.

She clutched at her neck again and pulled down, ripping the material from clavicle to armpit. A flap fell over her chest, exposing a metal collar identical to the man's. She fumbled with something in the back—a latch, he realized, when she pulled the collar off and hurled it to the ground.

Grimacing, she rubbed her throat, then her face. Her right hand slid around to the back of her neck, and she released a curtain of black hair. She scratched at her bare arm, then at the other through the material, then her legs. She placed her hands on her knees and stayed that way, catching her breath. Slowly she raised her face and gazed at him through strands of hair.

"That hurt," she said. More heavy breaths, then: "Well, what are you waiting for? Shoot."

[48]

Jagger's finger tightened on the trigger, then he relaxed it. "It doesn't have to end this way," he said. "Just—"

From their tall tower near the basilica, the monastery's carillon bells began chiming, loud in the still air. Nine bells of different sizes—a gift from the czars of Russia in 1871, Gheronda had proudly told them—peeled out a rhythmic tune that to Jagger's ears recalled the grating horror of the shower scene in *Psycho*. He focused more intently on the woman, thinking she'd use the distraction to get the upper hand.

When all she did was smile, he yelled, "Leave now and live. Stay and die."

She simply stared.

"Take your friend and go!" He hoped he wasn't making a second mistake of mercy. The way these people fought—the man and earlier the teen, who he was certain was part of them—they were people he didn't want to underestimate.

In the States, he'd have held the woman until the cops arrived, but he wasn't confident the Egyptians would do anything or that she wouldn't fight if she knew his intentions to turn them in.

He looked behind him, a quick glance, which his mind processed after his eyes returned to the woman. The terrace was clear, at least as far as the light reached before the shadows devoured it. Not that he would see someone creeping up, not if the attacker was invisible.

"How many are you?" he yelled at her over the ringing of the bells.

"Inside? Now?" she called. "Just me and him. There was a third. He took off for our vehicle when Phin"—she nodded toward the downed man—"radioed that he had what we came for. Now he says your son took it."

The details made him believe her. But what *would* she say? *Five more, and they're right behind you?* He could only hope she was telling the truth.

She held her palms out, showing she had nothing in them. She straightened and took a step toward the man—*Phin*, she had called him—then stopped and cocked her head.

He heard it too—barely audible between the clangs of the bells, growing louder: Tyler's rattling utility case. It was coming from the walkway on the other side of the arch, and Jagger knew what it meant. Tyler had circled around to reach his father from another direction. If he believed the woman was pursuing him, of course he would try to get back to Jagger without crossing her path.

"Tyler, no!" Jagger screamed, cursing the bells. "Stop!"

But the rattling drew closer, and Tyler appeared. He slammed into a side of the archway, grabbing it to stop himself. He was panting hard; beads of sweat glistened on his face. Immediately his eyes found Jagger, and he grinned and bolted for his dad.

"No!" Jagger said, holding up RoboHand, which was completely useless for making a stop gesture.

He realized the woman was moving, reaching across her chest to a pocket under her arm. She produced a pistol and swung it forward, sidestepping to avoid his aim.

He adjusted . . .

Tyler stormed up, arms wide. His shadow fell over Jagger, and Jagger sensed his dropping toward him.

She aimed.

Jagger pulled the trigger. *Click.* The firing pin came down on a spent casing or an empty chamber. He pulled again. *Click.*

She fired.

Tyler's face instantly changed. The smile snapped into a silent scream. His eyes flashed wide. Pain and surprise twisted his sweet face into a stomach-churning mask that would make angels weep. He flew into Jagger's arms. His head struck Jagger's chest and he crumpled into his lap, a rag doll.

Jagger screamed. He dropped the gun and lifted his boy, bringing his face close. Tyler's eyes rolled, found his, and communicated too much for Jagger to bear. His head dipped, came up, as though he were gripped by utter exhaustion, seconds from sleep. Through quivering lips he said, "Da-Dad?"

"I got you, Ty. You're okay, you're okay, you hear me?" Jagger said, wishing it, wishing it. He cupped a hand on the side of Tyler's head, then brushed his fingers down to touch his son's lips, as if trying to stop what might come out—blood, last words, a last breath. His fingertips left twin streaks of crimson across Tyler's cheek. Using the prosthesis to support his son, Jagger reached his other hand around to Tyler's back and felt warm wetness, so much of it.

"Dad?" Tyler said, barely more than a weak groan.

Do something, Jagger thought, but all he could think about was holding his son, holding him together, keeping him here.

"You're okay," he repeated automatically—the words coming out on gasping breaths. He turned his head away, whispered, "No, no, no, no . . ."

A shadow slid over him. The woman walked near and knelt. She held the pistol close to her chest, pointed at Jagger, and reached for Tyler's hand. Jagger turned away from her, pulling Tyler with him, but she grabbed Tyler's wrist, turned it. His hand opened, and a small black object rolled out. She took it and glared at the thing as though it were a bug that had crawled out of her ear.

"I was aiming for you," she said, just loud enough to be heard over the bells.

Jagger pushed his face into his son's neck. He inhaled Tyler's fragrance; it still smelled new, clean, free of the bitter tang of post-pubescent perspiration. But overpowering it like cigar smoke in a flower store was the sweetened coffee/metallic odor of blood, growing stronger with each breath.

"Go to hell," he said.

His tears poured onto his son as his hand found the hole in Tyler's shirt. He stuck his finger through and tore the material away. He rubbed bare skin, slick with the lifeblood that Tyler needed inside, not out. He ran his hand up to the bullet hole, gently pushing the blood back in. He stroked more liquid up, squeegeeing it off Tyler's skin, back into the hole, only vaguely aware that it was the act of an insane person. No matter how fast he worked, the blood kept coming, flowing out over his fingers, cascading down.

He shifted Tyler in his arms and realized the woman and injured man were gone. He leaned his son's head against his left bicep, stroked his face, ran his fingers through his hair, smearing blood everywhere.

Tyler watched him, lids half closed. With great effort he opened his eyes wider, questioning. Jagger read in them a need to know: *What's happening to me?* And more important, *What's going to happen next?*

"My boy," Jagger whispered.

Tyler smiled.

Jagger smiled back, but he couldn't hold it. His molars ground together, and he raised his face to the sky. "Not him, Lord," he whispered. "Me, take me instead. Please. Not him, not him ... ."

He lowered his head, touching his cheek to Tyler's. He tried to stop weeping and couldn't. He groaned. His head rolled back, and he was looking at the stars again. "Why!" he screamed, and the word became a long, loud wail.

As if realizing their defeat for domination of the night air, the bells clanged their last and faded away.

[49]

The helicopter settled onto the slightly sloping rock in front of St. Catherine's, and Owen climbed out. He stared at the smoking hole that used to be the front gate and realized he'd arrived too late. He leaned back into the cabin and spoke to the pilot, who switched on a joystick-controlled spotlight mounted to the nose of the copter. It bathed the destruction in white light. He started toward it and stopped.

A woman was coming out, carrying someone over her shoulder, only feet, legs, and backside visible from this angle. He pulled his pistol and saw a small handgun clutched in her fist. Squinting, she aimed it at him, each of them watching the other over the barrel of a gun.

"Stop!" he yelled over the sound of the helicopter's engine and rotors. "I can't let you take him."

She twisted her torso, showing him the man she carried. It wasn't Creed.

Owen gestured with his head for her to leave.

"Get that light off me," she said. "Or would you prefer I just shoot it?"

He signaled the pilot, and the light snapped off.

Pointing the gun, watching him, she stepped gingerly through the rubble. When she'd cleared the worst of it she picked up her pace, heading for the garden side of the monastery. As she passed his position, she rotated to keep her eyes and gun on him, sidestepping, then walking backward.

At the end of the great wall, she stepped back into the shadows and disappeared. Owen kept his pistol aimed at the spot and slowly made his way toward the entrance.

X I I I

As Jagger lowered his head and closed his eyes, the bells continued to resonate in his mind, clanging unmusically, pounding, settling into an unwavering, high-pitched tone, a scream sustained through eternity.

Something touched his head, and he raised it. Tyler was looking at him, through him, with unfocused eyes. His son's hand slowly smoothed the hair on the back of Jagger's head, caressing it. He coughed, too quietly to penetrate the scream that filled Jagger's skull.

Jagger said something—Tyler's name, soothing assurances—but the scream stole his voice as well. Then other sounds did break through, rhythmic pulses, as if from a variety of drums scattered around a pitch-black stadium: his heartbeat, footsteps pounding and echoing in the monastery, the *thu-thu-thu* of a helicopter's rotors.

They're leaving, he thought. What he wouldn't have given at that moment for a rocket launcher. But he'd give more, he'd give everything, to save his son—to *move* and get him help. *Move!* Scratching in a deep recess of his brain, like a fingernail, was the thought that if he just stayed there, if he continued to simply hold his boy, time would stop, the badness would stop. Hit the pause button, freeze-frame this moment forever, the two of them holding each other, and what would happen next never would.

But if he moved—if he did the very thing he knew he had to, what every cell in his body except that scratching fingernail *screamed* at him to do—then the movie would go on, fast-motion, rushing to events he didn't want to experience.

One of those drums in the darkness rose in volume, drawing close, then stopped. A scream—real now—reached him like a slap across his face. He looked over Tyler's head and saw Beth frozen at the end of the terrace. She rushed forward. Her body broke up, prisming into disjointed shards. Jagger blinked his tears away, and her pieces came back together.

"Stop!" Jagger said, shaking his head. Beth should be there, he knew. To be with her son, to give Tyler comfort, to force Jagger to *move*. But he didn't want her to see Tyler this way, bloody, barely holding on. It would rip her apart. "Beth . . . don't . . ."

She didn't slow but came full-on into his nightmare, tears already streaming down her face. She fell to her knees beside them. Her hands shot toward Tyler, stopped inches from him, hovered—wanting so much to touch him, but afraid her love would cause him pain, hurt him worse. Or was it, Jagger thought—*scratch, scratch, scratch*—that to her, physical contact and only that would make this horror real?

"Jag—What, what—?"

He heard the meaning behind each syllable. *Tell me he's fine! What do we do, what can we do?*

She groaned, a mother's agony. "Tyler—"

And what assaulted Jagger's mind was everything Tyler ever had been—the wrinkled pink newborn, mad as a hive of bees at being extracted from the warm cocoon he had known; the five-year-old planting his entire face in his birthday cake and coming up a laughing abominable snowman—and as he was now, the boy whose love and joy was a sun that could burn away his parents' gloomiest moods.

Beth's torment broke Jagger's paralysis.

"Give me your sweater," he said. She stripped it off, and when he moved his hand from Tyler's back to press the material against the wound, she caught a glimpse. She gasped as fresh tears poured down her face. She clamped a hand over her mouth. New energy surged through him, adrenaline and determination incited by the urgent distress of the woman he loved. In his weakest time she had become strong, willing and able to carry them both; now it was his turn.

"Keep this pressed over the wound," he said.

She nodded and pressed her hands against the balled-up sweater.

Tyler's legs were sprawled across Jagger's, his bare feet canted at awkward angles on the stone terrace. Jagger shifted and got a foot under himself. He rocked forward and rose up, pulling Tyler into his arms.

"What are you going to do?" Beth asked.

"We need Ollie's Jeep."

"Help!" Beth screamed over her shoulder. "Someone! Help!"

Jagger started to walk, Beth sidestepping with him, keeping her hands on the sweater. She said, "When I heard you and came out, I passed

Father Jerome. He said they turned on the bells to call for help from the town. Someone should be coming."

"Who?" Jagger said, shaking his head. There was a doctor in town who manned a little clinic. He'd met him once, to get a prescription for stronger painkillers when a persistent ache in his stump had kept him up three nights straight. The doc looked as old as the monastery and moved like he had glass shards in his joints. He doubted the guy had treated anything more severe than a few cuts and bruises from clumsy tourists, a stomach bug now and then. But he *was* a doctor; he'd have equipment, supplies. Jagger moved faster.

Before they'd crossed half the terrace, a stranger rushed up the stairs and pointed a gun at them.

[50]

Beth froze and Jagger turned, putting his body between the stranger and Tyler. The sweater fell away, hitting the terrace with a sickening *plop*. Frustration and anger made Jagger feel like a racehorse straining at the gate: he wanted to *move*, go crazy, stomp over anyone preventing him from getting help for his son. But giving in to that impulse would get him killed, and that wouldn't be in Tyler's best interest. So he held it in, waiting to explode.

"What?" he yelled, glaring over his shoulder at the man with the gun.

The man looked like a lumberjack: long-sleeved flannel shirt, worn workman boots, a shaggy mess of hair that flowed into an equally shaggy beard.

"*What do you want?*"

The man set the pistol on the terrace and kicked it away. "I'm sorry," he said, walking forward. "I saw the destruction at the gate. I didn't know who you were in the dark."

"Stay away," Jagger said.

The man stopped ten paces from them. He said, "I'm a doctor. I'm here to help."

"You're not from the clinic," Jagger said.

"My name is Owen Letois. A man called me. He had a head injury, and the monks had taken him in."

Jagger thought it through quickly and decided it made sense. If this Owen guy was one of the attackers, why would he come back? If the woman had meant them further harm, she'd had the opportunity and no doubt the constitution to do it herself. He turned around, and Owen hurried to him.

He dropped to his knees, reached into a pouch on his belt, and pulled out a penlight. He examined the wound. "No air. I don't think the bullet struck a lung. Heavy blood flow, but it's not pulsing out, so his major arteries are intact."

"But there's so much," Jagger said.

Owen stood and offered a weak smile. "I've seen worse."

Beth grabbed Owen's arm. "So he'll be okay?"

Owen frowned. "He could still bleed out, and I can't know what organs may have been damaged."

Beth covered her mouth again and shook her head.

To Jagger, Owen whispered, "What's his name?"

Jagger told him.

The man leaned close to Tyler, took the boy's head in his big hands, and gently turned it toward him. He ran his fingers over Tyler's skin, along his forehead. "How are you feeling, Tyler? Sleepy?"

Tyler nodded.

Owen spread open Tyler's eyelids and flashed the light into them. "I need you to stay awake, okay? Can you do that?"

Another nod.

"Do you feel sick, like you have to throw up?"

Tyler's eyes drooped shut.

"Tyler?" Owen said, slapping his face lightly. "Wake up, son."

"Thirsty," Tyler said.

"We'll get you some water soon." Owen ripped open the boy's khaki shirt. Buttons popped and tinked onto the terrace. He ran his hands over Tyler's chest, stomach, neck, into his armpits and down each side. "No exit wound. The bullet's still in there. If we move him too much it could do a lot of damage." He turned to Beth. "Go get a bed, one of the little ones the monks use. Not the—"

Gheronda and two monks appeared at the top of the stairs. Owen snapped his head toward them.

"You?" Gheronda said.

"A bed!" Owen yelled. "I need a bed, just the board, not the mattress or frame. *Now!*"

Gheronda spoke to the other monks, and they hurried down the stairs.

"And blankets!" Owen yelled after them. Gheronda repeated the call, then started toward them.

Owen said, "Do you have any saline or blood expanders—Hetastarch, Voluven, Pentaspan . . . ?"

"No," Gheronda said. He waved his arm. "Only the basics. Ointment, gauze—"

"Get them," Owen said. "Meet us out front at my helicopter."

"Helicopter?" Jagger said. "That was you . . . coming in?"

"I was in a hurry." That seemed to remind him of something, and he looked back at the retreating monk. "Gheronda." When the old man turned he said, "Creed called me. Is he—?"

Gheronda shook his head, then continued away. Owen lowered his face.

"What are we doing?" Jagger said. "We have to *do* something."

Owen's eyes snapped to his. "We need to stop the bleeding and get him on a board to keep him as immobile as possible." He reached into his pouch. "I have a blood-clotting gauze . . ." He pulled out an empty wrapper, crumpled it, and tossed it away. "I *did* have it." He shook his head, said, "It's fine." His hand went behind him and reappeared with a wallet. He flipped it open and pulled out a credit card, which he pressed against the hole in Tyler's back. "This will form a better seal over the wound than a compress alone. Ma'am, could you push that material over this?"

Beth looked at the sweater. "It's . . . *drenched*."

In one quick motion Owen grabbed the back of his collar and yanked his flannel shirt over his head, revealing a green, long-sleeved undershirt, as stained and tattered as the button-down. He handed it to Beth, who pressed it against the credit card.

Owen removed his belt and wrapped it around Tyler's torso and over the balled-up shirt. He cinched it tight.

Beth removed her hand. She stepped up to Tyler's head and began stroking it. "You're going to be fine, baby," she whispered.

Tyler's eyes rolled to look at her, and he tried to smile.

"What about the clinic?" Jagger said. "It's in town, just a mile."

"He needs more than it can offer," Owen said. "We'll take my helicopter to Sharm el-Sheikh. We can be there in forty minutes."

Forty minutes, Jagger thought. They'd already wasted . . . He clicked off the chronology of events since the woman had shot Tyler: his distress, Beth's arrival, Owen's, the monks'. He realized that what had seemed an emotional eternity and at least twenty real-life minutes had been no more than five. Five minutes of agonizing, soul-searing torture. But another forty? How many heartbeats was that, as Tyler drifted toward some point of no return? He felt as though he were standing on a shore watching currents carry his son toward a plunging waterfall while someone ran off to find a life rope.

He saw Tyler looking at him while Beth stroked the bangs off his forehead and whispered in his ear. A patina of sweat slicked his face. Even in the scant light from the terrace's single bulb, Jagger could see the gray hue of Tyler's skin. The muscles under that skin continued to tremble, the way a puddle vibrates as something huge approaches. His lids closed and opened, closed and opened. But what frightened Jagger the most was the missing sparkle in his eyes, that indefinable reflected glow of his spirit.

The two monks returned, stomping up the stairs and across the terrace, carrying a board between them, blankets draped over their shoulders. Owen beckoned them with an urgent hand, like a flagman signaling a plane. He touched Tyler's cheek and smiled at him. Then, in his excitement, he grabbed Jagger's collar.

"We're on," he said. "Let's move!"

[51]

Using a wad of gauze clamped in a hemostat, Toby dabbed at the bullet hole in Phin's right cheek and the much larger exit wound in his left. "Man," he said. "And I thought you were ugly *before*."

Phin moaned. His hand came up to strike Toby, but dropped back to the vinyl bench seat in the rear of the helicopter's cabin.

"Why's he falling asleep all the time?" Alexa said, reaching over her seatback to touch Toby's head. He was crouched between the bench seat and a row of captain's chairs, where she and Nev sat. In front of them, Ben occupied the copilot's seat.

"Pain," Toby said. "Head wounds hurt, and the bullet really messed up his mouth, tongue, and teeth."

"And his face."

"It'll heal." Toby taped squares of gauze over each wound, pushed a syringe of an analgesic-sedative cocktail—morphine, bupivacaine, and dexmedetomidine—into Phin's thigh, and returned to his seat beside Nevaeh. He slapped her shoulder. "So what's this?" he said. "You shot a kid?"

She glared at him. "I'll shoot *you* if you don't shut up."

"Like, how old was he?"

Nevaeh ignored him. Ben turned in his seat to look at her, then at Toby. "Tobias," he whispered, "our pilot's fidelity has already cost a king's ransom. Your mouth will make it two . . . if not unpurchasable at any price. We will sort everything out on the plane."

Toby glared into the back of the pilot's head. "Don't you think he heard the explosion? What about all those emergency vehicles we just flew over? The El Tour Road looked like a jeweled snake."

"Everyone has a line they won't cross." Ben returned his gaze to Nevaeh, who said, "It was an accident."

Toby waited for Ben to tell her what he'd told Toby a million times: *We don't* do *"accident,"* but the older man simply turned in his seat and stared out the windshield at the dark desert below.

[52]

The helicopter Owen called "his" was an Egyptian Air Force Mi-8MB *Bissektrisa*—his for the evening, he'd told Jagger, at a cost of 50,000 LE—roughly $9,000—and "the calling in of long-forgotten favors."

"The Egyptian military owed you favors?"

"Only some of the top brass."

Jagger suspected that Owen's chitchat—while carrying Tyler on the makeshift stretcher to the helicopter, waiting for Gheronda's meager medical kit, even checking Tyler's vitals and the compress's effectiveness—was intended to distract Beth and him from dwelling too long on how all of this might end. Little good it did: the possibility of Tyler's not pulling through was a black pool of stinking, noxious muck at the bottom of a pit with sloping, crumbling walls. No matter how hard Jagger tried to climb away from it, he always tumbled back in.

Between the far back seats and the pilot chairs was an open area that accommodated the stretcher with room to spare. Tyler lay on his side with Jagger's folded shirt under his head. Jagger felt naked in a black tee, his prosthetic arm fully exposed. But of course he would spend the rest of his life wandering through cities truly naked if in some truth-or-dare version of the universe it meant saving his son or even merely granting him some measure of comfort and peace.

While they carried Tyler to the helicopter, Beth had rushed back to their apartment for her purse. Now she and Jagger crouched near Tyler's head. Jagger kept a grip on Tyler's shoulder, partly to comfort him, partly to hold him still as the helicopter banked and maneuvered through gusts of wind. Beth stroked his face and hair, whispering words of comfort or prayers—although she would argue they were one and the same, Jagger had never been so sure as now that they weren't. But he wouldn't begrudge her—or Tyler—access to the one they thought was a loving God. His disagreement was between *himself* and God.

Owen spun out of the copilot's chair and knelt beside Tyler. He slapped a palm on Jagger's back. "The pilot's called ahead. He's cleared to land on the hospital's roof, and they're prepping an OR. Sharm International, very modern with all the latest technologies and world-renowned doctors. He'll get the best care."

The hospital's credentials didn't surprise Jagger; Sharm el-Sheikh was a ritzy playground for the rich and famous. What did surprise him was Owen's timely appearance and their ability to transport Tyler so quickly . . . "quick" only in relative terms: traveling the single road from St. Catherine's west to Dahab, then south to Sharm el-Sheikh would have taken a bumpy, excruciating three hours, not counting the innumerable checkpoints. He might have said both Owen and the transport were miracles, blessings, but wasn't the God who doled out such blessings the very one who had caused their need for them?

Deep inside, he feared that his anger would cause God to withdraw the blessings part of the equation: the helicopter would malfunction; the hospital would be missing an essential supply or piece of equipment or physician; or worse, Tyler wouldn't hold on long enough to receive the care he needed. That would be consistent with the God Jagger knew: to offer hope, only to snatch it away.

He let loose with a mental scream. This was the kind of thinking that would tick off the Guy Upstairs. If he couldn't thank him for Owen and his helicopter, then it was best not to think of him at all.

Just take each thing as it comes. It's a world of defeats and victories, of counterbalances. Things happen, they just happen.

Then Owen started praying. This gun-toting doctor with a penchant for grungy clothing and lax grooming, who racked up favors with Middle Eastern nations and had "seen worse" than Tyler's gunshot wound, laid his hand on Tyler's head and chest and prayed. He spoke softly, just above a whisper, but the sincerity and passion some televangelists tried to achieve through fervor and volume he evinced with a surety of words and a tone Jagger could not recall hearing before. More than anything, it spoke of *relationship*, a connectedness borne of time spent together, of battles won and battles lost, of pleasure and pain, grief and joy, and everything in between.

Jagger was awed by the seeming effortlessness of Owen's faith. He had slipped into prayer without preamble or apology, without the rolling-up-the-sleeves attitude of so many believers as they approached their time with God. He had flashed the penlight into Tyler's eyes, smiled, and said, "You're doing great. You're a brave young man," then started praying, as simply as checking a pulse.

A part of Jagger wanted to give Owen a solid shove, scream at him, *Don't you know you're wasting your time!* But a more powerful part said, *Yes! Do it!* After all, he'd accept help for his son from anyone, anything. He tried to push away the thought that from Owen's mouth came the words Jagger should have been saying, a heart-aching plea for Tyler's life. He closed his eyes, clamped his teeth together.

Is that what you want from me? Are you crushing me so low that I have nowhere else to turn? Ain't going to happen. I know how cruel you are. I know your games.

He felt a tap on his back and jumped. He turned to see the pilot holding up five fingers. Jagger patted Owen. "Five minutes!"

Owen nodded and continued to pray.

[53]

Nevaeh sat alone in the forward cabin of the Tribe's jet, a Bombardier CL-601: six recliners as fat, soft, and white as marshmallows, arranged in two rows flanking a central aisle. The lights were dimmed to a soft glow, and the sacred music of Gioachino Rossini—at the moment, *Tantum Ergo*—whispered through the air. Despite enough comfort and ambience to lull a binging crackhead to sleep, she was far from relaxed. Simply being at Mt. Sinai again, the memories it conjured, would have keyed her up for hours of soul searching and memory sifting—but shooting the boy, she'd be up for days grappling with that one. An accident, yes, but she wondered if it could have been avoided. Had she jogged right instead of left to avoid the man's aim, the boy would not have entered the bullet's trajectory.

Like a team of "cleaners" in a hit-man movie, sweeping in to scrub a crime scene of evidence, into her troubled mind marched her twin friends Justification and Rationalization.

"The boy interfered," said Justification, gruff as a police sergeant, sure as a judge. "That made him an accessory after the fact, equally expendable."

"Even if he was an innocent," said Rationalization, always in the gentle teaching tones of her long-forgotten father. "You know unfortunate casualties come with the territory. All for the greater good."

"The greater good," she repeated, liking the sound of it. "If I'd allowed him to steal the chip we couldn't carry on, we couldn't do our job."

"Given to you by God," Rationalization clarified.

"He was a meddler," Justification said. "And he paid the appropriate price."

"I don't know that I killed him," she said.

"All the better, if you didn't," intoned Rationalization. *"We don't need to be having this conversation."*

She shook her head. "He didn't look good."

"He should *be dead,"* said Justification. *"He sinned when he stole from Phin. He sinned by trying to stop you."*

"You did what you had to do," said Rationalization.

"Yes, only what I had to do."

"Our work here is finished," said Rationalization.

And with that the twins were gone.

Feeling better, Nevaeh spun her chair around to gaze toward the rear of the plane. Against the walls, in line with the chairs, were two floor-to-ceiling compartments, each containing two bunks. The doors were closed, and she had always thought of them as crypts, sealed off from the world, a place of rest, if only for a time. Toby and Alexa occupied the two bunks on the right. Phin lay in the other. They'd done everything they could for him, which amounted to dressing his wounds and drugging him into oblivion.

At the end of the aisle, between the compartments, a door led to a galley, a bathroom, and storage closets. She considered going back there and changing out of her invisibility suit. Instead, she rose and headed for the cockpit. Normally Elias would be piloting, but with him sent off to Trongsa—and certainly back home by now—Ben was at the controls. She slipped into the copilot seat. Outside the plane, the black Mediterranean Sea sparkled with the reflected light of a billion stars overhead.

"It's a tomb back there," she said without looking at Ben.

"You're complaining?"

"Just saying. Our numbers are dwindling." From the corner of her eye, she caught him looking at her and faced him. "Eight now, from forty."

"It was bound to happen," he said.

"We should talk to the ones who haven't died, build back up to fighting numbers."

"They're scattered," Ben said. "Lost causes."

"Ben—"

"Did you put the chip in the safe?"

She wanted to talk more about rebuilding the Tribe, going after the ones they'd lost, but she knew Ben had said all he would. She sighed and unzipped a breast pocket. She reached in and pulled out the microchip container.

"I'm not so sure technology is making our task any easier," she said, thumbing it open.

"Easier considering the size of our target. As you pointed out, we're only eight now, can you imagine . . ."

She stopped hearing his words. All of her senses narrowed into the container, which held a plug of polyethylene foam and nothing more. She used a fingernail to dig out the plug, examined it, peered into the empty cylinder. She patted the outside of her breast pocket, searched inside. She looked up and saw Ben watching her.

"Are you having fun with me?" he said.

"It was in the boy's hand," she said. "I just assumed."

Ben took it with the calm of a man learning that his flight would be a few minutes late. He punched buttons on the control panel, into the GPS. He said, "Remember what Phin said? He saw the chip in its container. That changed between then and when you found it. Either it fell out or the boy removed it. I'm betting on the boy."

"You think he stashed it somewhere?" Nevaeh said. If so, and the boy was dead, they'd never find it.

"Let's hope he had it on him," Ben said. "Call Sebastian. Tell him we need to know where the child is now. Have him check the area hospitals and morgues. We'll also need that helicopter again, and I want the same pilot."

Calm as he was, Ben had a way of communicating reproach with his eyes. He hadn't leveled condemnation at Nevaeh yet, and she wasn't going to hang around until he did. She plucked the satellite phone out of its dashboard-mounted cradle and stood, only to plop down again as Ben forced the plane around.

[54]

For Beth and Jagger, the hours Tyler spent in surgery were like flailing through a nightmare from which they couldn't wake.

Beth expressed it best: "I feel like I'm underwater," she said, sitting on the edge of a cushioned chair near the ER nurses' station, face lowered into her hands. "I mean *really*—in the ocean. The surface is way up there, like clouds, with the sun shimmering over it, but it's dark where I am. I can see Tyler close by, but I can't reach him. I just keep swimming and running, moving any way I can, but too slowly . . . so very slow. I'm exhausted, trying to get to him, but I'm not getting any closer." She sniffed and smiled weakly at Jagger, as if to say, *Isn't it crazy?* "And all around him are these sharks, and I know they're going to attack him any second." The tears came again, and she shifted to hug Jagger's arm.

He felt the same—at least the sense of it, until she put it into words, and then he was down there too, deep in the ocean. But in his tortured imagination, the sharks had already attacked. All Jagger could do was scream, a bubbling explosion of muffled anguish.

He tried to comfort Beth, all the while buffeted by an internal storm of anger, frustration, and worry. His thoughts flipped from images of Tyler in happier times—jumping into his arms, falling asleep on his lap—to should-have-been fantasies of sweeping the boy out of harm's way and somehow getting the upper hand on the woman: hopping up, dodging her bullets, making her eat the gun. He continually checked with the nurses and learned more than he wanted about bullet probes and forceps, resorbable microsurgical nerve and blood vessel sutures, and how infections have caused more deaths than blood loss in gunshot victims.

The physicians' frequent calls for blood—it sounded like *"Adem!"* in Arabic—were like fresh jabs at his heart with an ice pick. A nurse rushed out of the OR, her green smock bloody, her surgical mask spattered.

A thought pierced Jagger's brain: *That's my son on her, my son!*

She rambled in Arabic to the nurse at the station, rushed back to the OR door, and turned again. She waved her hand in a spinning circle and yelled an Arabic word Jagger understood: *"Haza! Haza!"* Now! Now!

The station nurse picked up a phone, replaced it, consulted a computer screen, picked the phone up again, and started dialing.

Jagger learned over the counter. "What is it? What's happening?"

The nurse ignored him, pushed the disconnect button, released it, dialed.

Jagger reached out and grabbed her arm. "What!"

"The pediatric surgeon hasn't shown up yet," she said in nearly perfect English. "I paged him twenty minutes ago. Please!"

He released her, and she continued dialing. She spoke into the phone, urgency imbuing every foreign syllable. When she hung up, Jagger said, "Where is he? Is he coming?"

She nodded. "Yes, yes. The ER surgeons are doing everything, but he too will be here soon. Don't worry, please."

Don't worry. Don't worry! If ever anything was easier said than done . . .

He sat on the edge of a chair and stared at the blue cotton slippers a nurse had asked him to put on over his bare feet. He thought about his boots on the steps near the burning bush, next to Tyler's sneakers. His boy had wanted to remove his shoes to approach the bush. What kind of kid thinks like that? What kind of god strikes him down?

Eventually a man came down the hallway, fast-walking with nurses scurrying around him, slipping off his watch and pushing scrubs over his arms and chest. He rushed into Tyler's OR. Jagger tried to follow, but two hefty orderlies stopped him.

Some time later—twenty minutes, an hour, a day; Jagger had

lost all sense of time—sharp calls emitted from the room, followed by the unmistakable *THUMP!* of a defibrillator. Both Jagger and Beth pushed through the OR door before the orderlies could stop them. Tyler's little body lay on the operating table, his skin too white under the blinding brightness of a Cycloptic lamp, blood everywhere, an army of doctors and nurses standing around, one holding defib paddles over Tyler's chest, then pressing them down and Tyler convulsing, all eyes on the EKG, blipping irregularly.

"No! Tyler! Tyler!" Beth yelled.

Someone barked out words, and the orderlies intensified their efforts to pull them away. Jagger knew that, unlike movie depictions, deliberators didn't restart flat-lined hearts. Mostly, they corrected ventricular tachycardia, which was the heart's equivalent of a last cry for help, telling anyone listening, "I'm going . . . I'm going . . ." which it often did within seconds—unless shocked back into a normal rhythm.

Behind Jagger someone said, "*Talitha Koum.*"

THUMP!

The bouncing green line on Tyler's EKG spiked, plummeted, began making a mountain range on the screen. The physician holding the paddles nodded and handed them to a nurse. Jagger let himself be pulled away.

He twisted out of the bouncer's arms and wrapped his arm around Beth to guide her. They nearly walked into Owen, who moved to Beth's other side and gripped her arm. Jagger realized it was he who had said those words, *Talitha Koum.* The man had disappeared sometime during the chaos of Tyler's arrival. Jagger was glad to see him; it felt like having someone else on their team, a friend. He didn't want to think of where they'd be, what would have become of Tyler, had Owen not been there.

[55]

Shuffling back to the chairs, Jagger could feel Beth shaking as violently as she would have standing naked on the Arctic tundra. He and Owen lowered her into a chair, and Jagger sat beside her. Owen crossed the room and sat on the floor, his back against the wall.

"What?" Beth said. "What was that?"

"I've heard that happens all the time during surgery." He hadn't. "The heart's response to low blood pressure, trauma."

"His *heart* . . . oh, Jagger . . ." She pushed into him harder and wept into his shirt.

Could anything be more emotionally wrenching or physically draining as watching your child fight for his life? All the love and protectiveness that fills every cell of your body like a third strand of DNA from the moment you learn of his existence, feelings that can't possibly grow stronger, but do with each of his smiles and tears and sounds and thoughts—that irresistible force that nurtures, guides, teaches, and tells dangers real and perceived, *Don't even think of coming near my kid* . . . All of it crashing head-on into an immoveable object made of helplessness and the fact that the human body is fragile in a world of hard, sharp things moving too fast, of diseases, stupidity, and malice. That point of impact, where neither side gives or flexes or compromises, creates an energy that can tear you apart.

Jagger felt that tension pulling at his sanity, and he held on to his wife as he would a tree in a hurricane. Like a tree, she was rooted in soil that was more solid than the tilled-up dirt of *his* life. Maybe that was cheating, depending on her strength, which flowed from a source he had blocked off and rejected; but she was his wife, and it was on *her* he trusted to help him survive this storm. In turn, he hoped to be someone she could hold on to. But he wondered how much help he could be when all he wanted to do was rage . . . at God, at the world, at the people who did this to his son.

He sat beside Beth, comforting her as best he could, then got up and walked to where Owen sat. The man's head was lowered, his hands clenched together in his lap.

"*Talitha Koum?*" Jagger said, crouching in front of him."

Owen raised his head and smiled. "Jesus said it when he raised Jairus's daughter from the dead. It means, 'Little girl, I say to you, get up!' It applies to little boys as well."

"A prayer?"

"A plea."

"You took off," Jagger said.

"There's a chapel on the third floor." He pushed himself up. "I hear it calling to me now. Do you hear it?"

Jagger rose, shook his head.

Owen gripped his arm. "Of course. You do your work here. I'll do mine there."

Jagger watched him disappear down a hall, then he started pacing. He thought about calling someone, even got the mobile phone out of Beth's bag. He stared at it, noticing for the first time in months the bars that indicated service. He opened the directory and found the number for Beth's parents, a little picture of them smashing their faces together to fit in the frame, laughing about it. But why put them through the agony of uncertainty? There would be time to call when they knew more. He dropped it back into the purse.

He found himself in the bathroom, staring at his own bloodshot eyes in the mirror, and Tyler's blood caked on his cheek. He splashed water over his face and scrubbed it off, a token to his belief, his *having* to believe, that Tyler would be fine. He watched the pink water swirling around the drain, going down, and regretted letting even that much of his son get away from him.

As he returned to the chairs, a surgeon pushed through the OR doors. Jagger tried to read his eyes, but didn't get anything until the man pulled his mask down, showing a tight smile. Beth ran up and grabbed Jagger's arm, afraid, Jagger thought, of collapsing regardless of the news. What the doctor said was a blur of contradictions: Tyler was in critical condition, but stable. They'd removed the bullet and repaired damage to his lung, several blood vessels, and muscles.

"He is not—what do you say?—away from the forest yet, but he is a very lucky little boy. The bullet missed his major arteries and his heart. Do you know what sort of gun was used?"

Jagger shook his head. "A pistol."

"It is interesting," the doctor said. "It appears to be a .25 caliber and extremely low velocity, not what we normally see."

Jagger understood: low-velocity bullets were special-order ammo, meant to be subsonic, so there would be no crack of a bullet breaking the speed of sound; combined with a small caliber, it was ideal for a sound-suppressed firearm—an assassin's weapon. The woman's gun hadn't been equipped with a suppressor, but he suspected that an inspection of its muzzle would reveal threads to accommodate one.

"Bullets cause tissue damage in three ways," the doctor was saying. Jagger almost interrupted, wanting only a bottom-line prognosis, but Beth nodded, her brows furrowed in concentration. Jagger appreciated her desire for knowledge, even when it was stomach-turning and hit close to home. The journalist in her. He pulled her closer as the doctor continued.

"Laceration and crushing from the bullet itself. Fragmentation, either from the bullet or from splintered bone. That's like getting shot again. Then there are shock waves and cavitation, caused by the energy radiating out from the path of the projectile. This can be more devastating than the bullet, which is why firearm injuries tend to be worse than those produced by blades. Eighty percent of nerve damage results not from the bullet but from shock waves. They've been known to even fracture bones several centimeters from a passing bullet."

Beth pulled in a breath and covered her mouth. The doctor patted the air reassuringly. He said, "That is not an issue with your son. In all cases, the greater the velocity of the bullet, the worse the damage.

Because the child was shot with a small caliber at low velocity, he sustained minimal shock wave damage, no bone breakage, and the bullet did not fragment, as far as we can tell at this point. As I said, a very lucky boy."

"Lucky?" Beth said. "He almost . . . almost died. He's still in danger, isn't he?"

"He is," the doctor said, "but considering his size, if he'd been shot with an ordinary round, the type we usually see . . ." He shook his head. "We need to monitor him for any internal bleeding we may have missed, and of course infection. He lost a lot of blood and his body went into shock. He seems to be bouncing back, but we will know more in twelve or so hours."

"Seems?" Jagger said. "He *seems* to be bouncing back?"

The doctor smiled. "The human body is a complex organism. It constantly surprises us, both for bad and for good. We'll move him to a private room in the ICU. He will sleep for some time, but please, be there with him. I believe he will"—he searched for a word—"*feel* your presence and will respond favorably."

"You couldn't drag me away," Beth said. She hugged Jagger, pressing her face into his chest and digging her fingers into his back.

Her tears soaked through his shirt, and he wished they were anyplace but here, doing anything but this. He wanted it so badly, the weight of it weakened his knees and pulled at him as though gravity had suddenly doubled its power. He braced himself, fighting the urge to collapse. If he ever had to be strong, it was now.

[56]

Five and half hours after Jagger and Owen had carried Tyler into the ER, the boy was lying in a hospital bed, canted to one side by foam wedges to keep pressure off his back. Jagger eyed the machines arrayed around his son. They beeped and hissed and occasionally squiggled out a few inches of paper, a permanent record of his vital signs at that particular moment. One IV dripped antibiotics into a tube that snaked to a needle in his arm. Another of saline kept him hydrated. A vinyl bag hanging on the bed by Jagger's knee caught urine from Tyler's bladder, and somehow to Jagger that captured the enormity of what had been done: his son couldn't even pee.

He held Tyler's hand and tried to see past the oxygen mask to his face. Pale, except for his eyelids, which were the color of storm clouds. He could tell they had cleaned him up, but had either been sloppy about it or too careful: the rim of his ear was caked with maroon blood.

Beth sat in a chair on the opposite side of the bed, stretching to hold Tyler's other hand. Her head was bowed in prayer, but as he watched she raised it and frowned at him. "God didn't do this," she said.

He closed his eyes and bit his tongue. She didn't want to hear his opinion on that.

"Jagger?"

He hated the pain in her eyes, the redness that he couldn't imagine ever going away.

She said, "Let this draw you closer, not push you away."

He wanted to yell at her to shut up about that, to open her eyes to the way God really was, merciless and spiteful. Instead, he ran his hand over his face and pushed his fingers through his hair. "I need some air," he said, turning toward the door. "And coffee. You want some coffee?"

She shook her head, and he stepped into the corridor. It was bright with fluorescents, reflecting off floors so polished they could have been liquid. Still, the place appeared as vacant as an office building on Sunday morning. To his right, at the far end of the corridor, a nurse crossed from her station and disappeared into a room. He turned the other direction and started walking. A wall of glass at the end, overlooking rectangles of undeveloped parcels and the low, white buildings of Sharm el-Sheikh to Naama Bay and the Red Sea. He spotted a door with a plaque showing a stick figure on stairs, pushed through, and descended.

At the first landing, he stopped. His lungs were keeping time with his racing heart, pumping air like a bellows in the hands of a spastic kid. Dizziness made his vision swim. He staggered and grabbed the railing, then stumbled into a corner and leaned his forehead against a pipe running from floor to ceiling. It was cold, and that's all he thought about: the pipe and the way it cooled his skin . . . not about Tyler or the woman who shot him or God or anything but the pipe and its temperature.

Tyler.

The woman.

God.

Jagger groaned, and it turned into a scream. RoboHand gripped the pipe, and he leaned back. His real hand was squeezed into a tight fist, hurting from being that way for a while. He threw it into the wall, making an indent. He punched again and again until he broke through, and continued striking the edges, widening the hole, leaving bloody streaks and spots around it.

A hand seized his shoulder and spun him around. He pulled his fist back to strike the intruder. It was Owen, right in his face, glaring. He grabbed Jagger's head, fingers curved around behind, palm over his ear, firm.

"I *know*," he said, the words *what you're going through* unnecessary, communicated through his gaze, and his expression said that he really did.

Jagger felt a measure of the chaotic jumble inside him flow out, as though taken by Owen, a burden shared. His fist opened, and his hand fell to Owen's shoulder. He wanted to say something, to explain himself, but the sense that Owen already knew everything was so great that all he could do was nod.

Jagger had never believed that sympathy or even empathy helped anyone; intense emotion, agony, was unique to each person: a million starving people in the world didn't help ease the stomach cramps of the man who hadn't eaten in three days. But this was different. It was shared anger, grief, and pain, coupled with a *solution*; it was the one-legged man throwing his arm over the shoulder of another one-legged man because together they could both walk.

Owen pushed a box into his arms. "I guessed size eleven."

Jagger lifted the lid to see new cross trainers and a package of socks. He nodded. "Thanks."

"There's a *kahwa* up the street." Owen smiled at Jagger's puzzlement. "A café. We have to talk."

Jagger returned to Tyler's room first, and Beth assured him there was nothing for him to do there at the moment, and she'd be fine if he grabbed coffee with Owen.

"Go get out of your head for a while," she said. "It'll do you good."

[57]

The two men walked four blocks into a neighborhood with dirt streets and none of the sparkle or forced Egyptian décor that made Sharm el-Sheikh attractive to tourists. They approached the *kahwa*—a converted house—at just past six in the morning, a smoldering orange glow singeing the eastern frays of a violet sky. When Owen pulled the door open for Jagger, the aroma of coffee, tobacco, and fried food wafted over them. Smoke hazed the cavelike interior, whose dim light came from dozens of candles lined up like soldiers on a narrow shelf running the length of each wall, a yellow bulb hanging over the service area behind a counter, and murky front windows.

Behind the counter, an old man tended to something sizzling in what appeared to be a household FryDaddy. A cigarette with three inches of ash dangled from his lips. Two other old guys sat in the back, coffee mugs and a tall *sheesha* water pipe on the table between them. Tubes ran from the *sheesha* to the corner of each of their mouths, and they sat there puffing as they watched Jagger and Owen.

Owen unslung the pack at his waist and dropped it on a heavy wooden table. The table was weathered and beaten; it looked like it might have been something else once, part of a ship or a door. Jagger sat, and Owen greeted the old man behind the counter in Arabic, then turned to Jagger. "Coffee? Sugar, cream?"

"Black."

Owen held up two fingers to the old man. "*Kahwascitto.*" He pulled back a chair and dropped into it with a loud sigh. He studied Jagger's face for a good ten seconds, then said, "I spoke to the doctor. He said the surgery went well."

Jagger shrugged. "Tyler's not in the clear yet."

"I'm sorry. I'm sorry it happened at all."

The old man shuffled over and placed mismatched mugs on the table. He grumbled something to Owen, who asked Jagger, "Breakfast? He's got *t'aamiyya*, kind of like falafel: ground fava beans, coriander leaves, sesame seed paste . . ."

Jagger was shaking his head. "I can't eat."

Owen said something, and the old man went back to his post. They sat in silence for a minute, Owen sipping his coffee, Jagger staring at his bloody knuckles. He tasted the brew, winced at the bitterness, and set down the mug. "Who was the guy they were after," he said, "the one you were coming to see?"

Thinking, Owen used a palm to flatten his beard, first one cheek and jawline, then the other side. He said, "He called himself Creed. He was part of a group, but he was trying to get away."

"So they killed him? Is it a cult, a Charles Manson thing?"

Owen shook his head. "Nothing like that. There's no charismatic leader brainwashing the others. They're all in it together, voluntarily. They think of themselves as a tribe, but really they're a family. Not blood related, but they've been together a long time, and they genuinely care for one another."

"Yeah," Jagger said. "We killed my brother when he wanted to leave home too."

Owen squinted at Jagger, a slight smile turning up one corner of his mouth. "The Tribe adheres to a fierce set of principles, the most important being *Protect the Tribe*. If Creed had wanted only to leave, they would have let him. He took something they needed, something that would not only stop them from what they believe they must do but could also destroy the Tribe."

Where's the boy? the woman had said. *He has something of ours.*

"What?" Jagger said, leaning forward. "What did Creed have they wanted so badly?"

"A computer microchip."

"With information? Data that would expose them, get them all busted?"

"I don't think so." Owen took a swig of coffee. "Creed said it would prevent them from completing their mission, and just having it would open doors, get people to listen and act to stop them."

"Mission? What is their mission?"

"Creed used a code word, *Agag*. It comes from the Bible, I Samuel. Agag was the king of the Amalekites. God ordered the Israelites to destroy the city of Amalek, every man, woman, and child. The code word meant something big was going down."

"Something big, like blowing-up-a-train big . . . or 9/11 big?"

The muscles of Owen's face tightened. "Like Hiroshima big."

Numbed to the cares of the world by the crisis with Tyler, Jagger was surprised to feel a pang of panic jitter through his stomach and into his heart. The thought of thousands—tens of thousands—of innocents like Tyler suffering, dying in fear and pain, was enough to cut through the fog of his own misery. "You think that chip controls a *nuclear bomb?*"

"Nuclear, or something just as destructive."

"Wait a minute." Jagger looked around the room, his eyes stopping on the old men in back, so dark in the shadows their eyes stood out like an animal's catching the moonlight. He said, "I figured these guys were pros, the way they attacked the monastery in a coordinated effort, the way they fought. Those invisibility suits, they aren't off the rack, not even issued to top-shelf black ops boys. They're DARPA or some foreign equivalent or maybe an off-the-charts elite private organization. Now you're telling me they've got nukes . . . or 'something just as destructive.' You're talking heavy backing, government backing."

"Just the Tribe," Owen said.

"How many?"

"I don't know for sure. Ten, fifteen maybe. Used to be more." He shifted in his chair, leaned back, and dropped a booted heel on the corner of the table, settling into the conversation. "But they're well connected. The favors I called in to get the military chopper? Nothing to them. For years, they've helped important people become important.

Everybody owes them. They're privy to the most secret information—classified *umbra* in the U.S., *Streng Geheim* in Germany, *Sirriy lil-Gāyah* here in Egypt." He waved a hand: *whatever*. "And once they know about something, all they have to do is ask. I'm sure that's how they got hold of that invisibility technology."

"What do they give in return?"

"Knowledge, for one thing. They're intelligent, freakishly so. Mostly about human nature, and no knowledge is more powerful than that. As a species, we're fickle, counterintuitive, vacillating between altruism and selfishness. We're influenced by loved ones, friends, enemies, colleagues, rivals, culture, movies, literature, who we hope to be, wish we were, our health and personalities and personal histories— more factors shape our decisions than shape our flesh. Anyone who can read those calculations with even a modicum of accuracy wields more power than a nuclear arsenal."

"Then why are they in the trenches, *shooting* people, planning another Hiroshima?"

"Because they're also people of action. They balance brain and brawn. Wars are won through strategy and tactics driving a physical force. That desire for action suits the other service they occasionally provide to powerful people, the elimination of opposition, embarrassments, trouble. They're highly efficient black operatives, killers. Best in the world, best in history."

"They didn't seem that way last night." A ribbon of smoke from the old men's *sheesha* drifted between Jagger and Owen, rippling and coiling like a snake.

"You mean the way they blasted in there?" He made a face. "Stealth is for James Bond movies. They do that too, but not every operation fits that approach. They used what worked for Genghis Khan, called the *Chen*—shock and thunder. The Germans called it *blitzkrieg*, lightning war. Fast, loud, powerful. It takes their enemies off guard, forces them to act impulsively instead of prudently. As far as I can tell, it worked."

Jagger remembered the woman taking something from Tyler's

hand. "If their objectives were to kill Creed and get back what he stole, then I guess it did."

Owen lowered his boot and leaned forward. "You know they got the microchip?"

"The woman said Tyler took something of theirs. After she . . ." He couldn't bring himself to even say it, the images it conjured. "Later, she took something from his hand."

Owen frowned, stood up, and carried his mug to the counter.

They shot my son, Jagger forced himself to think, handing the blame now to this mysterious group Owen described rather than merely to the woman. He recalled the crack of the gun that changed everything, starting with the way Tyler's face instantly went from joy to stunned pain.

Owen came back, blowing steam off the surface of his coffee. He sat and took a sip.

"I saw a tattoo," Jagger said, "right here." He touched the inside of his prosthetic forearm.

Owen nodded. "They all have it. Liquid gold ink, impossible to remove. As far as they're concerned, you really can't leave the Tribe, even if you're not physically with it anymore."

"They got you forever," Jagger said. "Sounds like a cult to me." He couldn't get the idea out of his head.

"Think of it as a birthmark."

"So, what . . . these people, the Tribe, they're just a bunch of brainy killers for hire?"

"It's not about money. They have plenty of wealth, accumulated over the years. They'd rather rack up favors; reciprocity from the right people is invaluable. I said they *occasionally* provide black op favors for powerful people. Typically, they're doing it on their own. When they do it for others, regardless of the other person's motive, the target has to meet their criterion."

"Which is?"

Owen squinted at him and tilted his head, as though Jagger should already have known. He said, "They have to be bad guys."

[58]

"Bad guys?" Jagger said, waving his hand through the smoke hovering over the table between them. "What does *that* mean?"

"People who've committed crimes and for one reason or another have escaped justice," Owen said. "For the most part, murderers, rapists, child molesters, but also kidnappers, white collar criminals, men who've severely and repeatedly battered their wives or children and just haven't killed them yet."

"They're vigilantes?" Jagger said.

"That puts a different spin on things, doesn't it?"

Jagger shook his head. "No."

"But you understand the feeling, wanting to take the law into your own hands? Especially when the system breaks down and bad guys get away."

"What are you getting at?"

"They've killed people who've used vehicles to murder innocents. Habitual drunk drivers."

Jagger reached across the table and grabbed Owen's wrist. "You've investigated me?"

"I did a little research."

"Why?"

"I'm getting to that," Owen said. "Right now I just want to know how you feel about vigilantes."

Jagger released Owen's wrist, leaned back. "Of course I understand vengeance. Who doesn't? Yes, I wish that drunk was dead, and there's a part of me that's angry with myself for not doing something about it. Maybe if it weren't for my family, I would."

"A lot of people think that way," Owen said. "Something stops them from acting. Their family, going to jail, lack of the knowledge of how to do it or lack of courage, their belief that God will sort it out. Nothing wrong with any of that." He picked up his mug and seemed to speak into it. "Do you want to kill the woman who shot your son?"

Jagger's jaw stiffened, his teeth ground together, sounding like ropes pulling tight. He closed his eyes and said, "Yes. But I would settle for her being caught, going to trial, spending the rest of her life in jail."

"Justice."

"Yes." He opened his eyes. "I said I understood vengeance, but I don't understand what this . . . this *tribe* is doing."

"They're filling the gap between what victims or the families of victims *want* to do and what they *can* do."

"I get that," Jagger said. "But who are they targeting? Just random criminals?"

"Sinners," Owen said. He set down the mug and pushed it away. "They target sinners."

"*Sinners?* In the religious sense?"

Owen smiled. "I don't know any other sense. A criminal breaks man's laws. Sinners break divine law. The Tribe doesn't have much regard for man's laws, except where they match God's, and that helps them find targets, because criminals, not sinners, make the news. They're much more interested in right and wrong as God defines the terms, and then meting out justice to those who escape it. That's the reason they exist, as far as they're concerned."

Jagger had called them vigilantes, but that wasn't quite it. The religious aspect added something: "Vigilantes for God."

"So they think."

"On a divine mission from God."

"It's a bit more complicated than that," Owen said, "but you can put it that way."

"I suppose their dog told them to kill for God?" Jagger grabbed his mug and took a big swig. The brew was lukewarm and even more bitter than before.

"Don't think about their motivations, just what they're doing: killing bad guys."

"Then they should kill themselves, what they did to Tyler. He wasn't their target. He's innocent."

"You said Tyler took the chip?"

"That's what the woman said."

"Then he wasn't innocent, not in their eyes. He got in their way. That made him guilty."

We were going to leave you alone, Phin had said. *But you got in our way—you and the kid—and that gives us permission. Not just that, an obligation.*

"That's twisted logic," Jagger said. "It makes almost anybody fair game for them."

Owen nodded, a slow bobbing of his head. "That's why I've been after them for years. Not constantly, they're much too cunning, too covert. By the time I get to the scene of one of their killings, they're long gone."

"That's how you know so much about them, by going after them when you can, trying to stop them?"

Owen smiled. "I would like nothing more than to call fire down from heaven to destroy them."

The old man from the counter sauntered over with a carafe. He topped off Jagger's mug and refilled Owen's.

"I'm going to be wired," Owen said, watching the man depart. Without lifting it, he wrapped his hands around the mug and leaned over it, getting closer to Jagger. "I've spoken to people who've left the Tribe. Most of them, like Creed, came to realize that killing is no way to please God. Sometimes it simply dawned on them. Sometimes what drove them to that realization was the death of an innocent— someone you and I would call an innocent." He paused, seeming to study Jagger's face again. "For Creed, it was the Agag."

"Hiroshima?" Jagger said. "Yeah, I think that would do it."

"But he didn't just leave. He was going to try to stop them."

"Of course. Anyone in their right mind—What?"

Owen was staring at him intently. "Creed can't do it. Someone else has to."

"You?" Jagger said. He shook his head. "This is too big, too important. You've got to inform someone, I don't know, *authorities*."

"Do you know how difficult it would be to get any law enforcement agency, any government, to believe there's going to be a major attack somewhere in the world, sometime soon—let alone care or do something about it? Even if it were possible, it would take too long."

"And you can do better? By yourself? How? You just said they're always a step ahead of you, gone by the time you get there."

Owen scooted his chair closer to the table and put his elbows on it. He moved his hands as if shaking a ball, excited. "While Tyler was in surgery, I tapped into the crime databases of INTERPOL, the FBI, the International Crim—"

"You can do that?" Jagger interrupted.

"Calling in more favors," Owen said. "Now, pinpointing vigilante killings is no easy task. Of course, I first searched for murder victims. Turns out there were about three hundred thousand worldwide in the last six months. Then I ran the list through a bunch of filters: which murder victims had been charged with a crime during the previous year . . . and got off on a technicality or hung jury . . . whose crime or release was reported by the local media. Even then, criminals tend to consort with unsavory types, so their deaths could have been infighting or flirting with the wrong woman or anything. So I looked for non-firearm deaths. The Tribe favors blades."

The door opened, letting in a warm breeze that cleared the smoke away from Jagger and Owen and caused the candle flames to flap like little pennants. Three people in their twenties entered, a woman and two men, all of them laughing. Jagger noticed the sky had brightened to the color of the baby blue paint he'd quickly slathered on Tyler's walls between his birth and bringing him home. The newcomers commandeered a table in the center of the café, and one of the men waved the old man over.

Owen watched the group for a few seconds before turning back to Jagger. "I've isolated a few cities, radiating from which are a number of possible vigilante killings, like animal bones near a predator's lair. One place is particularly interesting." He wiggled his finger over a spot on the table and started tapping in concentric circles around it. "The killings mostly occurred in outlying towns—only one in the city itself—which is what they would do, kill away from where they live."

"What city?"

"Paris," Owen said. "Le Mans, Orleans, Cergy, Beauvais, Reims—vigilante killings in all of them within the last half year. Only two days ago Philippe Gerard, the money manager who drained his clients' accounts, was found stabbed to death in his home in Versailles. And Paris fits their personal style too. They like big cities, nightlife, culture, enough air traffic that their own frequent trips don't attract attention."

"How long would it have taken them to reach St. Cath's from there?" Jagger said.

"Private jet"—he calculated—"five hours. Add time to get to the airport, then to a helicopter in Sharm el-Sheikh, fly to the monastery—nine, nine and a half hours."

Jagger nodded. "Creed showed up just after most of the tourists had started up the mountain at closing, about twelve thirty. Someone was watching from the crags. The Tribe attacked about ten thirty."

"Ten hours, it fits."

"One thing bothers me about your little plotting of the killings." Jagger tapped the table the way Owen had done. "You said these guys are globetrotters. They kill all over the world. Why would they kill anywhere near where they live? Why risk it?"

Owen grinned. "They can't help it. It's what they do. They may be experts in human behavior, but that doesn't mean they can completely control their own. They're Einstein smart, but they don't necessarily act like it; they're way beyond that. Their intelligence is a weapon they pull out of a drawer when they need it. Otherwise, they're just people with their own proclivities and demons, their own habits, compulsions, and hang-ups. One of them's a firebug, loves torching things. A couple of the killings I plotted around Paris ended in arson fires.

Covers their tracks in terms of trace evidence they might have left, but the fires themselves point to them."

He looked around the room, came back to Jagger, and sighed. "I saw that woman who shot your boy. She was leaving the monastery when I arrived. I recognized her, Nevaeh, unless she's changed her name recently."

Nevaeh. What kind of a name is that? Jagger thought about etching it into a live bullet casing.

Owen shook his head. "She's really something. Gorgeous as all get-out, but mean as they come. She loves her job, and that's just wrong when your job is killing people. Has a thing for death: graves, tombs, caskets. You can bet wherever they're holed up in Paris, it has some connection to death. Maybe a former mortuary or a cemetery caretaker's house."

"I saw some other tattoos on her," Jagger said, "besides the fireball thing. Crosses, a skull."

Owen nodded. "Every one about death—except for the crosses, but I guess you can say that has something to do with death too. She's got the grim reaper in hooded cloak, holding a scythe; an angel done in all black ink, with huge wings, pulling a man up to heaven by his wrist; lots of skulls, skeletons, things like that."

Jagger pictured the woman. Something about her—the fluid way she moved, catlike, her exotic beauty—was consistent with his idea of a painted lady: mysterious, rebellious, confident.

"You found all that about her on Google?" he said.

"I tracked the Tribe to L.A. once and spotted her going into a nightclub. She had on this skimpy top thing we used to call underwear, I'm sure just to show off her tattoos. The club was one of those Goth numbers, so she fit right in. The guy at the door wouldn't let me in, so I went around back to the kitchen and slipped a busboy a hundred bucks. But I couldn't find her. Found out later a drug dealer who specialized in peddling to middle school kids got knifed in the bathroom that night."

Jagger felt a faint twinge of admiration for the woman and hated her all the more for it. Even if she hadn't shot his son, everything about her should have repulsed him. She was a killer who had a strange fascination with death and for all he knew slept in a coffin. Still, he couldn't help but appreciate her taste in targets. He shook his head, disgusted with himself for acknowledging even the most trivial of qualities in this woman. His body was tired and his mind was numb, that's all. She had shot Tyler, and if he learned that she had a supernatural ability to instantly rid the world of every murderer, rapist, and pedophile, he'd still want to kill her.

The old men in the back seemed to be staring past the three twenty-somethings at him, as though they knew his thoughts and were waiting for a confession. He turned a shoulder to them and clunked his prosthetic arm on the table.

". . . tempted to leave them alone," Owen was saying, "if the only people they killed were drug dealers and other scum who prey on the innocent. But they're not. The Agag means blood, a lot of it, and it'll flow from good men, women, and children. They have to be stopped." He lifted his mug, set it down again. "And you're right," he said. "I can't do it alone." He paused until Jagger's eyes found his.

"Jagger," he said, "I need you to help me stop them."

[59]

It felt to him as though the only light coming into the café from the front windows was a single ray of sun falling directly in his eyes. He leaned forward, out of it. "What are you saying, help you stop them?"

"I need you to come with me, to watch my back, help find a way to stop them."

"But what does that mean, *stop* them? *Kill* them?"

"Whatever it takes," Owen said. "Kill them, take back the chip, find enough evidence to make someone pay attention . . . I don't know, exactly. But I don't want to wake up tomorrow or a week from now to find out somebody detonated a bomb in New York or London or anywhere, and know I didn't try everything to stop it."

"These guys are good," Jagger said. "They're coordinated and well connected, motivated and wealthy. They're in the middle or maybe the end of a game you haven't even started, and you don't know the rules. They're probably out of their minds. I mean, these are the kind of nuts people write books about and little kids cry over because they might be hiding under their beds. And by the way, they also happen to possess a nuke."

"Or something equally destructive."

"Right . . . well . . ."

The twentysomethings were staring at them now as well, and Jagger realized he was standing, leaning across the table to get into Owen's face. He straightened, pushing back his chair with his calves.

"I wish you luck with that," he said. "I really do." He turned and started for the door.

"Jagger . . . ," Owen said, "please."

Jagger stopped. After a pause, he returned to the table. He

stood looking down at Owen and said, "Why me? Why are you even asking me? Why are you trying to drag me into your secret war?" He pointed at the men and woman three tables away. "Ask them. Wouldn't hurt, right?"

"You're not just anyone," Owen said calmly. "You have the mind of an investigator, the skills of a soldier. And more than anything . . ."

"What?"

"You're a cauldron of molten hate. You're furious and frustrated. You have a young son fighting for his life, suffering for no fault of his own, and you want to make the people who hurt him pay. Normally I'd tell you revenge will eat your heart and make a hat out of your soul, but right now it's a flaming sword, white hot and powerful. And I'd be a fool not to use it to stop the Tribe. Why not avenge your son and in the process save thousands of lives?"

"Because I'm not leaving Tyler. Or Beth. What kind of man would I be if I left them like this?" His voice became quiet. "How would I live if . . . if Tyler slipped away and I wasn't here?"

"How will you live knowing you could have saved a city and didn't?"

"It's a suicide mission."

"Maybe," Owen said. "Maybe not."

Jagger shook his head. He cut through the smoke and stares and pushed out the door. Four blocks away, the hospital rose like a glass pyramid over the roofs of rundown houses. Kids kicked a soccer ball down the street, chasing it and kicking it again. A multicolored Fiat with the word *Taxi* spray-painted on its side chugged through an intersection, leaving a dense cloud of gray exhaust. He headed into it, toward the hospital.

The world goes on. But it all seemed like a dream. He tried to remember his son's last words to him, before he was shot, and his heart ached further when they came to him: *Dad, I'm scared.* Crouched down in the corner by the burning bush, big eyes staring up at him, wanting to be told everything was all right. So that's what Jagger had told him. And then he'd said, *Be brave, son.* He wanted to hear Tyler's voice again, that little-boy voice that could knock a train off its tracks.

He heard a rattle like maracas, and his heart leapt. Turning, he saw two little girls sitting on a front stoop, shaking out the contents of a piggy bank. So much like the sound of Tyler's utility case. How he loved that junk, and Jagger felt a weird sort of affection for the unknown people who'd dropped their coins or key fobs so his son could find them, making him smile.

Everything went away—the little girls, the houses, the street— as his mind grasped an image, a recent memory: Tyler dropping something in the case, the sound of its hard heaviness landing on candy and rocks. *Charon's obol*, the coin-looking thing he'd found in the cave where the teenager had been hiding. Ollie had said it would have been placed in a corpse's mouth so its soul could pay the ferryman for a ride across the River Styx. Could it be a coincidence that he'd found it where one of the Tribe had been, on the day another of them, a woman with a penchant for death, attacked the monastery?

You can bet wherever they're holed up in Paris, Owen had said, *it has some connection to death.*

Was the obol a clue to where they were, something the boy had picked up near his home?

A car horn honked, and Jagger jumped. He had stopped in the intersection. Six feet away, the grille of an ugly Ford sedan rattled in time with a revving engine. The horn blared again, and a hand waved at him out of the driver's window.

He debated going to the hospital and completely forgetting Owen. Then he headed back toward the café.

X I I I

He found Owen where he'd left him, at the table, his head bowed in prayer. He pulled a chair out and sat. "Owen?"

The man didn't move. The twentysomethings were laughing again, glancing at him. The old men and their *eyes*. Another man stood at the counter now, paying and carrying a mug and a fried pita thing on a plate to a table near the door. And Owen was smiling at Jagger.

Jagger raised his hand. "I didn't change my mind: I'm not going with you, so stop smiling. I have something that might help. Do you have a mobile phone?"

Owen fished inside his pack. "It's a satellite phone," he said, handing it to Jagger.

"Can it receive images?"

"Songs too, if you have any Leonard Cohen."

It was a little larger than Beth's iPhone, with a touch screen now showing a picture of Owen crouched among a group of children, straw huts in the background. "What do I do?"

"Tap it."

Jagger did, and a keypad appeared.

"Just dial, no special codes. The satellite assumes you're calling within the same region unless you enter a country code."

He dialed Beth's number.

[60]

Beth sat on the edge of a chair, her head resting on Tyler's bed, her hand gripping his. Some time ago, without noticing the shift, her praying had turned into a rambling monologue to her son. ". . . You were the cutest baby," she whispered. "I loved feeling your skin on mine. We'd lie in bed, with the sun warming us through the window, and I'd tell you all the things we'd do together, you, me, and Daddy. Camping . . . bowling . . . Disney World." She laughed a little. "Daddy said he was going to teach you how to shoot and throw a punch. I wanted to show you how to bake cookies and recognize the difference between Shakespeare and Francis Bacon. And you learned so fast. You could read along with *Green Eggs and Ham* when you were three. I was amazed! Your daddy just said, 'Of course he can, he's our son.' But I could tell he was amazed too . . . and proud, you always made us so—"

A machine chimed, and her head shot up, ready to scream for the nurses. The EKG beeped along normally. Nothing flashed on the other machines, just amber and green lights. The chime continued, and she realized it was melodic, a song. Not a machine at all: her phone. She stood and looked around, finally spotting her purse on a table near the bathroom door. She hurried to it, pulled out the phone, and saw a number she didn't recognize on the screen.

"Hello?"

"Beth, it's me. How's Tyler?"

She looked at her boy on the bed, a blanket pulled up over his shoulder, tubes and wires going into him, coming out. "No change," she said. "Where are you? Is anything wrong?" *God, let there be nothing wrong. I can't take any more.*

"I need you to get something for me," Jagger said. His voice

224

cracked on *something*, but she couldn't tell if it was his voice—was he crying? frightened?—or a transmission problem. "Do you still have Tyler's stuff?"

She went to a tall, narrow cabinet and opened the door. Drawers filled the bottom half; the top was open for hanging clothes. On top of the drawers was a large, clear bag containing the clothes the nurses had cut off Tyler. "It's here, in the bag they gave us. Jagger, what—?"

"Look in his utility case. There should be a coin, an old medallion. I gave it to him yesterday."

"Just a sec." She moved the bag to the table and opened the Ziploc. A raw odor like hamburger reached her; she held her breath and tried not to think about it. The first item she pulled out was his shirt, cut and torn and stiff with dried blood, so much of it. Her heart stopped, then pounded hard against her breastbone, an angry fist beating on a door. She recalled yesterday morning, when he came out of his room wearing it, the buttons misaligned with the holes. She'd rebuttoned it for him, saying he was just like his father and did he want chocolate chips in his pancakes.

She blinked tears out of her eyes and sniffed loudly. She heard Jagger say, "Beth?" but she was already setting down the phone.

She folded the shirt as nicely as its raggedy strips allowed and laid it flat beside the phone. His jeans too, stained and cut from waist to hem. Even his underwear was so soaked with blood only a few SpongeBobs remained visible, that goofy grin on his face. Only the utility case left, twin tails of canvas belt coming out from behind it, cut short on either side. She removed it and popped it open. Her fingers felt the things inside. Candy, empty wrappers, knickknacks—one feeling so peculiar she almost pulled it out. But a heavier object—feeling about right—nudged into her palm and she withdrew the coin, an ancient-looking disk two inches across.

"I have it," she said into the phone. She examined the skull stamped into one side, a banner in its mouth—*Tyler must love this thing*—and flipped it over to see a skeleton floating above a squiggly line, which possibly represented water. Three eggs formed a semicircle over the bones. "What exactly is this?"

"It's called an obol. It might help Owen find the people who hurt Tyler. Could you take pictures of it, front and back, and send it to this number?"

She flipped on a wall-mounted lamp and placed the coin on the empty bag that had contained Tyler's personal items. She switched to the camera app and hovered the phone over the coin until it appeared focused on the screen. She snapped the photo, turned the coin over, and did it again. She went to the photo gallery, selected the images, and hit Send. The number of Jagger's phone automatically filled the address box, and she pushed the button to send them to him.

"Done," she said. "What's going on?" She reached back into the case and found the item that had puzzled her earlier. It was a black octagon about the size of a thumbnail, with eight tiny golden pins poking from one side. She was pretty sure it was a computer chip.

Where in the world did he get this?

". . . they call themselves the Tribe," Jagger was saying.

"Who? I'm sorry."

"The group that attacked the monastery, the woman who hurt Tyler."

Beth pinched the chip between her thumb and forefinger, feeling pins poking at her flesh.

"I already told him I couldn't do it, but Owen thought—"

A hand came around Beth's head and clamped over her mouth, yanking her back into a body standing behind her. At the same time, the person grabbed her phone hand and squeezed, locking the phone in her fist. The person—a woman, Beth could tell now—leaned her head over Beth's shoulder to listen to Jagger talk.

"—we can stop them, this Agag thing."

The woman pulled Beth's hand farther over her shoulder and spoke into the phone. "Not if you want to see your woman again."

Beth twisted her hand out of the woman's and rammed her elbow back into her ribs.

The phone was dashed out of her hand, and Jagger's voice squeaked out of the tiny speaker: "Who is this? Beth!" Then it shattered on the tiles.

Beth spun, her forearm positioned to make contact with her attacker's nose, as Jagger had taught her. But the woman was already ducking and driving a fist into Beth's ribs. As Beth's arm sailed over her opponent's head, her enemy—moving as precisely as a fine watch's mechanisms—reversed away, rose and arched backward, hitched up a bent leg, and pistoned it into Beth's chest.

Beth crashed against Tyler's bed. The bed's locked metal wheels chirped against the tiles. The beeping of a machine jumped from adagio to adagio and back: a mother's concern flashed through her brain, wondering if the machine had been jarred or if it reflected a spike in her son's heartbeat at having been jostled. She sat hard on the floor, the bed frame behind her head. Her attacker stepped forward, her leather-covered fist telescoping toward Beth's face. Head caught between a metal frame and metal-like knuckles, she heard a crack like a hammer striking a nail, felt the brief onset of an instant, excruciating headache, then . . . nothing.

[61]

"Hello? Beth!" Jagger stood abruptly, knocking his chair over. "Hello?" He looked at the phone as though it would tell him something about what just happened. The call timer continued ticking off the seconds, indicating a connection. He returned it to his face. "Beth!"

"The Tribe's at the hospital," he told Owen and bolted for the door. Behind him, Owen called, "What? How do you—?"

Jagger pushed out the door, careened off a fat man who barked out Arabic words, and ran into the dirt street. A dog barked and started after him, yipping at his heels. He hit asphalt, and the yipping behind him trailed off. He came out of the neighborhood and cut diagonally across a field toward the hospital.

What does she want? Why did she come back? To finish the job?

That woman in the same room with Beth, with Tyler, was more than he could process.

I'll kill her, kill her, kill her . . . She won't know what hit her. Don't stop to talk, don't listen, just hit her, run into her at full speed . . . Get RoboHand on her neck and squeeze . . .

An image flashed in his mind—unexpected, unwanted—as if projected on a movie screen, put there by an evil projectionist bent on terror and intimidation: Tyler sprawled on the bed, blank eyes open, mouth agape in a frozen scream; Beth on the floor in an expanding pool of blood.

No! No! No!

He concentrated on running, pumping his legs as fast as possible, touching down and throwing each foot forward again. The hospital drew closer—its first floor like concrete ramparts; the next four floors, black glass slanting inward, the bottom of a pyramid; then atop that a smaller but complete pyramid; big parking structure behind it. On the roof beside the smaller pyramid, rotors moved slowly over a helicopter—an air ambulance—and Jagger remembered the terror of the night before, their rush to the hospital in just such a copter.

Owen's phone was still in his hand. He lifted it and used his thumb to hit the redial button. The call went to voice mail.

"Beth!" Jagger said. "I'm almost there. Call me back." Hoping she'd get the message, was *able* to, but not expecting she would. He disconnected and slipped the phone into his back pocket.

He reached the driveway leading to a portico in front of the emergency room, breath coming heavier now, feeling the muscles in his calves and thighs, a stitch in his side. He braked in front of the automatic glass doors and slipped through the tight opening as they parted, clanging RoboHand against the frame. He paused two seconds to get his bearings and decided against cutting through the emergency area, where guards would try to stop him. Instead, he turned and shot down a corridor, windows on his left and an unbroken wall of framed paintings on his right.

A sharp right at the first junction brought him to the ICU and, beyond its reception area, locked double doors. He pushed on them, slapped his palm onto a four-inch-square metal button beside them. They didn't budge.

Behind a counter a nurse stood, asking questions in Arabic, then English: "Sir, can I help you?"

"My son's here," he said, panting. "Tyler Baird." He held up his wrist, adorned with a plastic security bracelet they'd placed on him when Tyler was admitted. "My wife. They're in trouble. Please."

She waved him over, grabbed his hand to examine the bracelet, then pushed a button. The doors hissed open.

He rushed down the hall, eyeing the room numbers flashing past on the right: 102 . . . 104 . . . 106 . . . At the next room, he grabbed the doorjamb and shoved his shoulder into the door.

The blinds were drawn, turning the sunlight into a glowing thread tracing the square of the window. A fluorescent light bar cast its radiance over the equipment and bed. Tyler lay there—not sprawled or lifeless—just as Jagger had left him, inclined slightly to one side. The EKG showed his heart rate at 86; a blood-oxygen monitor read 92 percent. The blankets over his stomach rose and fell slowly.

And a little girl stood on the other side of the bed, holding his hand. She couldn't have been more than six years old. Espresso-colored locks tumbled to her shoulders and curled over her forehead, accentuating big green eyes.

"Hello?" he said. Her gaze moved off of Tyler's face to Jagger's. She smiled, model-adorable, rosy round cheeks. She released his hand and began stroking it, gently, as though it were a baby chick.

"Hi."

Jagger looked around the room. No sign of Beth. On the table beside the open bathroom door Tyler's utility case sat on the plastic bag that had held his possessions. His clothes lay in a bundle on the floor. He couldn't imagine Beth leaving them like that.

He turned back to the girl. She wore a pink summer dress, not the gown of hospital patients. Neither the hand stroking Tyler nor the one resting on the bed beside it displayed a security bracelet. He said, "Where's your mommy or daddy, honey?"

She giggled.

"Have you seen the lady who was in this room, Tyler's mommy? That's Tyler you're comforting."

She looked at Tyler. "He's sleeping. Is he all right?"

"He will be, but right now he's hurt."

She turned sad eyes to him. "I'm sorry."

"Thank you for visiting, but you have to leave now. Have you seen my wife?"

"She's gone." That smile.

"Gone? You saw her? Where'd she go?"

"Away," the little girl said. "You have to play the game."

Jagger's stomach tightened. "Game?"

"Don't try to stop us, and you get her back." Her head tilted sideways, precious . . . or precisely opposite. "Try . . . and you don't."

"What? Where is she?" He edged closer to the foot of the bed.

The girl didn't seem to notice. She said, "Nevaeh told me to tell you. Do nothing, and you win the game." She smiled. "That's silly, isn't it?"

He stepped closer. "I don't want to play the game. Tell me where my wife is."

"Those aren't the rules." She shook her head and gazed at him as though he had to be the dumbest person she'd ever met. "All you have to do is *nothing*. *Then* you get to see your wife again. Nevaeh said you'll know when the game's over and where to find Beth."

"You know what? I need to ask Nevaeh something about the game. Why don't you tell me where *she* is?" Another step, at the corner of the bed now.

"You silly. That's something." She made her eyes big and punctuated each word with a nod of her head: "All . . . you . . . have . . . to . . . do . . . is . . . noth—"

Jagger bolted for her, grabbing the bed to help him swing around to the far side. She ducked and was under the bed, out the other side before he realized it. He stooped to grab legs that were long gone. He rose, saw her darting out the door, and ran around the bed to follow. Out of the room, he saw her silhouette against the brightness of the window at the far end of the corridor. She was heading for the stairs, little feet slapping the tiles, tiny laughter wafting back at him.

"What is it?" Owen said, hurrying toward him from the ICU entrance.

"The little girl!" Jagger yelled, pointing and sprinting after her.

A nurse stepped out of a room carrying a tray.

"Stop her!" Jagger yelled.

The girl whipped around the nurse, laughing. Seconds later Jagger stormed past the stunned nurse. The girl disappeared through the stairwell door. It hadn't fully closed when Jagger hit it. Footsteps and giggles echoed down from above. He grabbed the railing and ascended, Owen a few steps behind.

"The helipad's up there," Owen said, and Jagger tried to put more energy into his legs, but they were already moving full-bore. He remembered the copter he'd seen, thinking it was an air ambulance. He cursed himself for not putting it together sooner. He could have done something differently, checked out the helicopter first or sent Owen up to do it.

Above him, a door banged open.

He reached the top landing and crashed through the door. Directly ahead of him, the little girl ran for the helicopter, her hair whipping like fire in the rotors' downdraft. The copter's side door was open, and the woman from the night before—Nevaeh—crouched on the floor, holding her arms out to the child. Other people sat in seats, their faces turned to watch the chase. On the floor behind Nevaeh, a body squirmed: Beth, hands bound behind her back, ankles taped together. She looked past Nevaeh, and Jagger saw that her mouth was also taped. Terror in her eyes. A swollen bruise on her right brow.

He was halfway across the roof when the girl leaped into Nevaeh's arms. Nevaeh twisted right, tossing the girl inside, then left to grab the door and close it. The helicopter rose, weaving back and forth as the skids lifted off the roof.

Jagger jumped. His fingers and the tip of the hook slapped a skid, and he fell to the roof. He hopped up as the copter rose and moved away. He followed, watching it.

"Beth! Beth! I'll find you! I'll get you!" Didn't matter if she couldn't hear him, he had to say it, but once the words were out, he realized nothing was good enough, nothing made anything better. *I love you!*

He stumbled forward, trying to get a glimpse of his wife, but the side windows were too high. Owen grabbed his shoulder, pulling him back. He realized he was at the roof's edge.

Nevaeh's face appeared in the window. She wasn't smiling, just looking. He fell to his knees. "*Nevaeh!*" he screamed.

The copter banked away and sped toward the Red Sea, continually rising. The thumping sound of its rotors faded to nothing.

Jagger turned away from the edge and seized hold of Owen's hand and shirt. "Where are they heading? Where would they go?"

Owen gazed at the diminishing copter. "The airport," he said. "Probably not Sharm el-Sheikh International. More likely Manguna. It's more private, the one celebrities and politicians use."

Jagger pulled himself up, couldn't spot the helicopter against the bright sky. He turned to Owen. "How fast can we get there?"

[62]

Owen gripped Jagger's arm, a compatriot. "Not fast enough, I'm afraid," he said. "They'll be at the airport in minutes, taking off in their jet in twenty. The best we can do is head to where they may be going."

Paris, Jagger thought . . . if Owen was right. "Can we track their plane somehow? Through their tail number?"

"Lack of cooperation between countries regarding air traffic makes it pretty easy to fly anonymously. And just to make sure their tracks are covered, the Tribe uses sophisticated equipment that provides false information to airport transponders. The equipment itself tracks other planes and makes sure it doesn't give conflicting numbers, like the number of a plane that just passed."

"How do you know what equipment they use?"

"Because *I* use it, and I learned about it trying to figure out why I could never find out where their plane was or where it'd been."

Jagger pulled the phone out of his back pocket. "What's the emergency number here?"

"What are you doing?" Owen said.

"Calling the police. They can stop them at the airport."

Owen snatched the phone out of his hand. "If they try, the Tribe will blow them away. Maybe there'll be a firefight. Do you want Beth in the middle of that?"

Jagger scanned the sky where he'd last seen the helicopter. Every part of him was tense, needing to do something; simultaneously, he felt defeated, a gutted corpse that didn't have enough sense to lie down.

"Nevaeh," he said. "She used a little girl to tell me she'd taken Beth, and if we try to stop this Agag thing, she'll kill my wife. She said to do nothing."

Owen said, "So what are you going to do?"

"Not nothing." Jagger looked Owen in the eyes. "Will she do what she said—kill Beth if we try to stop them?"

Owen looked out toward the sea. "She'd do it. But I think she'll wait until the last moment, thinking you'll finally realize that you can't beat her and give up."

"Can we beat her? Can we save Beth?"

Owen turned to Jagger. "I believe we can get Beth and stop the Agag. The question is, do you?"

He let out an airy sort of laugh. "I don't believe in much these days. My family, that's it, and look what's happened to them. I feel like I've been holding on to this rope, like it's the only thing keeping me from sliding down into a pit of . . . I don't know, vipers, fire, nothingness, whatever symbol you want to use for hell on earth. My lifeline is down to two strands: my son, who has a bullet hole in his back, and my wife, who's in the hands of a killer."

Owen raised his eyebrows and opened his mouth, then shut it without speaking.

"What?" Jagger said. "You were going to say something."

"You don't want to hear it."

"Tell me."

"Well." He took a breath. "There's a cable, a thick heavy metal cable, running down right beside your rope. All you have to do is grab it. Maybe that's why the rope's fraying. You've got all your weight on it, when it's the cable that's supposed to support you."

"You're right," Jagger said. "I don't want to hear it."

"Told you." Owen smiled and quietly added, "Not hearing it doesn't mean it's not there."

"So," Jagger said, "you're thinking Paris?"

"We can be there in six hours."

"I can't leave Tyler."

"There's nothing you can do for him here," Owen said. "How well do you know the monks—Gheronda, Leo, Jerome?"

Jagger nodded. "They're friends. At least I used to think so. Why?"

"Let them sit with Tyler. They'd love to, and I promise you can't find more dependable and capable men."

"I think Creed would argue that point." He started walking toward the stairwell door.

Owen fell in beside him. "There may be something to that . . . if you expect the doctors and nurses to attack Tyler with shotguns, swords, and explosives."

"Call them," Jagger said. "You must have their number. They told me they didn't even have a phone."

The words were brittle with bitterness. As far as he was concerned, it was the monks' secrets that led to all this. He believed they would take care of Tyler, but under ordinary circumstances, he'd think twice before turning his back to them.

X I I I

He was sitting on the edge of the bed stroking Tyler's hair when Owen stepped in. "Gheronda and Leo are on their way," he said. "They'll be here in a couple hours. We can take off now and—"

"No," Jagger said. "We'll wait for them." He brushed hair off Tyler's forehead. "I'm not leaving him alone."

"Of course. There's some paperwork you need to fill out at the nurses' station, giving the monks the authority to be here, make decisions about Tyler's care while you're away."

Jagger frowned.

"You can trust them, Jagger. They're smart and good men, and from what I gathered on the phone, they think the world of Tyler. They were in lauds when I reached Gheronda, all of them praying together. When they heard my request, they practically got in a fistfight over who'd come. Apparently your son has a way of endearing himself to people."

Jagger smiled. "That he does." He glanced at Tyler and turned back to Owen. "Look, I'm . . . Thank you for everything you've done. Last night, if it weren't for you . . ."

"Don't mention it. It's what I do."

"I thought you hunted the Tribe."

Owen stepped farther into the room, shut the door, and leaned back against it. "When I can, which isn't often. Most of the time I work with *Médecins Sans Frontières*. Sudan, Rwanda, Sierra Leone. Most recently, the Democratic Republic of Congo. Name a war zone, I've probably been there."

"Helping."

"What little I can do."

"You did a lot for us last night . . . everything, really." He shifted on the bed, lowering both feet to the floor. "Answer me something. How does kidnapping my wife, threatening to kill her if we go after them, fit into being vigilantes, especially ones that claim to be doing it for God?" He crossed his arms and breathed out heavily.

"You said it yourself in the café—twisted logic," Owen said. "Think about what being a vigilante means. You deal in death, and no one can know. It's a secret, has to be if you want to keep doing it, right? Anything kept in darkness too long, even something that started out with the best of intentions, is going to mutate, get twisted."

Jagger didn't know whether to nod or shake his head. Owen's explanation made sense, but in a sad, unhealthy way. He scooted back onto the bed where he could see and touch Tyler better, then twisted to address Owen again.

"I don't mean to be presumptuous, but while we're waiting, is there anything you can do? You know, so we can hit the ground running when Gheronda and Leo get here?"

Owen pushed off the door. "Absolutely." He unslung his pack, set it on the table, and walked around to the far side of the bed. He cupped Tyler's hand in his and placed his other hand on the boy's side. He leaned over, lowered his head, and quietly began to pray.

[63]

Usually when they weren't preparing for a mission, the cabin of their jet was serene and relaxing, but now it was giving Nevaeh a headache. Even the high she'd gotten from taking the woman wasn't suppressing the pounding in her head—which matched the pounding coming from one of the sleeping compartments.

"She's going to kick a hole through the wood," Toby said, swiveling his plush chair around to gaze toward the back of the plane.

"I think she's using her head," Nevaeh said, pinching the bridge of her nose. "This music isn't helping."

"Daft Punk!" Toby said. "Better than that artsy-fartsy stuff you listen to."

"Not a peep out of Phin," she said. Phin was in the other compartment, across from the woman's. "Do you have more of the sedative you gave him?"

"For you or Charlie Watts back there?"

Nevaeh nodded. "As long as one of us gets to sleep, I'll be happy." She looked at Alexa curled up in the chair across the aisle from her. She was dozing, using a threadbare, misshapen stuffed bunny rabbit as a pillow. Her thumb was in her mouth, despite her claims of having given up that habit long ago. With each bang and crash from the compartment, Alexa would flinch, probably without waking, and start sucking on her thumb.

The woman—Beth, she'd said her name was—commenced an especially loud attack on the compartment's sides and door. Toby grumbled and heaved himself out of the chair. He went to the compartment and beat on the wood with his palm. "Knock it off in there, you hear? You're not getting out that way!"

The pounding stopped, and he smiled. Before he reached his chair, it resumed. He spread his hands at Nevaeh. "Why do we have her anyway? We didn't find the chip? Are we holding her for ransom till we get it?"

"I got the chip," Nevaeh said.

"Then what?"

"Insurance."

Toby looked at her suspiciously and dropped into his chair. "I think you're messing around again, trying not to be bored."

"Not with this mission," she said.

He frowned and pulled a Kindle out of a pocket on the side of his chair. He flipped open the case, turned it on, cocked his foot up on the seat, and started reading.

"Let me guess," she said. "Ludlum."

Without looking up, he said, "Before all else, be armed."

"Machiavelli," she said. "Hmmm."

He looked up at her, his brows crunched in puzzlement. "There is one thing I don't understand."

"Yeah, I didn't totally get Machiavelli either . . . until I put him in the context of his situation," she said, loving that he would ask her. She tucked her feet under her and sat Indian-style in the chair. "Remember, both the Church and the Medici were suspicious of him, as they should have been. But because of that, *The Prince* is a *satire*. People don't get that."

"No, not this," Toby said, raising and lowering the e-reader. "You mentioned Ludlum. You know I like all those action/espionage/shoot-'em-ups. What I don't get is why no one in those stories ever has to go to the bathroom."

Nevaeh laughed, then realized he was serious. "This is what you think about?"

"I mean, they're like running, driving, chasing, hiding, shooting, fighting—and no one thinks, *Man, I really have to go to the bathroom.*"

"Who wants to read about that?"

"For realism," Toby said, like *Duh!* "That's what they're supposed to be about, all gritty and real. Well, let me tell you! I was sitting in that Jeep last night, after you blasted the gate, waiting for you guys to come back, and I really had to go. I mean *really*. I was dying."

"So what'd you do?"

"I got out and went." He smiled. "Ben caught me. He didn't say anything, but he gave me one of those looks, you know?"

She nodded. Toby. You couldn't help but love him. "Oh, I almost forgot." She felt the outside of her slacks pockets—having changed into street clothes upon boarding with Beth—and reached into one. She tossed the obol to him.

He caught it, and his face brightened. "*Seriously?* Yes!"

"Don't say I never did anything for you."

"But how?"

She tilted her head toward the banging. "The woman had it."

"Thanks." He kissed it, rubbed it, and leaned over an arm of the seat to push it way down into his pants pocket.

The cockpit door opened, and Ben appeared. He made a sour face at the racket coming from the sleep compartments. To Toby, he said, "Give her something to put her out." Toby shifted the medical bag from a shelf to his lap and began rummaging through it. Ben scowled at Nevaeh. "You don't really think taking her will stop them, do you?"

"If he loves her it will."

He squinted at her. "Are you really so out of touch with love that you believe that?"

Nevaeh said nothing.

Ben said, "When we get home, she goes free."

"No, she doesn't," Nevaeh said. In her peripheral vision she saw Toby stop what he was doing and look from her to Ben to her.

Ben gave her the look Toby had mentioned. He said, "You're only antagonizing them more, motivating them."

"She's my responsibility," Nevaeh said. "I'll take care of everything; you don't have to worry about it."

"I am worried about it. Very much so."

Toby inserted a needle into a vial of amber liquid and pulled back on the plunger, filling the syringe. He flicked his fingernail against the plastic barrel and released a squirt of liquid, making sure it was free of air bubbles.

"I have good news and bad news," Ben said. "The bad news—or

I should say, *potentially* bad news—is the DOD has moved the date of the drone field test."

"We knew they would," Nevaeh said.

"Yes, but this time they've moved it up by ten days. It will take place on Friday of this week."

"That's in three days," Toby said.

"We can't do it," Nevaeh said. "Toby's not ready, and Phin—"

"I am too!" Toby said.

"Sebastian told me—"

Ben stopped her with a raised hand. "I'm sure Toby's ready. He has the reaction speed of a teenager and he knows video games inside and out. This is no different. As for Phin, let's see what happens."

"What's the good news?" Nevaeh said.

"Sebastian's decrypted all the microchips and added his own bit of code so they can't be intercepted. We're good to go."

"All right then," Toby said, climbing out of his seat and heading toward the continuous banging. It was a wonder the woman hadn't beaten herself unconscious.

"Ben," Nevaeh said, "you're talking about sleeping tonight, leaving tomorrow, and going right into the mission."

"We've done this sort of thing enough times, I hope we can now be efficient and fast."

That was a new one, coming from Ben: speed over prudence. That suited Nevaeh just fine. She nodded. "Guess we got the missing chip just in time."

Toby opened the sleeping compartment, quieting the pounding but unleashing screams muffled by duct tape. He pushed and shoved as Beth tried to buck her way off of the bed.

"A little help here?" Toby said.

Nevaeh untangled her legs and started back toward him.

"And, Nevaeh?" Ben said. He pointed a finger at the commotion. "She is *not* coming with us." He shut the cockpit door.

[64]

"Wow," Jagger said.

He was standing on the private-plane tarmac of Sharm el-Sheikh International Airport, gawking at Owen's jet—a white bullet with wings. A barrel-shaped engine was mounted to the fuselage between the wing and tail, its front air intake rimmed in chrome. Forward of the door, big windows defined the cockpit, which merged into the nose, stretching to a point hawklike. Gold and green stripes zipped from nose to wing before making a wavish swirl up to the windows and flying back to the tail. Watching Owen—with his wild hair and beard, stained and threadbare undershirt and baggy jeans—swing open the door conjured images of a hobo breaking into a mansion.

"This is yours?" Jagger said. He stepped forward and ran his hand over a word painted in cursive under the side cockpit windows: *Boanerges. It's beautiful.*

Owen pulled down a set of steps and said, "Don't pass judgment yet."

Jagger didn't understand until he climbed inside. The cabin looked as though Owen had invited school kids to pile their homework inside and their parents to use it as a laundry hamper—and then flown somersaulting loops with the door open. Pinned to the walls, covering the windows, were maps, diagrams, newspaper clippings, photographs, sticky notes, napkins with doodles and food smears, seemingly anything that *could* be pinned up. Books, magazines, newspapers, binders, loose pages were pushed into nooks and crannies, stacked on the floor, seats, and a desk. The center of the desk had been cleared, like trees in an Amazonian jungle, to accommodate a flat-screen monitor and keyboard. As far as Jagger could tell, the only other surfaces free of paper products were an unmade bed—which apparently doubled as the desk's chair—and an old wooden chest at its foot.

"It's the cleaning lady's day off," Owen said. "Believe it or not, it's all organized, and I know where everything is."

"What is all this?"

"My work, my mobile office. Wherever I was in the world, I'd hide the jet, but I'd still manage to get to it a few times a week. I'd search news reports for signs of their activities, compile dossiers, histories of their activities, attempts to predict their next moves."

"Did you predict what they're doing now, the Agag?"

Owen pulled in the steps and slammed the door closed. When he stood, his eyebrows disappeared under the hair hanging over his forehead. "What they're planning is a black swan event—unpredictable and devastating, world-changing, even, like the Japanese tsunami or 9/11." He shook his head. "No, I didn't see this coming." His shoulders drooped. "But I should have."

"Why?"

"It's time." He seemed to think about his next words. "At least once a year, they do something outrageous . . . well, more outrageous than their typical hits on individual criminals. Once they stopped a gang of armed robbers who'd been hitting banks and armored cars for months—killed all of the thieves during a heist. Imagine the planning that went into figuring out when and where the robbers were going strike again, something even the cops and FBI couldn't do.

"A few years ago a U.S. platoon was pinned down for a week in the Korengal valley of Afghanistan by heavily armed insurgents. Then one night the hills lit up, explosions, gunfire not directed at the platoon's outpost. In the morning, all the insurgents were dead."

"You're saying the Tribe killed them?"

Owen stepped around Jagger and kicked through loose clothes on the floor. He stopped at the desk, walked his fingers down a foot-high pile of papers, and pulled out a photograph. "This was snapped by one of the automated cameras the troops had set up." Taken with a night vision lens, it showed a woman on the far left side of the image, about to step out of the frame. She was running with a machine gun in her hands; her belt was lined with what looked like soup cans but Jagger suspected were grenade-like explosives; something like a cannon was strapped to her back. She was caught in the act of turning her head to look at the camera, as though it had made a noise before snapping the shot. Her hair was pinned in back, flowing out of a tight beanie, and the active infrared technology made her eyes appeared to be glowing dimes, but it was clearly Nevaeh.

"I don't believe it," Jagger said. "In one night, a few ragtag Batman wannabes do what a platoon of soldiers couldn't?"

"Few, yes, but not ragtag. They've trained for years for this sort of thing. They're incredibly fit and disciplined, experienced in explosives, small arms, and other weapons, map-reading, orientation, small-unit tactics, stealth . . . As you've seen, they're often equipped with experimental advanced technology. They make James Bond look like a kid with a decoder ring."

"And Rambo look like a ninety-pound weakling. With glasses and a weak heart. And a popgun."

"A spork," Owen agreed, smiling. "But what really makes them effective is also what makes them dangerous: no rules, no restraints. Part of that platoon's mission was to protect and build relations with the civilian population. In wiping out the insurgents, the Tribe also killed at least three dozen civilians. They're not concerned about civil rights or jurisprudence. They rely on newspaper accounts and police records when they can tap into the computer systems, which is fairly easy for them. If it *looks* like you're guilty, in their eyes you are. And God help you if you get in their way."

The ceiling was too low for the men to stand fully upright, and Jagger was starting to get a kink in his neck from bending it sideways. He looked behind him and sat on a pile of books. "So I guess my family got in their way." He lowered his head.

Owen brushed past him and slipped into the cockpit. He didn't sit in the pilot's chair but leaned over it to flip switches and turn dials. Lights and screens on the dash lit up.

Jagger said, "So the Agag is a natural progression from their previous assaults?"

Owen backed out of the cockpit, turned and crouched, resting his arms on his knees. He said, "Last year they orchestrated a hit on the Russian mob. In one night in Moscow they killed eight crime bosses, their lieutenants, and bodyguards. Simultaneously, bombs blew up fourteen mob-owned businesses—strip joints, nightclubs, bars, a porn shop, a brothel, a car lot."

"The Russian mob?" Jagger said. "It's almost a shame to stop them." He said it, and intellectually he believed it, but the idea of *not* stopping them—of not getting Beth back and avenging Tyler—felt like acid in his veins.

"I'm not going to lie," Owen said. "There's a part of me that admires what they do. Besides all the typical organized crime activities, the Russians were heavily into sexual slavery: forced prostitution, kidnapping, child sex tourism. The Tribe freed scores of women and children and arranged for a private aviation firm to fly them out of the country."

"I remember that," Jagger said. "It was huge. Led to indictments all over the world."

"How can you not appreciate what the Tribe did, right?" Owen said. "People yearn for justice and protection, and sometimes the criminal justice system fails us. That's why Batman is so popular and all those *Death Wish*–type movies." He frowned. "But then I think of those innocent Afghani villagers who died or the Russian family who was driving past one of the bars when it blew up . . . or Tyler. Are you familiar with Blackstone's Formulation?"

Jagger shook his head.

"I'm sure you are, just not the reference. It's based on Genesis 18:

Then Abraham approached him and said: 'Will you sweep away the righteous with the wicked? What if there are fifty righteous people in the city? Will you really sweep it away and not spare the place for the sake of the fifty righteous people in it? Far be it from you to do such a thing—to kill the righteous with the wicked, treating the righteous and the wicked alike. Far be it from you! Will not the Judge of all the earth do right?'

The Lord said, 'If I find fifty righteous people in the city of Sodom, I will spare the whole place for their sake.'

Then Abraham spoke up again: 'Now that I have been so bold as to speak to the Lord, though I am nothing but dust and ashes, what if the number of the righteous is five less than fifty? Will you destroy the whole city for lack of five people?'

'If I find forty-five there,' he said, 'I will not destroy it.'

"Abraham continues pleading for the city," Owen said, "until God finally says, 'For the sake of ten, I will not destroy it.' William Blackstone, an English jurist in the 1700s, put it this way: 'It is better that ten guilty persons escape than that one innocent suffers.'"

For a few seconds he glanced around the cabin, thinking, and Jagger realized he was a tough-looking guy: jaw square enough to be obvious, even through the shabby beard; chiseled brow; brawny neck. He was the sort whose compassionate heart would pick you up off the ground, and whose exercised muscles would stop anyone from knocking you down again.

Jagger realized that he admired the guy—his fortitude and determination. It gave him hope.

Owen cast a serious expression at Jagger. "I hunt the Tribe not for the sake of the guilty's right to a trial, but for the innocent's right to live." He stood and stretched his legs, pushed his hands into the small of his back as he bent over them. "Sometimes I wonder if the innocent people they've killed total more than the guilty ones." He moved to reenter the cockpit, but turned back. "One thing's certain: if they're successful with the Agag, I won't have to wonder anymore."

[65]

Beth was in the hospital room, but instead of leaning over Tyler, whispering words of comfort, it was Tyler who was leaning over her. She felt his fingers on her cheek, caressing. She tried opening her eyes, but a light speared through them, making her brain throb.

"Don't be scared," Tyler said.

"Oh, Ty . . . Ty . . ." She forced her eyes open again, ignoring the pain. Everything was blurry, but there was Tyler, a silhouette against the light over him. She put her fingers over his hand on her cheek, wrapped them around it. She remembered him drooped in his father's arms, blood everywhere . . . the defib pads touching his chest—*THUMP!*—and his little body spasming . . . his cool, pale skin as he lay in the bed and her thinking that the machines were like gargoyles crouched over him, waiting to gleefully announce his passing. She began crying, pushing his hand into her face, turning to kiss his palm.

He snatched his hand away. "You *kissed* me," he said.

"Tyler?" she said, reaching for him. She blinked and tears spilled away. Yes, he was right there, right there, backing away from her. "Tyler, wait . . . I was so worried."

She lifted her head, heavy as a bowling ball, and wiped her eyes. A little boy stared at her with something like amazement on his face. Dark hair, cut like Tyler's—but *not* Tyler. This boy was a couple years older.

She began crying again, louder, and dropped her bowling ball head down. She felt a hand smooth her hair. "I'm sorry," the boy said. "I didn't mean to scare you."

He was kneeling beside her now, and she realized she was on a bed. He smiled, bending cherubic features into an expression of sheer joy, much the way Tyler could do. "Where am I?" she said.

"You're safe," he said. "With us."

She pushed a palm into her forehead, wanting to massage her aching brain. She groaned and remembered: grabbed at the hospital, taken by helicopter—Jagger running to save her!—to the airport and a jet plane, locked in the sleeping compartment, the teen opening it and sticking a needle into her arm. Keeping her hand on her head, she looked at the inside of her elbow. A square of gauze was taped there, a spot of blood showing through.

She touched her lips. They were sore, as was the skin around them. Her mouth had been taped, off now. She moved a leg, grateful that it was free. The other leg: a chain rattled, and her movement stopped short. She lowered it and kicked up, able to raise it only a few inches.

"For your own good," the boy said. "You don't want to get lost here or hurt yourself or . . ." His voice trailed off.

"Or what?" Beth said, hoping that the more she knew about her captors' thinking, the better chance she had of outwitting them. The boy looked sad. "It's okay, honey. Or what?"

"Or doing something that would force us to hurt you."

"Us?"

"Not *me*," he said, but his eyes didn't look so cherubic anymore. "One of the others, but only to protect us . . . if you do something. You know, like attack us or steal our things."

"Or escape?"

"Well, you can't escape. That would hurt us."

"How?"

"You could tell where we live. Then we couldn't live here anymore."

"Where's here?"

He blinked, his face expressionless. He'd been told not to say where they were. Maybe that was a good thing, maybe it meant they were planning on letting her go. If they planned on killing her, what would her knowing where she died matter? Still, she wanted to know:

what if she got to a phone or knowing her location helped her figure out how to escape?

He said, "Your lips are chapped. Want some water? I'll get you some water."

He hopped up and went to a stainless-steel sink in the corner of the room, a matching toilet beside it. This was a jail cell—not with bars, and larger than the cells she'd seen, but a jail cell nonetheless. It appeared to be carved from solid rock, no joints or seams anywhere, a few random cracks running down the walls like lightning. Stains spotted the floor, and she tried not to think about what had caused them. Marks on the walls, writing. She turned her head to look at the wall nearest her, touching the bed. Stick figures, hash marks, and words in foreign languages were scratched into it. Some were shallow, seeming to have been worn away, others deeper, more distinct, maybe newer, maybe simply carved with more determination. Whatever their stories, they gave her the impression that many people had been held here over a long period of time.

Water flowed into the sink, and she realized her mouth was dry and tasted like chalk. The boy came back with a plastic mug. He knelt again and held it to her. She rose onto one elbow and took it in her other hand. It had a metallic taste, but she thought it was the best water she'd ever drunk and downed it without pausing.

"Man, you must have been thirsty." He took the mug and rushed back to the sink.

"Sounds as though you like living here, huh?"

His back to her, he shrugged. His green T-shirt rose just enough to reveal a toy pistol in the back pocket of his jeans. So much like Tyler, so much a little boy. She felt a pang of pity for him. Was his room like this cell, windowless and dank? What kind of life must he have, living with people—his parents?—who would blow their way into a monastery, shoot a child, kidnap his mother?

"What do you like about it?" she said, fishing.

He turned off the water and headed back, mug in hand. "Finding things, exploring."

"Exploring what?"

He handed her the mug and smiled.

She said, "I used to explore around my house when I was a kid. The basement was the spookiest, but the attic was a close second. What's the spookiest place you've found?"

"You're pretty smart," he said. "Telling me what you explored so I'd tell you what I explored. Finding out about where you are, thinking about escaping."

She stopping drinking midgulp and blinked at him.

"That's okay," he said. "I'd do the same thing if I were you." He reached into his pocket and produced a key, which he hung in his fingers to show her. He nodded toward the chain around her ankle. "Nevaeh said I could unshackle you . . . if you were behaving yourself."

He moved toward the foot of the bed—no, it was less a bed than a cot, and her shackle was locked around its metal frame. He stopped and gave her a serious look. He reached behind him and drew out the toy gun. He pulled the slide back and let it snap shut with a metallic *ka-chunk!* That was no toy.

"I said I wouldn't hurt you. I meant I wouldn't *want* to. So don't try anything, okay? Nevaeh said she accidentally shot your son. I'm really sorry. Is he going to be all right?"

"I . . . uh . . ." She felt as though she were chasing thoughts the way a cat chases its tail. "I think so." The tears came again, welling in her eyes. She pushed them away with her fingers. "It's too early to tell. He was hurt really badly."

"How old is he?"

"Nine. How old are you?"

"How old do I look?"

"Eleven? You remind me of him."

Or did, she didn't say.

He smiled. "You seem like a nice lady, but you know, what happened to . . . what's his name, Tyler, right?"

She nodded, and he continued.

"What happened to Tyler and being here, all scared and every-thing, it can make you do crazy things." He shook his head gravely. "Don't."

He unlocked the bracelet around her ankle and backed away toward the door, holding the gun near his thigh. She noticed he hadn't curled his finger over the trigger, but extended straight past it, the way professional shooters are taught to do. He said, "We're going to eat soon. Elias is making shrimp curry. It's wicked good." He backed out the open door, pulled it shut, and locked it.

She stared at the door, wondering if that was the weirdest encounter she'd ever had or just close to it. Guess he'd answered her question about the kind of life he led here. She didn't know if she wanted to hug him or strangle him.

If it meant getting out of here alive?

The thought came unbidden, and she didn't want to answer it. But she did: no, she'd rather die here than hurt a child.

Maybe that's what her captors were counting on.

Let them.

She wasn't Nevaeh. The ends didn't justify the means.

She noticed someone had carved a five-foot cross in the wall by the door, and it made her smile. *Father, forgive them; for they know not what they do.* She laid her head back on a thin pillow and closed her eyes.

[66]

They were an hour out of Sharm el-Sheikh, and below them Egypt had given way to the Mediterranean, when Owen stepped from the cockpit into the cabin. He smiled at Jagger's initial shock and said, "George has the con. That's my autopilot. It's a zero-zero system, meaning it can take us all the way into Paris and even land the plane if necessary. Upgraded all the avionics a few years back. Cost more than the jet itself."

Jagger was sitting on the bed, back against the papered wall, filling a legal pad with everything he knew about the Tribe—from his own experience and Owen's narrative; what Nevaeh, Phin, the teenager, and the little girl had said; and their actions at St. Catherine's. From this, he attempted to decipher motivations and future behavior—classic FBI profiling. He decided that their thought processes were so alien to him, or so rooted in insanity, that he had no clue about their next moves. They could leave Beth behind or take her with them to whatever city they planned on attacking, kill her if they knew Owen and he were pursuing them, or leave her in some location that forced him to choose between her and them; they could go back and try to grab Tyler too—again, he didn't know why they would but he wouldn't put it past them; they could wait to ambush them or try to outrun them; they could be not thinking about Owen and Jagger at all. Bottom line: they were unknowable—the old "riddle wrapped in a mystery inside an enigma" Winston Churchill had used to describe Russia.

Hunching over, Owen came and sat beside him. He was holding his satphone, an image of the obol on its screen. "This is good," he said. "You know what an obol is, right?"

"A grave coin."

"Wealthier families had them made for their departed, usually with the family name. That's what I think this is." He pointed at the banner held in the skull's mouth.

"Choroutte? I can't quite make out the lettering."

"Chenevière, I think, like the French novelist. Not so common that old graves are filled with them, but common enough for me to recognize it. Where did you get this?"

Jagger described his encounter with the teen.

"I know the boy," Owen said. "You're sure he dropped it, and not Nevaeh?"

"I think—" Jagger started, and the plane bounced as though it had hit a speed bump. A beeping emanated from the cockpit.

"A little turbulence," Owen said, and the beeping stopped.

"I think the boy was their lookout, watching for Creed. I don't think Nevaeh and the others showed up until later. I'm not even sure the obol was his. It could have been sitting in that cave for—"

"No, it was his," Owen said. "Bedouins and tourists roam those hills like ants. It wouldn't have lasted long. And what made you think of it as something that could help in the first place? Too much of a coincidence."

"Does it matter that it belonged to him and not Nevaeh?"

"For our purposes, it does. I met the boy once, Tobias. Sweet kid, actually. At the time, he showed me a piece of a skull with Middle Persian writing engraved into it—the Sassanid version of an obol. The Tribe was using a Zoroastrian ossuary for their headquarters-slash-home. He likes to carry a token from his *current* home." He flipped his fingertip over the screen, moving to the next image: the obol's other side. "Nevaeh, on the other hand, cherishes grave mementos, has a large collection. She might have four or five on her at any given time, or just one that has special meaning to her for a particular mission. She gets them from anywhere, places she's been, other people. So you see, if it was his, we find where it came from, we find the Tribe."

Jagger shifted sideways and twisted to face Owen head-on. "You know more about the Tribe than you should. I was an investigator. The kind of intelligence you have doesn't come from Google searches and tailing them into nightclubs."

Owen appeared uncomfortable. Good.

"Do you have someone on the inside, a member of the Tribe?"

"No, but I did. He couldn't take it and defected."

"You spoke to the teen, Tobias. How'd that come about?"

"I confronted him, asked him to either be my inside man or to leave them." Owen shook his head. "It's no life for a child."

Jagger thought of the little girl. "What are they doing with kids?" he said. "Are the children their own, recruited, kidnapped; are they grooming them to carry on the vigilante tradition, perpetuate the Tribe?"

"Suffice to say the Tribe has been the Tribe, has been doing what they're doing now for"—he shook his head—"generations."

Jagger rose from the bed. He leaned over the desk and snatched an old photograph from the wall, its paper brittle and torn, and tossed it into Owen's lap. "This looks like the ruins of a Civil War encampment, dead soldiers everywhere, burnt tents. You think the Tribe did this? Some ancestral version of the Tribe?"

Owen picked up the photo and stared at it. "Confederate soldiers," he said. "They'd gone rogue, killing whole families for no reason. Raping the women . . . and girls."

"And you think the Tribe settled the score?"

Owen handed the photo back to Jagger. "Yes."

"*This* Tribe, *our* Tribe? Kids recruited into their way of life, their beliefs? You don't call that a cult?"

It made him wonder why they hadn't taken Tyler, or if they still would. Maybe his injury had saved him from that fate. Owen didn't say anything, so Jagger plucked another photo off the wall, this one depicting six men in suits sprawled on the floor near a wall, blood snaking away from them like roots. He held it up to Owen. "The Saint Valentine's Day massacre? Really?"

"That one worked almost perfectly," Owen said. "It turned two rival criminal gangs—Al Capone's and Bugs Muran's—on each other even more violently than before, and caused a public outcry that forced the feds to redouble their efforts to crush mob rule in Chicago." He watched Jagger toss the photo onto the desk, then continued. "They don't just want to kill, though they'd settle for that. They sincerely want to affect change: to draw public attention to the crimes going on under their noses but to which people have become inured; to tell the police and the courts that they're doing their jobs so badly, others have to do it for them. To turn criminal against criminal, or at the very least let criminals know that if the government doesn't make them pay, maybe someone will. They hope bad guys will think twice before abusing a child or taking money that doesn't belong to them or murdering a romantic or business rival."

Jagger selected another illustration, a line drawing of an old murder scene: men in overcoats and top hats standing around a bloodied woman lying in a cobblestoned street.

He showed it to Owen, who said, "Jack the Ripper. You don't think he just stopped killing, do you?"

Jagger tossed the paper over his shoulder. "I don't buy it," he said. "How does a group with such a specific purpose—an illicit, morally reprehensible, keep-it-secret-or-die purpose—sustain itself for, what, *hundreds* of years?"

"Thousands."

Jagger threw up his hands. "All the more unbelievable." He paced to the cockpit, turned back. "They'd have to be constantly recruiting, or raising their own kids or other people's in their way of life, which I can only imagine would be unbearable over time: always hiding, keeping secrets, killing. You said some people have broken away. Why didn't they go to the authorities? How have they not been caught, the Tribe dissolved? How are they so skilled? How is such a small group so powerful that they have governments doing them favors, giving them top clearance? I know what you said about their doing the governments' dirty work, but that's what we have the CIA for. Why use them?"

It was just too much. Too many questions, too many things that didn't make sense, too incredible. Mixing this garbage into the already poisonous brew of his emotions over Tyler and Beth, the possibility that the Tribe was planning the slaughter of thousands of people, and Owen's goal for the two of them to stop it—he was ready to explode.

Owen shifted on the bed. He scanned the walls, thinking. Finally he said, "Do you believe there are mysteries in the world we've yet to understand or even discover, things that defy what we think we know about the physical universe?"

"Of course," Jagger said. Quantum physics was a relatively new field that was turning human knowledge of the physical world on its head, such as the discovery of atoms that behaved differently depending on whether they were being observed or not—"conscious particles," he thought they were called. Tyler's doctor had said the human body frequently surprised the people who were supposed to know it best, meaning there was plenty the medical profession still didn't understand. These were things he'd classify as "not yet explainable, but someday will be," things that were simply outside the current understanding of science.

But Jagger also thought there were things humans would never understand, because they resided in the spiritual realm. Studies showed that ill people who were prayed for got well faster and more completely than people who were not, even when they don't know about the prayers. Scientifically inexplicable, now and forever. He didn't have to love God or believe God loved him to see him at work.

"Of course," he said again. "But what does that have to do with the Tribe?"

Owen pushed himself off the bed. He stood and fiddled with a stack of documents on the desk. He didn't select any, just fiddled. Finally he faced Jagger and said, "I feel like I should show you my best Jack Nicholson impression and say, 'The truth? You can't handle the truth!'"

He smiled, but Jagger simply stared, in no mood for humor.

Owen sighed. "I guess what I mean is, if I told you the truth, you wouldn't believe it."

"Try me," Jagger said.

[67]

Someone knocked at the door—*knocked? really?*—and Beth rolled over on the cot to face it.

"Come in," she said, feeling ridiculous, the prisoner inviting her captors in. She expected Jordan to come in with the food he'd promised, but it was a man, bald, goateed, intense dark eyes. He looked about sixty, but his physical fitness and facial musculature got her thinking he was younger. He wore slacks, a button shirt, and a velvet jacket—*a smoking jacket*, she thought, or the kind of thing an English lord would lounge around the manor in. He stood erect, shoulders back, a proud posture, someone reared to uphold the family name.

"Excuse me," he said, stopping midway to the cot. "My name is Ben. I understand yours is Beth."

She realized he was waiting for her to stand. She did, and he stuck his hand out. She glanced at it, then focused on his eyes. "You realize you kidnapped me? I'm a prisoner here?"

"I'm sorry," he said, no explanation. "I would be delighted if you would join me for dinner, nothing fancy, but I thought it would give us an opportunity to get to know each other a little better."

The games people play, she thought. *Why yes, thank you. I would love to see the layout of the place beyond my cell. Jordan and I were just talking about that, how knowing where I am would help me plan an escape.*

But she said, "Not to be rude . . . *Ben*, but I have no interest in getting to know you better. The who and why of my situation doesn't interest me, only changing it."

He smiled. "I understand, but you have to eat, and you may find our conversation stimulating. If we are to travel together, I think it best for us to be on more familiar terms, don't you?"

"Travel? Where?"

"Nevaeh has it in her head that you should accompany us on a mission. I tried to dissuade her, but the woman can be . . . stubborn."

His jaw muscles tightened, and Beth suspected this part to be true: It was Nevaeh who wanted her here. If Ben had his way, Beth would be released . . . or killed.

"We'll leave tomorrow. Call it a mystery trip; I don't want you leaving clues in case someone finds this place after we leave." He thought for a moment. "No one has discovered our home before, except a few unfortunates who stumbled onto it by accident. But now Nevaeh has motivated your husband to find us, and I won't underestimate the resourcefulness of a man pursuing his love." He smiled.

"Sounds like you know Jagger."

"I know people. Shall we dine?"

"I am hungry," she said, though she wasn't.

Ben bowed and swept his arm toward the door. "After you, madam."

She stopped in the doorway, startled by countless skulls facing her from the wall across a dimly lit tunnel.

"They don't bite anymore," Ben said. "Just up this way." He extended his arm past her and angled his hand to the left. She walked on, every sense on overdrive: dusty, damp smell, burning wax; the sound of silverware on plates, echoing slightly; muffled voices and explosions as if from a movie; a chill on her skin; eyes adjusting to the low light—candles in niches high on the wall, doors running the length of the long passage, some open, spilling out light, others closed.

They walked past an open door, and she saw a kitchen next to a dining area. Four people sat eating: a man with gray hair and beard, the teenaged boy who'd drugged her on the plane—*Toby*, she thought—the little girl from the helicopter, and Jordan, who grinned and waved at her. The others turned, but before their eyes fell on her, she had passed.

"My bedroom is the next door," Ben said. She gave him a look, and he said, "I'm sorry, space is limited, and each of our bedrooms must accommodate all of our needs. You may trust me to be a gentle-man, and of course we'll leave the door open."

She entered and was simultaneously surprised and unsurprised. Surprised because the large, well-appointed room was utterly at odds with the tunnel, the skulls, and her cell; unsurprised because she would have expected no less from the seemingly sophisticated Ben— more precisely, *half* of it fit him to a T. This half could have been a successful barrister's study: floor-to-ceiling bookcases with ornate carvings on the uprights and shelf edges; where no bookcases stood, the walls were richly paneled and decorated with gilded-framed paint-ings, brass lamps over them, and under them, busts and sculptures on sideboards. A large antique desk, leather sofa and chairs surrounding a marble coffee table whose base appeared to be authentic gargoyles from a medieval church. Tiffany lamps sat on two side tables and desk, bathing the room in a warm glow. The only luxury missing was a fireplace. The fragrance of leather, wood, and parchment invited long visits, perhaps to discuss the state of the world over brandy or to read classic literature.

The other side seemed more fitting for a pope: crosses of all sizes and styles; paintings of Christ and biblical events—David, depicted as a boy about Tyler's age, holding up Goliath's massive severed head; Aaron and Hur raising Moses's arms while Joshua and the Israelites battled Amalek's forces in the valley below; Christ's transfiguration, shining white between Elijah and Moses while Peter, James, and John watch in awe; similar sketches and etchings; what appeared to be bones, rocks, pieces of wood in glass cases. This side contained no furniture; only a woven mat on the floor in front of a short pedestal on which a large, thick book lay open.

Place settings were laid out on the coffee table in front of the couch and one of the chairs, glasses of water and ice beside them. "I'm afraid I don't have a dining table in here," he said.

"This is your bedroom? Where's the bed?"

"I roll out a mat on the floor between the two sections. I don't sleep much."

Beth wondered if he was aware of the symbolism of his sleeping between the two apparent devotions of his life, study and faith. Of course he was, she decided. She stepped up to a bookshelf and realized the distinctive halves were not so separate after all: Augustine's *De libero arbitrio* and *Confessiones*, Origen's *Hexapla*, *Ecclesiastical History* by Eusebius of Caesarea, John Calvin's *Institutes of the Christian Religion*, the Weimarer Ausgabe collection of Martin Luther's works. Latin, Greek, Hebrew, German, English—she stopped cataloging all the languages represented. The room, Ben's interests, weren't "study and faith," but the study *of* faith, specifically Christianity.

Astonished, she said, "*You're* a man of faith?"

[68]

"You sound surprised," Ben said.

She turned to him. "Your people blew up the monastery, shot my son, and kidnapped me."

He sat in a chair, gesturing for her to sit on the couch across from him. She had no intention of sitting. He said, "You find that contradictory?"

"One of you shot a nine-year-old boy! How does that square with your faith?"

"The Bible is replete with the death of children," he said. "But I don't believe that's what you're asking. I understand your son's injury was accidental."

"Only because the woman who shot him was aiming for my husband. What are you doing blasting into monasteries and carrying weapons in the first place?"

His face expressed genuine confusion. "Are not weapons and battle an integral part of God's word?"

"But God is love," Beth said.

"Is it not loving for a father to protect his children, even to kill, if necessary?" Ben said. "In Scripture, how many people were killed by God or for God?"

Beth thought this was a rhetorical question, until he answered it himself.

"Two million, four hundred-seventy-six thousand, six hundred and thirty-three, not counting those whose numbers are not stated, such as all but eight who died in the deluge and the number of first-born Egyptians who died during the tenth plague on Egypt."

"I've heard numbers like that thrown around before," Beth said. "Usually to illustrate God's cruelty."

"But do you think he is cruel?"

She knew how Jagger would answer, but she thought differently. "No."

"You can cite many reasons for these deaths—Belshazzar disrespected God; the people wiped out in Canaan threatened to corrupt God's people, turn them away from the one true God; Isaiah says the righteous are taken away to be spared from evil. But I submit that every reason leads to one: They were all killed in self-defense or in the defense of people who could not defend themselves. For anything that corrupts the spirit—such as witnessing crimes against God's law that go unpunished—threatens our eternal souls. And as precious life is here on Earth, isn't eternal life with God that much more precious?"

"Crimes that go unpunished," Beth repeated. "Where does God's forgiveness, his grace, come in?"

"Ah, but it's not really forgiveness, is it?" Ben said, obviously relishing the debate. "Our sins *are* paid for—by Christ on the cross. He bore our punishment, but we have to accept that, *believe* that he paid the price for us." He nodded. "I accept that, and we try very hard to make sure we don't extract payment from those whose debts are already paid through Christ."

He was losing her. "What do you mean, *you* extract payment?"

"'I will take vengeance; I will repay those who deserve it.' Deuteronomy 32:35."

"That's God speaking," she said. "'Vengeance is mine, *says the Lord.*'"

"Are you suggesting he doesn't work through his children? He can solve the problem of evil, smite the devil, like *that*." He snapped his fingers. "But he's doing it through his creatures, through us, as each of us turns to him instead of Satan. Some in the body are his eyes, others his head or feet. *We* are his fists."

She rubbed her temple, feeling her pulse there. "What does any of this have to do with attacking the monastery?"

The bearded man from the kitchen, a cigarette dangling from his lips, walked in carrying two streaming plates. He set them down on the coffee table: shrimp in sauce over rice. The smell was exotic and mouthwatering.

"Elias," Ben said, "have you met Beth?"

"Ma'am," his voice rumbled, and he dipped his head. He walked out, seeming uninterested in anything but the cigarette.

"I believe our conversation went astray," Ben said. "Sit, please; eat."

You mean it's encroaching into an area you don't want to discuss, she thought. He'd been elusive when she asked about their extracting payment, and now he shut down the conversation when she asked about the monastery. They were connected, the monastery and vengeance. Something against St. Catherine's. She'd told herself she didn't care about their motives, and yet she'd gotten sucked into Ben's twisted theology.

She sauntered toward the religious side of the room, scanning the book bindings as she did: Ignatius of Antioch . . . Polycarp . . . She stepped before the paintings. They were beautiful, and the rich, deep colors, intense light and dark shadow made her think they were all from the baroque period. Also indicative of the baroque style was the action depicted in each, unlike Renaissance art, which primarily showed scenes just *before* the action began—Michelangelo's relaxed David versus Bernini's fierce-faced David, caught in the act of slinging a stone at Goliath. They were—

She froze. Ben had arranged framed preliminary studies between the larger paintings. Her eyes had landed on one she recognized: a penciled sketch of a man raising a dripping blade, his face contoured in malicious ecstasy. It was a portion of the painting she'd been so horrified by in St. Catherine's library, the Israelites dancing around the golden calf. This was one of the figures Gheronda had covered, only the hand holding the knife rising from the cardboard redaction. It couldn't be a coincidence that Ben had the sketch, the monastery had the painting, and his people had attacked the monastery. Could it be the painting they'd been after?

For just a moment, she imagined telling Cyndi Bransford about this, the way she shared everything with her, usually over tea when the boys were in school. Cyndi would have said, "Too weird." And it was.

[69]

"What is this?" Beth said, pointing at the piece of golden calf art.

Ben leaned to see. "A pencil sketch from 1609," he said. "Not long after the pencil was invented, in fact."

"Why do you have it?"

"I collect . . . when the artist or subject matter has special meaning to me. The same artist painted that one too." He gestured to the wall behind her.

The painting was of a young man plunging a spear through a couple on a bed so forcefully the bloody spearhead protruded from the bottom of the bed. The faces of the man and woman were twisted in surprise and agony, rolled-up eyes, open-mouthed frowns. Like the golden calf painting, it was meticulously detailed: it was easy to imagine the spearman's muscles bulging and shaking with effort and fury, the lovers' violent death spasms, the warmth from a shaft of sunlight falling across all three of them.

Beth figured the enraged spearman was a spurned husband who'd found his unfaithful wife and her lover in their defiled bed. But something about the figure—perhaps the faint glow of his skin, the boldness of his actions, his posture—made him appear not a jealous murderer but heroic.

"That's Phinehas," Ben said. "Grandson of Aaron, Moses's brother. He's killing an Israelite adulterer and idolater and his Midianite lover, thus halting a plague that had already claimed twenty-four thousand Israelites. His courage and willingness to do what had to be done, even going against Judean civil law to do it, made him great in God's eyes."

Violence in God's name, again. It didn't take a genius to—

She leaned closer to the painting. On one side, in the shadows beyond the grotesque action, a man was parting the drapery, peering in. The beard was fuller and hair clung to the sides of his head like a wreath, but there was no mistaking that face as Ben's. The brush-strokes appeared consistent with the rest of the painting; the paint so similar in viscosity and hues, it could have come from the same palette. Either someone had expertly added Ben's face, or the entire painting was newer than it looked.

She turned her head to see Ben, a wry smile on his tight lips. He stood, walked around the coffee table and couch to a bookshelf. He selected a book from the shelf and carried it to her, flipping through the pages. He showed her the cover: *The Baroque View of Scripture.*

"Some time ago I lent this piece to the Kunsthistorisches Museum in Vienna," he said and spread the book open in his hands. The painting filled the right-hand page. On the opposing page, scattered among text, were five images: the painting hanging on a museum wall and close-ups of Phinehas's hands on the spear, his brow and eye, the contoured face of the impaled woman, and the witness peering through the drapery. The detail showed a dot in the corner of his left eye. She looked up at Ben, who was turning his head to show her a mole in the same spot.

She began reading the text. Like the golden calf painting at St. Catherine's, this one was unsigned, but assumed to be the work of Peter Paul Rubens. Based on papers provided by the anonymous owner and the opinions of experts who examined the piece, it was believed to be a private commission for a baron in Antwerp between 1614 and 1618. Several experts opposed the Rubens attribution, citing, among other things, two small initials painted on the reverse side.

"S.H.," Beth read aloud. "What's that?"

"Scarlit Hemel," someone said, and Beth turned to see Nevaeh leaning against the doorjamb. She wore all black, a zippered long-sleeved top and tight slacks. Her dark hair looked like a hood. "I'd come in, but Ben hates physical brawls."

"I don't want to fight you," Beth said. "Unless it'll get me out of here."

"You understand Nevaeh is the woman who shot your son?" Ben said gently, not to incite, but to clarify.

"I do," Beth said.

"And you harbor no ill feelings?"

"If my feelings could kill," Beth said, "she wouldn't be standing there." She gazed into Ben's eyes. "*I'm* not a fist. Who's Scarlit Hemel?"

"I am," Nevaeh said.

Ben chuckled. "In addition to her fascination with death, Nevaeh is obsessed with heaven."

"The first results in the second," Nevaeh said.

"*Hemel* is Dutch for heaven," Ben explained. "Over the years she's been Céu, Cielo, Taivas . . ."

"And *Nevaeh*," Beth said, "is *heaven* spelled backward." *Which would be appropriate*, she thought, *if backward meant opposite.*

Nevaeh stepped in, keeping an eye on Beth, and sat on the arm of the chair nearest them.

"I don't understand," Beth said. "The experts apparently agree this painting is from the early 1600s—if this is the one in the book."

"It is," Ben said.

She looked at Nevaeh. "Then how could you have painted it?"

"Have you seen Ben's other art?" Nevaeh said, glancing around the room.

Beth looked past her to a bust sitting on a side table. It was a young boy, hair below his ears, a cord like a crown on his head, lips slightly parted and irises shifted to look sideways, as if casually observing something he was unsure about. Beth squinted at it. "Is that . . . *Jordan?*"

"There's another like it in the Museo Nazionale del Bargello in Florence," Ben said. "This one was a gift from the artist, Andrea della Robbia, to his model."

Beth spoke in a whisper. "I've seen it on greeting cards." The colored terracotta bust included the upper chest and shoulders, showing what looked like a blue hoodie over a green T-shirt. She remembered thinking how cute it was that kids centuries ago dressed the way kids today did. "It's . . . *old.*"

"1470. Do you recognize the person there?" He pointed at another side table, on which sat a three-foot-tall sculpture of a boy sitting on a rock, withdrawing a thorn from the bottom of his foot.

Beth moved closer. She said, "It's a miniature version of the *Spinario—Boy with Thorn*, one of the world's most duplicated sculptures. Even the copies from the 1600s are on display in museums." She'd seen one at the National Gallery of Art in Washington.

"That miniature," Ben said, "is the artist's preliminary study, from . . . uh . . ." He looked at Nevaeh. "143 BC?"

Nevaeh shrugged. "Something like that."

"The original is a life-size bronze," Ben said. "It resides in Rome's Palazzo dei Conservatori."

Beth bent to look closely at the face. "It's that teenager . . . Toby." She stood to face them. "How . . ." Her gaze landed on a painting of two women beheading a man; the man was the bearded guy who'd brought their dinner. "How can this be?"

[70]

"They're immortal," Owen said.

He sat on the edge of the desk, where he'd spent the last thirty minutes tossing photographs—of live people and artwork—onto Jagger's lap as he sat on the bed. All around Jagger were purported images of the Tribe throughout history. Owen had started with Tribe members Jagger had seen in person:

Nevaeh as an Hellenistic bronze angel . . . a mother bathing her children in a Van Gogh painting . . . appearing opposite Charlie Chaplin in the 1914 short film *The Face on the Bar Room Floor.*

Phin—the man he'd shot in the face—as one of the crowd in Jean Auguste Dominique Ingres's 1827 painting *Apotheosis of Homer*; grinning at the camera, arm-in-arm with Jimmy Hoffa, whose smile seemed worried and unsure—by this time, Jagger's disbelief had already snapped like a rubber band, so he simply laughed; pointing a Luger pistol at the corpse of the Russian "mad monk" Grigori Rasputin on an autopsy table in a 1916 photograph.

The teenager Toby sculpted in bronze as the *Boy with Thorn*; clearly visible dancing with a half million other revelers in front of the stage at Woodstock—this one had been published in a 1969 issue of *Rolling Stone*; as the character Jim Hawkins, etched into the cover of a first edition of *Treasure Island.*

Jagger laughed again. "Oh, this is rich," he said. "*Immortals.* I don't know why you'd want me to think they were—or why *you* think they are—and I admit this is *good.*" He waved his hand around at the images Owen had shown him. "Someone knows his Photoshop. I don't know how you pulled this off—" He plucked the page that was supposedly ripped from an old *Rolling Stone* magazine off the bed. "It sure looks real. But you know what gives it away, what proves it's an elaborate hoax?"

Owen simply stared at him.

"It's a *cliché*," Jagger said. "They're immortal, so of course they're going to be part of all the important events throughout history, right? The Civil War, the Saint Valentine's Day Massacre, Jack the Ripper, Rasputin's death, Jimmy Hoffa . . . Come on!"

Owen grinned. "You're not getting it. These events are famous *because* the Tribe made them so. Remember, they *seek out* sinners. The worse their crimes . . . the longer they last . . . the more notoriety they get, the better. It means more attention to the fact that sin eventually catches up to you. Jack the Ripper murdered women from April 1888 to February 1891—plenty of time to draw the Tribe's attention and for them to reach London, from wherever they were in the world."

He reached to the desk and held up the picture of the wiped-out Civil War soldiers. "1863," he said. "Stories of atrocities had been circulating for at least a year. Hoffa's corruption and the rumors of his using violence and murder to tighten his grip on the trucking industry and line his own pockets went on for years before he disappeared. Same with Rasputin. His notoriety *drew* them. It's not a *coincidence* they were there at the end. They *caused* the end. It's what they do."

He shrugged. "I'll give you Woodstock, though. I have no idea why Toby was there, except to say he may be thirty-five hundred years old, but he has the *mind* of a teenager. If the Tribe was anywhere near New York at the time, he would have demanded to go. And besides, for every one of these incidents, I can show you hundreds of other historic events they *weren't* part of. And there are hundreds of events that no one remembers that they *were* part of—but where's the evidence? Take the Civil War picture. It's not a famous slaughter. But it did happen, and someone took a photograph. You see?"

Jagger nodded. It would be one thing to be "simply" immortal and happen to stumble onto something historic—and he supposed that would happen now and then, given their being around so long—but it was altogether different when they sought out atrocities and then did something about them. Would Jack the Ripper still be talked about today without the mystery of his disappearance? Would anyone care about Rasputin if his hideous and drawn-out death hadn't turned him into a legend? The Tribe had orchestrated the very things that made these events infamous. To use the events now as evidence against their being who Owen claimed they were was circular logic. But something still bothered him.

"What about the art?" he said. "They just happened to sit for some of the greatest artists in history?"

"No," Owen said, "not happened to. First, I've shown you only a few pictures of artwork—ones in which Tribe members appear— out of thousands of famous works of art. But I wouldn't call even these few times they've modeled for timeless art coincidence. Over the years they cultivated relationships with the influencers of their times, seeking patronage, information, political and cultural power. They've known emperors and kings, people like the Medicis, Robert Lewis Stevenson, Caligula."

"Did they participate in his assassination?" Jagger said, numb to any thinking more complicated than that.

"They were in the area at the time. Could be they incited it. They can be very charismatic. Add to that wealth, knowledge of practically everything, and whispered rumors of their immortality, and they were often welcomed into any seats of power, chamber, or studio they wished. So they were in a position to meet young artists who were becoming known because these influencers drew them, became their benefactors."

Owen shifted on the desk, propped one foot on the bed, and continued: "But more than that, some of the artists who became famous created stunning art because of the Tribe. They're master artists themselves. Think of it, they've had dozens of lifetimes to practice. They've mentored artists, with other members of the Tribe modeling. On top of that, they've witnessed new and obscure techniques and helped artists centuries later refine them."

Jagger looked down at all the faces staring at him from the photographs in his hands, on his lap, on the bed. He remembered encountering the invisible Nevaeh and thinking she was an angel or demon. Turned out not supernatural at all, just an invisibility suit that short-circuited on her. Now he had to amend his thinking again: the *invisibility* wasn't supernatural . . . *she* was. Or so this evidence indicated.

He frowned at Owen. "Immortal vigilantes . . . immortal kilers." He couldn't imagine anything worse.

Owen tilted his head in acknowledgment.

"But," Jagger said, "how . . . when?"

[71]

Beth sat on the couch and listened to Nevaeh's story about the origin of their immortality: waiting for Moses, forcing Aaron to craft a golden calf, the human sacrifice, the debauchery. How Moses found them that way and destroyed the first tablets he had received from God. How God's radiance washed over them, knocking them out and changing them forever.

Nevaeh seemed to be in a trace, staring off into a corner of the room and reciting details as though she were *there*, not remembering it, but living it. Her speech became increasingly feverish, fraught with passion and then remorse.

When she finished, she bowed her head and breathed heavily. Her shoulders rose and fell, slowly becoming less exaggerated as each second passed.

Beth realized her own lungs were pumping air like an athlete's after a sprint; her heart pounded, pounded. It was no longer difficult to believe Nevaeh was the artist who had painted the scene that had turned her stomach at the monastery. She felt now as she had then, sad and sickened.

Nevaeh raised her head and stared at Beth, as if seeing her for the first time. Ben handed her a glass of amber liquid, and she gulped it down. She smiled, like saying *wow*, shook her head, making her hair fan out in a ripple around her.

"So like everyone else, we wandered in the wilderness," she said. "I eventually married and had children, a son and daughter. Thirty-seven years later my husband was dead and my children were older than I was when I'd sinned so badly. But I hadn't changed. I looked as I do now. I had taken in the boy who woke with me that awful morning, and he was still a child after almost four decades."

"Jordan?" Beth guessed.

Nevaeh nodded.

"And the little girl I saw?"

"All of us who had been knocked out by God's light, who slept through the dismantling of the calf and its altar and woke together around where it used to be—all of us ceased to age."

"But . . ." Beth shook her head. "Why did God punish the *children*, the little girl especially?" She couldn't conceive of Tyler consciously committing a sin so heinous it would warrant such punishment, to be kept from God forever. She knew Catholicism commonly placed the age when children should know the difference between moral right and wrong at about seven. That was when they were accepted into the confessional, but Beth thought even seven was too young. And the little girl appeared younger than that. "Surely she hadn't reached the age of accountability, the age where she could have made up her own mind to sin."

Ben let out a quiet laugh. "Man is always trying to apply his own reasoning to God."

"I realize that," Beth said. "But common sense . . ."

"*Common* is the key word there. God is anything but common, at least as far as the mind of man is concerned."

"But his word does make sense," Beth argued. "When you look at everything in the Bible from a bird's-eye view, from the perspective of eternity, it's cohesive . . . consistent . . . it all works toward his glory and his love for us . . ." She couldn't find the right words to express her thoughts.

"I agree," Ben said. "But it doesn't mean we know everything. We can't, otherwise there would be no need for *faith*. Just try explaining the Trinity."

"The point is," Nevaeh said, a bit impatiently, "God does punish children. When he ordered the destruction of Amalek, Jericho—the children were killed too."

"I've come to believe," Ben said, "that it has to do with God's omniscient 'middle knowledge.' That is, he knows all things that have actually been, all things that will actually be, and all things that may have been in all possible worlds. He knew that the children of Amalek, for example, would never have accepted his plan for their salvation; they were as guilty as the adults—because he saw what was to be."

"And he knew," Nevaeh said, "that Alexa, our little girl, *would have* willingly participated had she been older, had she possessed the mental capacity to choose."

Beth shook her head. "I can't accept that."

"Then throw that out," Ben said. "It's above you."

Beth frowned. Ben was taking the cowardly egotist's way out: *If you don't agree with me, then you simply don't understand.*

He said, "Consider this: There is a spiritual connection between parent and child that is greater than the modern mind can grasp. We all want to be individuals, rewarded and punished for our own behavior, not the behavior of anyone else, our parents, ancestors, anyone. But that original sin has been passed down to all of us through Adam and Eve tells us differently. That the Bible clearly traces Jesus's lineage back to at least King David means there's something about bloodlines that matters to God. We don't understand it, but it's there. In that vein—no pun intended—children can be punished for the sins of their parents."

"Dathan and Abiram," Nevaeh said. "Look them up in Numbers 16, but we were there." She looked at Ben. "We saw what happened with our own eyes. They rebelled against God and denied Moses's authority. They were standing outside their tents with their families, their wives and children, including little ones younger than Alexa, babies."

Beth didn't have to look it up. "The ground opened up and swallowed them—and their households."

Nevaeh smiled at her. "It was an awesome display of God's might." She said it with true awe in her voice. Her attention seemed to drift away, remembering.

"And an example that God does punish children," Ben said. "We may not like it, but it's true. Alexa's father was there, at the golden calf."

"Did he become immortal?"

Ben nodded, a sad expression on his face. "He was one of us for a time. He departed some time ago."

"As in died?"

"Departed." Clearly something he didn't want to discuss.

Continuing their story of immortality, Nevaeh said, "Of course, other people noticed, and they brought us together before Moses. We had all come to the same conclusion: that our agelessness was God's punishment for our transgression. If we were never to die, then we would never dwell with him in heaven."

"We didn't think of it as heaven then," Ben said.

"We just knew what we would miss: peace with him," Nevaeh said. "Moses determined that because God had cursed us, we should not inherit the Promised Land. We were allowed to stay in the encampments until the crossing of the Jordan River, but he exiled us from our tribes."

"So we made our own," Ben said. "We became the Thirteenth Tribe, the Tribe of Olam."

"Hebrew for *forever*," Nevaeh explained.

"How many of you were there?" Beth said. "How many . . . who couldn't die?" She couldn't bring herself to say *immortals*.

"Forty," Ben said.

"But weren't there many more than that who worshipped the idol? Why only those forty?"

"As far as we could tell," Nevaeh said, turning her head away, "we were the only ones who . . . who tasted the blood."

"'I will set my face against any Israelite or any foreigner residing among them who eats blood, and I will cut them off from the people,'" Ben quoted.

Beth said, "I thought that was in regard to animal sacrifice."

"So how much greater was our sin?" Ben said. "Forty. That may not sound like many, but think about it. It's more than enough when none of you can die."

[72]

"But they *can* die!" Owen said, new excitement imbuing his words and face.

He was answering Jagger's mopey protest: "What's the point, then? We're after people we can't kill."

"And they can be stopped," Owen continued. "That may be more important right now. You put down Phin, right? Stopped him in his tracks. If you'd shot him as he entered the monastery, and the others too, you would have stopped their plans. Their being immortal doesn't mean they're unstoppable."

"Wouldn't shooting them as they entered the monastery have just slowed them down?"

"Considerably . . . long enough to have moved Creed and hidden or destroyed the microchip they were after." He gave Jagger a sideways smile. "Or long enough to finish the job."

"Kill them? How?"

"Separate their heads from their bodies."

Jagger threw his head back. "What is this, *Highlander*?"

"Well, they won't disappear in an explosion of lightning bolts, and you can't absorb their life essences, but . . . yeah, like that. Maybe the guys who made *Highlander* knew an immortal, huh? But more likely it just made sense: how do you keep living without a head?"

"Okay." Jagger said it slowly, trying to get his mind around it. "You cut off their heads."

"The Immortals heal really fast," Owen said. "Not Wolverine fast, but it's like a movie with the fast-forward button pushed. I'm pretty sure this rapid healing stems from the same genetic deformity that allows them to never age."

"Genetic deformity?" Jagger said. "I thought they became immortal through an act of God."

Owen had told him about getting the scoop from a Tribe defector, about how they traced their immortality back to God shazamming them at Mount Sinai for worshipping the golden calf.

"It *was* God, but he often does things in ways we eventually comprehend, even if our understanding doesn't mean we can duplicate it. It's still a miracle."

Owen paced to the cockpit, turned around and headed back, kicking clothes and trash out of his way as he did. "We live because our bodies replace worn-out cells through cell division. But every time a cell divides, its telomere—bits of DNA on the end of a chromosome required for replication—gets shorter. Eventually—on average, after about fifty-two divisions—the telomeres are gone, and the cell cannot divide anymore. It's called cellular senescence. Cells start dying without having created their own replacements, and that's when we start seeing the signs of aging: wrinkles, brittle bones, memory loss. We become more susceptible to age-related diseases."

He passed Jagger without pausing, reached the rear of the cabin, and came back.

"In laboratories, mortal cell lines have been immortalized—that is, their telomeres don't shorten during cell division, allowing them to divide forever—by activating their telomerase gene. All cells have them, but they're active in only a few cell types." He turned to Jagger and held up his hands as if to say, *Now bear with me.* "What if what God did to them was to activate their telomerase genes in all of their cells?" He grinned. "No cellular senescence, no aging, no biological death . . . ever."

[73]

"Some in the Tribe didn't get the significance of immortality at first," Nevaeh said. "They were just pleased as puppies to escape aging and death. But most of us were devastated. It was like being told, 'Hey, guess what, you're going to hell. You will never enjoy the experience of being in God's presence.' Our hell was on earth, but what did that matter? Hell is the absence of God."

"We prayed for forgiveness," Ben said. "Night and day we prayed. Let us grow old and die . . . take us now."

"Why not kill yourselves or each other?" Beth asked, but she thought she knew the answer.

"That would only secure our place outside of his kingdom," Nevaeh said. "Most Jews and Christians believe suicide is a mortal sin. After all, God gave you life, only he should call you back home, however he chooses to do it. And we *know* we're not in his Book of Life, because here we are, long overdue to be called home. But maybe there's a reason he hasn't just wiped us off the slate, sent us straight to hell."

"Why is that?" Beth said.

"Genesis says, 'And surely your blood of your lives will I require.' He has a purpose on earth for each of us, and we haven't accomplished that yet. When we do, maybe *that's* when we'll receive his forgiveness and can go home." She smiled at Ben. A pleasant thought.

"Back then," Ben said, "in the days of Moses, all we could think of doing was pray. And every day we looked for wrinkles, gray hair, were the kids getting taller? Nothing, ever." He walked to the painting of Phinehas spearing the two lovers and swept his hand over it. "And then this happened. We were at Ha-Shittim in the plains of

Moab, our forty-second encampment since leaving Pharaoh. It would be our final stop before Joshua led the other tribes across the Jordan into the Promised Land. One more chance for the Israelites to blow it with God, and they almost did."

He studied the painting as he spoke. "Balak, the king of Moab, called for the prophet Balaam to curse the Israelites, but when he tried, God instead made him prophesy blessings on them. Later, he went to Balak and told him, 'If you want to draw God's wrath on the Israelites, use your women to seduce them into adultery and idolatry,' which they did. So God sent down a plague on the Israelites and ordered Moses to hang the idolaters. Then Zimri defiantly brought a Midianite woman into the encampment and made a big show of cavorting with her right in front of Moses. He took her into his chamber. Phinehas went after them and . . ." He pointed at the painting.

"God proclaimed Phinehas a great man, loyal and brave, and halted the plague because Phinehas had atoned for their sins. He made Phinehas High Priest and said that he and his sons' sons would receive divine recognition for all eternity."

"That's when we knew what we had to do," Nevaeh said. "We would follow Phinehas's example and kill sinners."

"To regain God's favor?" Beth said.

"To please God the way Phinehas did."

"And you've been doing this . . . for thirty-five hundred years?"

"We'll do it another thirty-five hundred," Ben said, "if that's what it takes."

Beth caught Nevaeh frowning at him. She said, "But if it hasn't worked so far . . ."

"What is time to God?" He waved his hand dismissively. "Our sin was so great, our atonement must be great . . . in years, in the quality and quantity of our penance, maybe in a very special sinner we have yet to meet."

"But . . ." Beth paused. She was dumbfounded by their logic. Her eyes scanned across the shelves of books to the crosses on the wall. Finally she said, "You . . . know about Jesus?"

"*Know* about him?" Ben laughed. "We met him, followed him to the cross."

"Then you know what he came to teach us—forgiveness and grace."

"That's what we yearn for," Ben said, "and we pray to him for it constantly."

"While killing sinners," Beth said.

"It's what we are here for."

"But you can't *earn* your way into heaven." She looked from Ben to Nevaeh, their faces impassive. "That's what you're trying to do, you know that."

"Doesn't everybody try to earn God's grace?" Nevaeh said.

"That's not grace. Grace is freely given and freely received."

"Then why do people go to church, tithe, pray, try to do good things and not bad?" Ben said. "Don't kid yourself. You might say, 'To thank God for what he's already given.' And people might believe that, but it's not true. Deep inside, they're thinking, 'If I don't do this or if I do that, I will lose my favor with God.' Don't deny it, young lady."

Beth almost smiled. *Young lady.* If what he claimed was true, no female on earth *wouldn't* be a young lady to him.

She was a little stunned that people with 3,500 years of praying and studying Scripture could be so ignorant. Then again, the apostles had doubts and confusion after spending three years with Jesus and witnessing his miracles. She would have thought that such intimate exposure to God would be worth 10,000 years of study and prayer.

She gathered her thoughts for a moment, then spoke. "It doesn't matter what people think, does it? What matters is only what's true. 'For it is by grace you have been saved, through faith—and this is not from yourselves, it is the gift of God.' You either believe it or you don't."

Ben said, "'Behold, I am coming soon! My reward is with me, and I will give to everyone according to what he has done.'"

"'Not by works, so that no one can boast.'"

"'In the same way, let your light shine before men, that they may see your good *deeds* and praise your Father in heaven.'"

"Killing people constitutes 'good deeds'?"

Ben marched back to the painting of Phinehas and pointed at it. "Our only failing is that we have not killed enough."

[74]

"And some of these immortals *have* died?" Jagger said. The jet seemed to be handling Owen's absence from the cockpit well, and Jagger had almost forgotten that they were hurling toward Beth— and a confrontation with immortals—at something like 500 miles per hour.

"One was beheaded during the French Revolution."

"It wasn't Marie Antoinette, was it?"

Owen laughed and sat on the bed beside him. "No, but occasionally a Tribe member has . . . distinguished himself or herself and become quite well known."

"Like who?"

Owen slapped him on his knee. "Isn't your head swimming enough?" He thought for a moment. "Some have just died."

"What does that mean, 'just died'?"

"They simply keeled over. I guess God decided their time was up."

"And there're only ten or fifteen left? So twenty-five have died."

"I said there were ten or fifteen in the Tribe now, not ten or fifteen immortals in the world. Some defected and are still out there, as far as I know. I've been able to keep tabs on a few."

"What are they doing?"

"One's teaching at a university. Changes location and sometimes occupations about every ten years."

"And nobody notices that he doesn't age?"

"This one's a she, and you'd be surprised how long you can go without someone noticing. Adults don't change all that much in a decade, and the people who see you day in and day out don't notice. And there are things you can do to fool people. Start with longer hair, keep your body fat down. Then get shorter haircuts over time, pack on some pounds, maybe grow a beard. The women are masters with makeup." He glanced at Jagger, saw the question on his face, said, "I've been doing this a long time."

"What got you started?"

"Long story, and we have to start preparing. I need you to get on the computer, see if you can find any killings I missed in the Paris area. We need to narrow our hunting grounds a bit."

"But the obol . . . ?"

"If my expert helps at all, he could come back with three possible locations or ten or twenty. We should know which ones to hit first. The killings might give us a clue."

Jagger thought about the word *hit*. Hitting at immortals seemed a bit like taking on lions with a water gun. It wasn't even that they would just keep coming back if you failed to remove their heads; it was who they were because they'd been around so long.

Thinking out loud, he said, "They're as proficient as they are because they've been doing this so long."

"And it's all they do," Owen said. "Regular soldiers are pretty darned good at killing. But these guys don't just learn something and then get called in once in a while to exercise their skills. They do this day in and day out—acquiring targets, staking them out, planning the mission, making the hit, getting away."

His frustration was evident, and Jagger realized Owen had been wrestling with these facts for *years*—with these *people* who had frustrated, infuriated, and afflicted Jagger for fewer than twenty-four hours. He felt bad that he had grilled him, suggested he knew more than he was letting on. But then, Jagger was sure Owen did know more, that he was intentionally keeping things from him.

Owen seemed to read his thoughts—Jagger never did have much of a poker face. "I really have been after them for years. When I spotted a pattern to their killings, I saw they were concentrating on one area or going after a certain type of criminal, I'd go search for the targets they were searching for and try to intercept them. If I found them, I'd try to get one by himself, try to turn him to *my* way of thinking."

"Make him a mole," Jagger said.

"Or convince him to leave the Tribe."

Jagger's gaze roamed the photographs all around him. He said, "Has it ever worked, changing a Tribe member's ways?" He looked over his shoulder to see a lopsided smile on Owen's face.

"A few times. It's not easy pulling people out of a muck they've spent three millennia in, especially when they're giving evil people their due or preventing someone from being victimized. And they've got the 'God's on my side' attitude going." He let out a huff of air. "I'd much rather convince them than resort to their methods."

"*Have* you killed any of them?"

"I tried a time or two." He scooted off the bed and walked toward the cockpit. "When they wouldn't listen to reason." He stopped at the cockpit entrance and leaned against the wall. "And you need to know this. They yearn for death, but they will do everything in their power to stop you from killing them."

"Why?"

"Because anything less is the same as suicide, and they don't want to die before receiving God's forgiveness." He climbed into the pilot's seat.

"Hey, Owen?"

"Yeah?"

"We're not going to Paris so you can open up a dialogue with them, are we?"

Owen called back: "Don't worry, Jagger. This time our guns will do the talking."

[75]

Beth caught Ben staring intently at her, curiosity softening his features. But she also saw sadness in his eyes, and she wondered if it was because of her lack of understanding or something she possessed that he did not: limited time on this earth.

He dropped his gaze, said, "You didn't eat."

Beth looked at her plate on the coffee table. "Thanks anyway." She knew she should eat, but Nevaeh's golden calf story and Ben's *our only failing is that we have not killed enough* had destroyed her appetite.

Nevaeh leaned over from the chair, pulled the plate closer, and started shoveling it in.

Beth leaned back in the couch. She closed one eye and rubbed her fingers into her temple hard. Ben went behind his desk, opened a drawer, and brought her two pills. "Ibuprofen," he said.

She popped them with a swig of water. "I think I need to lie down."

"Come." He held out his hand.

She stood on her own and followed him out the door. They turned right, and she kept her eyes on the wall with the doors. She didn't need to see skulls at that moment; she'd had enough of death for one evening.

Ben slowed his pace and fell in beside her. "Do you believe us?" he said. "About our immortality?"

"Does it matter?"

"I'm curious."

She thought about it. "Everything I know about the world and life says you're either lying or delusional," she said. "But I don't know how you could have faked all that art or why you would. So, yeah, let's say I do."

Jordan and Alexa came burning around the corner at the end of the tunnel. When they saw Ben and Beth, they braked hard. Acting terrified, Jordan screamed loud and long, and Alexa joined him. They spun and disappeared back the way they'd come.

"They're thirty-five hundred years old?" Beth said.

"Forever children. There are neuroendocrine changes that occur in the brain during puberty, an extensive remodeling of the brain, if you will. It's not just the external, physical changes—the brain actually transforms so that we can *think* like adults. Since those two didn't go through that—and never will—they still think and act like children. And thank goodness; I don't believe I could tolerate adult language and ideas coming out of their little mouths."

"But they know how long they've been alive, don't they?"

"They have a vague sense of it. They have a much shorter memory than the rest of us, though they've retained impressive language skills. Each knows some thirty languages."

They reached Beth's cell, and she went in. Ben stopped in the doorway.

"Toby is similar. He's still a teenager in almost every way. We all just stopped developing at the ages we were when we became immortal. That's one reason we consider each other by that age and not our actual age. It makes it much easier to keep in mind the kids' cognitive abilities and emotional temperament when dealing with them or planning their role in a mission."

Beth felt sick. "They've killed too?"

"We try to limit their duties to supportive functions. Alexa's great at reconnaissance and intel gathering. The things people say around little kids . . . and if we need a quick peek inside a home, she's the gal for the job . . . *I'm lost, can I call my mommy?* Jordan's the best lookout, bar none. Toby . . . well, he has a habit of expanding his roles. Hard to keep him in check." He shrugged, that little tip of his head. "What are you going to do? Teenagers. Enjoyed our conversation." He backed out, pulling the door shut.

Beth sat on the bed, too many thoughts sparking in her brain.

She lay down and scrunched up the thin pillow under her cheek. She wanted to be back in their little apartment at the monastery, the three of them on the hard sofa, munching popcorn and laughing at something one of them did or said. She wanted that with everything inside her, but she might as well have wanted to fly.

She turned her face into the pillow and wept.

[76]

Jagger lifted his head from the pillow as Owen brought the jet into Le Bourget Airport in a northeastern suburb of Paris. He stretched, rubbed his face, and sat on the edge of the bed, getting his bearings and remembering why he was there: it felt like putting on filthy, blood-stained clothes.

The plane taxied awhile, then the engines wound down like a slain dragon exhaling its last breath. Jagger rose and stumbled to the lavatory at the rear of the cabin. He splashed water on his face, found a roll of paper towels in the cupboard under the sink, and dried off.

"Get some sleep?" Owen said, coming down the aisle toward him.

Jagger looked at his watch. "Almost two hours," he said. "I dreamt I was standing in a vast wasteland, nothing as far as the eye could see in all directions. Just dry, cracked earth . . . and two glass coffins. One was a mile away, the other a mile in the opposite direction. Tyler was in one and Beth the other, and both were filling with water, almost full already. I knew if I ran as fast as I could, I might be able to reach one in time." He shook his head and turned bloodshot eyes to Owen. "But not both."

Owen sat beside him and put a strong hand on his shoulder. "Tyler is fine. We'll rescue Beth. You'll have them both in your arms again."

Jagger nodded. "I need to use your phone."

He called the number Gheronda had given him, and Father Leo answered.

"I'm right here in his room," Leo whispered. "He hasn't woken, but the doctor said that was normal. His vitals are stable. I'll let you know if anything changes."

Jagger wanted to ask questions, but he knew there was nothing more to learn. He wished he were there, touching his boy, comforting him. He said, "Just . . . uh . . . talk to him. Can you talk to him, please? Let him know how much his mother and I love him."

"I have," Leo said, "and will continue. You do what you have to do, Jagger, and get back here so you can tell him yourself."

When Jagger disconnected, Owen stepped to the trunk at the foot of the bed and opened the lid. He lifted out a tray of socks and underwear to reveal a selection of pistols and revolvers, each nestled in its own custom black velour cut-out.

"Pick one," he said.

"What about customs?"

"I got it covered."

While Jagger handled each weapon, Owen pulled a black satchel—a doctor's bag—from under the bed. He removed a false bottom, took from the desk the Glock he'd wielded at St. Catherine's, and put it in.

"Lead-lined," he said. "On x-rays it looks like a really sturdy case, but customs at general aviation terminals rarely use x-rays. In my experience, they'd rather catch you moving cash than guns. Speaking of which . . ." He slid his hand under the socks in the top tray and produced a stack of cash, which he dropped into the case.

"What about the weight?"

"Those guys don't lift anything heavier than a rubber stamp. Watch, they'll slide this thing around a counter until they're finished. Got one?"

Jagger hefted a stub-nosed .357 Colt Python in his hand and a Taurus Judge .45 in RoboHand. "I can't decide."

"Bring 'em both," Owen said, spreading the bag open.

Stepping out of the plane, Jagger saw that Owen had parked it in a space between two other business jets.

He locked up and pointed across the tarmac to a building marked with a big 153. "That's where the *Bureau d'Enquêtes et d'Analyses pour la Sécurité de l'Aviation Civile*—customs—is located."

"You know this airport?"

"Been here a time or two." They started walking, and Owen said,

"This is where Charles Lindbergh landed after making the first solo flight across the Atlantic."

Jagger scanned the sky and marveled that night had already fallen. Considering that he'd risen at four thirty the morning before last— Tyler waking him to attend morning services—and had no rest last night, coupled with the emotional turbulence of his son's shooting and his wife's kidnapping, two hours' rest was nothing. He should have been dead on his feet, but he wasn't; riding waves of adrenaline and anxiety, he felt like he could go twelve rounds with Floyd Mayweather.

Owen was saying something about Hitler beginning his only tour of Paris from this airport when Jagger interrupted. "What's the plan, Owen? How do we find the Tribe?" *If he shrugs, I'll hit him.*

"I know a guy who can shed light on the obol. He's the curator of a museum."

"Just like that, he'll tell us where it came from?"

Owen looked at him from the corner of his eye. "Nothing's that easy, but if anyone can find what we need, it'll be this guy. He has death and burial records for all of France, maybe Europe, dating back centuries."

"We should have sent the images from the plane, got him started on the research."

"He doesn't have a phone."

"What, not even a landline?" Jagger couldn't imagine.

"He's odd that way, a throwback to simpler times."

"Not having a phone is simpler?"

Owen shrugged. He rented a car with a GPS, consulted his phone's directory, and punched in an address. "It's not far," he said.

The district they drove into—*Gare du Nord*—didn't seem capable of hosting a museum; in fact, if anyone had asked Jagger about it, he would have called it run-down. Posters for long-ago events peeled alongside the paint of the buildings on which they'd been plastered. People sat on sidewalks and leaned against walls, as though waiting for a bus or friends or opportunities that would never arrive.

They turned off rue la Fayette, and the degradation became even more pronounced, with whitewashed store windows, trash becoming part of the curbs, and graffiti—most of it obscene and masterfully rendered.

"Not quite the Paris I've seen in pictures," Jagger said.

"Every city has its more colorful neighborhoods."

"You said this guy curates a museum?"

"And here it is," Owen said, leaning close to the wheel to gaze through the windshield at a sign approaching on the left: *Musée de la Mort de Paris*.

"*Mort?*" Jagger said. "Doesn't that mean—?"

"Death," Owen said. "The Paris Museum of Death. You know a better place to learn about a grave coin? I'm telling you, this guy can point to the wall behind which somebody bricked up his wife in 1890, even if she never was found."

They rolled past, and through a cracked front window Jagger could see dim lights burning inside. The place looked like a pawnshop, the kind that deals in toaster ovens, broken guitars, and stolen jewelry. Owen kept driving, and Jagger said, "Aren't we stopping?"

"If the Tribe really is calling Paris home, I'm not taking any chances. From now on, we're going covert." He pulled down an alley and drove behind the building. He passed an overflowing Dumpster and parked next to a seventies-era Peugeot with a wired-down trunk lid. It was parked by a metal fire door with the museum's name stenciled on it, barely visible through a graffitied version of a Jackson Pollock painting. A light over the door turned the whole grubby setting into a black-and-white diorama that didn't seem quite real.

Owen killed the engine and said, "Wait here. I don't want to freak him out, showing up after years with a stranger."

"Is he a drug dealer?"

"I'll just make sure he remembers me, then wave you in." He climbed out, went to the fire door, and pounded on it. After a minute, Owen stepped back and the door opened. A man appeared under the light, startling Jagger. Maybe sixty, the guy was at least six and a half feet tall, thin as a tree, with a face long and gaunt; bald from forehead to crown, but with long salt-and-pepper hair hanging from the sides and back of his head to below his shoulders. He wore a crisp black suit and a fierce frown. Either the museum had, over time, transformed him into the perfect curator of death or he had shaped himself into that role; no one could possibly look that way naturally.

He stooped to squint with one eye into Owen's face; the frown became an equally fierce grin, and he enveloped Owen with spidery arms. It reminded Jagger of a black widow consuming her mate. Owen spoke and gestured toward the car. The man looked, frowning again, then Owen pulled him closer and appeared to whisper to him. The man listened and nodded. Owen waved Jagger over.

As Jagger approached, the man stuck out his hand, and Owen said, "Jagger Baird, this is Victor Grimm."

Taking the man's hand, Jagger said, "No!" and laughed.

The man's frown deepened. Owen was smiling.

"I'm sorry," Jagger said. "Nice to meet you."

Victor bowed his head. He spotted RoboHand and simply stared at it. In a heavily accented voice as deep and gravelly as a rock quarry, he said, "Where is the arm?"

"What?"

"The arm and hand," Victor said. "Did you keep it?"

Jagger had read an article about people holding funerals for their severed limbs, but he'd never heard of anybody keeping one. He said, "The hospital incinerated it."

"Oh," Victor said, scowling, "too bad." He rubbed his hands together. "I understand you require my services."

Jagger's judgment that the guy was more mortician than curator tilted into the red.

"Yes, has Owen filled you in?"

"An obol," Victor confirmed. "Come." He turned and stepped into the darkness beyond the door.

[77]

Jagger followed Victor into the Museum of Death, and an odor assailed him, something chemical like rubbing alcohol and gasoline; he wondered what embalming fluid smelled like. It was mixed with other, contradictory aromas, primarily flowers and dust. Just as unsettling was the gloominess; everything that wasn't an item on display was black: the walls and ceiling, the carpet, the cabinetry.

They traversed a central aisle, past a labyrinth of nooks, cubicles, and small rooms. Each area was lighted by candle- or oil-powered carriage lamps, strategically placed to cast their best light on a dominant feature. The first of these that Jagger saw was a bloodied guillotine attended to by a hooded mannequin, with the head of who could only be Marie Antoinette glaring from a basket. Hadn't he just been thinking about her on the plane?

Next came a serial-killer room, complete with framed letters and art, pictures, newspaper clippings, and tools of the trade, from scalpels and knives to nooses, bottles of poison, and firearms. One room explained Victor's interest in his severed arm: it contained tall glass jars of assorted severed body parts. A two-lamp setup illuminated the room's trophy: the left side of a head preserved in a Lucite cube, which magnified the cleaved brain, sinus cavity, and mouth components.

Jagger stopped looking into the exhibits.

Victor was far ahead, pushing through curtains into a slightly better lit room at the end of the aisle. His gait was the only part of him that didn't remind Jagger of a mortician. It was the long, fast stride of a man with a sense of purpose, as though the proximity of so much death reminded him how short life was. The room he'd entered was the museum's reception area, where visitors were teased with posters, pictures, and a few actual artifacts of death, more of which they could experience for 9,50€. There was also a rack of T-shirts and another of postcards.

In one corner sat a desk fashioned from a coffin. Behind it, more coffins standing upright without lids formed bookshelves. Except the one farthest on the right, in which a mannequin posed as a dead cowboy, complete with bullet holes in his shirt. Victor sat down behind the desk, slipped on a pair of reading glasses, and looked expectantly at Jagger.

Owen stepped forward and handed him the satphone.

"What is this?" Victor said, glaring at the image on the screen.

"The obol."

"*That* is not an obol." Victor opened a drawer and tossed a handful of medallions on the desk. "*These* are obols. That is a *picture* of an obol . . . on a *contraption*." He sounded disgusted, but he leaned closer to the screen and said, "A handsome piece. Engraved, even, with the family name, very rare."

"Chenevière," Owen said.

Victor nodded. "I think so, yes."

"Slide your finger over the screen. The next picture is the reverse side."

Victor looked at Owen as though he'd told him to pick his nose. Owen reached down and turned to the next image.

"Ah, yes, yes, beautiful," Victor said. He looked up, his face almost childlike, if the child were really grumpy and ugly. "Is it for sale?"

"We don't have it," Owen said. "We need to know where it came from, where it might have been found recently. The original grave."

"I can tell you that it has not been in its original grave for quite some time," Victor said. "Not for over two centuries."

"You know it?" Jagger said. "Where has it been?"

"I recognize elements of it. Look here." He pointed at the three ovals in the ten, twelve, and two o'clock positions and the heavy, irregular line at the bottom. "Three stones and the martyr's palm."

"Saint Stephen," Owen said. He told Jagger, "He was the first martyr of the New Testament, stoned to death for preaching Jesus's divinity."

"And the patron saint of the Church of St-Etienne-du-Mont, here in Paris," Victor said. "Now see here. It's not clear on this blasted device, but this small mark under the palm branch? If we had the original obol, you'd see it's an *N*, a *G*, and a *D* on top of one another—the mark of the engraver, Nicolas-Gabriel Dupuis." He looked from Owen to Jagger, impressed with himself. "From these things, we can surmise the deceased died before Dupuis did in 1771 and was interred in the cemetery at St-Etienne-du-Mont."

Now Jagger was impressed.

"In the late 1700s, all the graveyards in Paris were overflowing," Victor said, rising from the desk and walking through the curtains that led to the museum's exhibits.

Owen and Jagger followed.

"The decay created unsanitary conditions and threatened the water supply. The government decreed that no more bodies could be buried in Paris and the remains of the already buried had to be moved—over six million former residents of Earth. But no one knew where to put that many bodies."

"The catacombs," Jagger said.

Victor twisted to smile at him and stopped outside the entrance to a room. "Almost all the buildings of Paris are made of limestone," he said. "At the time of the corpse crisis, there were hundreds of miles of quarry tunnels in the city. It didn't take long to decide to put all those remains in the tunnels. They disinterred the bodies from the cemeteries and wheeled them by covered cart at night to their new resting place. A priest led the way, praying for the dead. They began in 1786, and it took over fifteen years to complete the work."

Jagger was thinking the catacombs would be like a stay at the Waldorf Astoria for death-obsessed Nevaeh, when Victor noticed Owen studying a sign over the entrance, painted to look like stone with crisp lettering carved into it: *Arrête, c'est ici l'empire de la Mort.*

"It's a replica of the sign above the catacomb entrance," Victor said, and his translation put to rest any doubts in Jagger's mind about where Nevaeh and the Tribe were holed up. "It says, 'Stop, this is the empire of Death.'"

[78]

The three men entered Victor's mini-empire of death. Lining the walls were poster-sized photographs of stacked skulls, many of them arranged into patterns like stars and hearts. There were also long bones placed to show their length when they were used to create a design; otherwise, only their knobby ends showed. In a corner, a glass case held what appeared to be the real things—discolored, cracked, incomplete.

In the center of the room was a display case with more skulls, each holding an obol between its teeth.

"Hey," Jagger said, almost touching his nose to the glass.

"You see?" Victor said, sweeping his hand over the display. "All of them found in the catacombs." He pointed to a side wall. It displayed framed documents and etchings from the time. One illustration showed the procession from graveyard to catacombs, much as Victor had said: wagons with black tarps covering large and bumpy payloads; a priest in full vestments and holding a tall cross marching ahead; grubby and downcast workers with shovels and wheelbarrows following. Another was of a church, its graveyard pitted with empty graves—evidence of a zombie apocalypse, Tyler would have said.

Dominating the wall was a large map, apparently hand drawn around the time of the catacombs' creation. The tunnels squiggled this way and that, seemingly without rhyme or reason, like the meandering network of tunnels in an ant farm. One tunnel stretched farther north than the others, and the overall shape of the tunnel system reminded Jagger of a digestive track. At the mouth were the words *Place d'Enfer*.

"What's this?" Jagger said, tapping his finger there.

"The Place of Hell," Victor said. "Now it is called *Place Denfert-Rochereau*. The old name was better, no? Much more colorful. It is the entrance to the catacombs. No, no . . . it is the *official* entrance." He waved his hand over the map. "There are a thousand ways to get in, most of them either unknown or walled up. But cataphiles—people who explore them regularly—keep finding new ways of breaking through the barriers."

"Do they cover a wide area?"

"There are hundreds of miles of tunnels, running under most of the south part of Paris."

Jagger looked at Owen. "How are we supposed to know where they are?"

"Who? Who is 'they' you seek?"

"More obols," Owen said quickly, before Jagger could push his foot deeper into his mouth.

"Yes, yes," Victor said. "More like this one would be worth looking for."

"But how are we supposed to find the exact spot, when there are hundreds of miles to search?"

"It is impossible," Victor said. "For a time, people lived down there. They turned whole sections into communities, with living quarters, stores, everything you would find in any neighborhood. Except sunlight and gardens, but they even built playgrounds and movie theaters. During World War II, the German army converted some of these areas into bunkers and command centers. They shored up crumbling tunnels, squared off caverns with brick and concrete, installed doors, and ran electrical conduits from the breaker boxes above them to the tunnels." He raised his hands in resignation. "But now nobody knows where most of the improved areas are. The early settlers and then the Germans hid the entrances well. Every now and then a cataphile or city employee working on utility lines stumbles into one of these rooms. I've heard experts estimate that eighty percent of what's down there hasn't been seen for sixty years or longer."

Jagger heard Victor's words, but his mind had stopped processing them after the third one. "Impossible?" he said. They had come here for nothing.

"Well . . . ," Victor said, teasingly. "There is a way to narrow it down, quite specifically, actually."

"How?" Jagger said.

Victor rubbed his chin and gazed at them with narrow eyes.

"We'll share any obols we find with you—*anything* we find," Owen said.

Victor smiled, a ghastly sideways smirk like the one Jagger suspected the devil put on whenever he tricked a desperate human out of his soul.

He looked down at the satphone screen showing the obol, used a spindly finger to flip to the first image, and stared at it awhile. "Chenevière," he said and repeated it. He turned and walked out of the room.

Jagger threw a puzzled expression at Owen and went after the old man. In the front room, Victor went to the cowboy's coffin and swung it forward like a door, exposing a narrow entrance into a pitch-black room. Without looking back, Victor raised his index finger and said, "Wait here." He went through, and with each step became shorter in six-inch increments. Jagger realized it wasn't a room, but a staircase. The light from Owen's phone glowed dully on a side wall made of brick and faded down and away.

Jagger turned to see Owen standing in the entrance to the exhibits, holding the curtain back and staring at the secret staircase. "Where's he going?"

"Hope he comes back with my phone," Owen said.

"Think they're really down there in the catacombs, the Tribe?"

"I should have thought of it before," Owen said. "It's perfect for them, especially if they stumbled onto one of those neighborhoods Victor talked about. Rooms, doors, electricity. They probably rigged something like a moveable fake wall between where they're living and the route to the surface."

He wandered into the reception room, lifted a T-shirt, and looked at the design—a wicked-looking face pointing a gun directly at the viewer. He dropped it and said, "But even if I knew they were hiding in the catacombs, I couldn't do anything about it without something like the obol telling me where to look—assuming Victor comes through. You can spend years down there and not find someone who doesn't want to be found."

Jagger walked to the front door and looked out. A woman on a bicycle rolled past. Three men came out of a bar across the street, two of them turning left, the other right. They waved and shouted *adieus* and *au revoirs* at each other. He stepped away and found himself facing the skeleton of a child holding a sign he couldn't read.

Coming up beside him, Owen said, "It says kids get in for half price."

[79]

A half hour after he'd vanished down the stairs, Victor returned. "This will take some time, a couple of hours." He pointed at the bar across the street. "Go eat, drink, come back later."

Jagger had a pint of Kronenbourg 1664 and some kind of sandwich, both of which were tasteless. Exhaustion hit him like a truck as soon as he sat at the table. He and Owen started conversations about the Tribe's intentions and motivations, what they should do when they found them, and Owen's experiences pursuing them, but each one trailed off after a few back-and-forths. Everything hinged on Victor's success at finding where the coin had spent the last two centuries, and Jagger couldn't mentally move beyond that.

Once he thought Owen had fallen asleep sitting up, but then he saw his lips moving slightly and realized he was praying again. Jagger stared at a rugby match on the TV above the bar, but it was just moving colors and sound.

Two hours to the minute after they'd left the museum, he stood, nudged Owen, and said, "Let's go back."

When they pushed through the front door, Victor was at the desk, surrounded by stacks of papers, books, and rolled documents. He looked up, his face grim, in his case meaning nothing. Addressing Jagger, he said, "Lock the door, *s'il vous plait*. Oh, and light the skull in the window."

Jagger turned the bolt and found the skull resting on an ancient electric chair facing the front window. He lifted off the top and saw a candle down inside. He lit it with a long match also on the chair and replaced the top. Its flickering eye sockets and nose holes were reflected in the glass.

"Come see," Victor said.

When Jagger and Owen leaned over the front of the coffin-desk, Victor placed his hand on a leather-bound book. "The Chenevières were a wealthy family in the Latin Quarter, mostly traders dealing in imports from Asia. Many of them were buried in the St-Etienne-du-Mont cemetery, where they had a family plot and mausoleum."

The cadence of his speech had taken on a perfunctory mechanical quality, like a bored professor's. Jagger hoped it meant he wanted merely to get through this preliminary information to the good stuff.

Victor continued: "When the government condemned all existing parish cemeteries within the city limits, the Chenevières attempted to bribe officials into leaving their dear departed where they lay and finally settled for buying them in a private part of the new catacombs."

"Did you find it or not?" Jagger said. "Where the obol came from?"

Victor seemed not to hear, but as he flattened a map before him, he said, "I'm getting to that." The map appeared old, thick and yellowed, with small tears along the edges where it had been folded. Like the map in the exhibit, it displayed the catacomb tunnels, but this one was more roughly drawn—scribbled, even—and included directional arrows and annotations.

"Most people know of the catacombs that are open to the public in the Denfert-Rochereau area." He showed them on the map. "What many do not realize is that human remains fill a much broader area." He ran a finger along one line, then another and another, stopping on each one far away from place Denfert-Rochereau. "The wealthier families paid to have their departed interred far from the heaping masses of the commoners' remains and kept together as families. I have in my archives many burial records, including disinterments and relocations into the catacombs. Unfortunately—"

A loud banging erupted from behind Jagger. He spun and saw a little boy about eight years old waving at him through the front door. The boy pounded his palm against the glass again.

Jagger turned to Victor, who said, "Let him in. *Entre! Entre!*"

As soon as Jagger opened the door, the boy rushed in. *"Est-ce que je suis trop tard? Ma mère vient de voir la lumière!"*

Victor tossed him a coin and said, *"Va chercher Adrien et Rèmy au bistro du coin. Dépeche!"*

Grinning wildly, the boy said, *"Oui!"* He ran to the lighted skull, blew out the candle, and darted out the door.

"He's going to get some men from a corner pub," Owen told Jagger. "See, who needs phones?"

"Who are the men?" Jagger said, returning to the desk.

Victor twisted his lips into what Jagger thought was a smile and said again, "I'm getting to that." He stared down at the map, running his hands over it. "Where was I?"

"Burial records," Owen said.

Jagger added, "You said *unfortunately.*"

"Ah. Unfortunately, I do not have the relocation records of the family Chenevière."

Jagger felt like he'd been punched in the gut.

"I did, however, find a letter from Mathilde Chenevière to her sister Adèle, explaining the transport of their father Charles Chenevière into the catacombs." He put on his glasses, flipped through a stack of papers, and pulled out a photocopy of a letter written in beautifully florid script. He read, translating as he did, "'Our family has secured a most favorable section of the ossuary. It is in the same passage as the de Gournays and not terribly far from the Fouquats.'"

He set the letter aside and smoothed his palm over the map. "This, *messieurs*, is the de Gournays' map to their family's place in the catacombs." He tapped an X on the paper, clinging to one of the far-off branches. Then he unrolled a modern street map over it and stood to hold both in front of a carriage lamp. "The scale is off, but this was the closest I could find. This is where you will find the place of the obol. Under rue de Sevres."

"Can we get to it?" Jagger said, all cool, though he felt like that little boy, jumping up and down.

"There is always a way," Victor said. "I checked several modern maps of the catacombs, ones cataphiles use and constantly update. The men I asked the boy to fetch are cataphiles. They can guide you to the Chenevières location. They will be thrilled to do it, to find this unexplored place. They will start tomorrow. You can wait, no?"

"No," Jagger said.

Owen touched his arm. "Yes, we can. We need sleep anyway. We'll get a room and return in the morning. What time, do you think?"

Victor waved a hand at him. "You will stay here." He read the panic that flashed on Jagger's face, and said, "Not *here* in the museum. I have rooms upstairs, an apartment. It is no trouble, and you will be here when they arrive."

[80]

"I can still smell it," Jagger said, "that chemical-orchid stench." He was lying in bed, staring at the ceiling with a hand and stump under his head. Owen lay in another bed against the opposite wall, a nightstand, clock, and lamp between them. Thankfully, nothing in the room was black. Red and yellow lights from the bar across the street came through the window and jumped around on the ceiling.

"Go to sleep," Owen said.

Out on the street, someone yelled and a different voice laughed. As the time ticked away, more people left the bar and their rowdiness increased. Glass shattered, and someone gleefully hooted.

Earlier, Jagger had called the hospital in Sharm el-Sheikh again, this time reaching Gheronda. He'd said Tyler had woken up, groggy but cognizant. The doctors were pleased but still watchful.

"Was he in pain?" Jagger had asked.

"A little. He misses you."

Jagger closed his eyes, hating himself for not being there. What Tyler must have felt to wake up with only Gheronda to comfort him. Tyler liked the old man—and Gheronda's affection for the boy was apparent—but he wasn't Dad, he wasn't Mom. There he was, in pain, in a strange place, without the two people most important to him.

Jagger had pressed: "Did he . . . did he cry?"

The line seemed to have gone dead, then: "A little. As he was falling back to sleep."

Jagger could not have felt worse if he'd pushed a knife into his heart. His boy, alone, frightened, injured, crying himself to sleep.

Staring at the colored lights now, Jagger's wrath turned to the

Tribe and the woman who shot his son. He said, "I've been thinking about the Tribe being expert fighters, soldiers."

Owen shifted to face him. "Yeah?"

The lights on the ceiling flickered and jumped. The sign above the bar's storefront windows had some kind of animated neon, a bottle pouring liquor into a glass, something like that. He said, "Doesn't matter. We have to do this."

"Are you trying to convince me . . . or yourself?"

Jagger turned his head to look at him. "They hurt my boy, they took my wife. I'm doing it."

"I'm with you," Owen said.

"But not because of Tyler."

"No, not for revenge," he said, "but for Beth and for all the other Tylers and Beths they will hurt if I don't stop them. The Agag—stopping it is what I was made for."

"You know that for sure?"

"I'm supposed to help, in whatever form that takes."

"Help what?"

"People," Owen said. "To ease the suffering."

"Don't you feel like a drop in the ocean?"

Owen was silent for a few moments. "It's not my place to question the plan or whether my contribution matters. I trust it does."

"You've seen some horrific things," Jagger said. "Evil at its worst. Don't you ever question what it's all about, why God lets it happen?"

"Sure. But never his love or his plan, just my understanding of it. Sometimes faith is like playing tennis in the pitch dark. You can't see the ball, but you know it's there, somewhere, so you swing. Sometimes you hit it, sometimes you don't, but after a while, your eyes acclimate and there it is."

Tennis in the dark, Jagger thought. You'd think a guy as serious as Owen, who'd seen the brutal side of life, would have found a more masculine metaphor—scaling a jagged precipice, fighting a barbarous gladiator . . . *Sometimes you have a broadsword, sometimes only the nail you pried from your hand after they pinned you to the wall . . .*

But then, maybe that's why he chose to go the mundane route; life wasn't always about blood and strength, war and death.

It only seemed that way.

The next thing Jagger knew, sunlight was streaming through the windows and someone was pounding on the bedroom door. He propped himself up on one elbow. "Yeah?"

The door opened, and Victor poked his head through. "The cataphiles are here." And he was gone again.

Owen was sitting up in bed, stretching and rubbing his face with so much vigor, Jagger expected his beard to start smoldering. "Sleep well?" he said.

"I don't remember."

Owen hopped up and began pulling on clothes. "Now that we can go," he said, "we better go fast. Finding an empty hideaway is no better than never finding it at all."

X I I I

On the way to rue de Sevres and the catacombs, Owen told their guides, "Get us close, then we'll go on alone. We're expecting trouble from some very nasty people."

At the wheel, Adrien Bertrand laughed, the kind of noise that rises above everybody else's at comedy movies. He was twenty-two and looked like what Jagger pictured when he heard the word *surfer*: long blond hair, bandana, tan, trim, and always seeming to be thinking about something else. Cool and laid back. The car was his, which they took because its trunk was filled with the gear they'd need.

Jagger was hyped up, and the idea of "gear" irritated him: just another stall tactic; the only gear he needed was slipped into his waistband and wedged into his sock.

"I'm serious," Owen said.

"I know, I know," Adrien said, nodding exaggeratedly, hair flying. "We bring you, you take obols." His English wasn't as fluent as Victor's, but at least Jagger understood him.

"If we find any," Owen said, "you'll get the obols, all of them."

Adrien's partner, Rémy Lefebvre, grinned back at them from the passenger seat. He was about thirty and quieter than Surfer Dude; only problem was he grinned constantly, making Jagger believe it was the consequence of cosmetic surgery gone wrong . . . or the guy was an idiot.

Rémy said, "Monsieur Grimm said take you to the obols."

"All right, turn around," Owen said. Jagger grabbed his arm and started to protest, but Owen held up his hand. "*Tourne-toi maintenant.* I mean it, turn around."

"*Bien! Bien!*" Adrien said. "We get close, we talk."

"No talk," Owen said. "I want your word."

"Okay, we take you close, that is all."

To Jagger's surprise, they motored their way into a suburban residential neighborhood, and Adrien slowed the car to a crawl. Jagger had it in his mind that all the catacombs were under city streets.

Adrien and Rémy spent the better part of an hour consulting Victor's map, parking at the curb, and looking for entrances to the 'combs—as they called them—in backyards, around basement foundations, and in storm drains. Jagger and Owen, too, scoured the area, and though they were less sure about the object of their quest, their determination to find it made them bold nearly to the point of criminal: they jumped privacy fences, investigated garages left open, tore through shrubs like tornados. Finally, their guides made the decision to retreat from the neighborhood and enter the tunnels from a place they knew.

"We will have to walk more, get through more tunnels," Adrien explained.

"What are our options?" Jagger said, leaning his shoulder against a tree, catching his breath. Leaves and playground bark clung to his hair and clothes.

Adrien shrugged, exaggerating the gesture, which Jagger started to realize was the man's way. "Stay here and keep looking . . . maybe we find it next minute, maybe never."

"Are you sure you can find the spot from below?" Jagger said. "If Victor's map is wrong about the entrance—"

"*Non, non,*" Rémy said. "Down there, nothing changes. Up here, houses, landscape, streets . . . always changing. Entrances get covered."

"Just get us down there," Jagger said.

Fifteen minutes later they were standing in an alley between a three-story brick building—stores on the ground floor, apartments and professional offices above—and a stone wall. On the other side of the wall, a grassy park hosted picnickers, dog walkers, and mothers with children too young for school. Adrien had pulled up so close to the building, all of them had to disembark through the driver's door, and now they stood behind the open trunk while Rémy handed out the gear: coveralls, thigh-high waders, coils of rope, and head-mounted lamps. He strapped on a daypack, loaded with food, water, a first-aid kit, and other articles he called *peut-êtres*—maybes.

By the time they were dressed like farmers confused about whether they were going fishing or spelunking, and Rémy had checked for stray items and closed the trunk, Adrien had removed five or six large stones from the wall. The exposed fissure turned into a gaping maw plummeting into the earth. Rémy backed into it and lowered himself, using rungs mounted to the wall of the hole.

Owen followed, and when it was Jagger's turn, Adrien stopped him. He glanced at RoboHand and said, "It can get rough down there. Are you sure you are up to it?"

"Don't worry about me," Jagger said and descended into the blackness.

[81]

Directly below the wall fissure, the four men gathered, nodded, and moved into the first tunnel. It was no wider than Jagger's hips, and they walked like robots for forty yards, then descended again, this time via a flight of circular metal stairs. With each step the staircase squealed like an animal caught in a trap and threatened to rip from its moorings. They reached a wide stone ledge, beyond which their lights lost their battle with the darkness before landing on anything.

Adrien retrieved a spotlight from Rémy's pack and shined it over the ledge. They were in a cavern, the farthest wall a football field away. Two stories below, helter-skelter passages we cut twenty feet into the stone floor, seeming never to intersect. Jagger recalled comparing St. Catherine's to a mouse maze, but *this* made the monastery look like the epitome of geometric perfection.

Adrien rambled on in French, perhaps tiring of struggling with English or too excited about the journey ahead.

Owen translated: "After we pass through this cavern, we'll be in tunnels that run on top of each other. Unlike the single plane of the surface world, we'll have to navigate layers of tunnels. We may have to double back now and then to take a different level."

"What are we waiting for?" Jagger said.

A foot of tepid water covered the maze's floor. They sloshed through, at times keeping their feet on the outer edges to avoid sinkholes that, according to Rémy, could drop you down to your neck or into an underground stream that would sweep you away. They turned into an intersecting tunnel and onto dry ground. Often the floor rose steadily for long stretches and then plunged straight down before continuing, as though the stone cutters had finally realized their mistake and made a sudden adjustment. Most of the drop-offs were already rigged with a rope, affixed to the upper wall by a cleat. Those that weren't, Rémy or Adrien remedied.

They traveled through tunnels of all shapes and sizes: wide corridors that would have allowed them to walk shoulder to shoulder, passages so narrow they had to shimmy through sideways, tall caverns, and rabbit holes that required crawling on elbows and toes. But two conditions never changed: the utter blackness, only temporarily disturbed by their bobbing, weaving lamps and the backsplash they made against the walls; and the silence—no dripping, no echoes, no sounds besides their own.

After an hour they came to a roomlike cavern that previous visitors—more like *occupants*, Jagger thought—had turned into a kind of den. They'd made a table out of a rusty old saw blade big enough to sleep on. A trio of lawn chairs made a semicircle around the table, but only two vinyl straps remained among all three. Jagger marveled at the effort it must have taken to provide the room with its central furnishing: a stained, threadbare couch with disgorged foam stuffing, like a dead buffalo ravaged by wolves. Scattered on the floor were empty plastic water bottles; energy bar wrappers; and paperback novels, moldy and water damaged.

Rémy pulled off his pack and sat on the sofa, his butt sinking to the floor and his legs hiking over its bare-wood front panel. He tossed everyone an energy bar, which got Jagger thinking that at least some of the old trash was Rémy and Adrien's.

Adrien found an ancient tool, a wrench or short crowbar, flipped it in the air, caught it. He jumped onto the saw blade, sat Indian-style, and started clanging the tool against the surface.

"*Eille!*" Owen said. When Adrien's light was on him, he opened his palm: *Let's not be stupid, okay?*

Glaring at Adrien, letting him know he meant it, Owen sat on the floor. Jagger joined him, rubbing an ankle through the rubber boots. He must have twisted it a little, but he didn't remember doing it.

Rémy passed around a water bottle. "You know," he said, with that grin again. "We are in the eastern part of the tunnels and heading farther east. Lots of stories about these sections, people seeing ghosts, vanishing like nothing." He snapped his fingers.

Owen and Jagger captured each other's faces in their lights. Owen's was cool, just looking, but his eyes were slightly wider than usual, saying, *Hey, that's interesting.*

Rémy patted the cushion beside him. "The two who moved this here," he said. "We met them, a man and woman." He scowled at Adrien. "*Quels étaient leurs noms?*"

"Uh, Tristan *et* . . . Aimée."

"*Non, non, non . . . Adèle!*"

"Adèle." Nodding.

"They wanted to move in," Rémy said. "Make a home. We told them, you're crazy, who wants to do that? No sun, too tight. They say for freedom down here. No rules, no people, uh . . . *condamnez.*"

"Judging them," Owen offered.

"*Oui*, judging."

"What about the police?" Jagger said. He'd heard there was a special squad just for the catacombs.

Adrien laughed. "We have entered here maybe three hundred times. Never have we seen the police. We hear about them sometime, looking for lost kids, chasing away noisy partyers too close to the tourist section."

Rémy nodded. "They stay near the tourists, make sure they do not get robbed or frightened. We are far from there now. That couple. We returned a week later, they were vanished." He glanced at Adrien, and for the first time his grin faltered. More quietly, he said, "There was blood."

Adrien nodded. "*Beaucoup*," he said.

"We think it was *meant* to scare us off," Rémy said, as if meaning that was enough reason to ignore it.

Jagger scanned the stone floor with his light. Any of the stains, all of them, could have been blood, or none of them. The couch too: way too filthy to identify specific substances.

"Shhh," Jagger said, though the only noise coming from the others was the rustling of the food wrappers.

"What?" Adrien said. He laughed. "You are spooked."

"Shhh."

"I hear it," Owen said. "Music."

Faint . . . wavering, as though carried on wind Jagger hadn't felt since entering the tunnels . . . bass notes more pronounced than treble notes . . . The music was so indistinct, it could have been classical or rock, produced by a single instrument or an entire orchestra.

"Where's it coming from?" Jagger said.

"Tourists?" Rémy suggested. "The surface? Who knows? Sound does not travel normally far down here. The tunnels are like a . . ." He thought about it. "A *baffle*, you know, like make-record studio." He shrugged. "But you never know. I followed music once. Took me two hours to find it, some guy with a boom box, painting a rainbow across a cavern's ceiling."

"How close are we to the unexplored area?"

Rémy frowned and shook his head. "An hour, maybe?"

"*Non*," said Adrien, jumping down from the table, swiveling and falling into the couch next to Rémy. He produced the map Victor had made and together they studied it, pointing, running their fingers along the lines, whispering.

Adrien's headlamp rose to shine in Jagger's face, panned to Owen's. He said, "We are almost there." He lobbed the tool into the air. It came down on the table with a loud clang.

The music stopped.

X I I I

Nevaeh kept her finger on the iPod's power button, her head tilted up like a rabbit detecting danger. "Did you hear that?"

"What?" Jordan said. He pushed a change of clothes into his daypack.

Alexa had been dancing on the lemon rug in her room, just shaking her rump and pumping her fists like she was polishing shoes. She said, "I like that song."

Nevaeh stared at the ceiling, listening. The men—Ben, Elias,

Sebastian, Phin, and Toby—had made a trip to the surface with the electronic equipment Sebastian needed for the Amalek Project. They weren't due back so soon.

"Stay here," she said and left their room. She strode past the other bedrooms and kitchen, and stopped at the next door. She unlocked it and opened it a foot, ready for anything. Beth sat on the cot, knees bent up in front of her. She looked up from the Bible Ben had given her.

"What are you doing?" Nevaeh said.

Beth lifted the book and her eyebrows. Nevaeh spotted the metal mug on the floor beside the cot. She let go of the thought that Beth was using it to make noise. She shut and locked the door, went back to the kids' room.

"Jordan, honey, go check it out."

"What?"

"The noise, a clang."

"I didn't hear it."

"Just go scope out the perimeter then," she said. "See if there's anyone outside the hidden doors."

"I thought we were leaving." A little whiny.

"What good are your surveillance points if you never use them?"

"I use them."

"Then do it now," Nevaeh said. "For me."

He grabbed a flashlight and shuffled for the door, head down.

"Hurry, please," Nevaeh said.

He started to run.

"Jordan?"

He stopped at the door.

"Be careful."

[82]

All four men shined their lights at an opening in the wall a foot above their heads. It was only slightly larger than a pizza, and Jagger figured the cataphiles wouldn't have trouble shimmying into it, but he and Owen had broader shoulders.

"What do you think?" Owen said, addressing him.

Before he could answer, Adrien said, "If you want to get to the obols, this is the way. It leads to a tunnel that marks the end of the map."

"For now," Rémy said. "Victor's map goes farther. Today, we are Columbus."

"Do it," Jagger said.

Adrien hoisted Rémy up. The man's legs wiggled and jerked and disappeared. Owen went next, groaning and grumbling, but making it. Jagger stepped into Adrien's stirrupped hands and forced himself in. He felt Adrien's tug on his foot and realized Surfer Dude was using him to pull himself up. Jagger followed Owen's rubber boots. His shoulders would wedge tight, and he'd back up a few inches, then try it again with his shoulders angled differently or his arms tucked in under him. A few times Adrien pushed at his feet. Jagger would lock his knees, and the extra momentum would get him through. He traveled that way for forty, fifty feet, then saw Owen's legs slip out of the hole, blackness beyond, a flash of light on a wall of round stones.

He slipped out of the hole into Owen's arms. Got his feet under him and turned to help Adrien. Their lights turned toward the opposite wall, made not of round stones but skulls and the ends of long bones stretching in both directions as far as their lights could reach.

X I I I

After leaving his bedroom, Jordan turned away from the route that led to the surface; that way was secure, the easternmost part of the tunnels, which no one knew existed. Heading west, he thought about the labyrinth of passages, all of them eventually coming either to a dead end—he loved that, "dead end" in this place of bones—or what looked like a dead end but really contained a hidden way out. Or *in*, and that was what had Nevaeh worried.

He didn't want to be checking for noises he didn't hear, looking for trespassers who never came. He'd set up observation points—peepholes and windows—for surveiling the areas outside their section—and even within it—like the towers and ramparts of a castle, but that was for fun, done when he was bored and looking for something to do. Now they *had* something to do, something big. They were minutes away from leaving. Why do this now?

He turned a corner, reached the end, and got on his hands and knees. He gripped the edges of a thick stone block and wiggled it toward him. When it was almost clear of the wall, he killed the flashlight and pulled it the rest of the way out. He nudged it sideways, lay on his stomach, and peered through. Nothing. Blackness. Though he couldn't see it, he knew the tunnel stretched a couple hundred yards, a main artery feeding a lot of smaller passageways. With Alexa's and Toby's help, he'd experimented and realized he could spot even the smallest light—a candle or one of those keychain bulbs—anywhere in the tunnel, and often caught the glimmer of light from the side tunnels. He remembered that Creed had helped too, and that made him sad.

He replaced the block, flicked on the flashlight, and headed for the next surveillance point. It was one of the funny ones he thought was clever. That picked up his spirits a little and got his feet moving faster.

X I I I

"Like in the tourist section," Adrien said, panning the wall of skulls. "Cataphiles always thought the people who made the 'combs put these here, far from the others, to mark the boundary."

"Here and no farther," Rémy said.

Adrien pushed long blond hair out of his face, tugging it back and letting the headlamp straps hold it in place. He pulled Victor's map from his coveralls' central chest pocket and unfolded it. He said, "But Victor says this is just the beginning." He cupped his hand over a skull and scanned the wall the way an archeologist would a newly unearthed doorway to a still-buried ancient temple. "And if the obols are over there, what else?"

"More grave treasures," Rémy said. "I have heard the men who moved the bodies here were careful to keep the dead's belongings with the dead. They were chosen for their respect and honesty."

"And motivated by guards who would make sure they joined the dead if they were caught stealing," Adrien added.

"*Oui.* But looters broke in later and became wealthy men."

While they spoke, Jagger walked into the darkness of the tunnel. He came to a dead end and returned. Hiking a thumb over his shoulder, he told Owen, "It stops down there, no other tunnels."

"That way too," Rémy said, turning his head and his light the other direction.

"How do we get to the other side?" Owen said.

"Could another level take us there?" Jagger suggested.

Adrien shook his head. "This level comes the farthest east. That is the reason for why we took it." He shone his light on the hole they'd come through. "We need to go back, move south, find another passage east."

"Maybe there isn't one," Owen said. "If the section past this was exclusively for the rich, it may have been chosen because it's accessible only from entrances that lead directly to it."

Adrien studied the map. "There are lines continuing from this side to that side, but you cannot trust them."

Rémy nodded. "We have followed even current maps, made by cataphiles we know, and found dead ends where there was shown a passage. These old maps, even worse."

"Is this wall entirely made of bones?" Jagger asked, trying to think of everything, pushing down the panic rising from his guts. This was taking too long. Owen had nailed it: *Finding an empty hideaway is no better than never finding it at all.*

"Solid stone behind them," Adrien said.

"Or more bones," Rémy said, gazing at the map in Adrien's hand. "Often, remains were piled in a chamber and they built these skull walls to hold them in."

"Retaining walls," Owen said.

Adrien ran his light over the skulls. "But usually, skull walls like this were built against stone ones. The masons, *skull*-masons, thought they were da Vinci, working with bone instead of paint. No artist wants his creation destroyed." He slapped a hand on a skull. "Solid."

"Should we try the residential neighborhood again?" Owen said. "That's the way Victor said to go."

Jagger's heart sank. It would take them hours to retrace their steps out of the tunnels, with no guarantee they'd find the entrance they couldn't find the first time. He said, "If the Tribe's hiding out over there, they would have hidden the passages."

"The what?" Rémy said. "Who?"

"I told you there may be bad people down here," Owen said. "We think they've already found the tunnels we're looking for."

Adrien spat out a string of French words that Jagger suspected would shock his mother. "We are not the first? They will take the treasure."

"No one said anything about treasure," Owen said.

"The obols!" Rémy said.

"We're not here for them."

Surfer Dude and Smiley launched into very uncool, unfriendly behavior: they ranted at each other, jabbing fingers at Owen and Jagger.

Owen stopped them. "Help us find the way in, and I'll pay you more than a hundred obols are worth."

"Oh yeah, sure, sure," Adrien said and spat.

Owen reached beneath his coveralls and pulled out the wad of cash he'd gotten from the trunk. He peeled off about a dozen bills and handed them to Adrien. "The rest when we get in."

The cataphiles counted them, each getting half. They shoved them into their pockets, and Rémy said, "Okay, we are here now, so we look for your hidden passage."

He and Adrien started walking down the tunnel, scanning the skulls from ceiling to floor, pushing at the skulls with their fingers, whispering to each other as they went.

Jagger and Owen took the other direction. Jagger didn't merely prod the skulls with his fingers; he shoved them, putting his weight behind his efforts. A few skulls shifted, one crushed under his hand, but nothing indicated a secret panel or way in. He tapped the skulls with his hook, thinking a change in the sound it made might lead to something. Owen followed, working lower on the wall.

Jagger's light emphasized the stark white and grays of skinless foreheads, jaws, and teeth, the black hollows of the eyes. With every movement of his head the skulls moved as well, seeming to shake with fright at these prodding, meddling intruders.

A splash of light panned quickly over the skulls he had not yet reached, and he jumped. The light had flashed past the impossible: one of the skulls still possessed flesh . . . and eyes, turned to observe him. He shined the light directly at it and let out a startled yell. Four feet away, chest level: a skull was missing, and in its place was the face of a very much alive young boy.

[83]

Momentarily blinded by the light, Jordan yanked his head out of the hole in the wall and shoved the skull into place. Someone yelled on the other side, and Jordan stumbled backward and fell. He had just stuck his face through to look when the light hit him. For a few seconds he'd frozen, a part of his mind unable to think. The part that did said, *Don't move! He won't notice.* But of course he had noticed.

He grabbed his flashlight, scrambled up, and ran out of the chamber.

"Nevaeh! Nevaeh!"

Years ago he had wanted to break away the back of a skull so that he could look through the sockets, but all the skulls he tried to modify had shattered. He should have tried harder; eyes were so much more covert than his whole face. What had he been thinking?

Behind him came the sounds of skulls falling to the floor, the wall shattering.

"Nevaeh!"

X I I I

"Over here!" Jagger yelled.

His racing heart pulsed blood past his eardrums in a deafening roar. The face had startled him, the flesh among so much bone, the glistening eyes after so many sightless sockets. Taking the shock to his system from *jump* to *scream* was the fact that the face had resembled Tyler's.

He jabbed at the skull with RoboHand. It fell back and sounded as though it struck stone. He bent over to look through.

Owen grabbed him. "Careful."

Jagger peeked, shifted away, peeked again. His light landed on a stone wall some fifteen feet away. He yanked off his headlamp and shined it through while he scoped the area. No boy, but a child's yell reached him from the other side: "Nevaeh!"

He sprang back. "It's them!" He kicked at the skulls. They vibrated, releasing a cascade of dust. He kicked again, punched a skull with RoboHand, collapsing its face into the brainpan. He punched again, and his hook broke through the wall. He didn't know which was more effective, kicking or punching, so he did both, switching between the strength of his foot and the hammerlike power of his prosthetic.

Owen kicked too, smashing the faces of skulls to bits, but the wall did not shake as it did under Jagger's pummeling.

Behind them, excited by the sudden action, Adrien and Rémy shouted encouragement—"Do it! Yeah!"—and spoke rapidly to each other in French. Their shaking headlamps added to the strobelike flashes of light on the skulls, making it all seem surreal.

"I think it's just here," Jagger said. "An opening." He kicked, and his leg plunged though the wall up to his knee. He fell to the ground on his back. Owen lifted him up, pulled him back until he'd extricated his leg.

"Kick around the edges of the missing skulls," he said and did it. A skull flew back into the blackness. Jagger kicked away another. Together they beat at the wall, alternating their blows like a team of railroad workers sledging in a spike. Above the hole they'd created, a head broke loose and fell, then another. They fell like drips of water, became a downpour.

Owen stepped back as the craniums spilled toward them into the tunnel and away into the dark chamber. Jagger covered his head and jumped over the remaining wall, crushing bone underfoot. He slipped the lamp harness over his head, adjusted it, tightened the straps. He reached for the pistol in his waistband and grabbed nothing but a handful of coveralls. He pushed the coverall's straps off his shoulders and peeled it down off his torso. The waders prevented complete removal, and he cursed. Always something.

He dropped to his butt among the skulls and held a foot up to Owen, stepping through the opening. "Pull these things off," Jagger said. "I can't maneuver with them."

Owen did, and Jagger stripped out of the coveralls. The place they'd broken through was at one time an arched portal between chamber and tunnel. Whoever had constructed the skull wall had simply ignored it. Owen was on the ground now, lifting a foot to Jagger. Jagger tugged the wader off and grabbed the other. He listened for shouts and footsteps coming at them from the tunnels on this side, but he heard nothing. Even the boy's yelling had stopped.

Rémy and Adrien clambered through the opening and darted past Jagger, who made a grab at Adrien's arm but missed. They disappeared through another arched portal, this one not blocked.

"*Hé! Tu m'as donné ton parole. Arrête!*" Owen yelled, and Jagger didn't need a translation.

He gave a fierce tug on Owen's heel, popping the wader off his leg. He spun around, drawing the magnum from his waistband. "Wait!" he yelled. "It's dangerous."

"Danger!" Owen yelled. "Danger! Idiots." He rose, climbed out the coveralls, drew his Glock, chambered a round, and said, "Let's go."

They caught up with the two stooges at the first place another tunnel crossed the one they were in. They were examining the map, debating which way to go. Owen marched up to them and snatched the paper out of Adrien's hands.

"*Hé!*" Surfer Dude protested.

"Hey, nothing," Owen said, his voice low. "We had a deal. We're in, now go." He whipped out the roll of cash and held it out. "And be quiet."

"You still need us," Adrien said. "Look at the map, can you read it?"

"Enough to get by."

"Where are we?"

Owen pointed at an intersection. Jagger nodded.

Adrien tapped the paper two inches from Owen's finger. "Not all the intersections are marked," he said. "Never are, there are too many." He gripped the top of the map, Owen refusing to relinquish it. "We go with you. You chase your *voyou*s away, we find the obols." He pushed away Owen's hand holding the cash. "We do not want the money, not so much. It is the *discovery*."

"Think about this also," Rémy said. "Without us, you will never find your way out."

"We don't have time for this," Jagger told Owen.

Owen let go of the map, instantly replacing it with his pistol. He held it up to Adrien's face. "Run and I'll shoot you," he said. "Unless it's back the other direction, away from the bad guys, in which case, drop the map. If you don't, I'll shoot you. Stay close to the walls and let me lead."

"What, you want me calling directions to you? Quiet, you said." Adrien smiled, turned, and started walking.

[84]

Owen sighed and followed. He kept his shoulder close to the right-hand wall. Jagger did the same on the left side, which consisted of more skulls. His shoulder bumped over them, like sliding over washboards. They passed side tunnels branching off to the left or right, a few cutting straight across. Adrien paused a time or two, glanced at the map, and pressed on.

They rounded a corner and had just come to a junction when Adrien stopped again. He took a few tentative steps, the others waiting, letting him get his bearings.

"What is that?" Adrien said.

In the darkness directly ahead—beyond the reach of their lights—a flame flickered, seeming suspended in the air.

A sound reached them: *click . . . click . . . click . . .*

"Out of the tunnel!" Jagger said. "*Now!*"

He shoved Owen into the side passageway, grabbed Rémy by the collar, and dived the other direction. As he left the main tunnel he saw the flame explode into a stream of fire, shooting through the air, lighting everything up. Adrien became a silhouette against a blinding orange burst.

Jagger hit the floor in the side tunnel, Rémy tumbling on top of him. A scream penetrated Jagger's ears—more hideous and wrenching than any nightmare could conjure or movie duplicate. Under it, like the breath that bore it, a rushing surflike sound; not water—fire, eating oxygen, roaring for something to consume. Which it found: Adrien flew backward past the side tunnels, already completely engulfed in flames, what looked like a fiery rope attached to his chest. Bits of burning clothes, hair, spattered fuel trailed behind, sailing up, dropping down like miniature bombs. He fell, rolling furiously between the walls. Everything he touched, the stone ground and walls, remained flaming after he passed. His screaming continued.

Jagger got to his knees, used the wall to stand, thinking of a way to help. Across the tunnel, Owen held up his hand, stopping him. Rémy crawled toward his friend—*"Adrien! Non! Adrien!"* Once again, Jagger seized the collar of his coveralls and yanked him back, pulling him away from the wall nearest to the man wielding the flamethrower.

A stream of liquid fire struck the side passage's wall at the corner where it met the main tunnel. Flames splattered. Jagger raised his prosthetic arm, shielding his face, and simultaneously backed farther into the tunnel, dragging Rémy. The temperature had shot up thirty degrees at least, wringing sweat from Jagger like a sponge.

The tunnel corner burned like a pillar of fire. Spatters on the wall and floor reminded Jagger of watching a valley at night, bonfires scattered across it, as far as he could see. A memory? Had he witnessed such a sight, sometime in his lost past, or had a movie put the image in his head? He shook the thought away.

A stream of flames hit the corner of Owen's tunnel. He covered his face with both arms and turned away. The stream fell to the ground, as water from a hose does, leaving a burning line on the ground. Jagger saw that one of Owen's sleeves was on fire, from cuff to shoulder.

Jagger darted across the gap, ripping the sweater off his waist as he did. Flamethrowers expel flaming napalm—thickened gasoline. It clings to whatever it hits like glue, burning, burning, burning, nothing anyone can do.

"Don't touch it!" he said, beating at Owen's arm with the balled-up sweater. Now both were burning. He grabbed Owen's cuff with RoboHand and yanked it up, ripping it along the path of the flames. He dropped the sweater and used both hands to tear the sleeve off at the shoulder. Owen pulled away, but Jagger seized his wrist to look for damage to his flesh—and on the inside of Owen's left forearm saw a gold tattoo of a fireball.

The men stared into each other's eyes.

"You? *You?*" Jagger said.

"I'll explain later," Owen said, no malice, no panic in his voice.

Jagger squeezed his arm, glaring into his face.

"Jagger, later. Beth first. Beth."

Jagger's head was swimming. He released his grip and jumped across the tunnel again. He needed to get away from Owen, even if only by six feet and for a few minutes. Owen was one of them. If he meant no harm, then why hadn't he told him? He pushed his back against the wall.

Not now, he thought. Owen's right. Beth was the goal. There would be time later to sort through Owen's . . . *betrayal.*

Adrien had stopped screaming, stopped moving. His body lay in the center of the tunnel, still aflame. Smoke roiled off him and the fires all around, gathering against the ceiling, growing heavier, lower, like a flood in reverse. Owen coughed. Jagger got down on the floor and saw Owen already there.

Rémy had crawled back into the darkness. Light from the flames barely reached him, showing a sitting figure, knees cocked up in front, arms wrapped around his legs. He was weeping, his headlamp shaking and bobbing, illuminating his rubber-booted feet.

Jagger wondered if the flamethrower man was coming closer. He turned off his light and edged to the corner, peered around. Visible now from the fires. Older guy, bushy gray beard, long hair, smoking a cigarette. While Jagger watched, the guy plucked the cigarette out of his mouth, turned his head to spit, and assessed his smoke before returning it to his mouth. Relaxed, cool about torching people. As far as Jagger could tell, he hadn't budged from his original position.

Jagger pulled in, scooted away. Why wasn't the guy moving forward? Biding his time, but for what? Only two possibilities: either the side tunnels were dead ends, from which they'd eventually be driven out by the smoke, or accomplices were even now coming through the side tunnels toward them. Neither prospect did anything to cheer him.

That whooshing sound preceded the stream of fire by a half

second. Flames splashed against the walls, sprayed over the junction's floor. Adrien got another wave and lit up anew. The stream dropped.

Jagger didn't know a lot about flamethrowers, and now wished he did. He was especially curious about whether the stream had a time limit per shoot and if it needed a few seconds to cool down or refill or whatever before shooting again. He couldn't vouch for it, but it seemed that the guy's sprays were about five, six seconds, and the intervals between twice that. Which meant the next attack should come . . . about . . . now.

Nothing.

Nothing.

Whoosh! Approaching fire lit up the tunnel. The stream hit the corner of his passage, swept across to Owen's, back to his. *Holding us here*, Jagger thought. The stream fell to the ground, a flaming whip that had served its purpose.

Jagger dropped to the ground and used his elbows to propel his upper body into the main tunnel. He aimed and fired, the .357 magnum sounding like a cannon in the tight confines. The man twitched but didn't move, except to swing the barrel of the flamethrower toward him. Jagger fired again. A spark sprang up from the barrel, and the man snatched his hand away. The barrel fell from his hands, swung down beside his leg; a strap over his shoulder prevented it from hitting the floor. He immediately reached for it.

Jagger pulled the trigger.

The man's left shoulder jerked back, and he reversed a step. He shifted his reach from the flamethrower barrel to his belt buckle—the gun Jagger knew must be tucked there.

Jagger slopped sweat out of his eyes, off his brow, and fired, missed.

The man lifted his hand, a big revolver in it.

Bam! Bam! Bam! Bam! Bam!—five rapid shots: Owen, leaning around the corner, plugging away.

The man staggered, jerked, dropped the gun. He turned and lurched away, growing dimmer as he distanced himself from the fire.

Bam! Bam!

Jagger took his cue from Owen and fired again. Something sparked on the man's back. The flamethrower tanks. He thought they were designed not to explode, one holding the napalm, another pressured gas. Neither by itself would blow up—this wasn't *Jaws* and he wasn't Roy Scheider.

Bam! Owen again.

Boom! Jagger's magnum.

No explosion, but one of the tanks did catch fire. It flamed like a torch stuck to the man's back; a stream of liquid fire poured out and stretched behind him, as though he were Satan showing off his tail. He shrugged out of the flamethrower's harness, and it dropped to the ground with a clang. Flames splashed against the wall. He dropped to his knees, rose again, teetered into a side wall, and kept walking. He turned a corner and disappeared.

[85]

Smoke swirled against the ceiling like storm clouds. Jagger coughed and pulled his shirt over his nose, trying to ignore the stench of charred meat, for once appreciating the stronger odor of fuel. He and Owen crouched low in the junction, their faces and arms glistening with sweat.

"Jagger, I didn't want—"

"Does it mean what I think it means?"

Owen studied Jagger's face before answering. "Yes," he said. "I was afraid you wouldn't trust me, that you'd run off and try to rescue Beth on your own."

"You're not one of them now, are you? Part of the Tribe? You defected?"

"I'm not one of them. I got away."

"How long ago?"

"Two thousand years."

Jagger blinked. That was a number, a length of time, he couldn't grasp. He looked along the tunnel at the burning flamethrower. "We have to get going."

Owen nodded toward Rémy. "What about him?"

"We can't leave him there," Jagger said. "I figure they're coming at us from the side tunnels. I can't think of another reason he'd hold there without advancing."

Owen frowned. "More likely to stall us while the rest of them make their escape."

Beth. Owen had to be right. They'd suspected that the Tribe would be leaving soon to fulfill the Agag, and they weren't about to let a few interlopers get in the way.

Jagger wanted to run, just barrel into the tunnels until he found them. He took a deep breath and closed his eyes.

The man who rushes into battle is the first to fall.

It wasn't merely wisdom from his fragmented databank; he could *hear* a man speaking to him. He couldn't remember the face or the situation, but that someone had told him those words was undeniable.

He heard himself reply, *But if time is critical, speed essential . . .*

Time is always critical. Why cut yours short by hurrying to death? Presence of mind, observing your opponent's environment and weaknesses, seeing the trap that awaits you—these things lay waste to speed. Will the thing you rush to be better off if you never arrive?

He didn't know the when or how or why, but he was certain these words had saved his life. Sometime in the past, he had heeded them and avoided death.

He flipped open the magnum's cylinder, turned it upside down, and ejected the six spent shells. "Ammo?"

"On the plane," Owen said. "I thought three handguns would be enough."

Jagger pulled the Taurus Judge from his sock. "I got five .45s right here. How many Tribe members did you say?"

Owen smiled. He stood and tucked his Glock behind him. "Don't make me fight you for Elias's handgun."

"Elias?"

"The firebug. I told you about him."

Jagger nodded, remembering. At the time, he had pictured some geek crouching in front of crumpled newspapers, striking paper matches—not this fire-breathing monster they'd faced. He stood and started for the end of the tunnel, where Elias had vanished. He stooped, picked up Elias's weapon, and handed it to Owen. "Ruger."

"If we see him," Owen said, "don't think he's unarmed."

"A flamethrower *and* two guns?"

"Maybe more, and grenades, knifes, and swords."

Jagger eyed him and decided he was serious. They approached the burning flamethrower.

"Those things ever blow up?" Owen said.

"I'm not sticking around to find out."

Jagger looked back the way they'd come. No sign of Rémy, who was most likely still sobbing and rocking himself in the side tunnel. As shell-shocked as the man was, Jagger was glad not to have to deal with him.

They reached the corner, and Jagger peered around it. "Light at the far end," he said. "Maybe a hundred yards."

"That's a lot of dark in between."

Jagger moved into the tunnel, Owen on his heels.

X I I I

Clutching a handgun, Elias lay on the floor and watched the two men come into the tunnel. The glow of the fire behind them was dim and growing dimmer. He saw the silhouettes of their heads, but as they came closer, he lost them. Then one of them turned on a flashlight. It was high and bobbed with his steps, and Elias recalled the headlamps they wore, right over their foreheads. He'd let them get closer, just to be sure his aim was true.

He pressed his fingers into his shoulder, sending a bolt of pain down his arm, into his head. He needed the stimulus. The three bullet wounds he'd sustained had drained him of too much blood. He was fading, couldn't even walk. But he could shoot.

He was dying for a cigarette. *Ha!* But having one would have been stupid, kind of like wearing a light on your head.

His vision blurred and came back. Had to take his shot now, while he could. They were forty yards away, an easy shot. He'd been rated a pistol marksman more than once. Pistol, shotgun, high-powered rifle, M16 . . .

Lying on his side, he took aim, using his other fist against the floor as a prop to steady his hand. He took a bead on the light, lowered his aim a few inches. *Between the eyes, a good kill to go out on.* He pulled the trigger, saw the immediate flash of return fire, and saw no more.

X I I I

Owen fired twice more. He waited, but no other shots came from the blackness. He said, "You okay?"

"My arm feels like a mule kicked it," Jagger said. He'd been gripping the headlamp with RoboHand, holding it out away from them as they walked near the wall. Owen had been in front, ready to shoot at any muzzle flashes. The bullet had struck the base of RoboHand's thumb-hook.

He rubbed his biceps, couldn't reach the stump, which had taken the brunt of the shock. He opened and shut the prehensor, making sure it still worked. It made a clicking noise it never had before, but otherwise it was good to go. Produced with carbon steel, carbon fiber, and aircraft cables, the thing was practically indestructible; a whole heck of a lot less damage-prone than flesh and blood.

He picked the headlamp off the floor, shined it on RoboHand, saw the dent but no other damage. He lifted the lamp again, and they continued. The light illuminated twenty feet of floor ahead of them and splashed a hazy line on the walls and ceiling. It washed over a body lying in a pool of blood. "Head shot," Jagger said. That wasn't uncommon when the target was a muzzle flash, if the shooter was good, and Owen was good.

He pried Elias's gun out of his hand and stuck it in his waistband. They moved toward the end of the tunnel and the light there.

[86]

Nevaeh stood outside the storeroom, a duffel of weapons and equipment slung over her shoulder. A backpack possessed her other treasures, the best of her death paraphernalia: obols, danakes, gold foil ghost coins, and lamellae; a bloody tunic; a tantō blade, used for the Asian seppuku ritual of suicide by disembowelment; a preserved piece of Eucharistic bread; a thorn. She stared toward the end of the tunnel, where she expected Elias to appear at any moment. The last round of gunfire—four shots from two guns—had been close. Elias must not have stopped them right away; they were driving him back.

She turned and headed in the other direction, then stopped at Sebastian's door. He was stuffing a bag with a laptop computer, hard drives, DVD-ROMs, handfuls of flash drives. "I thought you already brought everything up," she said.

He glanced at her. "That was for the mission. This is my other work."

She spotted Toby's Xbox on the desk next to the bag. "The Xbox, Sebastian?"

"So the boys can get a few more hours of practice on the plane."

"Time's up," she said. "Everybody out."

"Coming." But he reached into a desk drawer, grabbing more.

"Now, Sebastian!" She walked on, past the kids' room, Toby's, Phin's . . . She backed up. "Phin, what are you doing? We gotta go."

He was leaning over his bed, where an assortment of weapons was splayed out. He turned to look at her and grinned, the scabs on his face puckering, cracking, oozing.

"Thought I'd help Elias out," he said. He slammed a magazine into a pistol, chambered a round.

"No time for that. We're leaving."

At the last room, she produced a key and unlocked the door. She opened it to see Beth standing in the middle of the room, anxiety making her look old.

Nevaeh held up handcuffs by one finger and said, "Time to go."

X I I I

Jagger and Owen reached the lighted tunnel. Skulls filled the length of one long wall. The other was stone, with doors marching to its far end. They walked slowly, keeping to the skull side so they could get early glimpses into each room. Movement at the opposite end drew Jagger's attention. He snapped his gun up.

Beth stumbled out of a room, pushed from behind. Nevaeh appeared, holding handcuffs that bound Beth's wrists.

"Beth!" Jagger yelled. "Nevaeh, stop!"

Nevaeh forced Beth around to face Jagger and stepped behind her.

"Jagger!" Beth called, and got jerked forward and back for doing it.

A man stepped out of a room between them, a canvas bag slung over one shoulder and a plastic box in his hand.

"Sebastian," Nevaeh said. "Get over here."

Jagger shot the plastic box, letting them know he meant business. The box crashed to the ground and a piece bounced from it, hit a skull, and dropped. Sebastian staggered back, a flash of gold on the dark skin under his forearm: the tattoo. Jagger wished he'd blasted the guy's arm off.

He said, "Freeze, Sebastian."

Nevaeh said, "You do that with a knife at your wife's throat?"

Sure enough, Nevaeh was pushing a blade against the skin under Beth's jaw.

Be cool, he thought, and said, "Making sure you're listening, Nevaeh. Let her go or Sebastian's dead."

Sebastian shrugged. "Do it, man."

Another man came running out of a room farther along the tunnel, gun already raised, laughing maniacally. He dashed toward Jagger and Owen, shooting as fast as he could pull the trigger.

Owen fired, shattering a skull in front of their attacker, who yelled, "Kieran!" as though he couldn't believe the nerve, shooting back at him.

"Don't shoot!" Jagger told Owen. He threw himself against the opposite wall, ran three steps, and ducked into a room.

Owen flew in, crashing into him, spinning away.

Jagger said, "Don't risk hitting Beth," and jumped back to the door opening. He swung his arm around it, ready to shoot if the man was still coming and the angle of the shot wouldn't put Beth in jeopardy. But he had stopped in front of Sebastian and was ushering him back, reversing with him, gun pointed at Jagger. He let off a round, which pinged into the doorframe.

Jagger didn't move, just kept his aim on the man, trying to comprehend what he was seeing. The gun-toting man was the guy he'd shot in the face at the monastery. Circles of pink scar tissue marked the entry and exit wounds on his cheeks. The higher one on the right appeared to be bleeding. Jagger had shot him two days ago. No way should he be out of a hospital, let alone running around as though he'd suffered no more than a popped zit. Owen had said they healed fast, but hearing about it and witnessing it was the difference between gazing at the moon and walking on it.

Nevaeh said, "Phin, get Sebastian up top."

"I can get these guys," Phin said.

"That's not a priority right now, Phin." Calm, like she was ordering a sandwich. She pulled Beth back, stopping at the end of the tunnel where another passage intersected it, forming a T.

Sebastian reached the end and turned right. Phin stopped beside Beth and Nevaeh. "Go," Nevaeh told him.

"Nev—"

"Go! Make sure he gets up safely."

Phin sidestepped out of sight, heading the way Sebastian had gone.

Nevaeh started to move that way as well. Beth kicked back, striking Nevaeh's knee. She twisted out of her captor's grasp and started for Jagger, but Nevaeh leaped up, round-housing her leg into her. Beth flew sideways into the left passage. Nevaeh went after her.

"Beth!" Jagger called and sprinted for the junction. He heard Owen behind him. "Owen," he said, "go right. Stop them. No matter what happens, stop them."

He reached the intersection and braked in the center of it, gun raised, just as Nevaeh pulled Beth off the floor and swung her around, putting her between them again. They were forty feet apart, and he wondered if he dared to take a shot at Nevaeh's head, visible over Beth's shoulder. He was a crack shot, but if he missed . . .

Owen came up behind him. "Jagger—?"

"Stop them, Owen. Phin and Sebastian, whoever else is up there. Don't let them get away."

Owen rushed away, his footsteps fading.

"You're not taking her," Jagger said. He stepped forward.

"Unless I'm missing something," Nevaeh said, "it's not your choice."

"You're not going to hurt her. If you do, I empty this gun into your head." Nevaeh smiled, and he continued. "I'll follow you, step for step. One slip, and I shoot. Eventually, we'll meet up with Owen, and one of us will get the angle we need. Let her go now and save us the dance."

Beth mouthed, *I love you.*

He took her in, basked in everything she was, like the warmth of the sun . . . before dark clouds moved in. He said, "Right back in your face."

He expected Nevaeh to comment, some tired bad-guy quip like, *Ah, isn't that sweet?* or *Save it for her memorial service,* insert wicked laughter here. But the brief glance he gave her showed only sadness. She was a sad soul who knew only how to make others sad as well.

Between them, at the bottom of the right-hand wall, a large block of stone moved. It slid out, seemingly on its own. It came free of the wall, and two thin arms trailed it, pushing. A boy appeared through the hole, stood up, and slapped the dust off his jeans.

"Jordan!" Nevaeh said, angry.

He turned to look at Jagger. His was the face that had replaced the skull. Jagger understood why he had been reminded of Tyler back there. This child was close to the same age, had the same coloring, the same innocent features.

"Is he yours?" Jagger asked Nevaeh. She'd asked him the same thing about Tyler.

"You can say that."

Jagger shifted his aim to the boy.

"Jagger, no!" Beth said—nothing he hadn't already told himself. What was he doing? Could he shoot the boy? He'd survive, wouldn't he? Couldn't be killed, not unless he cut the kid's head off.

Then he realized what really gnawed at him about seeing the tattoo on Owen's arm: it made everything he had said suspect. Was everything just an elaborate hoax? There were no immortals . . . had he really bought into that guff?

Yes, he had: all those pictures, and Owen's detailed explanations. And why would anyone create such a lie? What had he hoped would come of it? Was he trying to get Jagger to blast away at everything that moved, thinking he wasn't shooting humans, but monsters? Or trying to put into Jagger's head that he wasn't *killing* anyone, just putting them down for a while—but in reality, he *would* be killing?

He was overthinking it, and at the worst possible time. Owen had said to forget the immortality part, and Jagger decided to do just that. He'd shoot whoever he had to shoot to rescue Beth, and not harm anyone he wouldn't have if Owen hadn't told him they were immortal. That way, if it were all a load of bull, he wouldn't regret his actions.

But could he shoot a kid? Nevaeh had shot *his* son. But he wasn't Nevaeh, and it made his stomach sour that he had even threatened to hurt the child, was *pointing his gun at him*. Nevaeh didn't know him, though; she couldn't possibly believe without a doubt that he *wouldn't* do it. If she loved this boy the way he loved Tyler, a hairsbreadth of uncertainty would be enough to forfeit the game.

All this raced through his mind in a nanosecond.

The boy—she had called him Jordan—raised his arms straight

out from his body, exposing himself to Jagger's aim. "Go ahead," he said. "Shoot me."

What's with these people? Jagger thought. Even if he were immortal, wouldn't it be agonizing? Phin had screamed like a banshee and passed out.

Hurt, not kill.

Don't think that! Go on the assumption they're mortal humans.

Jordan said, "Go, Nevaeh. I got you covered."

Shockingly, Nevaeh began backing up, tugging Beth along with her.

He could never shoot the kid, but he could definitely kick him aside, clobber him, knock him out, enabling him to continue putting the pressure on Nevaeh. He thought he'd had her, before the boy arrived. Take him out of the picture, and he would have her again. He considered how to do it: just rush him and let him have it. *Sorry, kid.*

Then Jordan changed the equation. He reached over his shoulder and came back with a sword, a gleaming three-foot blade Jagger thought was called a katana, a Samurai sword. This one was shorter; maybe they came in kids' sizes.

Nevaeh and Beth were in the shadows now, drifting farther away.

Jordan swung the sword in a downward arc, whipped it up over his head, crossed it in front of his chest. Before Jagger realized it, the sword had changed hands, and the boy was performing the maneuvers again.

The kid knows how to use it. There was going to be no slapping it aside and cracking the gun upside his head. So, now what? Shoot him in the leg? Jagger couldn't do even that. Even as Nevaeh disappeared down the tunnel with his wife, he couldn't shoot the boy. And he knew Beth felt the same. She wouldn't want to be saved if it meant resorting to violence on a child . . .

If Jordan attacked him with the sword . . . yeah, maybe then. But he'd try to evade the blade first, parry it. He found himself wishing that to happen.

Jordan glanced over his shoulder, checking Nevaeh's progress. He backed away from Jagger, who followed. The boy paused, blurring the sword with quick maneuvers.

Far behind him, Nevaeh took Beth around a corner.

Still Jordan waited. He said, "Are you going to shoot me?"

"I'm thinking about it."

"I like your wife."

"Then why are you letting this happen to her?"

"I like the Tribe more."

"Jordan, listen. All I want to do is get my wife back. She's not part of all this. Let me get her from Nevaeh, and you guys, the Tribe, can go do whatever you're doing."

"She's not part of this?" Jordon said, saying it like, *You're not from this planet?* "Looks like she is to me."

"Only because Nevaeh thought taking her would stop me," Jagger said, frustrated. "Look how that worked out."

Gunshots reverberated against the tunnel walls behind him. He spun that way, and when he turned back, Jordan was running the other direction, toward where Nevaeh had taken Beth. Jagger ran after him.

At the corner he paused, approached it wide. Candles lit the passage; it was gloomy but visible. He didn't see anyone, so he plunged in, heading for another T. He passed a side tunnel and wondered if that's where they'd gone, how Jordan had disappeared so quickly. He stopped before reaching the end. *Which way?*

More gunfire, far away.

"Beth! Beth!"

He darted to the T. This new tunnel was pitch black in both directions. He pulled the headlamp from his back pocket, strapped it on, and flipped the switch. He went right, in the direction of the shooting. He calculated that he was walking in a tunnel parallel to the one in which he'd last seen Beth, the same one where Jordan had made his stand. But were these tunnels really that straight, that gridlike? He could be moving away from Beth, maybe even heading for a different level.

"Beth!"

He turned around and ran back to the candle-lit passageway. The lighted tunnel, Beth's tunnel, was a few hundred feet away. He went for it, realizing as he did that backtracking would not find Beth, was putting more distance between them.

Maybe not, he thought.

Nevaeh was taking Beth with them. Surely Jordan was going too. They had to be heading "up top"—as she'd told Phin—all of them rendezvousing for the trip. He began running. Phin and Sebastian had apparently taken a direct route to their meeting place. They'd gone right instead of left out of the tunnel with the rooms. Owen had followed and then turned at the first left.

It was more information than he had about the routes Nevaeh, Beth, and Jordan had taken.

He ran past the tunnel of rooms, calling Beth's name.

[87]

Beth stumbled ahead of Nevaeh, pushed through a dark tunnel lit only by a small penlight Nevaeh shined over her shoulder. The handcuffs dug into her wrists, Nevaeh's pulling and pushing on them intensifying the pain.

Worse was the pressure in her chest; seeing Jagger had reminded her of the life she'd been ripped from, the man who always made her feel loved and safe. After the crash, in what she'd come to think of as the dark time, he'd pushed her and Tyler away, acting sullen and irritated; but she recognized his behavior as confusion, grief, and fear, his rejection of her and Tyler as a way of protecting them from the beast inside him that he couldn't control. He did not want them sucked into his black abyss, so he'd snapped and barked and scared them away. But he always came back, often late at night after a day of torturing himself, to seek her forgiveness, comfort, and warmth. It hadn't always been easy to give, but she knew his heart and wanted it to heal.

The other night—just the other night? It seemed ages ago now— she had told him that his grief ran as deep as his love, and it was true. Everyone had a well of emotions, some deeper than others. She saw it as her duty—as his wife, friend, and fellow human—to help him replace the poison that had seeped into his well after the crash with the good stuff that used to be there.

She wanted to believe that what had driven him to find her, to face her kidnappers, was love for her rather than hate for them, but in her heart she suspected it was a bit of both. And in the end that was okay, maybe the way it was supposed to be: sometimes loving something meant hating anything that could hurt it.

A gunshot brought her back to the tunnel, her aching wrists,

Nevaeh pushing her around a corner. At the end of a short passage, Phin was taking cover and shooting down a perpendicular tunnel. He saw them and yelled, "Shoot and you could hit the woman!"

"Beth," Nevaeh said.

"Beth! You'll shoot Beth!" He told Nevaeh, "Go, he won't shoot."

"Wait for Jordan."

"Phin nodded."

Nevaeh pushed Beth into the junction, keeping herself glued to Beth's back. Flickering light came from behind them, illuminating the tunnel ahead, their shadows stretching long on the floor. Beth saw Owen peering around a corner.

"Beth," he said. "You okay?"

"For now. Where's Jagger?"

"I thought he went after you."

Jordan stomped up to Phin, breathing hard. Nevaeh said, "Jordan, go, get up top."

He ran behind the woman and Beth, his feet pounding on stairs.

"Phin, you're next," Nevaeh said.

Phin followed Jordan. Nevaeh tugged Beth backward, step after step.

Owen said, "Don't do this, Nevaeh. Leave the woman."

"Oh, but she makes all of this so much more interesting, don't you think?"

"Can't you see how wrong this is? What happened to you?"

Nevaeh pulled Beth into a doorway. "Life happened. Too much life."

"Beth!" Jagger's voice, near.

Nevaeh yanked Beth again. The light was bright here, dozens of candles on stone ledges. Phin was pressed up against the other side of the doorway. Another tug and Beth's heels struck something. She realized it was a step, she went up.

Owen's face disappeared, and Jagger stepped out into the tunnel. "Beth!"

"Jagger!" Yanked up another step.

Phin swung around, fired at Jagger, who dived away. Phin laughed and slammed a heavy metal door, lowered a metal plank into brackets mounted to the walls and door. The door rattled; pounding came from the other side, and "Beth! Nevaeh! Beth!"—faint through the stone and metal. Nevaeh pulled Beth up a flight of stairs, Phin following, grinning. She spun her around and marched her through a tight tunnel. At the end, metal rungs rose through a rabbit hole in the ceiling.

"I'm going to uncuff you so you can climb," Nevaeh said. "Try to escape, I'll cut your throat and leave you for hubby to find. Then I'll make a special trip to visit your son. Understand?"

Beth nodded and felt the cuffs come off. She climbed the rungs, hands shaking, wrists throbbing. At the top, Ben grabbed her, helping her through an A-shaped crack in concrete. They were in a garage, barely large enough to park the two white panel vans there. The rolling door in front of them was closed. Toby was at the wheel of one van, Sebastian in the passenger seat, Alexa peering out the driver's window from behind Toby.

Beth turned to see Ben helping to pull a large duffel bag through the breach, Nevaeh pushing it through from the other side. She climbed through, then Phin. "'Bout time," he said.

Phin laughed. "They're still pounding on the door down there. It'll take them hours to get out of the 'combs." He pushed a rolling tool cabinet in front of the crack.

Beth felt her arms pulled behind her, the cuffs slapped on her wrists again. Phin rushed to the front of the van, and the garage door rattled up, filling the space with sunlight. Outside were low buildings, lined with rolling doors: a storage facility.

"Everybody in," Nevaeh said, pushing Beth toward a van. Its side door opened, and Jordan smiled out at her. He started to say something, but Nevaeh stopped him. "No yapping. I have a headache, and we have a long flight ahead."

[88]

Owen seized Jagger's shoulders and pulled him back from the door. "It's no use," he said. "Come on, we'll have to go back the way we came."

Jagger kicked the door, the bang resounding around him. He turned, blinding himself in Owen's headlamp. He squinted and looked away. His own light slashed against the tunnel walls, making the darkness beyond look that much darker. The thought of trudging through all those tunnels while Beth was taken increasingly farther away felt like a thousand hands clawing at him, pulling him into the ground.

"There must be another exit in this part of the catacombs," he said.

"We'll never find it," Owen said. "I can get us back to Rémy, if he's still there. He can guide us out."

"We don't have that much time! Owen, they're getting away . . . with Beth!"

As though he had to be told. The idea that Owen had set this up somehow, that he was helping the Tribe get away, touched his mind like a hand in a dark, empty room, and he again comprehended the great damage caused by his seeing Owen's tattoo. No, not by his *seeing* the tattoo—by Owen's *having* the tattoo.

"We don't have any choice, Jagger. I'm sorry."

"Where are they going? How are we ever going to find them now?" That panic again, rising up, clutching his brain.

Owen thought a moment. "We search their living quarters. Come on."

X I I I

They'd already torn through the rest of the bedrooms when they stepped into a room Owen said was Sebastian's. "The computers and monitors—Sebastian's a tech-head. If there's anything to be found, it'll be in here." But the computers were military-issue, the ports and front controls protected by metal doors with heavy locks.

"I can pry those open," Jagger said.

"Don't bother. Any tampering will activate a degaussing pulse through the hard drive, wiping it out, and a blast from a thousand-volt battery, frying the motherboard, RAM chips, and just about everything else."

"How—?"

"I have one. But look here." He was picking what looked liked blue plastic Chiclets out of a drawer. "Flash drives," he said, dumping them into his pocket. "We'll check them on the plane." Back in the tunnel, he pointed and said, "What's that?"

"An Xbox," Jagger said. "For video games. Tyler had one in Virginia.'"

"What's it doing here in the tunnel . . . with a bullet hole in it?"

"Sebastian had it. I shot it."

"Well, I doubt he was taking it for fun," Owen said. "See if you can open it." He walked on, saying, "There are a few more rooms up this way."

Jagger watched him for a moment. The man was decisive and quick. It would have taken Jagger ten times as long to go through the rooms and determine if anything was worth further investigation. He seemed resolute about uncovering clues and moving on to whatever it was they were going to do next. If Owen was jerking him around, he was a good actor.

Jagger used RoboHand to rip the Xbox apart. In the DVD tray he found a disk without the silkscreened graphics of commercial games. Someone had written one word on it in permanent marker: *Amalek*. He ran to show Owen, meeting him coming through a door.

"I found this on the floor in the kitchen," Owen said. He showed Jagger a paper airplane made out of twenty-dollar bill. "American. They're heading for the U.S."

"You know that from a paper airplane?"

"Ben's obsessive about keeping currency organized. If you go to the U.K., you get a stack of pounds. Rest of Europe, it's euros. Yen for Japan. When you come back, he collects the leftover. He doesn't want anyone caught with the wrong currency, to avoid both a financial need and unwanted attention. If he distributed U.S. dollars recently, it's for one reason: that's where they're going. What'd you find?"

Jagger showed him the disk.

"Jackpot," Owen said. "It must be information about their current mission."

"I thought that was Agag."

"Agag is the code word for 'something big going down.'"

Jagger nodded. "Hiroshima. I remember."

"Agag is the book. Amalek is the chapter."

Owen started fast-walking toward the end of the tunnel that would lead them to Rémy and the way out. "We'll pick up an Xbox on the way to the airport. I'll get us airborne, heading for the States, and you check out the disk and the flash drives." He stopped at a door, went through it, and a moment later came out with a sword.

"What's that for?"

Owen gestured with his head and said, "Elias. The flamethrower guy. Time to send him home."

But Elias was gone. Blood, no body.

"Did he . . . immortalize?" Jagger said. "Just get up and walk away?"

"Injuries like that don't heal *that* fast. He might have dragged himself away."

Jagger scanned the floor with his light: besides the pools and rivulets of blood, he spotted a bloody boot print and a few smears. Nothing that indicated that Elias had crawled to safety.

"More likely," Owen said, "someone came and got him." He tossed the sword down, loud in the tunnel. "Another day, Elias."

Adrien's charred corpse lay smoking in the center of the tunnel. Rémy was still huddled in the dark side of the passage, clutching his legs, shaking, and leaking from eyes, nose, and mouth.

Jagger hooked his hands in Rémy's armpits and pulled him up, saying, "Let's go, man. We have to get out of here, and you're leading the way."

[89]

Beth sat in the cabin of the Tribe's jet, leaning her head against a Plexiglas window and watching clouds glide past below her. Her eyes closed, and she said prayers for Jagger, Tyler, herself. She couldn't imagine her life without them or any one of them without the others. They needed each other.

They'd been so *there*, so whole. Even in the aftermath of the crash, they'd held it together, and she'd known that they were going to make it through . . . stronger than before. Because they'd had each other.

And into this serenity came a spider. Worse than that: venomous creatures with *malicious intent*. They had attacked, leaving her son for dead and kidnapping her, forcing Jagger to risk his life to rescue her.

She rolled her head to look at Ben, in the chair across the aisle from her. He was studying something on an iPad. Toby slouched in the chair behind him, snoring softly, a Kindle in his lap. The others were in the sleeping compartments or the cockpit. They looked so normal. How could they have become such vile, hurtful beings?

Ben shifted to return her gaze. He smiled, and she wanted to slap it off his face. He said, "You're troubled."

"You think?" She turned to watch the clouds streaming past and pinched the skin of her knuckle with her teeth.

"I have a question," he said.

She ignored him.

"What you said yesterday," he continued, "about not *earning* heaven. Do you believe it?"

She spoke without looking at him. "It's what the Bible says. You either believe it or you don't."

He remained silent for a minute, then said, "I'm only trying to understand."

She swiveled her chair to face him. "That's your problem. Yes, Christianity is a thinking person's religion. Everything fits together with everything else, if you really look. God is consistent. But it's also about faith, and you can't *think* faith. You're making it all about this"—she tapped her head—"and you've forgotten this." She touched her chest over her heart.

"But look at the Bereans," he said. "They were—"

She turned back to the window, shaking her head.

A few moments later he said, "Please."

She closed her eyes. *God, what do you want from me? I can talk for a year and not say anything this man hasn't already heard a hundred times. Even if I had the answer he's looking for, why should I give it to him? Anyone but him.*

His silence pressed against the back of her head.

Lord, don't ask me to minister to this monster. Even if I could.

She thought about how Jesus often preached to people hostile to him: traitors and spies, the Romans and Pharisees. He hadn't waited for the perfect audience, for people with ears to hear. Even under the pain of a brutal lashing and the terror of imminent death, he spoke about his father. He spoke the truth.

But what can I possibly say? The guy's been studying theology for centuries.

Outside the jet, the setting sun turned the clouds gold and the sky behind them red, blending into purple. It was beautiful, and she thanked God for giving that to her, for reminding her of his presence. She slowly rotated her chair to face Ben.

"A sunset," she said and held his gaze. "A flower, a baby, mountains, the ocean, the smell of lavender or leather or old books, Bach's *St. Matthew Passion*, Handel's *Messiah* . . . Close your eyes and *feel* the objects as though you're experiencing them."

His lids sealed, and she continued, more slowly: "Gentle rain over a green valley . . . the *sound* of rain . . . the warmth of the sun . . . the taste of an apple or pear or strawberry . . . a million stars in a dark sky . . . God."

She watched him relax, breathing slowly, the faintest of smiles creasing his lips. He stayed that way a long time. At last his eyes opened, and he sat looking at her.

"Those are all beautiful things that bring happiness, joy, peace. For me they do, anyway. Even though they can be analyzed—which notes for which instruments combine to create the *St. Matthew Passion?*— they don't have to be picked apart to enjoy them. In fact, they're better if you don't. At least not *while* you're trying to enjoy them. *Feel* God's love. *Be* his child."

"I don't know how *not* to think," he said.

"Insanity is doing the same thing over and over again and expecting different results."

He nodded. "Albert Einstein."

"Try something different," she said. "A different way to reach God. Do something you believe is right, loving . . . and do it before you think your way out of it. *Trust* it's right."

[90]

They'd been off the ground for twenty minutes when Owen stepped out of the cockpit into the cabin. "Anything?" he said.

"Not on these flash drives," Jagger said. He was sitting on the bed, opening and closing documents from each of the blue "Chiclets" Owen had found. They were lined up on the desk beside the keyboard, and he pointed at each one as he described their contents: "Every issue of *Popular Mechanics*, *Popular Science*, *Scientific American*, and *Wired* . . . scanned pages of some old-looking journal in a language I can't read . . . topographical maps, I think, of every place on earth . . . and this one—" He pointed at the screen, which displayed a shark the size of a Buick lunging out of the water toward a man on a small boat. "So far, it's nothing but shark photos and videos."

"That's Sebastian. He's a shark groupie."

"I'll set up the Xbox next."

"We have some time, about nine hours to New York. I have to stop in the Azores to refuel. Why don't you catch a little shut-eye?"

Jagger stared at the screen and said, "Because, frankly, I don't know if I'll ever wake up."

"That tired?"

He glared at him. "Not tired."

"I don't understand."

"I think you do." He stood to face Owen in the aisle and pointed at Owen's arm, now covered by the sleeve of a new shirt. "The fireball tattoo."

"It's the burning bush, actually."

"I don't care what it is. You're one of them. No wonder you know so much. With all the talking we did, all the looking at photographs . . ."

He stood and pulled a photo off the wall to fling it across the cabin like a Frisbee. "You didn't think, 'Hey, maybe I should tell him I used to belong to the group that shot his son and kidnapped his wife'? *Used to belong*—I can't even be sure of that."

"I left a long time ago."

"Two thousand years, right? Wow. How am I supposed to know that? What happened to make you leave? Did you tick off Nevaeh? Chase some pretty girl to the other side of the world? Kill an innocent?"

"I met Jesus Christ," Owen said.

"You—" Jagger stopped. "You mean, in *person*?"

Owen smiled. "He said to me, Ὁν εφιλει ο Ιησους.'"

"What does that mean?"

"That he loved me."

Jagger sat on the bed. "Well, sure. I mean, he was Jesus, right?"

"I listened to him, watched him. He was a man of peace and love. You can't know him, truly know him, and go back to what the Tribe is doing."

"But I thought you said they were Christians. Why didn't they turn from their ways?"

"If we claim to have fellowship with him and yet walk in the darkness, we lie and do not live out the truth."

"So they're not? Believers, I mean."

"You believe in him," Owen said. "But do you love him?"

Owen might as well have stuck a knife in his heart, but Jagger got his point: he knew the truth, but couldn't get over his anger.

"Like you, the Tribe keeps a kernel of bitterness in their hearts. It may be small, but it's enough to poison their souls. You went to St. Catherine's thinking the proximity of godly things would soften your heart, dissolve that kernel. In the same way, they kill sinners. They're believers the way a lot of people are believers. They're still trying to figure out what it means, how to align their lives with what they know in their hearts is true."

Jagger shook his head. "You'd think after thirty-five hundred years, they'd figure it out."

"Some know as children, others on their deathbeds. It's up to God when it happens. What's thirty-five hundred years to him?"

"Did he—Jesus—know you were immortal?"

"What do you think?"

"I think if you turned to him, he would have forgiven you, let you die."

"He changed my curse to a blessing. He restored me to the table of the twelve tribes, no longer part of the thirteenth tribe. I know my purpose . . . and when I'll go home."

"You know when you'll die? When?"

He simply smiled, then said, "That's between me and him."

"And what's your purpose—to stop the Tribe?"

"In part. I'm here to help others, to be a light. Same as others who believe."

Jagger gazed at the computer screen. *This is too much.* But then he thought: *Maybe that's what Owen's counting on. He's distracting me, overwhelming me with fantastical, unverifiable details.* He stood again. "That doesn't change your hiding the fact that you are part of them."

"Were."

"How can I trust anything you say, not telling me, keeping it a secret. Makes me wonder why."

"I didn't want to scare you off."

The two faced each other in the jet's narrow, trashy aisle as if in some dark alley.

"Yeah, I know . . . I might try to rescue Beth myself. My thinking right now is that's exactly what I should have done. Couldn't be any worse off. For all I know, you're still one of them. How convenient you showed up at the monastery just when we needed you—with a helicopter even. Pulling me into the café, telling me wild stories . . . then Beth gets kidnapped. I don't know what kind of game this is, I don't know why you chose me, but my boy is fighting for his life with a bullet hole in his back, my wife is in the hands of a death-loving certifiable loony toon, and I gotta ask myself, what's wrong with this picture? Right now, it's you."

"Jagger, listen—"

"Uh-huh, you want me to listen *now*. What else haven't you told me?"

"A lot."

That knocked the fighting words right out of him, Owen being so blunt. More quietly he said, "Like . . . what?"

Owen turned his back on him and started for the cockpit. Jagger grabbed his shoulder. Owen turned around, a pistol in his hand.

Jagger took a step back, raising his arms. "Owen?"

Owen backed away from him, sidestepping in the aisle awkwardly.

Jagger glanced over his shoulder toward the back of the plane, where a thick wooden partition separated the cabin from the bathroom and storage area. Owen was angling his position so a bullet wouldn't jeopardize the integrity of the jet. He *meant* to do it.

"Owen, don't—!"

"I'm sorry," Owen said and shot him.

[91]

Jagger woke on the bed, his right side throbbing as though first kicked by a horse, then stabbed. Pain shot down into his hip and leg, rippled over his rib cage, and jabbed into his shoulder. He couldn't have been out long. Owen was cutting away Jagger's shirt, his hands so red he could have been wearing gloves.

Jagger tried to shove him away. Owen stood, leaned over, and grabbed both shoulders, pushing them against the mattress.

"Believe it or not," he said, "you're going to be all right. The bullet was a through-and-through, just under the ribs, way off to the side. No vital organs."

Jagger turned his head, looking for something to use as a weapon.

Owen gripped his chin and forced his face back to him. He held his palm against Jagger's cheek. "Now this you *must* believe: I'm on your side. I'm your friend."

"You're crazy's what you are," Jagger said, groaning, swinging RoboHand at him. Owen dodged it. He slid back to his knees in the aisle and pressed gauze to Jagger's side.

Jagger gritted his teeth, twisted one way then the other, trying to find a position in which the agony wasn't so great.

"I gave you some painkillers," Owen said. "You should start feeling better soon."

"Feeling better?" He cursed at him. "You shot me. I knew I shouldn't have trusted you."

Owen sponged away the blood around the wound, every stroke like a broken bottle raked across Jagger's side. He dried it and taped gauze over it. "Lean over the other way," he said and dressed the exit wound as well. He walked to the galley and brought back a bottle of water. He lifted Jagger's head and helped him drink. He stood, leaned his rear on the desk, screwed the cap on the bottle, and set it aside. He pulled a key from his breast pocket and unlocked the top, left-hand desk drawer. He stuck his hand in, rustled some papers, but drew nothing out. Crossing his arms, he took a deep breath, let it out, and proceeded to simply watch Jagger.

Jagger squirmed in pain, his legs kicked. He pressed his hand over his eyes. *Oh, Tyler*, he thought. *Did you experience this kind of pain? Worse? I am so, so sorry.*

Gradually he stopped moving. He lay there, hand over his eyes, and breathed, just breathed. He slid his hand off his face and stared at the dirty ceiling. The pain had subsided to a dull ache. He touched the bandages and flinched at an electric bolt that zapped his guts. He rose to his elbows and shifted around to a sitting position, his back against the side of the cabin, leaning a bit on the chest of guns, which was taller than the bed and formed a makeshift headboard. He decided to stay that way awhile, feeling very little pain now.

He squinted at Owen, was aware his own mouth had formed into something you'd expect a snarl to come out of. "You didn't shoot me for nothing," he said. "Tell me everything, and start with your real name. They called you Kieran."

Owen shook his head. "They called *you* Kieran."

"Me? What? Why?"

Owen pulled a paper from the desk drawer and tossed it onto Jagger's lap. Even before he lifted it, Jagger felt the plane dissolve around him. Everything faded away until he was sitting on nothing in a vast void of gray, holding a picture of himself, looking over his shoulder at the camera as he ran away from it. He held a gun in his hand, and smoke billowed up from somewhere to the left of the cameraman, obscuring the top right corner of the shot. He was running across a city street toward a 1970s-era station wagon with faux wood paneling on the sides. Phin stood on the far side, at the driver's door, looking at the source of the smoke, laughing. Nevaeh leaned out the passenger door, gripping the handle, craning her head around to shout at him. Alexa and Jordan watched him from the rear windows.

"Kieran was your name the last thirty years you were with the Tribe," Owen said.

Jagger shook his head and stared at the photo. Elias, Mr. Flamethrower, was running from an alley a block away. Jagger felt dizzy: Elias wasn't actually in the picture. But he was certain Elias was there, making his way back to the car after watching the rear exits.

"No," he said. "It can't be."

"Do you want the catalog of images? Artists loved you, especially during the Classical period, Ancient Greece. Handsome, manly. They thought you cut a perfect Poseidon or Zeus. There's a bronze sculpture in the Athens National Archaeological Museum—you'd think you were looking in the mirror."

"But—" Jagger didn't know where to start asking questions. Hundreds presented themselves, each flashing into his mind before another pushed it away.

"That photograph was taken at a Tribe bombing of the Oakland headquarters of the Symbionese Liberation Army in 1974. A young child was killed, and you left the Tribe shortly after. I tried to recruit you to help me stop the Tribe's activities, but you said you needed to find who you were outside of the Tribe first. You traveled, attended various universities, and eventually wound up at the University of Virginia, where you met Beth and fell head over heels. Said you wanted a normal life and asked me not to contact you again."

"No . . . I remember my childhood, my parents . . ."

"You remember the story you made up after you met Beth."

"I can *see* them . . . in my mind . . . I remember their voices."

"You watched videos, Jag. Movies of normal American families. Then movies about kids who've lost their parents, wound up in foster homes. You took scenes from those movies and fabricated the life you wish you had lived, so your new life with Beth could be as normal as possible."

Jagger remembered a time in college, shortly after meeting Beth, when he watched movie after movie, taking notes while he did. A part of him said it was for a class, Introduction to Cinema, something like that. But was it research for a different purpose . . . to *deceive* the one he loved?

He looked at the photo in his hand, and it seemed to become animated. He saw the kids waving . . . himself—climbing into the backseat, sliding across to make room for Elias, who slammed the door and smiled at him . . . the car squealing away from the curb, everyone laughing . . .

[92]

"My life," Jagger said. "It's all been a lie?"

"Not your time with Beth, with Tyler . . . that's all real. You did it for her. You loved her so much, you wanted so badly to be normal, to live a normal life with her, you created a new past, one she would accept."

Jagger's heart ached. "I . . . can't believe I would have lied to her." He cast a pained expression at Owen. "And for so many years . . . about something so big."

"If it's any consolation, you lied to yourself first. You forced yourself to believe the past you constructed and blocked out your history before that. After you left the Tribe, you and I"—he smiled a little—"we would meet about once a year, old friends catching up. I caught up with you at UVA. You told me what was going on. You asked me not to contact you again."

"Did you think it would work?"

"I knew there was a going to be a time when it would all unravel, when you'd have to tell her the truth." He looked around the cabin, then back at Jagger. "You were so determined. You didn't want to just not talk about the previous thirty-five hundred years—you *truly* wanted to forget them, mentally make it as though they never were. You almost convinced me you could do it. I often thought about you, wondered if you'd succeeded. I even imagined you becoming shocked that you weren't aging." He grinned. "You'd visit all these doctors, and everyone would be puzzled. Then I thought, what if you *did* age? What if you wanted it so much that God let you forget, and your forgetting was symbolic of *his* forgetting and he released you of your immortality? Wouldn't that be something? I prayed that for you."

"But . . ." Jagger looked at his prosthetic arm. "The tattoo."

Owen nodded. "The one thing you couldn't leave behind. I asked you about that. Wouldn't that, if nothing else, keep reminding you of your past, keep you anchored to it?"

"What did I say?"

"You had a story for that too, that it was something you and a close buddy got upon graduation from high school. When he died in a car accident, the tattoo became a painful memory. You were going to ask Beth never to speak of it."

"Why don't I remember having it, even during my time with her?"

"Funny thing, what happened to you in that crash. It seems that your mind shattered—the memory part of it, anyway. Came back together instantly, so it couldn't be classified as amnesia."

"They call it fragmentation."

Owen's head bobbed up and down slowly. "I got hold of your medical records. Of course they don't tell the whole story, but they gave me a leaping-off point for research, which helped me come to some theories. I think your subconscious shattered like glass, and when you put it back together, you selected only the shards you wanted, only the pleasurable ones. Do you have any bad memories of the ten years prior to the crash?"

Jagger thought about it and came up with family picnics, birthdays, cozy gatherings on the couch together. Recently Beth had shown him a picture of a seven-year-old Tyler with a cast on his arm and told him how Tyler had wailed, rushing into the house after falling out of a tree. Apparently Jagger had swooped him up and rushed him to the hospital . . . but he couldn't recall the event at all.

"No."

"And since you were trying so hard to forget your past before Beth, you certainly wouldn't pick up any of those shards . . . including the tattoo."

"But I did pick up some *plastic* shards, some false memories," Jagger said. "And I can't tell the difference between those and real ones."

"It's not unheard of," Owen said. "In fact, there are dozens of documented cases a year in which trauma victims completely erase bad memories. Sometimes there are just blank spots in their memory, but who remembers what they don't remember?" He smiled. "Someone has to tell them what's missing, or there's evidence of it, a scar or a gravestone. Other times, those gaps are filled in with false memories, something they've seen on TV, or even someone else's memories they heard about." He tapped his temple. "Crazy thing, the mind."

Jagger gripped his forehead. He didn't know if losing his bad memories—3,500 years' worth—was evidence that he possessed absolutely no control over his life, as much as he liked to believe he did, or that he possessed ultimate control.

"I'll also share this suspicion with you," Owen said. "Complete hypothesis, but I think it's a pretty good one. The crash damaged your parahippocampal gyrus, which shattered your memories, right?"

"It didn't show damage."

"Not by the time they got around to checking. In normal people it heals slowly, giving their minds time to organize their memories correctly, more or less. Yours healed quickly, grabbing whatever memories it could, most likely the ones at the front of your conscious-ness—your life with Beth and the fabrications you've spent the last decade convincing yourself were real. It never had time to reach the ones you pushed deep down, all those memories you wanted to forget. Maybe it snagged a few, but you wouldn't know what they were all about, out of context, fragmented."

Jagger thought of his vivid "confabulated" memories—sailing on a pirate's ship, battling with shield and sword—and nodded. His heart felt sore, as though gremlins had pounded on it with bats. Immortality. Deceiving his family. Beth kidnapped. Tyler shot. But what kept roll-ing back to the front of his consciousness was the thought of watching Beth grow old and die, while he stayed just the way he was. Did he ever really think he could stand that? And Tyler too?

He said, "Tyler . . . is he . . . mortal?"

"Other children of Tribe members have been. They exhibited signs of inheriting some of our traits: they tend to lead long lives, to a hundred, hundred and five, and heal faster than normal, but not anything like an immortal. That aspect is probably what saved his life the other day. It was a devastating wound, especially for someone so small."

At least there's that, Jagger thought. As devastated as he was about this news, he'd gladly accept it if it meant saving Tyler's life.

He shifted on the bed and felt a pang flare up in his side, but it was nothing. More like a stitch from running than a gunshot wound: the painkillers, or a side effect of immortality? He thought of Phin, how he'd healed so quickly from being shot in the face.

Something confused him. "How . . ." He started again. "Why didn't the doctors notice anything unusual about the way I healed after the crash?"

"You'd passed out," Owen said. "Loss of blood, pain. Where did you wake up?"

"In the hospital."

Owen kept looking at him.

Jagger remembered: "In a private room, a *suite* of rooms. The drunk's insurance company . . ."

Owen was shaking his head.

"That was you?"

"The monks arranged it. The hospital staff thought you had an eccentric rich uncle."

"Monks? St. Cath's monks?" He hadn't met Gheronda or any of the monks until he took the job in Egypt.

"They help us when they can. How do you think Dr. Hoffmann came to contact you for the position?"

"He told me a former client referred him."

Owen shook his head. "Gheronda. At my request. We take care of our own." His eyes lowered to the prosthetic arm, which Jagger was absently rubbing through his shirtsleeve. "Unfortunately, by the time the Helpers arrived at the hospital, the OR team had already amputated your arm. I understand it was pulverized, so it may not have survived anyway. I mean, I've seen immortals survive horrendous inflictions: burning, impaling, crucifixion. I myself got thrown into boiling oil."

"Ow." Jagger really didn't know what else to say.

"Serious *ow*. But pulverization? I don't know."

"You said helpers. You mean the monks?"

"The doctors and nurses who tended to you after your initial surgery, they were ours, five of maybe a dozen mortals—not counting the Keepers, the monks—who know about us."

"They never let on."

"No, they wouldn't have. When you told me what you were doing to create a new life with Beth, you asked me to spread the word: no contact from anyone. You didn't want the past to crash your party."

"And they agreed?"

"I passed your request on to the monks. They're sort of a clearinghouse of immortal communications. Not a lot of trust among us."

"You're trying to kill them."

Owen shrugged. "Anyway, the Tribe sent their acquiescence with a single word: 'Who?' When you left the Tribe, you became dead to them anyway. They're very good at making things dead, even figuratively."

We were going to leave you alone, Phin had said, the scarcest of hints, in no way an acknowledgment.

"Even now," Jagger said, "at the monastery and in the catacombs—they didn't say anything."

"Dead isn't dead if you keep popping up. As far as they're concerned, you're just another guy. Besides, I think it's crossed their minds, too, what if you're onto something? Lose your past and find a new future. They've tried everything else." He pushed himself off the desk and bent backward, cracking his spine. "But don't think they won't cut your head off if they get a chance."

Jagger didn't think his heart could ache any further, but he thought of Beth and it did. She was with them, the Tribe, killers who knew who . . . *what* he was. That seemed like more of a reason to hurt her. They were all about revenge—what they called justice. He'd left them, something they obviously don't respond well to. Would they hurt her just to hurt him?

He leaned forward, said, "We have to get Beth away from them."

"We're already doing everything we can, as fast as we can. I want her back in your arms as much as you do."

Jagger sighed. "That's not possible."

Owen started for the cockpit, but Jagger stopped him.

"Why did you tell me? Why now?"

"Because I need your help, as I said in the café. I really do. I need you to trust me, so I'm laying it all out, everything I know."

Jagger bent sideways, felt the tug of the tape on his skin, but no real pain. "And you shot me because . . . ?"

"How's the wound?"

Jagger peeled the tape off one side and flipped the gauze over. The bleeding had stopped, and pink new skin formed a thin ring around the hole. A thread of skin stretched across it.

"Pictures or not," Owen said, "would you have believed me any other way?"

[93]

After Owen stopped in the Azores to refuel, Jagger felt well enough to contribute to their goal of finding the Tribe. Now he sat in front of Owen's computer monitor, which he'd connected to the Xbox. He found a set-up screen that displayed a slowly rotating unmanned aerial vehicle—a drone. Specifically, an MQ9-Reaper. It showed armaments of four Hellfire II air-to-ground missiles and a M134 Gatling-style machine gun—when Jagger moved the cursor over it, a little box popped up: *Known as the Minigun, this multi-barrel heavy machine gun fires 4,000 7.62 mm rounds per minute.*

Under the dominant image of a single Reaper was a row of smaller Reapers, numbered 1 through 12. A bracket under the first six said *Pilot A*, and under the next six *Pilot B*.

Jagger turned, feeling a pain under his ribs, like a pencil jab from a classmate who'd miscalculated his thrust. "Owen," he called, "you better check this out."

Owen exited the cockpit and sat next to him. "Oh no."

"At least they're not nuclear," Jagger said.

"Tell that to the people they kill."

Jagger clicked an onscreen Start button, and five new buttons appeared:

Take Control
Take Off
Approach
Attack
Land

Clicking Take Control divided the screen into six panels, each showing the nose of a drone and a runway ahead of it. Two lights at the bottom of each panel: red and green. In quick succession, the red lights clicked off and the green ones clicked on.

"We need to know what their target is," Owen said.

Jagger selected Take Off and realized he controlled only one of the drones. And even that one was nearly too much to handle. After some wild flying and near misses with the ground he got the drone under control and began buzzing through the air over a military base.

"That's where they're getting them from," Owen said. "Try to find out where they're sending them."

The heads-up display showed a radar in the bottom left corner, four missiles and a Minigun in the upper right, a dimmed AP in the lower right.

"That's autopilot," Owen said. "Try to activate it."

Jagger began pushing buttons on the controller. A missile streaked out and struck a cinderblock building, turning it into rubble. The Minigun rattled, and tracer bullets stitched a line from the bottom of the screen to the ground, where dirt flew up until it hit a Jeep, which exploded. Finally the AP turned yellow. The drone immediately banked left and traveled over desert terrain, dirt roads and two-lane roads, a larger highway . . . then a city rose up from the horizon. Closer, closer. The drone flew over houses, industrial buildings, and banked to streak over a major thoroughfare. Lights blinking everywhere, despite the daylight setting. Crowded streets. Mobs of pedestrians. The Eiffel Tower approached on the right.

"What the . . . ?" Jagger said.

But it didn't look right: too small, standing among buildings not in a park. The Statue of Liberty came into view . . . a big black Pyramid . . .

"Las Vegas," Owen said.

"We have to tell someone."

"Who? They wouldn't believe us."

"Describe the base and the drone. Someone will know where that is. Maybe there's something happening soon with the drones, an air show or field test. Owen, we have to warn someone."

He nodded. "I'll make a few calls." He headed for the cockpit. "We'll have to stop for fuel again. Wouldn't you know it'd be three-quarters across the country."

"I don't think it matters. Reapers are remotely piloted through satellite uplinks. They could be anywhere in the world."

"But they're not. We know they left Paris for the States. Still, the most—and least—we can do is get to that base and warn them. Maybe they can batten down their little killing machines for a while until we find *our* little killing machines."

On the screen, the Reaper let loose a barrage of missiles into the grand façade of the Bellagio Hotel.

[94]

Robert McManus sat at his dining-table-sized desk in his Pentagon office, scrolling through reports on his computer monitor. A knock came from the door, and one of his assistants entered.

"Sir, you asked that any communication about the Reaper II program come directly to you."

McManus felt his scalp tighten. "Yes."

"A man on the phone. He won't give his name, and DIA is trying to track the call, but it appears to be encrypted through multiple satellites."

"What about him?" McManus demanded.

"He claims to have information about the Thor drone program, specifically a terrorist plot to—"

"Put him through. Now. Stop the trace, delete any recordings and records of the call."

"Sir?"

"This is umbra level, Colonel," he said, as if speaking to a child.

"Yes, sir."

McManus smoothed his hair and looked out his window at a massive parking lot and the Potomac River beyond. Ten seconds passed before his phone chimed. He picked up the receiver and pushed a flashing red button.

"Who is this?"

"Call me Ishmael."

"Cute. Why are you calling?"

As the caller spoke, McManus thought he recognized the voice. Perhaps it wasn't such a good idea to cancel the trace. He was thinking about reinitiating it when the caller hung up.

X I I I

At thirteen, Nicole Richmond was painfully aware of her developing body and could have killed herself for letting her mother pack for their trip. Why would the woman think she would wear the new bikini swimsuit in Las Vegas when she wouldn't even wear it at the Y back home?

"Honey," Mom said from the lounge chair beside her, "look around. Everyone's wearing them."

Nicole pulled the white terrycloth towel with the Bellagio's logo embroidered on it tighter around her and turned her shoulder to her mother. "I don't care."

"Next year you'll be begging us to let you go swimming in it." Conspiratorially, her mother whispered, "Let your father get used to it now, before you fill out too much."

"*Mom!*" It was bad enough having braces, but *this* too?

Water splashed over her, cold finger-jabs all over. She flashed a scowl at her twin brother, laughing as he clung to the edge of the pool.

"Mom, Jason's splashing me."

"Jason," Mom said, not looking away from her magazine.

He splashed again, and she picked up a folded towel and threw it at him.

"Aha," he yelled, pulling it into the water. "Ammo."

"Don't you dare," Nicole said. She hated this trip. Who took their kids to Las Vegas anyway?

Jason hefted the soaked towel, preparing to hurl it at her.

"Jason, put that down." Their father strolled past him to sit on the lounge chair on the other side of Nicole from Mom. He was wearing a Hawaiian shirt and Bermuda shorts—a nice change from his uniform of suit and tie, but his legs were white enough to blind her. He was looking at a guide book. "Let's go, guys. Lots to see."

"Like what?" Nicole said. "Strippers and a bunch of old guys playing cards?"

"Strippers!" Jason chimed from the pool.

"There's the Adventuredome . . . King Tut's Tomb . . ." He flipped a page. "The Tournament of Kings show."

"I want to go to M&M's World," Jason said.

"You're going to get zits," Nicole told him.

"I don't get zits," he said with a *nah-nah* face. "You do."

It was true and it was unfair.

"You don't need the chocolate, honey," her mother said, and that settled it.

"Do they have pink ones?" she said.

"Every color you can imagine," Dad said. "Whattaya say?" She nodded, and he stood and kissed the top of her head. "Okay, everyone! Get dressed. It's going to be a great day."

The tone of his voice, the sun glowing down on her—Nicole almost believed him.

X I I I

Ben watched Toby and Phin ready themselves in front of the twin consoles in their motorhome-cum-control center. Pieces of the drone-control stations had been constructed at different sites around the country, using experts McManus had provided, then shipped to a private hangar near Vegas's McCarran International Airport, where they'd been assembled. Upon their arrival, Ben had driven the big Gulf Stream RV out to its current location, among the rugged foothills of the Toiyable mountain range between Creech Air Force Base and Las Vegas. The others had followed in an SUV.

Sebastian leaned between Toby and Phin, adjusting the monitors' brightness and contrast. At the moment, they displayed only test patterns, but soon they would show the culmination of months of hard work.

Ben's phone beeped out a Morse code–like pattern, and he knew instantly who was calling. He dug the phone out of a satchel on a chair by the door and left the building, stepping from cool conditioned air to the dry heat of the desert. He went down the RV's three retractable steps and walked up a small rise. Only then did he push the answer button.

"Robert, how are you?"

"Not happy, Ben. I just received a call from someone who knows what you're doing out there. You weren't to tell anyone about me, not even other members of the Tribe."

"I didn't." Ben continued up the rise and stopped at the crest. "How much does this caller know?"

"Las Vegas. Drones. Soon. I don't need to tell you, that's an awful lot."

"Relax. We're online here. In a matter of hours it'll all be over."

He looked down the other side of the hill and frowned. Nevaeh was coming up the hill from their SUV, pulling Beth by her shirt. Beth's hands were bound behind her. Nevaeh's insistence on bringing Kieran's wife along infuriated him and was probably the root cause of the call he was now negotiating. It jeopardized the mission—and not just here on earth.

"Do you know who this person is who called me?"

"I have an idea."

Pause. "Are you going to tell me?"

"Let me look into it first," Ben said. "No sense pointing fingers at innocent people."

"I assume this matter is resolved, not anything I have to worry about?"

"That's right."

McManus disconnected.

Ben watched Nevaeh tugging on Beth and shook his head.

X I I I

McManus hung up and stared at the phone for a long time. This thing had better not blow back on him. He'd worked too long and too hard to reach his current position to throw it away on one of Ben's passion projects. But it was a good one, the sort of thing he'd dreamed about facilitating as he moved from office to office, ever closer to the one that mattered, and he was only a few years away from reaching it. Next administration, for sure. However, now that he was deputy secretary of defense, he wondered if that was the better position than the top dog's: all the power, a fraction of the visibility. He'd have to weigh his next moves carefully.

He rose from his desk, eyeing the phone as though it was not a line to Ben, but Ben himself. As ambitious and impacting as Ben's project was, McManus believed he could do so much more. Not small city stuff, but Ben-type projects on a global scale. He went into his private bathroom and shut the door. He turned on the water and rolled up his sleeves. Three splashes of cold water on his face made him feel better, more clear-minded. He dried his face, hands, arms, slowing as he rubbed the golden tattoo on the inside of his forearm.

[95]

Ben stepped and skidded down the hill to their rented SUV, glad now that he'd made Alexa and Jordan stay in the jet at the airport: he didn't want their eyes on him right now, and he didn't want to see them get hurt. He opened the back hatch and rummaged through the bags and boxes until he found what he was looking for.

Back up the hill and down the other side to the motorhome. Beth was sitting on the stairs, her arm raised to a railing where Nevaeh had handcuffed her. Ben squatted in front of her. "Nevaeh inside?"

Beth nodded.

Ben showed her the phone he'd taken from the SUV. "This is yours, isn't it?"

She looked and said, "Yeah." Tentative.

"I understand your husband called you from Owen's satphone."

"I was in Tyler's hospital room, talking with Jagger when Nevaeh grabbed me."

He held out the phone to her. "Show me."

Beth took the phone, punched in her security code, and went to the recent calls list. She handed it back. "It's the top number."

Ben looked. "Thank you." He stood and stuck his hand in his pants pocket. He held his fist out to Beth, who gave him a puzzled expression and opened her hand. He dropped a key into it. "For your handcuffs," he said. "Don't use it now. She'll just catch you and bring you back. You'll know when it's time."

She stared at him, those intense eyes. "Thank you," she whispered.

Looking at the phone, he turned and started walking into the desert, with the scrub oak and yucca and sand. He stopped and half turned to look at her.

He smiled and said, "I'm not *thinking.*"

[96]

Somewhere under the papers on the desk, Owen's satphone rang.

"Phone!" Jagger called, scanning the mess on either side of the monitor. "Should I answer it?"

"No," Owen said. He rolled out of the pilot's seat and, hunched over, walked down the aisle. Jagger located the phone and handed it to him.

"Yes?" he said. He listened, said yes a few more times, then: "Hold on, hold on." He patted his pocket, opened the desk's center drawer, forcing Jagger to lean back, and took out a pen. He scribbled on the back of a photo. "Why are you doing this?" More listening. "God bless you."

He pushed the disconnect button and set the phone down on a pile of papers, keeping his hand on it while he thought. He turned to Jagger.

"I know where the Tribe's control center is."

[97]

From the control tower at Creech Air Force Base, thirty-five miles northwest of Las Vegas, Lt. Col. Arnold Jackson watched the armaments crew wheel the empty missile carts away from the fleet of drones on the tarmac and into a hangar. He walked along a row of cubicles, seeing that every primary screen within displayed the nose of a drone and the runway that lay before it. Other screens showed side and rear views, maps, and aircraft stats, such as fuel level, altitude, GPS coordinates, and weapons remaining onboard. Two men manned each console, a pilot and his sensor operator who ran the cameras and deployed the weapons.

Col. Jackson was heading back to the observation windows when the commotion started behind him. Twenty-four voices rose in confusion and alarm. From where he stopped and turned he could see into a half-dozen cubicles, and he watched each screen blink off, going black on down the row. He started for the consoles—"What happened?"—then froze again when he heard the sound of a dozen drone engines power up. He ran to the windows.

The drones were already moving, gaining speed as they ate the runway. Two of them lifted off the ground . . . three more . . . the remaining seven. At least half the personnel from the cubicles ran toward the windows, their shiny black shoes clicking on linoleum tile like chattering monkeys.

Col. Jackson pointed and yelled at his flight commander, sitting at a nearby console. "Scramble the jets! Scramble now!"

He watched the drones climb steeply, begin to bank away. Twelve fully armed hunter-killer Reapers taking flight . . . no one in his command at the controls.

X I I I

"Yeah, baby!" Phin said and laughed.

Toby hooted, concentrating on his monitor. Six panels showed six different views of the sky. He toggled through the drones under his control, turning the autopilot on as he did. The clouds swept past, off each of the panels as the drones leveled out at a mere 2,000 feet. At different times, the tallest of the buildings in the distance slid to the center of each panel and rolled closer.

[98]

Nevaeh looked from Toby's screen to Phin's and back to Toby's. She grinned at Sebastian, standing near her, mirroring her crazy smile. He raised his palm for a high five. She ignored it and looked around. "Where's Ben?"

Sebastian shrugged.

Nevaeh pushed through the door and stood on the stoop. There he was: way out in the desert, kneeling. *Praying*, she thought. *Well, it's working.*

"Ben! Ben! They have control! The drones are in the air!"

He didn't stir, and she went down the stairs, brushing past Beth. She jogged toward Ben, calling. Twenty feet away, she slowed to a walk. "Didn't you hear me?"

No movement. Deep in prayer. He got that way sometimes, almost in a trance as he talked—and more important, listened—to God. But now was not the time. Their first Agag in more than a century, and he was missing it.

"Ben." She walked around him. His eyes were open, an unseeing gaze. She whispered, "Ben?"

This was no prayer, no trance.

She touched his shoulder, and slowly he tilted and fell sideways to the ground, his face in the dirt. The one eye she could still see . . . staring.

Nevaeh dropped to her knees and covered her face. Tears welled out of her eyes, pooled where her palms pushed into her cheeks. He was gone, God had taken him. Thoughts and emotions rose and popped into her mind like balloons.

My friend . . . my enemy . . . my comrade in arms . . . for so many years!

Why him? Why not me?

What did he do? What did he say?

Not dead . . . he can't be . . . yes, just a trance!

Dirt was sticking to his eye.

Dead! He beat me to it!

She shuffled closer on her knees and grabbed his face in her hands, lifted it toward her. She gazed into his eyes.

"What do you see, Ben? Show me. Please!"

She looked for heaven in his eyes, but saw only the dark brown irises she knew so well, lines fanning out from the pupils like lost suns. She lowered his head.

He clutched something in his hand, held close to his chest. She pried it away from him. A cell phone. The woman's cell phone.

She looked past Ben's body, saw Beth staring from the Gulf Stream's steps.

She rose and yelled, "What did you do?" She stepped over Ben's corpse . . . his *corpse*! "What did you do?"

From its sheath at her hip she withdrew her dagger, focused on Beth—rising to her feet now, tugging on the handcuffs, turning toward the door but unable to reach it.

Only vaguely aware of the sound of an approaching jet overhead, Nevaeh ran toward Beth.

[99]

Owen brought the jet low over the motorhome.

"There's Beth!" Jagger said, rising up from the copilot seat to look out the window. He tried to push away the pain that was coming back into his side, throbbing again. He touched it, saw bloody fingers.

Never mind that.

Beth!

"Something's wrong," he said. "I think she's stuck there, hand-cuffed."

"Human shield," Owen said.

"Go back around and climb higher."

"What are you thinking?"

Jagger climbed over the seat, stumbled back, and grabbed Owen's shoulder. "Do you have a parachute?"

X I I I

The white business jet buzzed the RV, right over Beth, but she was watching Nevaeh. The woman gripped a big knife or short sword, and she was running for her. Beth fumbled with the key, tried to get it slipped into the cuff's keyhole.

Nevaeh was yelling now, some kind of maniacal warrior bellow. Running. Bellowing. Closer.

The key slipped in, and she turned it. The cuff opened. Beth clambered off the steps, turned, and made her feet churn.

X I I I

"Beth got free," Owen yelled from the cockpit.

Standing in front of the door, Jagger cinched the last strap of a parachute tight around him. He backed up until he could see Owen in the pilot's seat. "I'm still jumping," he said.

"What are you waiting for? Nevaeh's chasing her." He craned his head around to look at Jagger. "You've done this before," he said. "You and I skydived in Taupo, New Zealand, 1985. Do you remember?"

"I wish I did," Jagger said. "But I do remember parachuting in the army. I'll be fine." He stepped toward the door.

"Wait, wait!" Owen said. Something in his face defied the chaotic situation they were in. "My real name isn't Owen."

"I didn't think it was." Any more than *his* given name was Jagger or Kieran. He may never know who he really was, and that was fine with him.

Owen pulled something out of a pocket on the side of his chair. "My journal," he said. "I think you'll find something in there you can use." He tossed him the small book. "Page fifty-two, when you get a chance."

Jagger smiled and slipped it into a pocket. "Tell me in person when all this is over. Thank you, for everything."

"You too."

Jagger pushed the latch down, expecting the door to fly away. It didn't even budge. He rammed his shoulder into it. Nothing.

"Don't try to open it the normal way," Owen called. "See the emergency release above it?"

It was a fat red button under glass, mounted in a red housing flush with the cabin wall. *Now you tell me.*

"Hold on a sec," Owen said. "I'm almost in position."

Jagger used his hook to break the glass. RoboHand kept moving, depressing the button. With the sound of an explosion, the door disappeared, whipped away by the wind.

Jagger went with it.

X I I I

Beth hurdled over boulders and yucca, barreling away from the motorhome, away from Nevaeh. She wondered if she should take a stand, just turn, grab a rock, and take on Cruella De Vil. She could do it, go crazy and pound the tar out of the woman who shot her son, kidnapped her, and was now attacking a million innocent people. Then again, Nevaeh was a warrior: strong, skilled, and armed. Beth decided she wanted to kiss her husband again and hold her son more than she wanted to put a crazy immortal in her place, and she angled for a gap in the small rolling hills.

The jet was back, swooping down toward her, and something fell from it—a person, falling fast. Three seconds later a chute snaked out behind him, caught the wind, and opened into a square blue canopy. The person snapped up at the end of long lines under the canopy. He—she assumed he, but she couldn't tell—settled, swinging a bit, and drifted down.

She glanced over her shoulder. Nevaeh was closing in, moving fast, pumping her arms—at the end of one of them, the blade.

The parachutist appeared to be heading for the other side of one of the hills ahead of Beth, then the chute dipped on one side, and he drifted toward the top of the hill.

Beth beelined it for him.

[100]

They were headed out of the store with Nicole staring into her tall cellophane cone of M&M's when Jason shoved her from behind. She stumbled into an old lady coming in, and her M&M's went flying. She didn't know whether to grab the lady's arm or try to catch the candy, so she did neither.

The lady braced herself against the door and flashed Nicole a nasty look that must have taken her years of practicing in the mirror to perfect.

"I'm so sorry!" Nicole said. She turned and slapped at Jason's bag of candy, really meaning to knock it out of his hands, but he turned it away from her. "Half my M&M's are on the ground, jerkwad!"

They continued through the glass doors and onto the sidewalk, where a thousand shoes were stomping her pink candies into the concrete.

She was about to punch her brother when he gave her a look that almost always defused her anger. "I'm sorry," he said. "I didn't know you were going to fly like that." He grinned despite himself. "Here." He held his bag out to her.

"I didn't want black and red," she said quietly, but reached in for a handful.

Having stopped to discuss a six-foot M&M with arms and legs and eyes, Mom and Dad finally came out of the store. "Nicole, is that your candy all over the ground?" Mom said. "You really need to be more careful, honey."

"See what's next door, guys?" Dad said. "GameWorks. Look, Jason. It's got a seventy-five-foot climbing wall."

Nicole looked at Jason to catch his reaction; he loved climbing walls.

But her brother wasn't paying attention. His eyes were transfixed on something in the sky, and she turned to see what was so fascinating.

Birds, ten or twelve of them. No, not birds: these things looked like small planes or big missiles, sleek and black and turning as one to fly down the street.

"Dad," Jason said behind her, then she saw his arm stretching over her shoulder to point. "What are those?"

"What are what? Oh. I . . ." His voice trailed off.

As they approached, the things started to drift apart from the pack, some staying high, others swooping lower and lower. One was flying right at them.

Nicole tried to step back, but collided with Jason.

She saw now that they were planes, with what looked like bombs lined up on their underside. Three of them screamed past, forty feet over the roofs of cars in the street. Flashes of fire erupted from either side of the tip of the mini-plane heading for them.

Ga-ga-ga-ga-ga-ga-ga! Fast, like someone slamming hammers on a steel drum over and over.

The three-story plastic display over the store's entrance—three M&M characters pouring out a bag of candies—shattered.

Mom screamed, and Dad spread his arms and heaved into them, pushing them into the street, away from the falling shards of plastic, coming down like huge guillotines and icicles.

"Come on!" Dad said, grabbing Jason's hand and tugging him into the street, where cars screeched to a stop and swerved into one another. But Mom threw her arms around Nicole and spun her back toward the store.

A man on the sidewalk dodged a windshield-sized piece of falling sign and grabbed the store's door handle. The green-tinted glass that spanned the storefront shattered, and big bloody holes appeared on the man's back. He tumbled to the concrete, as the windows seemed to turn into raindrops and fall with him. People in the store were falling too.

Nicole and her mom turned back toward the street. Dad and

Jason were halfway across when a car five cars away exploded. It flipped up, tumbling in the air. A millisecond later the car in front of it exploded as well . . . and the one in front of that . . . It was as if a missile had struck the first car and was piercing all of them in a row like a barbecue skewer. Fire and metal, glass and smoke shot up and rolled toward Dad and Jason like a boiling wave.

Mom was screaming, her voice joining the din of destruction and terror. Nicole's mouth was open, but fear had its icy talon on her throat, sealing it closed.

Dad turned and rushed back toward them, pushing Jason ahead. Smoke roiled at his back and something hulking rose high behind him. Nicole's eyes stretched wide as she recognized a taxi—off the ground and perfectly vertical—flipping, arching toward her dad and brother.

"Daddy!" she managed to scream. "Jason!"

Dad looked over his shoulder as the taxi dropped toward him. At the last moment, he shoved his son. Jason seemed to dive, as though pushing off a starting block at a swimming meet. He hit the ground hard and slid.

The taxi came down on Dad. He was there, then the taxi was there.

As Nicole's lungs pulled in more air than they had ever before demanded, Jason began to scream.

Then her own screams came, and they would not stop.

X I I I

"First strike!" Phin yelled, pumping his fist in the air.

On his monitor, one of the six panels showed churning smoke, then instantly, blue skies, clouds.

"Shut up," Toby said, narrowing his eyes at his own screen. He clicked a few buttons and pushed forward on a thumb control. Three drones dived toward the traffic below.

"Buildings, please, gentlemen," Sebastian said behind them. "We have only so many missiles. Let's make them count."

[101]

Descending, Jagger saw Beth running toward him. She had just started up the hill, Nevaeh close behind. He approached the crest of the hill at sixteen feet per second. Leave it to Owen to have the best parachute available—a cruciform T-11, used by the army. The square canopy made the chute highly maneuverable and decreased the descent speed, allowing for softer landings.

Or so claimed the experts.

Fifteen feet off the ground, Jagger pulled down on the toggles, tucking in the edges of the canopy and further slowing his fall. His feet touched down on sand and rocks, twisted out from under him, and he tumbled, rolling toward the slope up which Beth was frantically scrambling. The wind, stronger than he expected, caught the chute and dragged him backward, over the crest, and down the other side. Jagger grabbed at the lines and yanked, pulling the canopy in. He found the cut-away handle and pulled it. A group of lines on his right side snapped back and away; the ones on the left snagged RoboHand, keeping the canopy anchored to him. Fighting its lopsided tug, he made his way back up the hill.

By the time he reached the top he had the lines and canopy reeled in. Beth rose up in front of him and threw her arms around him. For a moment he thought he felt her heart beating against his chest, his own heart responding, together coming into synch.

"Jagger!"

He'd never wanted to kiss her so badly. Below them, sunlight glinted on metal, and he spun her around as Nevaeh's blade flashed forward. It sliced into his calf, and he fought to stay up. He pushed Beth away, forcing her to stumble down the incline, away from Nevaeh.

He kicked at his attacker, striking her arm. She reeled back, seemed about to lose her footing on the steep slope, and knelt to stabilize herself. The parachute canopy fluttered on the ground like a giant beached jellyfish, its tentacles stretching to ensnare his fake arm. He yanked them free and tossed them on the ground.

Slicing at his legs, forcing him back, Nevaeh scrambled onto the crest. Jagger reached into his back pocket and withdrew the Taurus Judge .45. He swung it around and forward, and while it was still moving, Nevaeh's foot collided with it. It flew out of Jagger's hand. Nevaeh completed her roundhouse kick by spinning, then stopping in a crouched, ready-for-more position. She pointed her blade at him. He recognized it without knowing how: favored in medieval India, it was a *suwaiya*, whose H-shaped handle made the two-foot blade appear to extend from her knuckles and was nearly impossible to disarm.

She smiled up at him. "Jagger. The name suits you, all jagged and broken." She lunged, spearing the blade at his face. He parried it with RoboHand. The different metals *chinged* as sharply as a gunshot. She pulled it back and thrust it at his chest. He lowered his arm, then brought it up, clamping the hooks over the blade. She twisted her wrist, forcing the blade to turn, opening the hooks. She plucked it free and thrust again. But it was a feint: his parrying arm swung past the tip, rotating his body a quarter turn away from her.

She lifted the suwaiya and swung it down. The weapon sliced over his shoulder blade, producing a burning pain as if from the strike of a whip and severing one of the two nylon straps holding his prosthesis in place. He felt his fake arm loosen from the stub, held now only by the second strap. One of the cables that allowed his shoulder and back muscles to operate the prehensor also snapped, paralyzing RoboHand into an inanimate hook.

Nevaeh raised the blade high to facilitate a powerful downward strike. Hunched over, Jagger lifted his useless arm over his head, hoping the blade wouldn't push past it to his body. He executed the only offensive move he could think of: he leaped under the suwaiya and tackled her.

She landed hard on her back, Jagger's full weight pinning her. The parachute canopy billowed and flapped a few feet away. She punched him in the temple, and he grabbed her wrist with his real hand. From the other side, the sword swung toward him. He shoved her arm to the ground with his fake one. The prosthesis jarred up, flopped down, and rested on top of her arm like a length of firewood.

Her grin showed that she realized what had happened. Her hand and the sword it wielded propelled from the dirt, pushing the fake arm ahead of it as though it didn't exist. Jagger released her left wrist and twisted to reach her right one, knowing it was pointless, knowing the sword would reach him before he could stop it.

The point of the blade stopped six inches from his face, jerked three inches back, and remained there, shaking. Jagger saw two hands gripping Nevaeh's wrist and followed the arms up to Beth's face, straining with effort, teeth bared under furled lips. She crouched beside the two fighters, pulling at Nevaeh's arm, which strained to plunge forward and drive the suwaiya into Jagger.

Instead of diving away, Jagger rolled under the blade and onto Nevaeh's arm. Nevaeh rolled with him, punching his rib cage. Beth maintained her grip on Nevaeh's wrist and pounded the woman's hand against the ground. But Jagger knew there was no forcing the weapon out of her fist.

Nevaeh stopped punching him. Her hand went to a pocket on her thigh, her fingers lifting the flap, finding their way inside.

The canopy billowed up and settled over them, turning the light the color of pool water and blocking Jagger's view of Nevaeh's hand. She had to be reaching for another weapon, a gun or knife. He pushed off her arm and launched for the place he believed her other hand was, the pocket, the unknown weapon. He felt Nevaeh twist under him in an explosion of movement, rolling with him.

"Jagger!" Beth yelled. "Her hand's free! She got free!"

The blade sliced through the canopy and ran across his bicep like a bow over violin strings.

They rolled again, entangled in the canopy and its lines. Jagger slid himself down, toward Nevaeh's legs, lifting and pushing the parachute material off him as he did. A cord snagged on his ear, then snapped past. Nevaeh's knee struck his chin. He rolled onto the ground and kept pushing himself away . . . scrambling . . . slipping under and around lines, the flapping canopy . . . twisting. He slipped out from under the canopy and stood.

Nevaeh squirmed under the canopy. Beth was crouched near her head. When she saw Jagger, she duckwalked backward. She rose, holding a cantaloupe-sized rock in both hands. She raised it high, glaring at the billowing canopy, under which was Nevaeh's head. Jagger couldn't tell if she hesitated in hopes the fluttering material would settle and give her a precise target or she didn't have it in her to kill, even an evil being like Nevaeh.

Two gunshots rang out. Beth startled and dropped the rock.

"Run, Beth!" Jagger said. "Now!" He sidestepped as Nevaeh let another bullet fly. He didn't see the hole it made in the canopy, but knew she'd aimed at his voice.

Beth was frozen, her eyes flicking in a cycle from rock . . . to canopy . . . to Jagger . . .

"Beth, go!" Jagger said.

The gun cracked again.

She moved off the crest, descending down the slope away from the RV 400 yards in the distance. Jagger's gaze followed her, and he caught something in the sky: Owen's jet, heading right for him, only its nose and wings visible. It was about a mile away, maybe twenty seconds from screeching over the hill. Jagger visually traced its trajectory and understood what Owen was up to.

Another shot.

He looked to see the far edge of the canopy inching toward its center, pulled by a hand he couldn't see. Nevaeh was trying to get at least her head clear so she could shoot him. If he jumped on her, even just kicked at her, all he'd be doing was giving her a target. If he ran, she'd be up in no time and pick him off . . . then Beth.

He had an idea, sure to fail, but why not? He looked at the jet: bigger, closer, fifteen seconds. He jumped and waved his arms—the prosthetic flopping back against his biceps. He pointed, gestured.

The jet's left wing dipped, then the right—the universal avionic signal of acknowledgment.

He leaned over, gripped the edge of the canopy nearest him, and began gathering it into his arms. The far edge slipped over Nevaeh's face, then arms. She was pointing the gun at him. He continued pulling, gathering.

She shook her head and smiled. "You realize the gun's just to put you down? Then I'm going to cut your bloody head—"

He tossed the canopy into the air. It started to flutter down, then the wind caught it, puffing it into a glowing square of blue over their heads.

Nevaeh scowled. Her eyes followed the lines to where they entangled her body: over one shoulder, a couple looped around her stomach and chest. She snapped her head toward the jet, its engines now roaring in their ears, growing louder. It was almost on top of them.

"Come back in a hundred years, Nevaeh!" Jagger yelled. "I'm not ready yet!"

He dropped down, and the jet blasted over them. Its nose missed the canopy. An instant later the left wing ripped into it like a child's plastic sword striking a bedsheet drying on a line. He caught a flash of shock on Nevaeh's face, then she was gone, yanked away faster than he could blink, leaving a plume of dust where she'd been. Tangled in the parachute lines trailing under the wing, her body flew in an arc and slammed into the fuselage beneath the tail fin. There it fluttered like a flag.

The jet dipped, its wings waggling a bit, then it crashed into the motorhome.

At first, no explosion, no fire. It was like witnessing toys collide. It tore the mobile control center in half. Its wings caught the pieces and hurled them forward. The nose plunged into the ground, and the fuselage snapped like a dry bone. Two seconds after hitting the motorhome it exploded, and everything disappeared behind veils of flame and smoke. The cacophony that reached Jagger made him think of shrieking, howling souls breaking through the gates of hell.

[102]

The drone streaked toward the entrance of the Venetian Resort. Modeled after its Italian namesake, it was all stone and arches and glass. A water-filled canal cut in front of the façade like a moat; gondolas ferried lovers and families to nowhere. A wide arching bridge linked the modern bustle of the Strip to this faux-foreign land. And everywhere, tourists screamed and ran. A hundred of them streamed over the bridge toward the drone's very target. A crowd in front of the entry doors jostled left and right, unsure which way to run and too packed together to move anywhere.

As it sailed over the bridge, the drone suddenly shot nearly straight up. Across the city—around the Bellagio, the Luxor, Mandalay Bay—drones climbed into the sky like black-robed angels on an emergency call to heaven. They rose to 4,000 feet and turned toward Creech Air Force Base, following a program that returned them safely to their hangars in the event they lost contact with their controllers.

X I I I

Nicole lay sprawled on the sidewalk, glass cutting into her arms and hands and cheeks and legs. She sobbed and moaned. All around her, people screamed and cried, car security alarms wailed like babies, fire crackled, small explosions—probably fuel tanks—erupted. Heavy smoke glided over her like a shadow, and she coughed.

She raised her head. Bodies lay everywhere, and for an instant her crazed mind believed someone had rolled out a shiny red tarp for them to lie on—where was hers?—but then she noticed its scalloped edges and the way it spread to the curb and flowed over. It was blood, so much of it, and she started to retch.

She recognized a voice yelling for help, hoarse and raw sounding. She realized she had been hearing it all along, so regularly it had become part of the audio landscape. She turned her face toward the street. Jason lay there, his legs pinned by the taxi. Her mother knelt by his side, holding his hand and tilting her mouth to the sky to howl for help.

Her brother was still, but his eyelids fluttered, and she tried to smile. Then her eyes focused on the thing directly behind her mother: a taxicab lying on its crushed roof and hood. From its exposed undercarriage, smoked billowed up and black fluid flowed down. She saw the puddle it made, and her stomach churned when she realized the black was mixing into a pool of crimson.

She pulled her arm in, dragging it over beads of broken glass, and dropped her head onto it. All sound faded—the cries for help, the sirens—and the only thing she heard was her own gentle weeping.

X I I I

Jagger turned from the smoking wreckage and gazed down the other side of the hill. Beth stood at the bottom, looking up, anxiety carving deep lines in her face. He smiled and started down. She began to climb. He held out his good arm and she grabbed his hand, walking her fingers up his arm as he brushed past her to stand on lower ground. This put them eye to eye, hers teary, his trying to take in all of her radiance at once. He cupped his palm over her cheek, and she gripped his face like she'd never let go.

They moved in and stopped before their lips touched. Jagger tasted her breath, breathed in her essence, felt himself come alive with her spirit.

Their lips touched, and for a few minutes everything in the world was exactly right.

[103]

Jagger and Beth sat on opposite sides of Tyler's hospital bed, each holding one of his hands. The head of the mattress was canted up so Tyler could smile down on his parents. He was pale, but that old spunk was returning.

"I can't wait to show Addison," he said. "Do you think she's ever seen a bullet hole before . . . or a bullet that was *in someone*?"

The doctor had given him the slug they had removed from his body. Beth wanted to throw it away, or better still, grind it into dust the way Moses had ground the golden calf. Then if she ever saw Nevaeh again—Jagger had told her not to rule out that possibility: no bodies had been recovered from the site of the Tribe's makeshift drone control center or the wreckage of Owen's jet—she would make her drink it.

But Tyler had convinced her he should keep it.

"It's like . . . like a monster that tried to kill me but couldn't," he'd said.

"A memento of your victory. Going to put it in your utility case?"

He'd shaken his head. "Too noisy. I'll keep it in my pocket."

Now he squeezed their hands and said, "Can I go home?"

"Soon," Jagger said. "Maybe in a few days."

Tyler made a face. "I want to see the wall that got blowed up before they fix it. And that guy who chased me—he went *over* the roof of one of the monk cells. I didn't know you could *do* that."

"*You* can't!"

"But, Mom . . ." He pronounced *mom* with two syllables.

Jagger waggled Tyler's hand. "There's plenty of time to explore and plenty of places that need exploring. Let's get you better first."

Tyler looked from his father to his mother and back again. "Does that mean we're staying? We don't have to leave St. Cath's?"

"I don't know why we would," Jagger said. "I've just begun exploring its mysteries myself."

Tyler smiled and took a deep breath. As he let it out, his eyelids drooped. Within a few minutes he was asleep.

Jagger's and Beth's eyes found each other. Jagger released Tyler's hand and reached for hers. He took in her features, so perfectly formed, the glow of her complexion. He remembered thinking that her beauty was something to bask in, better than the sun, and it was truer now than ever. And like the sun, she wasn't just beautiful. She was strong and bright, energizing and life-giving, warm . . . and hot. That made him smile, a big stupid grin. She smiled in return, but hers appeared a little sad.

"So," she said. "Immortal."

"I'm sorry."

"Don't be sorry for being who you are."

"For keeping it from you. I don't know why I did."

"You don't? Before we got married, there's nothing you could have done or said that would have made me believe you. I would have thought you were crazy."

"But if somehow you came to believe?"

Her eyes dropped to their hands. "I don't know. I loved you, but did I love you enough to watch you stay young and vital while I drifted away on a sea of wrinkles, gray hair, sagging flesh, aching bones, infirmity? I don't know."

"And now?"

She looked him right in his eyes. "Yes," she said. "I do. It'll be hard . . . sad . . . terrible. But if you're in it to the end—"

"I am. The end and longer."

"Then let's take it one wrinkle at a time. How could I deny the love of a lifetime just because that lifetime is only mine?"

"And mine."

"Forever is a long time."

"I'll love you forever," he said. "No matter where I am or where you are."

"I'll help prepare a place for you," she said.

He smiled, and basked. Then he turned to watch Tyler sleep. His heart felt heavier, thicker, knowing that one day—not today and maybe not for a hundred years, but someday, he would stand over his son's grave. A tear spilled from the corner of his eye.

"Think of it this way," Beth whispered. "You get to enjoy him for a long, long time. Longer than I will."

He squeezed her hand. "We'll make the time we have together count."

"I'm glad we're staying at the monastery."

"I was just starting to get into those five a.m. services." He saw the question on her face and said, "If God's still talking, I'm ready to listen."

"Not angry at him?"

He waggled his head left and right. "I have some issues, but what relationship doesn't? I certainly don't understand his ways, but I guess I'm not supposed to." His voice grew playful. "When Anger and Depression knock on the door, I'll let Joy answer it. She really kicks their butts."

"Joy, huh?"

He gave Tyler a long look and then Beth. "Yeah." He shrugged. "So, we'll see."

Beth stroked Tyler's hand and gazed at her son. She said, "Sometimes I think about what would have happened if Owen hadn't shown up. Thank God for that man."

Remembering something, Jagger grinned. "I can't believe I didn't get this before. But I did some research . . ."

"On what?"

He pulled a notepad from a duffel on the floor. Flipping through the pages, he said, "Did you know that most theologians believe the twelve apostles represent the twelve tribes of Israel?"

She nodded.

"The name of Owen's jet was *Boaerges*. It means 'sons of thunder.'"

"That's what Jesus called James and John, because of their impetuosity. But he also called John his beloved."

"Right. And get this. In John 21, Jesus said about John, 'If I want him to remain alive until I return, what is that to you?'"

"Is he saying John is immortal?"

Jagger smiled. "His death was never recorded. According to the early Christian author Tertullian, the Romans tried to kill John by plunging him into a cauldron of boiling oil, but it didn't work. He walked away. So they exiled him to the Greek island of Patmos, where he wrote Revelation."

"Okay . . . ?"

"You ready?" Jagger said, grinning.

"For what?"

"What is Owen's last name?"

She shook her head.

"When we first met him he said it was Letois—the original name of Patmos." Jagger began talking quickly, rolling it all out. He said he survived boiling oil and that Jesus restored him 'to the table of the twelve tribes.' Interesting way of wording it, isn't it? I picture the Last Supper. Jesus called him Ου εφιλει ο Ιησους. He told me it meant Jesus loved him, but the literal translation is 'beloved disciple.'"

"Are you telling me—?"

He handed her the book Owen had given him. "It's a travel-sized New Testament, but he called it his journal."

Jagger had marked page fifty-two with an unopened Band-Aid, and when Beth turned to it, she started to weep:

The Gospel According to John

Acknowledgments

Thanks to the usual crew for their efforts: my wife and first reader, Jodi, my infinitely patient children, Melanie, Matt, Anthony, and Isabella; my editor, Amanda Bostic; my "other" editor, L.B. Norton; my publisher, Allen Arnold; the entire fiction team at Thomas Nelson; and my agent, Joel Gotler.

More thanks to:

Larry Hama, for weaponry assistance

Peggy Chenoweth and Sean McHugh, for sharing their experiences as amputees

Jeffrey Lyle, MD, for emergency medical guidance

John Fornof, Tom Manzer, and Mark Nelson, for theological counsel

Julie Jammers, for foreign language advice

Mae Gannon, for research assistance

Jordyn Wall for helping around the office

Tim Casey, Wayne Pinkstaff, Mike Landon, Paul and Jennifer Turner, James Rollins, Doug Preston, Rel Mollet, Mark Lavallee, Dave Rhoades, Nicole Petrino-Salter, Jake Chism, Joe Cuchiara, and Kim, Ben and Matthew Ford, for their constant friendship and encouragement

Special thanks to the Blue Monkeys from the Ragged Edge conference, who gave me early feedback and kind reviews: Stephanie Karfelt, Reuben Horst, Lynnell Koehler, Linnette R. Mullin,

LaDonna Cole, Kimberly Robertson, Kelsey Keating, Kathleen Edwards, John Michael Den Hartog, Jennifer Thompson, Jennifer Fancher, Jason L. Fancher, Heather Sudbrock, Hannah R. Lee, Frank Lattimore, Donna Marie McChristian, Donna M. Kilgore, Devin Berglund, Daniel Eness, Cory Kruse, Chadd Baltzley, Britton Peele, Donna Spivey, and Taylor Bomar.

Reading Group Guide

1. The Tribe received immortality as a curse for their transgression with the golden calf. They faced a future without access to heaven or God. What are your views of this? For you, what would be the advantages of living on Earth forever? What would be the drawbacks?

2. In *The 13th Tribe*, God's curse of immortality extended to children. Ben cited some biblical examples of children suffering God's wrath because of the behavior of their parents (such as Deuteronomy 11:5–6). Our modern society subscribes to the doctrine of the "age of accountability," also known as the "age of reason," which says that children under a certain age are not responsible for their actions because they are too young to know better. What do you think? At what age should children be accountable? What do you think God's position is on this?

3. After witnessing how Phinehas's killing of two sinners pleased God and ended the plague brought on by the heresy of Peor (Numbers 25:1–15), the Tribe decided to become vigilantes. And while discussing the criminals the Tribe has killed, even Owen admits, "There's a part of me that admires what they do." What are your views of vigilantism? Has there ever been a time when you heard about a crime that seemed to go unpunished and wished someone, anyone would bring the culprit to justice? Do

you think that there is ever a time when "frontier justice" (retribution outside the law) is appropriate, even biblical?

4. Ben says that most Christians think, deep down, "If I don't do this or if I do that, I will lose my favor with God." Have you ever felt this way? Is loving God and keeping his commandments always a matter of appreciation for the grace he has freely bestowed to us . . . or is there an element of earning his favor in our doing right?

5. Jagger lost his faith in God's love when a car crash cost him his arm and the lives of the Bransford family. Why does God allow such tragedies? Have you ever experienced a tragedy that tested your faith? How did you respond? Is there anything that could happen that would cause you to question God's love?

6. Beth is a woman of strong faith. How does this present itself in the story? Because of her faith, she is able to be strong while Jagger struggles with his. Have you ever had to be strong for others? Who in your life could you count on for strength and support if you ever needed it?

7. Nevaeh says she knows God's will through prayers and dreams, and that she believes God confirms her plans by allowing them to be achieved, or condemns them by hindering her attempts. How do you know when you're doing what God wants you to do? Do you believe he guides you and directs your actions? How does he do that?

8. God talked to Moses from a burning bush; during the Exodus, he appeared as a pillar of fire (Exodus 13:21–22); Jesus performed many miracles, only some of which were recorded (John 21:25). Why do you think God doesn't show himself in such obvious, physical ways today? Or does he? Can you name a few ways in which he makes his presence known to us?

ABOUT THE AUTHOR

Robert Liparulo has received rave reviews for both his adult novels (*Comes a Horseman, Germ, Deadfall*, and *Deadlock*) and the best-selling Dreamhouse Kings series for young adults. He lives in Colorado with his wife and their four children.

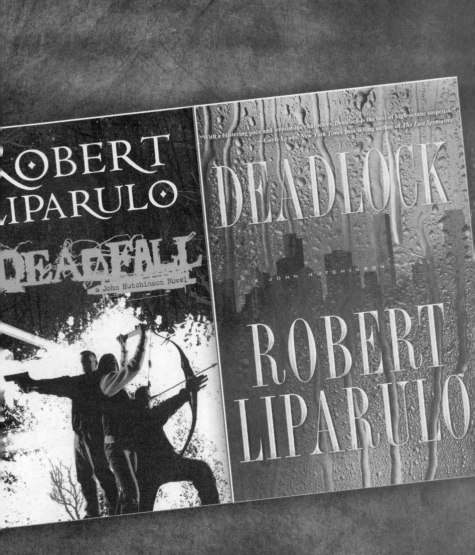